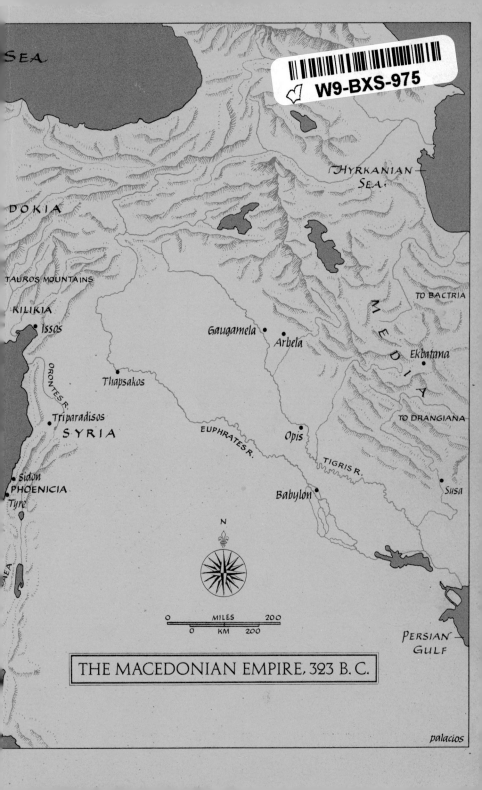

SEA

HYRKANIAN
SEA·

DOKIA

TAUROS MOUNTAINS

KILIKIA

Issos

ORONTES R.

Triparadisos

SYRIA

Sidon
PHOENICIA
Tyre

Gaugamela   Arbela

Thapsakos

EUPHRATES R.

TO BACTRIA

M
E
D
I
A

Ekbatana

TO DRANGIANA

Opis

TIGRIS R.

Susa

Babylon

N

MILES   200

KM   200

PERSIAN
GULF

THE MACEDONIAN EMPIRE, 323 B. C.

palacios

FUNERAL GAMES

FUNERAL GAMES

MARY RENAULT

Pantheon Books
New York

Renault, Mary.
Funeral games.

1. Alexander, the Great, 356–323 B.C.—Fiction.
I. Title.
PR6035.E55E45   1981   823'.912   81–47273
ISBN 0–394–52068–8   AACR2

"I foresee great contests at my funeral games."

—Reported deathbed words
of Alexander the Great

PRINCIPAL PERSONS

Invented characters are italicized; all those in roman type are historical. Persons marked * are dead before the story opens. Minor characters making a brief appearance are omitted.

ALEXANDER III   The Great. All further references to Alexander refer to him unless his son, Alexander IV, is specified.

ALEXANDER IV   His posthumous son by Roxane.

ALKETAS   Brother of Perdikkas, the general.

*AMYNTAS   Son of Philip II's elder brother, King Perdikkas. An infant when Perdikkas died, he was passed over in favor of Philip, after whose murder he was executed for treason. Husband of Kynna, father of Eurydike.

ANTIGONOS   General of Alexander; Satrap of Phrygia. Later a king, and founder of the Antigonid dynasty.

ANTIPATROS   Regent of Macedon during Alexander's years in Asia, and at the time of his death.

ARISTONOUS   A staff officer of Alexander; later loyal to Alexander IV.

ARRIDAIOS   See Philip III.

ARYBBAS   A Macedonian nobleman, designer of Alexander's funeral car. His real name was Arridaios; he is here given a rather similar Epirote name to distinguish him from Philip Arridaios.

Badia   A *former concubine of King Artaxerxes Ochos of Persia.*

BAGOAS   A young Persian eunuch, favorite successively of Darius III and Alexander. Though a real person, he vanishes from history after Alexander's death, and his appearance in this story is fictional.

*DARIUS III   The last Persian Great King; murdered by his generals after his defeat by Alexander at Gaugamela.

DEMETRIOS   Son of Antigonos. (Later known as The Besieger, he became King of Macedon after Kassandros' death.)

DRYPETIS   Younger daughter of Darius III; widow of Hephaistion.

EUMENES   Chief Secretary and general of Alexander; loyal to the royal house.

EURYDIKE   Daughter of Amyntas and Kynna. Her given name was Adeia; Eurydike was the dynastic name conferred on her at her marriage (or betrothal) to Philip III. She was the granddaughter of Philip II and of Perdikkas III, his brother.

*HEPHAISTION   Alexander's lifelong friend, who died a few months before him.

IOLLAS — Son of Antipatros the Regent of Macedon, younger brother of Kassandros; formerly Alexander's cupbearer.

KASSANDROS — Eldest son of Antipatros; lifelong enemy of Alexander. (Became King of Macedon after the murder of Alexander IV.)

Kebes — *Tutor to the boy Alexander IV.*

KLEOPATRA — Daughter of Philip II and Olympias, sister of Alexander. Married to King Alexandros of Molossia, which she ruled after his death in Italy. Her father, Philip, was assassinated in her wedding procession.

Konon — *A Macedonian veteran, attendant on Philip Arridaios.*

KRATEROS — Alexander's highest-ranking officer, absent on a mission to Macedon when Alexander died.

KYNNA — Daughter of Philip II by an Illyrian princess, from whom she learned the skills of war. Widow of Amyntas, mother of Eurydike.

LEONNATOS — Staff officer and kinsman of Alexander; betrothed to Kleopatra before his death in battle.

MELEAGER — (Greek spelling Meleagros.) A Macedonian officer, enemy of Perdikkas, supporter of Philip III.

NIARCHOS — Boyhood friend and admiral of Alexander.

NIKAIA — Daughter of the Regent Antipatros, married and divorced by Perdikkas.

NIKANOR — Brother of Kassandros; general in Eurydike's army.

*OCHOS — (King Artaxerxes Ochos.) Great King of Persia before the short reign of Darius III.

OLYMPIAS — Daughter of King Neoptolemos of Molossia; widow of Philip II; mother of Alexander.

PEITHON — Staff officer of Alexander, later of Perdikkas.

PERDIKKAS — Second in command to Alexander after Hephaistion's death. Betrothed to Kleopatra after death of Leonnatos.

*PERDIKKAS III — Elder brother of Philip II, who succeeded him after his death in battle. (See Amyntas.)

PEUKESTES — Staff officer of Alexander; Satrap of Persia.

*PHILIP II — The founder of Macedonian supremacy in Greece; father of Alexander.

PHILIP III — (Philip Arridaios.) His son by Philinna, a minor wife. The royal name of Philip was conferred at his accession.

POLYPERCHON — Staff officer of Alexander; Regent of Macedon after Antipatros' death.

PTOLEMY — (Greek spelling Ptolemaios.) Staff officer, kinsman, and reputed half-brother of Alexander. Later King of Egypt, founder of the Ptolemaic dynasty, and author of a history of Alexander extensively used by Arrian.

ROXANE   Wife of Alexander, married on campaign
              in Bactria. Mother of Alexander IV.

SELEUKOS   Staff officer of Alexander. (Later King of
              the Seleucid empire in nearer Asia.)

SISYGAMBIS   Mother of Darius III, befriended by Alex-
              ander.

STATEIRA   Daughter of Darius III, married in state
              by Alexander at Susa.

THEOPHRASTOS Aristotle's successor as head of the Lyceum
              University at Athens, patronized by Kas-
              sandros.

THESSALONIKE Daughter of Philip II by a minor wife;
              later wife of Kassandros.

FUNERAL GAMES

3 2 3 B. C.

THE ZIGGURAT OF BEL-MARDUK had been half ruinous for a century and a half, ever since Xerxes had humbled the gods of rebellious Babylon. The edges of its terraces had crumbled in landslides of bitumen and baked brick; storks nested on its ragged top, which had once held the god's golden bedchamber and his sacred concubine in his golden bed. But this was only defacement; the ziggurat's huge bulk had defied destruction. The walls of the inner city by the Marduk Gate were three hundred feet high, but the ziggurat still towered over them.

Near by was the god's temple; this Xerxes' men had succeeded in half demolishing. The rest of the roof was patched with thatch, and propped on shafts of rough-hewn timber. At the inner end, where the columns were faced with splendid but chipped enamels, there was still a venerable gloom, a smell of incense and burnt offerings. On an altar of porphyry, under a smoke-duct open to the sky, burned in its bronze basket the sacred fire. It was low; the fuel-box was empty. Its shaven acolyte looked from it to the priest. Abstracted though he was, it caught his eye.

"Fetch fuel. What are you about? Must a king die when it serves your laziness? Move! You were got when your mother was asleep and snoring."

The acolyte made a sketchy obeisance; the temple discipline was not strict.

The priest said, after him, "It will not be yet. Maybe not even today. He is tough as a mountain lion, he will die hard."

Two tall shadows fell at the temple's open end. The priests who entered wore the high felt miters of Chaldeans. They approached the altar with ritual gestures, bowing with hand on mouth.

The priest of Marduk said, "Nothing yet?"

"No," said the first Chaldean. "But it will be soon. He cannot speak; indeed he can scarcely breathe. But when his homeland soldiers made a clamor at the doors, demanding to see him, he had them all admitted. Not the commanders; they were there already. The spear-bearers, the common foot-men. They were half the morning passing through his bedchamber, and he greeted them all by signs. That finished him, and now he is in the death-sleep."

A door behind the altar opened to let in two Marduk priests. It gave a glimpse of a rich interior; embroidered hangings, a gleam of gold. There was a smell of spiced meats cooking. The door closed on it.

The Chaldeans, reminded of an old scandal, exchanged glances. One of them said, "We did our best to turn him from the city. But he had heard that the temple had not been restored; and he thought we were afraid of him."

A Marduk priest said stiffly, "The year has not been auspicious for great works. Nebuchadrezzar built in an inauspicious year. His foreign slaves rioted race against race, and threw each other off the tower. As for Sikandar, he would still be fortunate, sitting safe in Susa, if he had not defied the god."

One of the Chaldeans said, "It seems to me he did well enough by the god, for all that he called him Herakles." He looked round, pointedly, at the half-ruined building. He might as well have said aloud, "Where is the gold the King gave you to rebuild, have you eaten and drunk it all?"

There was a hostile silence. The chief of the Marduk priests said, with emollient dignity, "Certainly you gave him a true prediction. And since then have you read the heavens?"

The tall miters bent together in slow assent. The oldest Chaldean, whose beard was silver against his dark face and purple robe, signed to the Marduk priest, beckoning him to the broken end of the temple. "This," he said, "is what is foretold for Babylon." He swept round his gold-starred wand, taking in the crumbling walls, the threadbare roof, the leaning timber-props, the fire-stained paving. "This for a while, and then . . . Babylon was."

He walked towards the entry and stood to listen; but the night noises were unchanged. "The heavens say it begins with the death of the King."

The priest remembered the shining youth who, eight years before, had come offering treasure and Arabian incense; and the man who had returned this year, weathered and scarred, the red-gold hair sun-bleached and streaked with white; but with the deep eyes still burning, still ready with the careless, reflex charm of the youth beloved, still terrible in anger. The scent of the incense had lasted long on the air, the gold much longer in the treasury; even among men who liked good living, half was in the strongroom still. But for the priest of Bel-Marduk the pleasure had drained out of it. It spoke now of flames and blood. His spirit sank like the altar fire when the fuel was low.

"Shall we see it? Will a new Xerxes come?"

The Chaldean shook his head. "A dying, not a killing. Another city will rise and ours will wane. It is under the sign of the King."

"What? Will he live, then, after all?"

"He is dying, as I told you. But his sign is walking along the constellations, further than we can reckon in years. You will not see it setting in your day."

"So? Well, in his life he did us no harm. Maybe he will spare us dead."

The astrologer frowned to himself, like an adult seeking words to reach a child. "Remember, last year, the fire that fell from heaven. We heard where it fell, and went there, a week's journey. It had lit the city brighter than full moon. But we found, where it had struck, it had broken into red-hot embers, which had charred the earth around them. One had been set up by a farmer in his house, because that day his wife bore twin sons. But a neighbor had stolen it for its power; they fought, and both men died. Another piece fell at a dumb child's feet, and speech came back to him. A third had kindled a fire that destroyed a forest. But the Magus of the place had taken the greatest piece, and built it into the fire-altar, because of its great light while it was in the sky. And all this from the one star. So it will be."

The priest bowed his head. A fragrance drifted to him from the precinct's kitchen. Better to invite the Chaldeans than let the meat spoil with waiting. Whatever the stars said, good food was good food.

The old Chaldean said, looking into the shadows, "Here where we stand, the leopard will rear her young."

The priest made a decent pause. No sound from the royal palace. With luck, they might get something to eat before they heard the wailing.

The walls of Nebuchadrezzar's palace were four feet thick, and faced with blue-glazed tiles for coolness; but the mid-summer heat seeped in through everything. The sweat running down Eumenes' wrist blotted the ink on his papyrus. The wax glistened moistly on the tablet he was fair-copying; he plunged it back into the cold-water tub where his clerk had left it, with the other drafts, to keep the surface set.

Local scribes used wet clay; but that would have set hard before one could revise on it. For the third time he went to the doorway, seeking a slave to pull the punkah cord. Once again the dim hushed noises—soft feet, soft voices furtive or awed or grieving—sent him back behind the drawn door-curtain to his listless task. To clap the hands, to call, to shout an order, were all unthinkable.

He had not sought his clerk, a garrulous man; but he could have done with the silent slave and the waft of the punkah. He scanned the unfinished scroll pinned to his writing-board. It was twenty years since he had written with his own hand any letter not of high secrecy; why now was he writing one that would never go, short of a miracle? There had been many miracles; but, surely, not now. It was something to do, it shut out the unknown future. Sitting down again he retrieved the tablet, propped it, dried his hand on the towel the clerk had left, and picked up his pen.

And the ships commanded by Niarchos will muster at the river-mouth, where I shall review them while Perdikkas is bringing the army down from Babylon; and sacrifices will be made there to the appropriate gods. I shall then take command of the land force and begin the march to the west. The first stage . . .

When he was five, before he'd been taught to write, he came to me in the King's business room. "What's that, Eumenes?" "A letter." "What's the first word that you've written big?" "Your father's name. *PHILIP*, King of the Macedonians. Now I'm busy, run back to your play." "Make me my name. Do, dear Eumenes. Please." I gave it him written, on the back of a spoiled despatch. Next day he'd learned it, and carved it all over the wax for a royal letter to Kersobleptes of Thrace. He had my ruler across his palm . . .

Because of the heat he had left open his massive door. A brisk stride, half hushed like all other sounds, approached it. Ptolemy pushed aside the curtain and drew it to behind him. His craggy war-weathered face was creased with fatigue; he had been up all night, without the stimulus of action. He was forty-three, and looked older. Eumenes waited, wordlessly.

"He has given his ring to Perdikkas," Ptolemy said.

There was a pause. Eumenes' alert Greek face—not a bookish one, he had had his share of soldiering—searched the impassive Macedonian's. "For what? As deputy? Or as Regent?"

"Since he could not speak," said Ptolemy drily, "we shall never know."

"If he has accepted death," Eumenes reasoned, "we may presume the second. If not . . . ?"

"It's all one, now. He neither sees nor hears. He is in the death-sleep."

"Do not be sure. I have heard of men who were thought already dead, and who said later that they heard everything."

Ptolemy suppressed an impatient gesture. These wordy Greeks. Or what is he afraid of? "I came because you and I have known him since he was born. Don't you want to be there?"

"Do the Macedonians want me there?" An ancient bitterness pinched, for a moment, Eumenes' mouth.

"Oh, come. Everyone trusts you. We shall need you before long."

Slowly the Secretary began to put his desk in order. He said, wiping his pen, "And nothing, to the last, about an heir?"

"Perdikkas asked him, while he could still get a whisper out. He only said, 'To the best man. *Hoti to kratisto.*'"

Eumenes thought, They say dying men can prophesy. He shivered.

"Or," Ptolemy added, "so Perdikkas told us. He was leaning over. Nobody else could hear."

Eumenes put down the pen and looked up sharply. "Or *Kratero?* You say he whispered, he was short of breath." They looked at one another. Krateros, the highest-ranking of all Alexander's staff, was on the march to Macedon, to take over the regency from Antipatros. "If *he'd* been in the room . . ."

Ptolemy shrugged. "Who knows?" To himself he thought, If Hephaistion had been there . . . But if *he'd* lived, none of this would have happened. He'd have done none of the crazy things he's dying of. Coming to Babylon in midsummer—boating about in the filthy swamps down river . . . But one did not discuss Hephaistion with Eumenes. "This door weighs like an elephant. Do you want it shut?"

Pausing on the threshold, Eumenes said, "Nothing about Roxane and the child? Nothing?"

"Four months to go. And what if it's a girl?"

They moved into the shadowy corridor, tall big-boned Macedonian and slender Greek. A young Macedonian officer came blundering towards them, almost ran into Ptolemy, and stammered an apology. Ptolemy said, "Is there any change?"

"No, sir, I don't think so." He swallowed violently; they saw that he was crying.

When he had gone, Ptolemy said, "That boy believes in it. I can't yet."

"Well, let us go."

"Wait." Ptolemy took his arm, led him back into the

room, and dragged-to the great ebony door on its groaning hinges. "I'd best tell you this while we've time. You should have known before, but . . ."

"Yes, yes?" said Eumenes impatiently. He had quarreled with Hephaistion shortly before he died, and Alexander had never been easy with him since.

Ptolemy said, "Stateira is pregnant, too."

Eumenes, who had been fidgeting to be gone, was struck into stillness. "You mean Darius' daughter?"

"Who else do you suppose? She *is* Alexander's wife."

"But this changes everything. When did . . . ?"

"Don't you remember? No, of course, you'd gone on to Babylon. When he came to himself after Hephaistion died" (one could not avoid the name forever) "he went to war with the Kossaians. My doing; I told him they'd demanded road-toll, and got him angry. He needed to be doing something. It did him good. When he'd dealt with them, and was heading here, he stopped a week at Susa, to call upon Sisygambis."

"That old witch," said Eumenes bitterly. But for her, he thought, the King's friends would never have been saddled with Persian wives. The mass wedding at Susa had gone by like some drama of superhuman magnificence, till suddenly he had found himself alone in a scented pavilion, in bed with a Persian noblewoman whose unguents repelled him, and whose only Greek consisted of "Greeting, my lord."

"A great lady," said Ptolemy. "A pity his mother was not like her. *She* would have had him married before he set out from Macedon, and seen that he got a son. He could have had an heir of fourteen by this time. *She'd* not have sickened him with marriage while he was a child. Whose fault was it that he wasn't ready for a woman till he met the Bactrian?" Thus, unofficially, did most Macedonians refer to Roxane.

"Done is done. But Stateira . . . Does Perdikkas know?"

"That's why he asked him to name his heir."

"And still he would not?"

" 'To the best,' he said. He left it to us, to the Macedonians, to choose when they came of age. Yes, he's a Macedonian at the last."

"If they are boys," Eumenes reminded him.

Ptolemy, who had been withdrawn into his thought, said, "And if they come of age."

Eumenes said nothing. They went down the dim corridor with its blue-tiled walls towards the death-chamber.

Nebuchadrezzar's bedroom, once ponderously Assyrian, had been Persianized by successive kings from Kyros on. Kambyses had hung its walls with the trophies of conquered Egypt; Darius the Great had sheathed its columns with gold and malachite; Xerxes had pegged across one side the embroidered robe of Athene, looted from the Parthenon. The second Artaxerxes had sent for craftsmen of Persepolis to make the great bed in which Alexander now lay dying.

Its dais was covered with crimson tapestries worked in bullion. The bed was nine feet by six; Darius the Third, a man seven feet tall, had had ample room. The high canopy was upheld by four golden fire-daimons with silver wings and jeweled eyes. Propped on heaped pillows to help him breathe, and looking small among all these splendors, the dying man lay naked. A thin linen sheet had been spread half over him when he had ceased to toss about and throw it off. Damp with sweat, it clung to him as if sculpted.

In a monotonous cycle, his shallow rattling breath grew gradually louder, then ceased. After a pause during which no other breath was drawn in the crowded room, it started again, slowly, the same crescendo.

Until lately there had been scarcely another sound. Now

that he had ceased responding to voice or touch, a soft
muttering began to spread, too cautious and muted to be
located; a ground-bass to the strong rhythm of death.

Perdikkas by the bed's head lifted at Ptolemy his dark
heavy eyebrows; a tall man, with the Macedonian build but
not the coloring, and a face on which authority, long habit-
ual, was growing. His silent gesture of the head signaled
"No change yet."

The movement of a peacock fan drew Ptolemy's eye
across the bed. There, as he had been for days, seemingly
without sleep, seated on the dais was the Persian boy. So
Ptolemy still thought of him though by now he must be
three-and-twenty; with eunuchs it was hard to tell. At sixteen, he had been brought to Alexander by a Persian general involved in Darius' murder, to give exonerating evi-
dence. This he was well placed to do, having been the
King's minion, with inside knowledge of the court. He had
stayed on to give his story to the chroniclers, and had never
been far from Alexander since. Not much was on view
today of the famous beauty which had dazzled two kings
running. The great dark eyes were sunk in a face more
drawn than the fever-wasted one on the pillows. He was
dressed like a servant; did he think that if he was noticed
he would be turned out? What *does* he think, Ptolemy
wondered. He must have lain with Darius in this very bed.

A fly hovered over Alexander's sweat-glazed forehead. The
Persian chased it off, then put down the fan to dip a towel
in a basin of mint-scented water, and wipe the unmoving
face.

At first Ptolemy had disliked this exotic presence haunt-
ing Alexander's living-quarters, encouraging him to assume
the trappings of Persian royalty and the manners of a
Persian court, having his ear day and night. But he was a
fixture one had grown used to. Through Ptolemy's own

grief and sense of looming crisis, he felt a stir of pity. Walking over, he touched him on the shoulder.

"Get some rest, Bagoas. Let one of the other chamberlains do all this." A knot of court eunuchs, ageing relics of Darius and even of Ochos, advanced officiously. Ptolemy said, "He won't know now, you know."

Bagoas looked round. It was as if he had been told he was condemned to immediate execution, a sentence long expected. "Never mind," said Ptolemy gently. "It's your right; stay if you wish."

Bagoas touched his fingers to his forehead. The interruption was over. With his eyes fixed once more on the closed eyes of Alexander, he waved the fan, shifting the hot Babylonian air. He had staying power, Ptolemy reflected. He had weathered even the brainstorm after Hephaistion's death.

Against the wall nearest the bed, on a massive table like an altar, Hephaistion was still enshrined. Enshrined and multiplied; here were the votive statuettes and busts presented by condolent friends, assiduous place-seekers, scared men who had once had words with the dead; commissioned by the best artists found at short notice, to comfort Alexander's grief. Hephaistion stood in bronze, a nude Ares with shield and spear; precious in gold armor with ivory face and limbs; in tinted marble with a gilded laurel crown; as a silver battle-standard for the squadron which was to bear his name; and as a demigod, the first maquette for the cult-statue of his temple in Alexandria. Someone had cleared a space to put down some sickroom object, and a small Hephaistion in gilded bronze had fallen over. With a quick glance at the blind face on the pillows, Ptolemy set it up again. Let them wait till he's gone.

The small sound drew Eumenes' eye, which quickly looked away again.

Ptolemy thought, You've nothing to fear now, have you?
Oh yes, he could be arrogant now and then. Towards the
end, he thought he was the only one who understood—
and how far was he wrong? Accept it, Eumenes, he was
good for Alexander. *I* knew when they were boys at school.
He was somebody in himself and both of them knew it.
That pride you didn't like was Alexander's salvation; never
fawning, never pushing, never envious, never false. He
loved Alexander and never used him, kept pace with him
at Aristotle's lessons, never on purpose lost a match to him.
To the end of his days he could talk to Alexander man to
man, could tell him he was wrong, and never for a moment
feared him. He saved him from solitude, and who knows
what else? Now he's gone, and this is what we have. If he
were alive, we'd all be feasting today in Susa, whatever the
Chaldeans say.

A frightened physician, pushed from behind by Perdikkas, laid a hand on Alexander's brow, fingered his wrist,
muttered gravely and backed away. As long as he could
speak, Alexander had refused to have a doctor near him;
and even when he was light-headed, none could be found
to physic him, lest they should later be accused of having
given him poison. It was all one now; he was no longer
swallowing. Curse that fool quack, Ptolemy thought, who
let Hephaistion die while he went off to the games. I'd
hang him again if I could.

It had long seemed that when the harsh breathing
changed, it could only be for the death-rattle. But as if the
doctor's touch had stirred a flicker of life, the stridor took
a more even rhythm, and the eyelids were seen to move.
Ptolemy and Perdikkas each took a step forward. But the
self-effacing Persian by the bed, whom everyone had forgotten, put down the fan and, as if no one else were in
sight, leaned intimately over the pillowed head, his long

light-brown hair falling around it. He whispered softly. Alexander's grey eyes opened. Something disturbed the silky cloak of hair.

Perdikkas said, "He moved his hand."

It was still now, the eyes shut again, though Bagoas, as if transfixed, was still gazing down at them. Perdikkas' mouth tightened; all kinds of people were here. But before he could walk up with a reprimand, the Persian had resumed his station and picked up his fan. But for its movement, he could have been a statue carved from ivory.

Ptolemy became aware of Eumenes speaking to him. "What?" he said harshly. He was near to tears.

"Peukestes is coming."

The huddled functionaries parted to admit a tall well-built Macedonian dressed as a Persian, even—to most of his countrymen's shocked disapproval—down to the trousers. When given the satrapy of Persis he had adopted the native dress to please Alexander, not unaware that it suited him. He strode forward, his eyes on the bed. Perdikkas advanced to meet him.

There was a low buzz of talk. The eyes of the two men exchanged their message. Perdikkas said formally, for the benefit of the company, "Did you receive an oracle from Sarapis?"

Peukestes bowed his head. "We kept the night-watch. The god said at dawn, 'Do not bring the King to the temple. It will be better for him where he is.'"

No, thought Eumenes, there will be no more miracles. For a moment, when the hand had moved, he had almost believed in another.

He turned round looking for Ptolemy; but he had gone off somewhere to put his face in order. It was Peukestes who, coming away from the bedside, said to him, "Does Roxane know?"

⊙   ⊙   ⊙

The palace harem was a spacious cloister built around a lily-pond. Here too were hushed voices, but differently pitched; the few men in this female world were eunuchs.

None of the women whose home the harem was had set eyes on the dying King. They had heard well of him; they had been kept by him in comfort and unmolested; they had awaited a visit that never came. And that was all, except that they knew of no male heir who would inherit them; in a little while there would even, it seemed, be no Great King. The voices were muted with secretive fear.

Here were all the women Darius had left behind him when he marched to his fate at Gaugamela. His favorites, of course, he had taken with him; these who remained were something of a mixture. His older concubines, from his days as a nobleman unplaced in line for the throne, had long been installed at Susa; here were girls found for him after his accession, who had failed to retain his interest, or had come too late to be noticed by him at all. As well as all these, there were the survivors of King Ochos' harem, who could not in decency be put out of doors when he died. An unwelcome legacy, they formed with one or two old eunuchs a little clique of their own, hating the women of Darius, that usurper they suspected of complicity in their master's death.

For Darius' concubines it was another matter. When brought there they had been fourteen, fifteen, eighteen at most. They had known the real drama of the harem; the rumors and intrigues; the bribery to get first news of a royal visit; the long intricacies of the toilet, the inspired placing of a jewel; the envious despair when the menstrual days enforced retirement; the triumph when a summons was received in a rival's presence; the gift of honor after a successful night.

From a few such nights had come one or two little girls of eight or so, who were dabbling in the pool and telling each other solemnly that the King was dying. There had been boys too. When Darius fell, they had been spirited away with every kind of stratagem, their mothers taking it for granted that the new, barbarian King would have them strangled. Nobody, however, had come looking for them; they had returned in time and now, being of an age to be brought out from among women, were being reared as men by distant kindred.

With the long absence of any King from Babylon, the harem had grown slack. At Susa, where Sisygambis the Queen Mother lived, everything was impeccable. But here they had seen little even of Darius, nothing of Alexander. One or two of the women had managed to intrigue with men from outside and run away with them; the eunuchs, whom Ochos would have impaled for negligence, had kept it quiet. Some girls in the long idle days had had affairs with one another; the resulting jealousies and scenes had enlivened many hot Assyrian nights. One girl had been poisoned by a rival; but that too had been hushed up. The Chief Warden had taken to smoking hemp, and disliked being disturbed.

Then, after years in the unknown east, after legendary victories, wounds, perils in deserts, the King sent word of his return. The harem had aroused itself as if from sleep. The eunuchs had fussed. All through the winter, the Babylonian season of gentle warmth, when feasts were held, he was expected but did not come. Rumor reached the palace that a boyhood friend had died—some said a lover—and it had sent him mad. Then he had come to himself, but was at war with the mountain Kossaians. The harem slipped back into its lethargy. At last he was on his way, but had broken his march at Susa. Setting out again, he had been met by embassies from all the peoples of the earth, bringing him golden crowns and asking him for counsel. Then, when late spring was heating up for summer, the earth had shaken under the horses and the chariots, the elephants and the marching men; and the palace had seethed with the long-forgotten bustle of a king's arrival.

Next day, it was announced that the King's Chief Eunuch of the Bedchamber would inspect the harem. This formidable person was awaited with dread; but turned out, shockingly, to be little more than a youth, none other than the notorious Bagoas, minion of two kings. Not that he failed to impress. He was wearing silk, stuff never seen within those walls, and shimmered like a peacock's breast. He was Persian to his fingertips, which always made Babylonians feel provincial; and ten years at courts had polished his manners like old silver. He greeted without embarrassment any eunuchs he had met in Darius' day, and bowed respectfully to some of the older ladies. Then he came to business.

He could not say when the King's urgent concerns would give him leisure to visit the harem; no doubt he would find in any case the perfect order which declares respect. One or two shortcomings were obliquely hinted at ("I believe the custom is so-and-so at Susa") but the past was left unprobed. The wardens were concealing sighs of relief, when he asked to see the rooms of the royal ladies.

They led him through. These rooms of state were secluded from the rest, and had their own courtyard, exquisitely tiled. There had been some dismay at their abandoned state, the dry plants and withered creepers, the clogged fountain with green scum and dead fish. All this had been seen to, but the rooms still had the dank smell of long disuse. Silently, just opening his delicate nostrils, Bagoas indicated this.

The rooms of the Royal Wife, despite neglect, were still

luxurious; Darius, though self-indulgent, had been generous too. They led him on to the smaller, but still handsome rooms for the Queen Mother. Sisygambis had stayed here in an early year of her son's short reign. Bagoas looked them over, his head tilted slightly sideways. Unconsciously, over the years, he had picked up this tic from Alexander.

"Very pleasant," he said. "At any rate it can be made so. As you know, the lady Roxane is on her way here from Ekbatana. The King is anxious that she should have an easy journey." The eunuchs pricked up their ears; Roxane's pregnancy was not yet public news. "She will be here in about seven days. I will order some things, and send in good craftsmen. Please see they do all they should."

In a speaking pause, the eunuchs' eyes turned towards the rooms of the Royal Wife. Those of Bagoas followed them, inexpressively.

"Those rooms will be closed at present. Just see they are well aired and kept sweet. You have a key for the outer door? Good." No one said anything. He added, blandly, "There is no need to show these rooms to the lady Roxane. If she should ask, say they are in disrepair." He left politely, as he had come.

At the time, they had decided that Bagoas must have some old score to pay. Favorites and wives were traditional antagonists. The rumor ran that early in her marriage Roxane had tried to poison him, but had never again tried anything, so dreadful had been the anger of the King. The furniture and hangings now sent in were costly, and the finished rooms lacked nothing of royal splendor. "Don't be afraid of extravagance," Bagoas had said. "That is to her taste."

Her caravan duly arrived from Ekbatana. Handed down the steps of her traveling-wagon she had proved to be a young woman of striking, high-nosed beauty, with blue-black hair and dark brilliant eyes. Her pregnancy hardly showed except in opulent softness. She spoke fluent Persian, though with a Bactrian accent which her Bactrian suite did nothing to correct; and had gained a fair command of Greek, a tongue unknown to her before her marriage. Babylon was as foreign to her as India; she had settled without demur in the rooms prepared for her, remarking that they were smaller than those at Ekbatana, but much prettier. They had their own small courtyard, elegant and shady. Darius, who had held his mother in awe as well as in esteem, had always been attentive to her comfort.

Next day a chamberlain, this time of venerable age, announced the King.

The eunuchs waited anxiously. What if Bagoas had acted without authority? The King's anger was said to be rare, but terrible. However, he greeted them courteously in his scanty, formal Persian, and made no comment when shown to Roxane's rooms.

Through chinks and crannies known in the harem since the days of Nebuchadrezzar, the younger concubines glimpsed him on his way. They reported him handsome in countenance, for a westerner at least (fair coloring was not admired in Babylon); and he was not tall, a grave defect, but this they had known already. Surely he must be older than thirty-two, for his hair had grey in it; but they owned that he had presence, and awaited his return to see him again. They expected a lengthy vigil; but he was back in barely the time it would take a careful woman to bathe and dress.

This made the younger ladies hopeful. They cleaned their jewels and reviewed their cosmetics. One or two, who from boredom had let themselves get grossly fat, were derided and cried all day. For a week, each morning dawned full of promise. But the King did not come. Instead, Bagoas reappeared, and conferred in private with the Chief Warden. The heavy door of the Royal Wife's room was opened, and they went inside.

"Yes," said Bagoas. "Not much is needed here. Just there, and there, fresh hangings. The toilet-vessels will be in the treasury?"

Thankfully (they had tempted him more than once) the Warden sent for them; they were exquisite, silver inlaid with gold. A great clothes-chest of cypress-wood stood against the wall. Bagoas raised the lid; there was a drift of faded fragrance. He lifted out a scarf stitched with seed-pearls and small gold beads.

"These, I suppose, were Queen Stateira's?"

"Those she did not take with her. Darius thought nothing too good for her."

Except his life, each thought in the awkward pause. His flight at Issos had left her to end her days under the protection of his enemy. Under the scarf was a veil edged with green scarab-wings from Egypt. Bagoas fingered it gently. "I never saw her. *The loveliest woman of mortal birth in Asia*—was that true?"

"Who has seen every woman in Asia? Yes, it well may be."

"At least I have seen her daughter." He put back the scarf and closed the chest. "Leave all these things. The lady Stateira will like to have them."

"Has she set out from Susa yet?" A different question trembled on the Warden's lips.

Bagoas, well aware of it, said deliberately, "She will be coming when the worst of the heat is over. The King is anxious she should have an easy journey."

The Warden caught a sharp breath. Fat old chamberlain and slender glittering favorite, their eyes exchanged the immemorial communication of their kind. It was the Warden who spoke first.

"So far, everything has gone smoothly *there*." He glanced

towards the other set of rooms. "But as soon as these apartments are opened, there will be talk. There is no preventing
it. You know that as well as I do. Does the King intend to
tell the lady Roxane?"

For a moment, Bagoas' urbane polish cracked, revealing a deep settled grief. He sealed it off again. "I will remind
him if I can. It is not easy just now. He is planning the
funeral of his friend Hephaistion, who died at Ekbatana."

The Warden would have liked to ask if it was true that
this death had sent the King out of his mind for a month
or more. But Bagoas' polish had hardened, warningly.
Quickly the Warden smoothed away curiosity. They said
of Bagoas that, if he chose, he could be the most dangerous
man at court.

"In that case," said the Warden carefully, "we might
delay the work for a while? If I am asked questions, without any sanction from the King . . . ?"

Bagoas paused, looking for a moment uncertain and
still quite young. But he answered crisply, "No, we have
had our orders. He will expect to find them obeyed."

He left, and did not return. It was reported in the harem
that the funeral of the King's friend surpassed that of Queen
Semiramis, renowned in story; that the pyre had been a
burning ziggurat two hundred feet high. But, said the
Warden to anyone who would listen, that was a little fire
to the one he had had to face when the Royal Wife's rooms
were opened, and news reached the lady Roxane.

At her mountain home in Bactria, the harem eunuchs
had been family servants and slaves, who knew their place.
The ancient dignities of the palace chamberlains seemed
to her mere insolence. When she ordered the Warden a
flogging, she was enraged to find no one empowered to
inflict it. The old Bactrian eunuch she had brought from
home, despatched to tell the King, reported that he had
taken a flotilla down the Euphrates to explore the swamps.

When he got back she tried again; first he was busy, and then he was indisposed.

Her father, she was sure, would have seen to it that the Warden was put to death. But the satrapy conferred on him by the King was on the Indian frontier; by the time she could hear back from him, her son would have been born. The thought appeased her. She said to her Bactrian ladies, "Let her come, this great tall flagpole from Susa. The King cannot abide her. If he must do this to please the Persians, what is that to me? Everyone knows that I am his real wife, the mother of his son."

The ladies said in secret, "I would not be that child, if it is a girl."

The King did not come, and Roxane's days hung heavy. Here, at what was to be the center of her husband's empire, she might as well be encamped in Drangiana. She could, if she wished, have entertained the concubines. But these women had been living for years in royal palaces, some of them since she had been a child on her father's mountain crag. She thought with dread of assured Persian elegance, sophisticated talk tossed spitefully over her head. Not one had crossed her threshold; she had rather be thought haughty than afraid. One day however she found one of the ancient crannies; it passed the time to lay an ear to it and hear them talking.

So it was that, when Alexander had been nine days down with marsh-fever, she heard a palace chamberlain gossiping with a harem eunuch. From this she learned two things: that the sickness had flown to the King's chest, and he was like to die; and that the daughter of Darius was with child.

She did not pause, even to hear them out. She called her Bactrian eunuch and her ladies, threw on a veil, brushed past the stunned Nubian giant who guarded the harem, and only answered his shrill cries with, "I must see the King."

The palace eunuchs came running. They could do noth-

ing but run after her. She was the King's wife, not a captive; she stayed in the harem only because to leave it was
unthinkable. On the long marches, out to India and back
to Persia and down to Babylon, wherever the King pitched
camp her baggage wagons had unpacked the wicker screens
which had made her a traveling courtyard, so that she
could leave her covered wagon and take the air. In the cities
she had her curtained litter, her latticed balconies. All this
was not her sentence but her right; it was only whores whom
men displayed. Now, when the unprecedented happened,
to lay hands on her was inconceivable. Guided by her
trembling eunuch, her progress followed by astonished eyes,
she swept through corridors, courtyards, anterooms, till she
reached the Bedchamber. It was the first time she had
entered it; or, for that matter, his own sleeping-place anywhere else. He had never summoned her to his bed, only
gone to hers. It was the custom of the Greeks, so he had
told her.

She paused in the tall doorway, seeing the high cedar ceil-
ing, the daimon-guarded bed. It was like a hall of audience.
Generals, physicians, chamberlains, stupid with surprise,
stood back as she made her way to him.

The heaped pillows that propped him upright gave him
still the illusion of authority. His closed eyes, his parted and
gasping mouth, seemed like a willed withdrawal. She could
not be in his presence without believing that everything
was still under his control.

"Sikandar!" she cried, slipping back into her native dialect. "Sikandar!"

His eyelids, creased and bloodless in sunken sockets,
moved faintly but did not open. The thin skin tightened,
as if to shut out a harsh glare of sun. She saw that his lips
were cracked and dry; the deep scar in his side, from the
wound he had got in India, stretched and shrank with his
laboring breath.

"Sikandar, Sikandar!" she cried aloud. She grasped him by the arm.

He took a deeper breath, and choked on it. Someone leaned over with a towel, and wiped bloody froth from his lips. He did not open his eyes.

As if she had known nothing till now, a cold dagger of realization stabbed her. He was gone out of reach; he would no longer direct her journeys. He would decide nothing, ever again; would never tell her what she had come to ask. For her, for the child within her, he was already dead.

She began to wail, like a mourner over a bier, clawing her face, beating her breast, tearing at her clothes, shaking her disheveled hair. She flung herself forward, her arms across the bed, burying her face in the sheet, hardly aware of the hot, still living flesh beneath it. Someone was speaking; a light, young voice, the voice of a eunuch.

"He can hear all this; it troubles him."

There was a strong grasp on her shoulders, pulling her back. She might have recognized Ptolemy, from the triumphs and processions seen from her lattices; but she was looking across the bed, perceiving who had spoken. She would have guessed, even if she had not seen him once in India, gliding down the Indus on Alexander's flagship, dressed in the brilliant stuffs of Taxila, scarlet and gold. It was the hated Persian boy, familiar of this room she had never entered; he, too, a custom of the Greeks, though her husband had never told her so.

His menial clothes, his haggard exhausted face, conceded nothing. No longer desirable, he had become commanding. Generals and satraps and captains, whose obedience should be to her, who should be rousing the King to answer her, to name his heir—they listened, submissive, to this dancing-boy. As for her, she was an intrusion.

She cursed him with her eyes, but already his attention was withdrawn from her, as he beckoned a slave to take the bloodstained towel, and checked the clean pile beside him. Ptolemy's hard hands released her; the hands of her attendants, gentle, supplicating, insistent, guided her towards the door. Someone picked up her veil from the bed and threw it over her.

Back in her own room, she flung herself down in a furious storm of weeping, pummeling and biting the cushions of her divan. Her ladies, when they dared speak to her, implored her to spare herself, lest the child miscarry. This brought her to herself; she called for mare's milk and figs, which she chiefly craved for lately. Dark fell; she tossed on her bed. At length, dry-eyed, she got up, and paced to and fro in the moon-dappled courtyard, where the fountain murmured like a conspirator in the hot Babylonian night. Once she felt the child move strongly. Laying her hands over the place, she whispered, "Quiet, my little king. I promise you . . . I promise . . ."

She went back to bed, and fell into a heavy sleep. She dreamed she was in her father's fort on the Sogdian Rock, a rampart-guarded cavern under the mountain's crest, with a thousand-foot drop below. The Macedonians were besieging it. She looked down at the swarming men, scattered like dark grains upon the snow; at the red starry campfires plumed with faint smoke; at the colored dots of the tents. The wind was rising, moaning over the crag. Her brother called to her to fit arrowheads with the other women; he rebuked her idleness, and shook her. She woke. Her woman let go her shoulder, but did not speak. She had slept late, the sun was hot in the courtyard. Yet the wind soughed on; the world was full of its noise, rising and falling, like its winter voice when it blew from the immeasurable ranges of the east . . . But this was Babylon.

Here it died down and there it rose, and now it came close at hand, the high wailing of the harem; she could hear now its formal rhythm. The woman beside her, seeing her awake, at once began lamenting, crying out the ancient phrases offered to the widows of Bactrian chieftains time out of mind. They were looking at her. It was for her to lead the dirge.

Obediently she sat up, dragged at her hair, drummed with her fists on her breast. She had known the words since her childhood: "Alas, alas! The light is fallen from the sky, the lion of men is fallen. When he lifted his sword, a thousand warriors trembled; when he opened his hand, it shed gold like the sands of the sea. When he rejoiced, it gladdened us like the sun. As the storm-wind rides the mountains, so he rode to war; like the tempest that fells great forest trees, he rode into the battle. His shield was a strong roof over his people. Darkness is his portion, his house is desolate. Alas! Alas! Alas!"

She laid her hands in her lap. Her wailing ceased. The women, startled, stared at her. She said, "I have lamented; I have finished now." She beckoned her chief waiting-woman and waved the rest away.

"Bring my old traveling-gown, the dark-blue one." It was found, and dust shaken out of it from the Ekbatana road. The stuff was strong; she had to nick it with her paring-knife before it would tear. When she had rent it here and there, she put it on. Leaving her hair uncombed, she ran her hand over a dusty cornice and smeared her face. Then she sent for her Bactrian eunuch.

"Go to the harem, and ask the lady Badia to visit me."

"Hearing is obedience, madam." How did she know the name of Ochos' first-ranking concubine? But it was clearly no time for questions.

From her listening-place, Roxane could hear the fluster in the harem. Some were still wailing for the King, but most were chattering. After a short delay for preparation, Badia

appeared, dressed in the mourning she had put on for King
Ochos, fifteen years before, smelling of herbs and cedar-
wood. For Darius she had not worn it.

Ochos had reigned for twenty years, and she had been a
concubine of his youth. She was in her fifties, graceful once,
now gaunt. Long before his death she had been left behind
in Babylon while younger girls were taken along to Susa.
But she had ruled the harem in her time, and did not forget.

Some minutes were passed in orthodox condolences.
Badia lauded the valor of the King, his justice, his bounty.
Roxane responded as was proper, swaying and keening
softly. Presently she wiped her eyes, and made a few broken
answers. Badia offered the immemorial consolation.

"The child will be his remembrance. You will see him
grow to rival his father's honor."

All this was formula. Roxane abandoned it. "If he lives,"
she sobbed. "If Darius' accursed kindred let him live. But
they will kill him. I know, I know it." She grasped her hair
in both hands and moaned.

Badia caught her breath, her lean face shocked with
memory. "Oh, the good God! Will those days come again?"

Ochos had achieved the throne by wholesale fratricide,
and died by poison. Roxane had no wish to hear reminis-
cences. She flung back her hair. "How can they not? Who
murdered King Ochos when he lay sick? And the young
King Arses and his loyal brothers? And Arses' little son, still
at the breast? And when it was done, who killed the Vizier
his creature, to stop his mouth? Darius! Alexander told me
so."

("I used to think so," Alexander had told her not long
before, "but that was before I'd fought him. He'd not
spirit enough to be more than the Vizier's tool. He killed
him after because he was afraid of him. That was just like
the man.")

"Did the King say so? Ah, the lion of justice, the redresser of wrongs!" Her voice rose, ready to wail again; Roxane lifted a quick repressive hand.

"Yes, he avenged your lord. But my son, who will avenge him? Ah, if you knew!"

Badia raised sharp black eyes, avid with curiosity. "What is it, lady?"

Roxane told her. Alexander, still sick with grief for his boyhood friend, had gone before, leaving her in safety at Ekbatana, to purge of bandits the road to Babylon. Then, weary from the winter war, he had stayed to rest at Susa, and been beguiled by Queen Sisygambis; that old sorceress who, if truth were known, had set on her son, the usurper, to all his crimes. She had brought to the King the daughter of Darius, that clumsy, long-legged girl he had married to please the Persians. Very likely she had drugged him, she was skilled in potions. She had got her grandchild into the King's bed, and told him she was with child by him, though who was to know the truth? And, since he had married her in state in the presence of the Persian and Macedonian lords, what could they do but accept her infant? "But he married her only for show, for policy. He told me so."

(Indeed it was true that before the wedding, appalled by Roxane's frenzy, deafened by her cries, and feeling remorseful, Alexander had said something to this effect. He had made no promises for the future, it being a principle of his to keep the future open; but he had dried her tears, and brought her some handsome earrings.)

"And so," she cried, "under this roof she will bear a grandchild to Ochos' murderer. And who will protect us, now that the King is gone?"

Badia began to cry. She thought of the long dull peaceful years in the quiet ageing harem, where the dangerous outside world was only rumor. She had outgrown the need of men and even of variety, living contentedly with her talking bird and her little red-coated monkey and her old gossiping eunuchs, maintained in comfort by the wandering, distant King. Now there opened before her dreadful ancient memories of betrayal, accusations, humiliation, the waking dread of the new day. It had been a cruel rival who had displaced her with King Ochos. The peaceful years fell from her. She sobbed and wailed; this time for herself.

"What can we do?" she cried. "What can we do?"

Roxane's white, plump, short-fingered hand grasped Badia's wrist. Her great dark eyes, which had cast their spell upon Alexander, were fixed on hers. "The King is dead. We must save ourselves as we best can."

"Yes, lady." The old days were back; once more it was a matter of survival. "Lady, what shall we do?"

Roxane drew her near and they talked softly, remembering the crannies in the wall.

Some time later, quietly by the servants' door came an old eunuch from Badia's household. He carried a box of polished wood. Roxane said, "It is true that you can write Greek?"

"Certainly, madam. King Ochos often called on me."

"Have you good parchment? It is for a royal letter."

"Yes, madam." He opened the box. "When the usurper Darius gave my place to one of his people, I took a little with me."

"Good. Sit down and write."

When she gave him the superscription, he almost spoiled the scroll. But he had not come quite ignorant of his errand; and Badia had told him that if Darius' daughter ruled the harem, she would turn all Ochos' people out in the street to beg. He wrote on. She saw that the script was even and flowing, with the proper formal flourishes. When he had done, she gave him a silver daric and let him go. She did not swear him to silence; it was beneath her dignity, and Badia would have seen to it.

He had brought wax, but she had not sealed it in his presence. Now she drew off a ring Alexander had given her on their wedding night. It was set with a flawless amethyst the color of dark violets, on which Pyrgoletes, his favorite engraver, had carved his portrait. It was nothing like the royal ring of Macedon, with its Zeus enthroned. But Alexander had never been conventional, and she thought that it would serve.

She turned the stone in the light. The work was superb, and though somewhat idealized had caught a vivid look of him. He had given it her when they were at last alone in the bridal chamber; something to serve them in place of words, since neither could speak the other's tongue. He had put it on her, finding a finger it would fit at the second try. She had kissed it respectfully, and then he had embraced her. She remembered how unexpectedly pleasing his body was, with a warm freshness like a young boy's; but she had expected a harder grasp. He should have gone out to be undressed and have a wedding shift put on him; but, instead, he had just tossed off his clothes and stood there stark naked, in which state he had got into bed. She had been too shocked at first to think of anything else, and he had thought she was afraid of him. He had taken a good deal of trouble with her, some of it quite sophisticated; he had had expert tuition, though she did not yet know whose. But what she had really wanted was to be taken by storm. She had adopted postures of submission, proper in a virgin; for anything livelier on the first night, a Bactrian bridegroom would have strangled her. But she could feel he was at a loss, and had a dreadful fear that there would be an unstained bridal sheet for the guests to view next morning. She had nerved herself to embrace him; and afterwards all was well.

She dropped the hot wax on the scroll and pressed in the

gem. Suddenly a piercing memory came to her of a day a few months ago in Ekbatana, one summer afternoon by the fishpool. He had been feeding the carp, coaxing the old sullen king of the pool to come to his hand from its lair under the lily-pads. He would not come in to make love till he had won. After, he had fallen asleep; she remembered the fair boyish skin with the deep dimpled scars, the soft margins of his strong hair. She had wanted to feel and smell him as if he were good to eat, like fresh-baked bread. When she buried her face in him, he half woke and held her comfortably, and slept again. The sense of his physical presence came back to her like life. At last, alone, in silence, she shed real tears.

She wiped them soon. She had business that would not wait.

In the Bedchamber, the long days of dying were over. Alexander had ceased to breathe. The lamenting eunuchs had drawn out the heaped-up pillows; he lay straight and flat in the great bed, restored by stillness to a monumental dignity, but, to the watchers, shocking in his passiveness. A dead man, a corpse.

The generals, hastily called when the end was plainly coming, stood staring blankly. For two days they had been thinking what to do now. Yet, now, it was as if the awaited certainty had been some mere contingency with which their imaginations had been playing. They gazed stupefied at the familiar face, so finally untenanted; feeling almost resentment, so impossible did it seem that anything could happen to Alexander without consent of his. How could he die and leave them in this confusion? How could he throw off responsibility? It was quite unlike him.

A cracked young voice at the outer door suddenly cried

out, "He's gone, he's gone!" It was a youth of eighteen, one of the royal body-squires, who had been taking his turn on guard duty. He broke into hysterical weeping, which rose above the keening of the eunuchs around the bed. Someone must have led him away, for his voice could be heard receding, raw with uncontainable grief.

It was as if he had invoked an ocean. He had blundered, sobbing, into half the Macedonian army, gathered around the palace to await the news.

Most of them had passed through the Bedchamber the day before; but he had known them still, he had remembered them; they, most of all, had good cause to expect a miracle. Now a huge clamor rose; of grief, of ritual mourning; of protest, as if some authority could be found to blame; of dismay at the uncertainties of the shattered future.

The sound aroused the generals. Their reflexes, trained to a hair by the dead man on the bed, snapped into action. Panic must be dealt with instantly. They ran out to the great platform above the forecourt. A herald, wavering at his post, was barked at by Perdikkas, lifted his long-stemmed trumpet, and blew the assembly call.

The response was ragged. Only yesterday, believing the call to be from Alexander, they would in silent minutes have sorted themselves into their files and phalanxes, each troop competing to get into formation first. Now, nature's laws were suspended. Those in front had to shout back to the rear that it was Perdikkas. Since Hephaistion's death he had been Alexander's second in command. When he roared at them, it gave them some sense of security; they shuffled and shoved themselves into a semblance of order.

The Persian soldiers fell in with the rest. Their mourning outcries had counterpointed the Macedonians' clamor. Now they grew quiet. They were—they had been—soldiers of Alexander, who had made them forget they were a con-

quered people, given them pride in themselves, made the
Macedonians accept them. The early frictions had been
almost over, Greek soldier slang was full of Persian words,
a comradeship had begun. Now, suddenly, feeling themselves once more defeated natives on sufferance in an alien
army, they looked at each other sidelong, planning deser-
tion.

At Perdikkas' signal, Peukestes strode forward, a reassuring figure; a man renowned for valor, who had saved Alexander's life in India when he took his near-mortal wound.
Now, tall, handsome, commanding, bearded in the fashion
of his satrapy, he addressed them in Persian as correct and
aristocratic as his dress. Formally he announced to them
the death of the Great King. In due course, his successor
would be proclaimed to them. They might now dismiss.

The Persians were calmed. But a deep muttering growl
arose from the Macedonians. By their ancestral law, the
right to choose a king belonged to them; to the Assembly
of all male Macedonians able to bear arms. What was this
talk of a proclamation?

Peukestes stood back for Perdikkas. There was a pause.
For twelve years, both of them had watched Alexander
dealing with Macedonians. They were not men who could
be told to hold their peace and await authority's pleasure.
They had to be talked to, and he had done it; only once, in
all the twelve years, without success. Even then, once they
had made him turn back from India, they were all his own.
Now, faced with this disorder, for a moment Perdikkas
expected to hear approaching the brisk impatient footsteps;
the crisp low-spoken reprimand, the high ringing voice
creating instant stillness.

He did not come; and Perdikkas, though he lacked magic,
understood authority. He fell, as Alexander had done at
need, into the Doric patois of the homeland, their own

boyhood tongue before they were schooled into polite Greek. They had all lost, he said, the greatest of kings, the bravest and best of warriors, that the world had seen since the sons of the gods forsook the earth.

Here he was stopped by a huge swelling groan; no voluntary tribute, but an outburst of naked misery and bereavement. When he could be heard again, he said, "And the grandsons of your grandsons will say so still. Remember, then, that your loss is measured by your former fortune. You out of all men, past or to come, have had your share in the glory of Alexander. And now it is for you, his Macedonians, to whom he has bequeathed the mastery of half the world, to keep your courage, and show you are the men he made you. All will be done according to the law."

The hushed crowd gazed up in expectation. When Alexander had talked them quiet, he had always had something to tell them. Perdikkas knew it; but all he had to tell was that he himself was now, effectively, the King in Asia. It was too soon; they knew only one King, alive or dead. He told them to go back to camp and wait for further orders.

Under his eye they began to leave the forecourt; but when he had gone in, many came back by ones and twos, and settled down with their arms beside them, ready for night, to keep the death-watch.

Down in the city the sound of lamentation, like a brushfire with a high wind behind it, spread from the crowded streets nearest the palace, on through the suburbs to the houses built along the walls. Above the temples the tall thin smoke-plumes, which had been rising upright in the still air from the sacred fires, one after another dipped and died. By the heap of damp ashes in Bel-Marduk's brazier, the priests reminded each other that this was the second time in little more than a month. The King had ordered it on the day of his friend's funeral. "We warned him of the omen, but he would hear nothing. He was a foreigner, when all is said."

Theirs was the first fire quenched. In the temple of Mithra, guardian of the warrior's honor, lord of loyalty and the given word, a young priest stood in the sanctuary with a water-ewer in his hand. Above the altar was carved the symbol of the winged sun, at war with the dark, age after age till the last victory. The fire still burned high, for the young man had been feeding it extravagantly, as if it had power to rekindle the sinking life of the King. Even now, when he had been ordered to extinguish it, he put down his ewer, ran to a coffer of Arabian incense, and flung a handful to sparkle into fragrance. Last of the officiants, it was not till his offering had lifted into the summer sky that he poured the water hissing upon the embers.

On the Royal Road to Susa, a courier traveled, his racing dromedary eating the miles with its smooth loping stride. Before it needed rest he would have reached the next relay-post, whence a fresh man and beast would carry his charge on through the night.

His stage was halfway of the journey. The parchment in his saddlebag had been passed to him by the man before, without pause for questions. Only the first stage out from Babylon had been run by a rider unknown to his relief. This stranger, when asked if it was true that the King was sick, had replied that it might be so for all he knew, but he had no time for gossiping. Silent haste was the first rule of the corps; the relief had saluted and sped away, showing, wordlessly, to the next man in the chain, that his letter was sealed with the image of the King.

It was said that a despatch by Royal Messenger would outstrip even the birds. Winged rumor itself could not overtake it; for at night rumor stops to sleep.

Two travelers, who had reined in to let the courier past, were nearly thrown as their horses squealed and reared at the detested smell of camel. The elder man, who was about thirty-five, stocky, freckled and red-haired, mastered his mount first, wresting back its head till the rough bit dripped blood. His brother, some ten years younger, auburn and conventionally good-looking, took longer because he had tried to reassure the horse. Kassandros watched his efforts with contempt. He was the eldest son of the Regent of Macedon, Antipatros, and was a stranger in Babylonia. He had reached it lately, sent by his father to find out why Alexander had summoned him to Macedon and sent Krateros to assume the regency in his stead.

Iollas, the younger, had marched with Alexander, and till lately been his cupbearer. His appointment had been by way of an appeasing gesture to their father; Kassandros had been left behind on garrison duty in Macedon, because he and Alexander had disliked each other since they were boys.

When the horse was quiet, Iollas said, "That was a Royal Messenger."

"May he and his brute drop dead."

"Why is he riding? Perhaps—it's all over now."

Kassandros, looking back towards Babylon, said, "May the dog of Hades eat his soul."

For some time they rode in silence, Iollas looking at the road before him. At last he said, "Well, no one can turn Father out now. Now he can be King."

"King?" growled Kassandros. "Not he. He took his oath and he'll keep it. Even to the barbarian's brat, if it's a boy."

Iollas' horse started, feeling its rider's shock. "Then why? Why did you make me do it? . . . Not for Father? . . . Only for hate! Almighty God, I should have known!"

Kassandros leaned over and slashed his riding-quirt down on the young man's knee. He gave a startled cry of pain and anger.

"Don't dare do that again! We're not at home now, and I'm not a boy."

Kassandros pointed to the red weal. "Pain's a reminder. You did nothing. Remember, nothing. Keep it in your head." A little way further on, seeing tears in Iollas' eyes, he said with grudging forbearance, "Like as not he took fever from the marsh air. By now he must have drunk dirty water often enough. The peasants down river drink swamp-water, and *they* don't die of it. Keep your mouth shut. Or *you* might die of it."

Iollas swallowed and gulped. Dragging his hand across his eyes, and streaking his face with the black dust of the Babylonian plain, he said huskily, "He never got back his strength after that arrow-wound in India. He couldn't afford a fever . . . He was good to me. I only did it for Father. Now you say he won't be King."

"*He* won't be King. But whatever name they call it, he'll die the ruler of Macedon and all Greece. And he's an old man now."

Iollas gazed at him in silence; then spurred his horse and galloped ahead through the yellow wheatfields, his sobs catching their rhythm from the pounding of the hooves.

Next day in Babylon the leading generals prepared for the Assembly that was to choose a ruler of the Macedonians. Their law did not demand primogeniture as inalienable. It was the right of the men in arms to choose among the royal family.

When Philip had died, it had been simple. Almost all the fighting-men were still at home. Alexander at twenty had already made a name for himself, and no other claimant had been so much as named. Even when Philip, a younger brother, had been chosen before the child of King Perdikkas, lately fallen in battle, that had been simple too; Philip had been a tried commander, the child an infant in arms, and they were at war.

Now, Macedonian troops were scattered in strongpoints all over central Asia. Ten thousand veterans were marching home for discharge under the command of Krateros, a youngish man, whom Alexander had ranked next after Hephaistion, and who was one of the royal kindred. There were the garrison troops in Macedon, and in the great stone forts which commanded the passes into southern Greece. All this the men at Babylon knew. But no one of them questioned that theirs was the right to choose a king. They were the army of Alexander, and that was everything.

Outside on the hot parade ground they waited, disputing, conjecturing, passing rumors on. Sometimes, as their impatience and disquiet mounted, the noise would surge like a breaker on a pebbled beach.

The generals inside, the high command known as the Royal Bodyguard, had been trying to get hold of the chief officers of the aristocratic Companions, with whom they wished to confer in their dilemma. Failing in this, they ordered the herald to blow a call for quiet, and summon them by name. The herald, knowing no army call for quiet alone, blew "Assemble for orders." It was received by the impatient men as "Come to Assembly."

Clamorously they poured through the great doors into the audience hall, while the herald shouted against the din the names he had been given, and the officers he named, those who could hear him, tried to shove themselves through the crowd. The crush inside grew dangerous; the doors were shut, in desperation, on everyone who had entered, authorized or not. The herald, gazing helplessly at the milling, cursing mob left in the courtyard, said to himself that if Alexander had seen it, someone would soon be wishing he'd never been born.

First to get in, because others had made way for them, were the men of the Companions, the horse-owning lords of Macedon, and any officers who had been near the doors. The rest of the crowd was a mixture of high and low, thrown anyhow together. The one thing they had in common was a deep unease, and the aggressiveness of worried men. It had come home to them that they were isolated troops in conquered country, half their world away from home. They had come here through faith in Alexander, in him alone. What they craved now was not a king but a leader.

The doors once closed, all eyes sought the royal dais. There, as often before, were the great men, Alexander's nearest friends, standing around the throne, the ancient throne of Babylon; its arms carved into crouching Assyrian bulls, its back recarved for Xerxes into the winged image of the unconquered sun. Here they had seen the small, compact, bright figure, needing a footstool, glowing like a jewel in too large a box, the spread wings of Ahura-Mazda above his head. Now the throne was empty. Across its back was the royal robe, and on its seat the diadem.

A low, sighing groan ran through the pillared hall. Ptolemy, who read the poets, thought it was like the climax of a tragedy, when the upstage doors are flung open, disclosing to the chorus that their fears are true and the King is dead.

Perdikkas stepped forward. All Alexander's friends here present, he said, would witness that the King had given him the royal ring. But, being speechless, he could not say what powers he was conferring. "He looked at me fixedly, and it was clear he wished to speak, but his breath failed him. So, men of Macedon, here is the ring." He drew it off, and laid it beside the crown. "Bestow it as you choose, according to ancestral law."

There were murmurs of admiration and suspense, as at a play. He waited, still downstage, like a good actor who could time his lines. So Ptolemy thought, glancing at the alert arrogant face, now set in impassive dignity; a well-carved mask; a mask for a king?

Perdikkas said, "Our loss is beyond all measure, that we know. We know it is not to be thought of that the throne should pass to anyone not of his blood. Roxane his wife is five months with child; let us pray it will be a boy. He must first be born, and then he must come of age. Meantime, whom do you wish to rule you? It is for you to say."

The voices murmured; the generals on the dais looked restively at each other; Perdikkas had not presented another speaker. Suddenly, unannounced, Niarchos, the admiral, stepped forward; a spare, lean-waisted Cretan, with a brown weathered face. The hardships of the dreadful voyage down the Gedrosian coast had put ten years on him; he looked fifty, but still wiry and fit. The men quietened to hear him; he had seen monsters of the deep, and put them to flight with trumpets. Unused to public speaking upon the land, he used the voice with which he hailed ships at sea, startling them with its loudness.

"Macedonians, I put before you as Alexander's heir the son of Darius' daughter Stateira. The King left her pregnant when last he passed through Susa." There were surprised, disconcerted murmurs; he raised his voice over them, as he would have done in a noisy storm. "You saw their wedding. You saw it was a royal one. He meant to send for her here. He told me so."

This wholly unexpected news of a woman who, barely

glimpsed on her bridal day, had vanished at once into the recesses of the Susa harem, caused a surge of confusion and dismay. Presently a broad-spoken peasant voice called out, "Ah, but did he say aught about the bairn?"

"No," said Niarchos. "In my belief he meant to bring up both sons under his eye, if both were sons, and choose the better one. But he's not lived to do it; and Stateira's child has right of rank."

He stepped back; he had nothing more to say. He had done what seemed his duty, and that was all. Looking out over the sea of heads, he remembered how Alexander, lean as a bone and hollow-eyed from the desert march, had greeted him when he brought the fleet safe back, embracing him with tears of relief and joy. Since they were boys, Niarchos had been in love with him in an unsexual, undemanding way; that moment had been the climax of his life. What he would do with the rest of it, he could not begin to think.

Perdikkas' teeth were set with anger. He had urged the men to appoint a regent—who but himself? Now, they had been sidetracked into debating the succession. Two unborn children, who might both be girls. It was in the family; Philip had sired a horde of daughters, and only one son unless you counted the fool. The regency was the thing. Philip himself had started out as regent for an infant heir, but the Macedonians had not wasted much time in electing him King. Perdikkas himself had a good strain of the royal blood . . . What had possessed Niarchos? There was no heading the men off now.

Their debate grew noisy and acrimonious. If, in their view, Alexander had had a fault, it was letting himself get Persianized. The Susa weddings, a serious manifesto, had caused much more unease than the campaign marriage with Roxane, the sort of thing his father used to do time and again. They had been indulgent towards the dancing-boy, as towards a pet monkey or dog; but why could he not have married a girl from a decent old Macedonian family, instead of two barbarians? Now this was what had come of it.

Some argued that any offspring of his must be accepted, half-breed or not. Others said there was no knowing if he would have acknowledged either; and you could be sure, if either of those women had a stillbirth or a girl, they would smuggle something in. They were crawling on their bellies to no Persian changeling . . .

Ptolemy watched the scene with grief and anger, longing to be gone. From the time when Alexander's death had become a certainty, he had known where he wished to go. Ever since Egypt had opened its arms to Alexander as its liberator from the Persian yoke, Ptolemy had been entranced by it, its immemorial mellow civilization, its stupendous monuments and temples, the rich life of its sustaining river. It was defensible as an island, protected by sea and desert and wilderness; one had only to win the people's trust to hold it secure forever. Perdikkas and the rest would gladly give him the satrapy; they wanted him out of the way.

He was dangerous, a man who could claim to be Alexander's brother, even though from adultery when Philip was in his teens. His paternity was unproved and unacknowledged; but Alexander had always had a special place for him, and everyone knew it. Yes, Perdikkas would be glad to see him off to Africa. But did the man think he could make himself Alexander's heir? That was what he was after; it was written all over him. Something must be done; and now.

The soldiers, when Ptolemy stepped forward, broke off their disputes to give him a hearing. He had been a boy-

hood friend of Alexander; he had presence without Perdikkas' arrogance; men who had served under him liked
him. A group of them gave him a cheer.

"Macedonians. I see you do not wish to choose a king
from the offspring of the conquered."

There was loud applause. The men, who had all come
armed—it was the proof of their voting right—beat their
spears on their shields till the high hall echoed. Ptolemy
raised a hand for quiet.

"We do not know if either wife of Alexander will bear
a boy. If one or both should, when they come of age they
must be brought before you and your sons, for Assembly to
decide whom the Macedonians will accept. In the meantime, you await Alexander's heir. But who will act for him?
Here before you are those whom Alexander honored with
trust. Lest too much power go to one man, I propose a
Council of Regency."

The voices were tempered. Reminded that in fifteen
years or so they could still reject both claimants, they saw
where the day's serious business lay. Ptolemy said into the
new quiet, "Remember Krateros. Alexander trusted him
like himself. He sent him to govern Macedon. That is why
he is not present now."

That got home to them. They honored Krateros next to
Alexander; he was of royal stock, capable, brave, handsome
and careful of their needs. Ptolemy could feel the eyes of
Perdikkas, red-hot in his back. Let him make the best of it;
I did as I had to do.

As they buzzed and muttered below, Ptolemy thought
suddenly, Only a few days back we were all alike the Friends
of Alexander, just waiting for him to get up again and lead
us. What are we now, and what am I?

He had never set great store on being Philip's son; it had
cost him too much in childhood. Philip had been a no-

body, a younger son held hostage by the Thebans, when he was born. "Can't you make your bastard behave?" his father would say to his mother when he was in trouble. Philip had won him more than one boy's share of beatings. Later, when Philip was King and he himself a royal squire, his luck had turned; but what he had learned to care for was not being Philip's son, if indeed he was. He had cared, with affection and with growing pride, to be Alexander's brother. Never mind, he thought, whether it is the truth of my blood, or not. It is the truth of my heart.

A new voice broke his brief reverie. Aristonous, one of the Bodyguard, came forward to point out that whatever Alexander might have meant, he had given his ring to Perdikkas. He had looked around first, and knew what he was doing. This was fact, not guesswork; and Aristonous was for abiding by it.

He spoke simply and frankly, and carried the Assembly. They shouted Perdikkas' name, and many called to him to take back the ring. Slowly, scanning them, he took a few steps forward towards it. For a moment his eye met Ptolemy's, noting him in the way a man notes a newfound enemy.

It would not yet do, Perdikkas thought, to look over-eager. He needed another voice in Aristonous' support.

The hall, crowded with sweating men, was stiflingly close and hot. To the stink of humanity was added that of urine, where a few men had surreptitiously relieved themselves in corners. The generals on the dais were growing stupefied by their varied feelings of grief, anxiety, resentment, impatience and frustration. Suddenly, shouting something indistinct, an officer elbowed his way forward through the crowd. What, they all thought, can Meleager have to say?

He had been a phalanx commander since Alexander's

first campaign, but had risen no higher. Alexander had confided to Perdikkas, one night at supper, that he was a good soldier if one did not stretch his mind.

He arrived below the dais, red-faced with the heat, with anger, and, by his looks, with wine; then lifted a harsh furious voice which stunned the crowd almost silent. "That's the royal ring! Are you letting that fellow take it? Give it him now, he'll keep it till he dies! No wonder he wants a king who's not yet born!"

The generals, calling for order, were barely heard above the sudden roar. Meleager had aroused, from a kind of restless torpor, a mass of men who had not been heard before, the mental lees of the crowd. They took notice now, as they would of a knife-duel in the street, a man beating his wife, or a vicious dogfight; and shouted for Meleager, as if for the winning dog.

In the camp, Perdikkas could have restored order in minutes. But this was Assembly; he was not so much Commander-in-Chief as candidate. Repression might seem to forecast tyranny. He made a gesture of tolerant contempt, meaning "Even such a man must be heard."

He had seen the naked hatred in Meleager's face. The rank of their fathers had been much the same; they had both been royal squires to Philip; both had looked with secret envy at the tight-knit circle round the young Alexander. Then, when Philip was assassinated, Perdikkas had been the first to run down the fleeing assassin. Alexander had praised him, noticed and promoted him. With promotion came opportunity; he had never looked back. When Hephaistion died, he had been given his command. Meleager had remained an infantry phalanx leader, useful if not too much was put on him. And, as Perdikkas saw, the knowledge that burned him was that they had started equal.

"How do we know," Meleager shouted, "that Alexander

gave him anything? Whose word do we have for it? His and his friends'! And what are they after? Alexander's treasure here, which all of us helped to win! Will you stand for that?"

The noise turned to turmoil. The generals, who had thought that they knew men, saw incredulously that Meleager was beginning to lead a mob; men ready to sack the palace like a conquered town. Chaos broke out around it.

Perdikkas summoned, desperately, all his expert powers of dominance.

"*Halt!*" he thundered. There was a reflex response. He barked his orders; sufficient men obeyed them. Solid ranks with locked shields formed before the inner doors. The yelling sank to growls. "I am glad to see," said Perdikkas in his deep voice, "that we still have here some soldiers of Alexander."

There was a hush, as if he had invoked the name of an offended god. The mob began to lose itself in the crowd. The shields were lowered.

In the uncertain pause, a rustic voice, from somewhere deep in the press, made itself heard. "Shame on you all, I say! Like the Commander says, we're soldiers of Alexander. It's *his* blood we want to rule us, not regents for foreign children. When we've Alexander's true-born brother, here in this very house."

There was an astonished silence. Ptolemy, stunned, felt all his well-considered decisions shaken by a surge of primitive instinct. The ancient throne of Macedon, with its savage history of tribal rivalries and fratricidal wars, reached out its beckoning spell. Philip—Alexander—Ptolemy . . .

The peasant spearman below, having gained a hearing, went on with gathering confidence. "His own brother which King Philip himself acknowledged, as every one of you knows. Alexander always cared for him like his own. I do hear say he was backward as a boy, but it's not a month since the both of them were sacrificing for their father's soul at the household altar. I was on escort, and so were my mates here. He done everything right."

There were sounds of assent. Ptolemy could barely repress the stare and dropped jaw of utter stupefaction. *Arridaios!* They must be mad.

"King Philip," persisted the soldier, "married Philinna lawful, which was his right to have more wives than one. So I say, pass by the foreign babes, and let's have his son, which is his rightful heir."

There was applause from law-abiding men, who had been shocked by Meleager. On the dais, the silence was general and appalled. Simple or devious, not one of them had thought of this.

"Is it true?" said Perdikkas quickly to Ptolemy through the noise. "*Did* Alexander take him to the shrine?" Urgency overcame enmity; Ptolemy would surely know.

"Yes." Ptolemy remembered the two heads side by side, dark and fair, the apprentice piece and the sculptor's. "He's been better lately. He's not had a fit in a year. Alexander said he must be kept in mind of who his father was."

"Arridaios!" came a growing shout. "Give us Alexander's brother! Long live Macedon! Arridaios!"

"How many saw him?" said Perdikkas.

"The Companion escort and the foot-guard, and anyone looking on. He behaved quite properly. He always does . . . did, with Alexander."

"We can't have this. They don't know what they're doing. This must be stopped."

The speaker, Peithon, was a short wiry man with a foxily pointed, rufous face and a sharp foxy bark. He was one of the Bodyguard, a good commander, but not known for the spirit of persuasion. He stepped out, forestalling Perdikkas, and snapped, "Alexander's brother! You'd do better to choose his horse!"

The bite in his voice produced a brief, but not friendly silence; he was not on the parade ground now. He went on, "The fellow's a halfwit. Dropped on his head as a baby, and falls down in fits. Alexander's kept him like a child, with a nurse to tend him. Do you want an idiot for a king?"

Perdikkas swallowed a curse. Why had this man ever been promoted? Competent in the field, but no grip on morale in quarters. He himself, if this fool had not stepped in, would have recalled to the men the romantic winning of Roxane, the storming of the Sogdian Rock, the victor's chivalry; winning back their minds to Alexander's son. Now their feelings had been offended. They saw Arridaios as a victim of obscure intrigues. They had *seen* the man, and he had behaved like anyone else.

Alexander was always fortunate, thought Ptolemy. Already people wore his image cut on rings, for luck-charms. What spiteful fate inspired him, so near his end, with this kindly impulse towards a harmless fool? But, of course, there was a ceremony to come, at which he *must* appear. Perhaps Alexander had thought of that . . .

"Shame!" the men were shouting up to Peithon. "Arridaios, Arridaios, we want Arridaios!" He yapped at them; but they drowned his voice with boos.

Nobody noticed, till too late, that Meleager was missing.

It had been a long, dull day for Arridaios. No one had come to see him except the slave with his meals, which had been overcooked and half cold. He would have liked to hit the slave, but Alexander did not allow him. Someone from Alexander came nearly every day to see how he was, but today there had been no one to tell about the food. Even old Konon, who looked after him, had gone off just after getting-up time, saying he had to attend a meeting or some such thing, and hardly listening to a word he said.

He needed Konon for several things: to see he had something nice for supper, to find him a favorite striped stone he had mislaid, and to say why there had been such a terrible noise that morning, wailing and howling which seemed to come from everywhere, as if thousands of people were being beaten at once. From his window on the park, he had seen a crowd of men all running towards the palace. Perhaps, soon, Alexander would come to see him, and tell him what it was all about.

Sometimes he did not come for a very long time, and they said he was away on a campaign. Arridaios would stay in camp, or sometimes, as now, in a palace, till he came back again. Often he brought presents, colored sweets, carved painted horses and lions, a piece of crystal for his collection, and once a beautiful scarlet cloak. Then the slaves would fold the tents and they would all move on. Perhaps this was going to happen now.

Meantime, he wanted the scarlet cloak to play with. Konon had said it was far too hot for cloaks, he would only make it dirty and spoil it. It was locked in the chest, and Konon had the key.

He got out all his stones, except the striped one, and laid them out in pictures; but not having the best one spoiled it. A flush of anger came over him; he picked up the biggest stone and beat it on the table-top again and again. A stick would have been better, but he was not allowed one, Alexander himself had taken it away.

A long time ago, when he lived at home, he had been left mostly with the slaves. No one else wanted to see him. Some were kind when they had time, but some had mocked him and knocked him about. As soon as he began to travel with Alexander, the slaves were different and more polite, and one was even afraid of him. It seemed a good time to get his own back, so he had beaten the man till his head bled and he fell down on the floor. Arridaios had never known till then how strong he was. He had gone on hitting till they carried the man away. Then, suddenly, Alexander had appeared; not dressed for dinner, but with armor on, all dirty and splashed with mud, and out of breath. He had looked quite frightening, like a different person, his eyes pale grey and large in his dirty face; and he had made Arridaios swear on their father's head never to do such a thing again. He had remembered it today when his food was late. He did not want his father's ghost to come after him. He had been terrified of him, and had sung with joy on hearing he was dead.

It was time for his ride in the park, but he was not allowed to go without Konon, who kept him on a leading-rein. He wished Alexander would come, and take him again to the shrine. He had held everything nicely, and poured on the wine and oil and incense after Alexander did, and had let them take the gold cups away though he would have liked to keep them; and afterwards, Alexander had said he had done splendidly.

Someone was coming! Heavy feet, and a clank of armor. Alexander was quicker and lighter than that. A soldier came in whom he had never seen before; a tallish man with a red face and straw-colored hair, holding his helmet under his arm. They looked at one another.

Arridaios, who knew nothing of his own appearance, knew still less that Meleager was thinking, Great Zeus! Philip's face. What is inside it? The young man had, in fact, much of his father's structure, square face, dark brows and beard, broad shoulders and short neck. Since eating was his chief pleasure he was overweight, though Konon had never allowed him to get gross. Delighted to see a visitor at last, he said eagerly, "Are you going to take me to the park?"

"No, sir." He stared avidly at Arridaios, who, disconcerted, tried to think if he had done anything wrong. Alexander had never sent this man before. "Sir. I have come to escort you to Assembly. The Macedonians have elected you their King."

Arridaios stared at him with alarm, followed by a certain shrewdness. "You're telling lies. *I'm* not the King, my brother is. He said to me, Alexander said, 'If I didn't look after you, someone would try to make you King, and you'd end up being killed.'" He backed away, eyeing Meleager with growing agitation. "I won't go to the park with you. I'll go with Konon. You fetch him here. If you don't, I'll tell Alexander of you."

His retreat was blocked by the heavy table. The soldier walked right up to him, so that he flinched instinctively, remembering boyhood beatings. But the man just stared into his eyes, and, very slowly, spoke.

"Sir. Your brother is dead. *King Alexander is dead.* The Macedonians are calling for you. Come with me."

Since Arridaios did not move, he grasped his arm and guided him to the door. He came unresisting, not heeding where he was led, striving to come to terms with a world which Alexander did not rule.

So expeditious had Meleager been that the crowd in the hall was still shouting "Arridaios!" when he himself appeared upon the dais. Confronted by this sounding sea of men, he gazed in a numb astonishment, giving a brief illusion of dignified reserve.

Most of the dumbfounded generals had never seen him before; only a few of the men had glimpsed him. But every

Macedonian over thirty had seen King Philip. There was a
pause of perfect silence; then the cheers began.

"Philip! Philip! Philip!"

Arridaios sent a terrified look over his shoulder. Was his
father coming, had he never been really dead? Meleager
beside him caught the revealing change of countenance
and whispered swiftly, "They are cheering *you.*" Arridaios
gazed about, slightly reassured, but still bewildered. Why
did they call so for his father? His father was dead. *Alexander* was dead . . .

Meleager stepped forward. So much, he thought triumph-
antly, for that upstart Perdikkas and his unborn ward.
"Here, Macedonians, is the son of Philip, the brother of
Alexander. Here is your rightful King."

Spoken loudly and almost in his ear, it reached Arridaios
with awful comprehension. He knew why all these men
were here and what was happening. "No!" he cried, his
high plaintive voice issuing incongruously from his large
hirsute face. "I'm not the King! I told you, I can't be King.
Alexander told me not to."

But he had addressed himself to Meleager, and was
inaudible beyond the dais, drowned by the cheering. The
generals, appalled, all turned upon Meleager, talking across
him. He listened with mounting fear to the loud angry
voices. Clearly he recalled Alexander's large deep-set eyes,
fixed upon his, warning him of what would happen if they
tried to make him King. While Meleager was quarreling
with the tall dark man in the middle of the dais, he bolted
for the now unguarded inner door. Outside, in the warren-
like passages of the ancient palace, he wandered sobbing
to himself, seeking the way back to his familiar room.

In the hall, new uproar began. None of this had prece-
dent. Both the last two kings had been elected by acclamation, and led with traditional paeans to the royal palace

at Aigai, whence each had confirmed his accession by directing his predecessor's funeral.

Meleager, wrangling with Perdikkas, had not missed his fugitive candidate till he was warned by sounds of derision from the floor. Feeling was swinging against him; the powerful presence of Perdikkas had appeal for men seeking some source of confidence and strength. Meleager saw that only instant resource would avail. He turned and ran, followed by boos, through the door Arridaios had used. The most vocal of his supporters—not the loot-hungry mob, but kinsmen and fellow-clansmen and men with grudges against Perdikkas—took alarm and hurried after.

Before long they ran down their quarry, standing where two passages met, debating with himself which way to turn. At sight of them he cried out, "No! Go away!" and started to run. Meleager grasped his shoulder. He submitted, looking terror-stricken. Clearly in this state he could not appear. Gently, calmingly, Meleager changed his grip to a protective caress.

"Sir, you must listen. Sir, you've nothing to fear. You were a good brother to Alexander. He was the rightful King; it would have been wrong, just as he said, for you to take his throne. But now he is dead, and *you* are the rightful King. The throne is yours." A flash of inspiration came to him. "There is a present for you on it. A beautiful purple cloak."

Arridaios, already soothed by the kindly voice, now brightened visibly. No one had laughed; things were too urgent and too dangerous.

"Can I keep it all the time?" he asked cannily. "You won't lock it up?"

"No, indeed. The moment you have it, you can put it on."

"And have it all day?"

"All night too, if you wish." As he began to guide his prize along the passage, a new thought struck him. "When the men called 'Philip!' it was you they meant. They are honoring you with your father's name. You will be King Philip of Macedon."

King Philip, thought Arridaios. It gave him confidence. His father must be really dead, if his name could be given away, like a purple cloak. It would be well to take them both. He was still buoyed by this decision when Meleager steered him onto the dais.

Smiling around at the exclamations, he saw at once the great swath of color draped upon the throne, and walked briskly towards it. Sounds which he had mistaken for friendly greetings died; the Assembly, arrested by his changed demeanor, watched the drama almost in silence.

"There, sir, is our present to you," said Meleager in his ear.

To a ground-bass of restless murmurs, Philip Arridaios lifted the robe from the throne, and held it up before him.

It was the robe of state, made at Susa for the marriage of Alexander to Stateira daughter of Darius, and of his eighty honored friends to their Persian brides, with the whole of his army as his wedding guests. In this robe he had given audience to envoys from half the known world, during his last progress down to Babylon. It was of a wool as dense as velvet and soft as silk, dyed with Tyrian murex to a soft glowing crimson just tinged with purple, pure as the red of a dark rose. The breast and back were worked with the sunburst, the Macedonian royal blazon, in balas rubies and gold. A sleeveless dalmatic, it was clasped on the shoulders with two gold lion-masks, worn at their weddings by three kings of Macedon. The hot afternoon sun slanted down from a high window on the lions' emerald eyes. The new Philip gazed at it in rapture.

Meleager said, "Let me help you to put it on."

He raised it, and slipped it over Philip's head. Radiant with pleasure, he looked out at the cheering men. "Thank you," he said, as he had been taught when he was a child.

The cheers redoubled. The son of Philip had come in with dignity, looking like a king. At first he must simply have been abashed and modest. Now they were for the royal blood against the world.

"Philip! Philip! Long live Philip!"

Ptolemy felt almost choked with grief and anger. He remembered the wedding morning, when he and Hephaistion had gone to Alexander's room in the Susa palace to dress the bridegroom. They had exchanged the jokes which were traditional, along with private ones of their own. Alexander, who had been planning for weeks this great ceremony of racial concord, had been almost incandescent; one could have taken him for a man in love. It was Hephaistion who had remembered the lion brooches and pinned them on the robe. To see it now on a grinning idiot made Ptolemy long to spit Meleager on his sword. Towards the poor fool himself he felt horror rather than anger. He knew him well; he had often gone, when Alexander was busy, to make sure he was not neglected or ill-used; such things, it was tacitly agreed, were better kept in the family. Philip . . . ! Yes, it would stick.

He said to Perdikkas, who was beside him, "Alexander should have had him smothered."

Perdikkas, unheeding, strode forward, blazing with rage, trying vainly to be heard above the din. Pointing at Philip, he made a sweeping gesture of rejection and scorn.

Shouts of support came from just below him. The Companions, foremost by right or rank, had had the clearest view. They had heard of the fool; they had watched, in silent grief or sheer incredulity, the assumption of the robe.

Now their outrage found vent. Their strong voices, trained in the piercing war-paean of the charging cavalry, overpowered all other sound.

It was as if the robe of Alexander had been a battle-standard, suddenly unfurled. Men started to put their helmets on. The hammering of spears on shields grew to a volume like the sound of onset. Nearer, more deadly, came the hiss and whisper of the Companions' unsheathed swords.

In alarm Meleager saw the powerful aristocracy of Macedon rallying in force against him. Even his own faction might fall off from him, unless forced to commit themselves beyond retreat. Each common soldier now shouting "Philip!" was, after all, the tribesman of some lord. He must divide them from tribal allegiances, create new action. With the thought, the answer came to him. His own genius amazed him. How could Alexander have passed such a leader by?

Firmly, but imperceptibly, he guided the smiling Philip to the edge of the dais. The impression that he meant to speak procured a moment's quiet, if only from curiosity. Meleager spoke into it.

"Macedonians! You have chosen your King! Do you mean to stand by him?" The spearmen replied with defiant cheers. "Then come with him now, and help him confirm his right. A King of Macedon must entomb his predecessor."

He paused. He had real silence now. A ripple of shock could almost be felt, passing through the packed, sweat-stinking hall.

Meleager lifted his voice. "Come! The body of Alexander awaits its rites. Here is his heir to perform them. Don't let them cheat him of his heritage. To the death-chamber! Come!"

There was confused, seething movement. The sounds had

changed. The most determined of the infantry surged forward; but they did not cheer. Many held back; there was a deep mutter of opposing voices. Companions began to clamber on the dais, to guard the inner doors. The generals, all trying to protest at once, only added to the confusion. Suddenly, rising above everything, came the cracked new-broken voice of a youth, hoarse with passionate fury.

"Bastards! You bastards! You filthy, slave-born bastards!"

From a corner of the hall alongside the Companions, shoving through everyone regardless of age or rank, yelling as if in battle, came the royal squires.

The watch on duty had been with Alexander till he died, standing on after sunrise. They had been several years in attendance on him. Some of them had turned eighteen and had a vote, the rest had crowded into Assembly with them. They leaped and scrambled up on the dais, waving their drawn swords, wild-eyed, crop-headed, their fair Macedonian hair shorn raggedly almost to their scalps in mourning. There were nearly fifty of them. Perdikkas, seeing their fanatic rage, knew them at sight for the readiest killers in the hall. Unless stopped they would have Philip dead, and then there would be a massacre. "To me!" he shouted to them. "Follow me! Protect the body of Alexander!"

He ran to the inner door, Ptolemy neck-and-neck with him, the other generals close behind, and then the squires, so fierce in their rush that they outdistanced the Companions. Pursued by the angry cries of the opposition, they ran through the King's reception room, through his private sanctum, and on into the Bedchamber. The doors were closed, not locked. The foremost men burst through them.

Ptolemy thought, with a shuddering realization, He has lain here since yesterday! In Babylon, in midsummer. Unconsciously, as the doors burst open, he held his breath.

There was a faint scent of almost burned-out incense;

of the dried flowers and herbs which scented the royal robes and bed, mixed with the scent of the living presence which Ptolemy had known since boyhood. In the vast forsaken room he lay on the great bed between its watchful daimons, a clean fresh sheet drawn over him. Some aromatic sprinkled on it had cheated even the flies. On the dais, half propped against the bed with an arm thrown over it, the Persian boy lay in an exhausted sleep.

Roused by the clamor, he staggered dazedly to his feet, unaware of Ptolemy's touch upon his shoulder. Ptolemy walked to the bed's head and folded back the sheet.

Alexander lay in an inscrutable composure. Even his color seemed hardly changed. His golden hair with its bright silver streaks felt, to the touch, still charged with life. Niarchos and Seleukos, who had followed Ptolemy, exclaimed that it was a miracle, that it proved Alexander's divinity. Ptolemy, who had been his fellow-student with Aristotle, looked down in silence, wondering how long a secret spark of that strong life had burned in the still body. He laid a hand on the heart; but it was over now, the corpse was stiffening. He drew the sheet over the marmoreal face, and turned to the ranks that were forming to hold the bolted doors.

The squires, who knew the room in detail, dragged up the heavy clothes-chests to form a barricade. But it could not last for long. The men outside were well used to pushing. Six or seven ranks deep, they leaned upon the doors as, ten years back, they had leaned with their fifteen-foot sarissas on Darius' levies; and, like the Persians at the Granikos, at Issos, at Gaugamela, the doors gave way. Grinding along the floor, the bronze-bound chests were heaved aside.

As the foremost thrust in, Perdikkas knew himself unable to cut them down, and be first with the shame of bloodshed in this room. He called back his men to bar the way to the royal bed. In a brief pause, the attackers looked about them. The ranks of the defenders screened the body, they saw only the spread wings of the gold daimons and their fierce alien eyes. They shouted defiance, but came no nearer.

There was movement behind them. Philip came in.

Though Meleager was with him, he was here of his own accord. When a person died, his family must see to him. All motives of policy had passed over Philip like unmeaning noise; but he knew his duty.

"Where's Alexander?" he called to the bristling barrier before the bed. "I'm his brother. I want to bury him."

The generals gritted their teeth in silence. It was the squires whose yells of wrath and spat-out insults broke the loaded pause. They had no reverence for the dead, because in their central consciousness Alexander was still alive. They shouted for him as if he were lying on a battlefield senseless with wounds, beset by cowards who would not have faced him on his feet. Their whoops and war-cries set off all the young men in the Companions, who remembered their own days as squires. "Alexander! Alexander!"

From somewhere in the press, making a little whiffling sound as the spin-strap launched it, a javelin hurtled across and rang on Perdikkas' helmet.

In moments more were flying. A Companion knelt pouring blood from a severed leg-vein; a squire who had come helmetless had a slashed scalp and was masked in scarlet, his blue eyes staring through. Till it came to close quarters, the defenders were sitting game. They had brought only their short curved cavalry sabers, symbol of their rank, to what should have been a purely civil occasion.

Perdikkas picked up the javelin that had struck him and hurled it back. Others, plucking them from the bodies of the wounded, held them to serve as spears. Ptolemy, taking a step back to avoid a missile, collided with someone, cursed, and turned to look. It was the Persian boy, blood staining his linen sleeve from a gashed arm. He had thrown it up to ward a javelin from Alexander's body.

"Stop!" shouted Ptolemy across the room. "Are we wild beasts or men?"

From beyond the doors, the hubbub still continued; but it trailed off, damped by the hush of those in front to a kind of shamefaced muttering. It was Niarchos the Cretan who said, "Let them look."

Grasping their weapons, the defenders made a gap. Niarchos uncovered Alexander's face and stood back, silent.

The opposing line fell still. The crowd behind, jostling to see, felt the change and paused. Presently in the front a grizzled phalanx captain stepped a pace forward and took his helmet off. Two or three veterans followed. The first faced around to the men behind him, lifted his arm and shouted, "Halt!" Somberly, in a kind of sullen grief, the parties looked at one another.

By ones and twos the senior officers unhelmed themselves and stood forth to be known. The defenders lowered their weapons. The old captain began to speak.

"There's my brother!" Philip, who had been elbowed aside, pushed forward. He still had on the robe of Alexander, pushed askew and crumpled. "He has to have a funeral."

"Be quiet!" hissed Meleager. Obediently—moments like this were familiar in his life—Philip let himself be hustled out of sight. The old captain, red-faced, recovered his presence of mind.

"Gentlemen," he said, "you are outnumbered, as you see. We have all acted in haste, and I daresay we all regret it. I propose a parley."

Perdikkas said, "On one condition. The body of the King shall be left inviolate, and every man here shall swear it by the gods below. I will take my oath that when a fitting bier is ready, I will have it taken to the royal burial ground in Macedon. Unless these vows are solemnized, none of us will leave this place while we can stand and fight."

They agreed. They were all ashamed. Perdikkas' words about the royal burial ground had brought them sharply down to earth. What would they have done with the body if they had taken it? Buried it in the park? One look at that remote proud face had sobered them. A miracle he was not stinking; yet you would have thought he was still alive. A superstitious shiver had run down many backs; Alexander would make a powerful ghost.

On the terrace a goat was slaughtered; men touched the carcass or the blood, invoking the curse of Hades if they were forsworn. Owing to their numbers it took some time; as twilight fell they were still swearing by torchlight.

Meleager, the first to swear under Perdikkas' eye, watched, brooding. He had lost support and knew it. Only some thirty, the hard core of his partisans, still rallied round him; and even those because they were now marked men, frightened of reprisals. He must keep them, at least. While the sunset dusk hummed with the noises of an anxious fermenting city, he had been giving the matter thought. If he could separate the Bodyguard . . . thirty to only eight . . .

The last men had scrambled through their oaths. He approached Perdikkas with a sober placating face. "I acted rashly. The King's death has overset us all. Tomorrow we can meet and take better counsel."

"So I hope." Perdikkas frowned under his dark brows.

"All of us would be ashamed," went on Meleager smoothly, "if the near friends of Alexander were kept from watching beside him. I beg you"—his gesture embraced the Bodyguard—"return and keep your vigil."

"Thank you," said Niarchos, quite sincerely. He had hoped to do it. Perdikkas paused, his soldier's instinct indefinably wary. It was Ptolemy who said, "Meleager has taken his oath to respect Alexander's body. Has he taken one for ours?"

Perdikkas' eyes sought Meleager's, which shifted in spite of him. All together, with looks of profound contempt, the Bodyguard walked off to join the Companions encamped in the royal park.

Presently they sent messengers to the Egyptian quarter, summoning the embalmers to begin their work at dawn.

"Where were you all day, Konon?" said Philip, as his hot clothes were lifted off him. "Why didn't they fetch you when I said?"

Konon, an elderly veteran who had served him for ten years, said, "I was at Assembly, sir. Never mind, you shall have your nice bath now, with the scented oil."

"I'm King now, Konon. Did they tell you I'm the King?"

"Yes, sir. Long life to you, sir."

"Konon, now I'm King, you won't go away?"

"No, sir, old Konon will look after you. Now let me have this beautiful new robe to brush it and keep it safe. It's too good for every day . . . Why, come, come, sir, you've no call to cry."

In the Royal Bedchamber, as the evening cooled, the body of Alexander stiffened like stone. With a bloodstained towel round his arm, the Persian boy put by the bed the night-table of malachite and ivory, and kindled the night-lamp on it. The floor was strewn with the debris of the fighting. Someone had lurched against the console with the images of Hephaistion; they lay sprawled like the fallen after a battle. In the faint light, Bagoas took a long look at them, and turned away. But in a few minutes he went back and stood them up neatly, each in its place. Then, fetching a stool lest sitting on the dais he might sleep again, he folded his hands and composed himself to watch, his dark eyes staring into the dark shadows.

The harem at Susa was Persian, not Assyrian. Its proportions were elegantly balanced; its fluted columns had capitals sculpted with lotus-buds by craftsmen from Greece; its walls were faced with delicately enameled tiles, and the sunlight dappled them through lattices of milky alabaster.

Queen Sisygambis, the mother of Darius, sat in her high-backed chair, a granddaughter on either side. At eighty she kept the hawk-nosed, ivorine face of the old Elamite nobility; the pure Persian strain, unmixed with Median. She was brittle now; in her youth she had been tall. She was robed and scarved in deep indigo, but for her breast, on which glowed a great necklace of polished pigeon-blood rubies, the gift of King Poros to Alexander, and of Alexander to her.

Stateira, the elder girl, was reading a letter aloud, slowly, translating it from Greek to Persian. Alexander had had both girls taught to read Greek as well as speak it. From affection for him, Sisygambis had allowed him to indulge this whim, though in her view clerking was somewhat menial, and more properly left to the palace eunuchs. However, he must be allowed the customs of his people. He could not help his upbringing, and was never purposely discourteous. He should have been a Persian.

Stateira read, stumbling a little, not from ignorance but from agitation.

ALEXANDER KING OF THE MACEDONIANS
AND LORD OF ASIA, *to his honored wife Stateira.*
Wishing to look upon your face again, I desire you to set out for Babylon without delay, so that your child may be born here. If you bear a boy, I intend to proclaim him my heir. Hasten your journey. I have been sick, and my people tell me there is ignorant talk that I am dead. Do you pay no heed to it. My chamberlains are commanded to receive you with honor, as the mother of a Great King to be. Bring Drypetis your sister, who is my sister also for the sake of one who was dear to me as myself. May all be well with you.

Stateira lowered the letter and looked down at her grandmother. The child of two tall parents, she stood nearly six feet without her slippers. Much of her mother's famous beauty had passed to her. She was queenly in everything but pride. "What shall we do?" she said.

Sisygambis looked up impatiently under her white brows. "First finish the King's letter."

"Madam grandmother, that is all."

"No," said Sisygambis with irritation. "Look again, child. What does he say to *me?*"

"Madam grandmother, that is the end."

"You must be mistaken. Women should not meddle with writing; I told him so, but he would have his way. You had better call a clerk, to read it properly."

"Truly, there is no more writing on the paper. *May all be well with you.* See, it stops here."

The strong lines of Sisygambis' face slackened a little; her years showed like sickness. "Is the messenger still here?

Fetch him, see if he has another letter. These men tire on the road and it makes them stupid."

The rider was brought, gulping from his meal. He pledged his head he had received one letter only, one from the King. He shook out his wallet before them.

When he had gone, Sisygambis said, "Never has he sent to Susa without a word to me. Show me the seal." But her sight had lengthened with age, and even at arms' length she could not make out the figure.

"It is his likeness, madam grandmother. It is like the one on my emerald, that he gave me on my wedding day; only here he has a wreath, and on mine he wears a diadem."

Sisygambis nodded, and sat awhile in silence. There were earlier royal letters in the care of the Head Chamberlain; but she did not like to let such people know that her eyes were failing.

Presently she said, "He writes that he has been sick. He will be behindhand with all his business. Now he is over-taxing himself, as his nature is. When he was here, I saw he was short of breath . . . Go child, fetch me your women; you too, Drypetis. I must tell them what to pack for you."

Young Drypetis, the widow of Hephaistion (she was seventeen) moved to obey, then ran back to kneel beside the chair. "Baba, please come with us to Babylon."

Sisygambis rested her fine-boned old ivory hand on the young girl's head. "The King has told you to hurry on the road. I am too old. And besides, he has not summoned me."

When the women had been instructed, and all the flurry had moved to the girls' bedchamber, she sat on in her straight-backed chair, tears trickling down her cheeks and falling upon King Poros' rubies.

In the Royal Bedchamber of Babylon, now redolent of spices and of niter, the Egyptians who were the heirs of their fathers' art pursued the elaborate task of embalming the latest Pharaoh. Shocked at the delay which would surely undo their skill, they had tiptoed in by dawnlight, and beheld the corpse with awed amazement. As their slaves brought in the instruments, the vessels and fluids and aromatics of their art, the single watcher, a white-faced Persian youth, extinguished his lamp and vanished like a ghost in silence.

Before slitting the torso to remove the entrails, they remembered, far though they were from the Valley of the Kings, to lift their hands in the traditional prayer, that it might be lawful for mortals to handle the body of a god.

The narrow streets of ancient Babylon hummed with rumor and counterrumor. There were lamps burning all night. Days passed; the armies of Perdikkas and Meleager waited in armed truce; the infantry around the palace, the cavalry in the royal park, beside the horse-lines where Nebuchadrezzar had kept his chariots for the lion-hunt.

Outnumbered four to one, they had discussed moving to the plains outside, where there was room for horse to deploy. "No," said Perdikkas. "That would concede defeat. Give them time to take a look at their booby King. They'll come round. Alexander's army has never been divided."

On the parade ground and in the palace gardens, the men of the phalanx bivouacked as best they could. Stubbornly they clung to their victors' pride and their rooted xenophobia. No barbarian should rule their sons, they told each other across the campfires, where their Persian women, whom Alexander had induced them to marry lawfully, were stirring their supper-pots. They had long ago spent Alexander's dowries; not one man in a hundred meant to take home his woman when he was paid off.

They thought with confused resentment of the young

bloods in the Companions, drinking and hunting beside the sons of Persian lords with their curled beards and inlaid weapons and bedizened horses. It was well enough for the cavalry; *they* could afford to Persianize without losing face. But the foot-men, sons of Macedonian farmers, herdsmen and hunters, masons and carpenters, owned only what the wars had won them, their little hoards of loot, and, above all, the just reward for all their toils and dangers, the knowledge that whoever their fathers might have been, they were Alexander's Macedonians, masters of the world. Clinging to this treasure of self-esteem, they spoke well of Philip, his modesty, his likeness to his great father, his pure Macedonian blood.

Their officers, whose affairs took them into the royal presence, came back increasingly taciturn. The enormous business of Alexander's empire could not come to a standstill. Envoys, tax-collectors, shipbuilders, officers of the commissariat, architects, disputing satraps seeking arbitration, still appeared in the anterooms; indeed, in augmented numbers, many having waited for audience through Alexander's illness. Not only had they to be dealt with; they had to find a visible, believable King.

Before each appearance, Meleager briefed Philip carefully. He had learned to go, unled, straight to his throne, without wandering off to speak to some chance person who had caught his eye; to keep his voice down so that he was seen, but not heard to speak, enabling Meleager beside him to proclaim suitable replies. He had learned not to call while enthroned for lemonade or sweets, or to ask permission from his guard of honor when he wanted to go outside. His scratching himself, picking his nose and fidgeting could never be quite controlled; but if his appearances were kept short, he presented as a rule a quiet and sober figure.

Meleager had appointed himself to the post of Chiliarch,

or Grand Vizier, created for Hephaistion and inherited by
Perdikkas. Standing at the King's right hand, flamboy-
antly panoplied, he knew that he looked impressive; but he
knew too, all too well, what a soldier thinks when the chief
to whom he has come for orders speaks through an inter-
mediary and never looks him in the face. His officers, all of
whom had had free access to Alexander, could not be kept
out; nor could the royal guard. And all of them, he felt it
through his skin, were looking at the stout stocky figure on
the throne, the slack mouth and wandering stare, and seeing in mind's eye the dynamic vanished presence, the alert
responsive face, the serene authority, that now lay stilled
forever in the locked Bedchamber, submerged in the embalmers' bath of niter, preparing to abide the centuries.

Beyond all this, Persian officers appointed by Alexander
could not be refused audience, and were not fools. The
thought of a concerted rising, against a mutinous divided
army, gave him waking nightmares.

Like other men who have indulged a long rancorous hate,
he blamed all adversity upon its object, never considering
that his hatred, not his enemy, had created his predicament.
Like other such men before and after him, he saw only one
remedy, and resolved to seek it.

Philip was still in his old apartments, which, having been
chosen for him by Alexander, were pleasant and cool, at
least for Babylon in midsummer. When Meleager had tried
to move him into more regal quarters, he had refused with
shouts so loud that the palace guard had come running,
thinking murder was being done. Here Meleager sought
him, taking with him a kinsman, a certain Duris, who carried writing things.

The King was occupied happily with his stones. He had
a chest full, collected over thousands of miles of Asia as he
trailed along after the army; pebbles he had picked up for

himself, mixed with bits of amber, quartz, agate, old seals, and colored glass jewels from Egypt, which Alexander or Ptolemy or Hephaistion had brought him when they happened to remember. He had arranged them in a long winding path across the room, and was on his hands and knees improving it.

At Meleager's entrance he scrambled guiltily to his feet, clutching a favorite lump of Scythian turquoise, which he hid behind his back lest it be taken away.

"Sire!" said Meleager harshly.

Philip, recognizing this as a severe rebuke, hastened over to the most important chair, carefully stuffing the turquoise under the cushion.

"Sir," said Meleager standing over him, "I have come to tell you that you are in grave danger. No, don't be afraid, I will defend you. But the traitor Perdikkas, who tried to steal Alexander's body and rob you of the throne, is plotting to take your life, and make himself King."

Philip jumped to his feet, stammering incoherently. Presently Meleager made out, "He said . . . Alexander *said* . . . He can be King if he wants to. I don't mind. Alexander told me they mustn't make me King."

With some trouble, Meleager freed his arm from a grip he had feared would break it. "Sir, if he is King his first act will be to kill you. Your only safety is in killing *him*. See, here is the paper ordering his death." Duris set it, with pen and ink, upon the table. "Just write *PHILIP* here, as I taught you. I will help you, if you like."

"And then you'll kill him before he kills me?"

"Yes, and all our troubles will be over. Write it here."

The blot with which he began did not efface the writing; and he produced, after that, a quite tolerable signature.

⊙   ⊙   ⊙

Perdikkas' lodging was one of the grace-and-favor houses built in the royal park by the Persian kings, and bestowed on his friends by Alexander. Around it were encamped the royal squires. They had attached themselves to Perdikkas as Alexander's chosen Regent. Though they had not offered to wait upon his person, and he had known better than to ask it, they rode with his messages, and guarded him in their accustomed rota by day and night.

He was consulting with Ptolemy when one of them came in. "Sir. An old man is asking for you."

"Thirty at least," said Ptolemy flippantly. Perdikkas said crisply, "Well?"

"He says, sir, he's the servant of Arridaios." The honorific Philip was not used on the Companions' side of the river. "He says it's urgent."

"Is his name Konon?" said Ptolemy sharply. "Perdikkas, I know this man. You had better see him."

"So I intended." Perdikkas spoke rather stiffly. He found Ptolemy too easygoing and informal, traits which Alexander had regrettably not discouraged. "Bring him in, but search him for weapons first."

Old Konon, profoundly ill at ease, gave an old soldier's salute, stood to attention, and said nothing till given leave.

"Sir, with permission. They've made my poor master sign a paper against you. I was in his bedroom, seeing to his things, they never thought to look. Sir, don't hold him to blame. They took advantage of him. He never meant harm to you, not of his own accord."

"I believe you," said Perdikkas frowning. "But it seems that harm is done."

"Sir. If he falls into your hands, don't kill him, sir. He was never any trouble, not in King Alexander's day."

"Rest assured we have no such wish." This man could be useful, his charge more useful still. "When the army returns to duty, I will have your master well cared for. Do you want to stay with him?"

"Sir, yes sir. I've been with him nearly from a boy. I don't know how he'd go on without me."

"Very good. Permission granted. Tell him, if he will understand you, that he has nothing to fear from me."

"I will, sir, and God bless you." He left, saluting smartly.

"An easy favor," said Perdikkas to Ptolemy. "Did he think we could afford to kill Alexander's brother? Meleager, now . . ."

Later, his day's business done, Perdikkas was sitting down to supper when raised voices sounded outside. From the window he saw a company of a hundred foot-soldiers. The squires on duty numbered sixteen.

He was too old a campaigner to have changed into a supper-robe. In moments, with the speed of two decades' practice, he had whipped his corselet from the stand and clasped it on. A panting squire dashed in, saluting with one hand while the other waved a paper.

"Sir! It's a summons from the rebels. A royal warrant they call it."

"Royal, eh?" said Perdikkas calmly. The missive was brief; he read it aloud.

"*PHILIP SON OF PHILIP KING OF THE MACEDONIANS AND LORD OF ASIA, To the former Chiliarch Perdikkas. You are hereby summoned to appear before me, to answer a charge of treason. If you resist, the escort has orders to use force.*"

"Sir, we can hold them. Do you want a message sent?"

Not for nothing had Perdikkas served directly under Alexander. He laid his hand on the boy's shoulder, shaping his austere face into the needed smile. "Good lad. No, no message. Guard, stand to arms. I will talk to this squad of Meleager's." The squire's salute had the faint reflection of a remembered ardor. Perhaps, thought Perdikkas, I can show Acting Chiliarch Meleager why I, and not he, got promoted to the Bodyguard.

He had had twelve years to absorb a basic Alexander precept: Do it with style. Unlike Alexander, he had had to work for it, but he knew what it was worth. On his own account, needing instruction from no one, he could deliver a memorable dressing-down.

Striding bareheaded onto the porch, the summons in his hand, he paused formidably for effect, and began to speak.

He had recognized the officer—he had a good general's memory—and reviewed in detail the last campaign in which they had all served under his own command. Alexander had once spoken highly of them. What did they suppose themselves to be doing, disgracing themselves like this; they who had once been men, and even, God help them, soldiers? Could they face Alexander now? Even before he was King, the wittol bastard had been used in intrigue against him; anyone else would have had him put out of the way; but he in the greatness of his heart had cared for him as a harmless innocent. If King Philip had wished a fool to bear his name, he would have said so. King Philip! King Ass. Who would believe that men of Alexander's could come here as servants of Meleager, a man he had known too well to trust with a division, to sell the life of the man he himself had chosen to command them? Let them go back to their comrades, and remind them who they had been, and what they had sunk to now. Let them ask themselves how they liked it. They could now dismiss.

After an uneasy, shuffling silence, the troop captain rapped out gruffly, "About turn! March."

Meantime, the squires on watch had been joined by

every squire in hearing. When the troop departed, they gathered round Perdikkas and cheered. Without effort this time, he returned their triumphant grins. Almost, for a moment, he felt like Alexander.

No, he thought as he went in. People used to eat *him* alive. They had to touch him, his hands, his clothes. I've seen them fighting to reach him. Those fools at Opis, when he'd forgiven them for rioting, demanded the right to kiss him . . . Well, that was his mystery, which I shall never have. But then, nor will anyone else.

Slowly, against the stream, the rowers' labor lightened sometimes by a flaw of wind from the south, the canopied barge meandered along the Tigris. On linen cushions stuffed with wool and down, waving their fans, the two princesses stretched like young cats, luxuriating in smooth movement and the cool air off the water, after the jolting heat of their covered wagon. Within the awning, their duenna was fast asleep. Along the towpath trundled the wagon and the baggage-cart, the escort of armed mounted eunuchs, the muleteers and the household slaves. When the caravan passed a village, all the peasants would gather on the bank to stare.

"If only," sighed Stateira, "he had not told us to hurry. One could go all the way by water, downstream to the Gulf, and up the Euphrates to Babylon." She settled the cushions in her back, which had the ache of pregnancy.

Drypetis, fingering her dark-blue widow's veil, looked over her shoulder to be sure the duenna was sleeping. "Will he give me another husband?"

"I don't know." Stateira looked away at the riverbank. "Don't ask him yet. He won't like it. He thinks you still belong to Hephaistion. He won't let Hephaistion's regiment ever have another name." Feeling a desolate silence behind her, she said, "If I have a boy, I'll ask him." She lay back in the cushions and closed her eyes.

The sun, splintering through tall clumps of papyrus, made shifting patterns in the rose-red light that filtered through her eyelids. It was like the sun-glowing crimson curtains of the wedding pavilion at Susa. Her face burned, as always when the memory came back to her.

She had been, of course, presented to the King before. Grandmother had ensured that she made the deepest curtsey, before he took his tall chair and she her low one. But the wedding ritual could not be evaded; it had followed the Persian rite. She had been led in by her dead mother's brother, a fine tall man. Then the King had risen from his chair of state, as the bridegroom must, to greet her with a kiss and lead her to the chair beside him. She had performed, for the kiss, the little genuflection Grandmamma had taught her; but then she had had to stand up, there was no way out of it. She was half a head taller, and ready to die of shame.

When the trumpets had sounded, and the herald announced that they were man and wife, it was Drypetis' turn. The King's friend, Hephaistion, had stood up and come forward, the most beautiful man she had ever seen, stately and tall—with his dark-gold hair, he could have been one of the fair Persians—and taken her sister's hand, matching her height to a hair. All the King's friends, the other bridegrooms, had given a kind of sigh; she knew that when the King had stepped out to meet her they had been holding their breath. At the end, he and she had had to lead out the procession to the bridal chambers. She had wished that the earth might swallow her.

In the crimson pavilion with its golden bed, he had likened her to a daughter of the gods (her Greek was quite good by then), and she had seen that he meant well; but since nothing could do away those dreadful moments, she

would have preferred him to keep silence. He was a powerful presence, and she was shy; though the defect was his, it
was she who had felt like an ungainly tent-pole. All she had
been able to think about in the marriage bed was that her
father had run away in battle, and Grandmother would
never speak his name. She must redeem the honor of her
house by courage. He had been kind, and hardly hurt her;
but it had all been so strange, so overpowering, she could
hardly utter a word. No wonder she had not conceived, and
that though he had paid her visits of compliment while still
at Susa, and brought her gifts, he had never once had her to
bed again.

To crown these miseries, she had known that somewhere
in the palace was the King's Bactrian wife, whom he had
taken along to India. A stranger to sexual pleasure, Stateira
knew no sexual jealousy; but its fiercest torments could
hardly have been more wounding than her thoughts of
Roxane, Little Star, favorite and confidante. She pictured
them lying side by side in tender love-making, intimate
talk, amusing gossip, laughter—perhaps at her. As for
Bagoas the Persian, she had heard nothing of him at her
father's court, and nothing since. She had been carefully
brought up.

The King's sojourn at Susa had gone by, its great political
events dimly heard of and little understood. Then he had
gone on his summer progress to Ekbatana. He had called to
take leave of her (would he have done even that, except to
see Grandmother?) without a word of when he would send
for her or where. He had gone, taking the Bactrian woman;
and she had cried all night from shame and anger.

But last spring, when he had come to Susa after the
mountain war, it had all been different; no ceremony, no
crowds. He had been shut up alone with Grandmother, and
it almost seemed that she had heard him weeping. In the

evening they had all dined together; they were his family, he said. He looked lean, weather-beaten and weary; but he talked, as she had never heard him do before.

At the first sight of Drypetis in her widow's veil, his face had frozen in a dreadful grief; but he had covered it quickly, and enthralled them with tales of India, its marvels and its customs. Then he spoke of his plans to explore the coast of Arabia, to make a road along north Africa and extend his empire westward. And he had said, "So much to do, so little time. My mother was right; long before now, I should have begotten an heir."

He had looked at her; and she had known it was she, not the Bactrian, who was the chosen one. She had come to him in a passion of gratitude, which had proved as efficacious as any other ardor.

Soon after he had gone, she knew that she had conceived, and Grandmother had sent him word. It was good that he had summoned her to Babylon. If he was still sick, she would tend him with her own hands. She would make no jealous scenes about the Bactrian. A king was entitled to his concubines; and, as Grandmother had warned her, much trouble could spring from quarrels in the harem.

The soldiers sent to arrest Perdikkas had seen, as he had advised, what had become of them, and did not like it. They went among their comrades, reporting his courage and their discomfiture; and relating, what he himself had first revealed to them, that Meleager had meant to have his head. They had been anxious, restless, volatile. While Meleager was still digesting failure, suddenly they were roaring at his doors like a human sea. The guards on duty abandoned their posts and joined them.

In a cold sweat, he saw himself dying, like a boar at bay,

in a ring of spears. With the speed of desperation, he made
for the royal rooms.

In a cheerful lamplight, Philip was seated at his evening
meal, a favorite dish, spiced venison with pumpkin fritters.
A jug of lemonade stood by him; he was not reliable if
given wine. When Meleager burst in, he expressed annoy-
ance with his eyes, since his mouth was full. Konon, who
was waiting at table, looked up sharply. He was wearing
his old sword; he had heard the noise.

"Sir," panted Meleager, "the traitor Perdikkas has re-
pented, and the soldiers want him spared. Please go and
tell them you have pardoned him."

Philip bolted his mouthful to reply indignantly, "I can't
come now. I'm having my dinner."

Konon took a step forward. Looking Meleager in the eye,
he said, "He was taken advantage of." His hand rested, as
if by chance, on his well-polished sword-belt.

Keeping his head, Meleager said, "My good man, the
King will be safer on his throne than anywhere else in
Babylon. You know that; you were at Assembly. Sir, come
at once." A persuasive argument occurred to him. "Your
brother would have done so."

Philip put down his knife and wiped his mouth. "Is that
right, Konon? Would Alexander go?"

Konon's hand fell to his side. "Yes, sir. Yes, he would go."

As he was steered to the door, Philip looked back regret-
fully at his dinner-plate, and wondered why Konon was
wiping his eyes.

The army was placated for the time, but far from satisfied. Audiences in the Throne Room were going badly. The
envoys' regrets for the late King's untimely death grew less
formal and more pointed. Meleager felt his power increasingly unstable, and discipline crumbling by the day.

Meantime, the cavalry had taken counsel. Suddenly one morning they were found to have disappeared. The park was empty of everything but horse-droppings. They had made their way through the crumbling outer walls, and deployed to invest the city. Babylon was under siege.

Much of the terrain outside was swampy; it needed no great force to close the solid causeways and the firm open ground. As planned, the refugees were unmolested. At all the gates, with a hubbub of shouting men, wailing children, burbling camels, bleating goats and cackling poultry, the country people who feared war were pouring into the city, and the city people who feared famine were pouring out.

Meleager could have dealt with a foreign enemy. But he knew too well that he could no longer trust his troops for even the briefest contact with their former comrades. They were forgetting the threat of unborn barbarian heirs, and homesick for the familiar discipline of the old triumphant days, the officers who had linked them to Alexander. Less than a month ago, they had been limbs of a well-knit body directed by a fiery spirit. Now each man felt his isolation in a foreign world. Soon they would take revenge for it.

In this extremity, he went to consult Eumenes.

Throughout the turmoil since Alexander's death, the Secretary had gone quietly about his business. A man of humble origins, discovered and trained by Philip, advanced by Alexander, he had been, and remained, uncommitted in the present strife. He had neither joined the Companions nor denounced them. His work, he said, was to carry on the kingdom's business. He had helped with replies to the envoys and the embassies, drawing on his records, and had drafted letters in the name of Philip, but without the title of King (it had been added by Meleager). When pressed to take sides, he would only say that he was a Greek, and politics were the concern of the Macedonians.

Meleager found him at his writing-table, dictating to his clerk, who was taking it down on wax.

Next day he bathed again, and sacrificed the appointed offerings, and after the sacrifice remained in constant fever. Yet even so, he sent for the officers, and ordered them to see that everything was ready for the expedition. He bathed again in the evening, and after that became gravely ill . . .

"Eumenes," said Meleager, who had been standing ignored in the doorway, "let the dead rest awhile. You are needed by the living."

"The living need the truth, before rumor pollutes it." He motioned to his clerk, who folded his tablet and went out. Meleager outlined his dilemma, aware as he went that the Secretary had long since assessed it all, and was waiting impatiently for him to finish. He trailed to a lame conclusion.

Eumenes said without emotion, "My opinion, since you ask it, is that it is not too late to seek a compromise. And it is too late for anything else."

Meleager had already been driven to this view, but wanted to have it confirmed by someone else, whom he could blame if things went wrong. "I accept your advice. That is, if the men agree."

Eumenes said drily, "Perhaps the King can persuade them."

Meleager ignored the double edge. "One man could do it: yourself. Your honor is unquestioned, your experience known. Will you address the Macedonians?"

Eumenes had long since taken his measure. His own sole loyalty was to the house of Philip and Alexander, who had lifted him from obscurity to prestige and power. Had Philip Arridaios been competent, he would have felt divided loyalties; but he knew what the elder Philip had thought about that, and was for the son of Alexander, unborn, unseen. Yet Philip was the son of Philip his benefactor, who had seen fit to acknowledge him; and Eumenes would protect him if he could. He was a dry, cool man, whose inward feelings few suspected; he had no taste for protestations. He said, "Very well."

He was well received. A man in his fifties, spare and erect, with the subtler features of the south yet a soldier's bearing, he said what was needed and no more. He made no attempt to emulate Alexander, whose sense of his audience had been an artist's gift. Eumenes' talent was for sounding reasonable, and keeping to the point. Reassured by hearing their confused misgivings reduced to logic, the Assembly accepted his conclusions with relief. Envoys were sent to the camp of Perdikkas, to treat for terms. As they rode out at sunrise from the Ishtar Gate, crowds of anxious Babylonians watched them off.

They were back before noon. Perdikkas would raise the siege and reconcile the armies, as soon as Meleager and his accomplices gave themselves up to justice.

By now, any discipline still left among the troops in Babylon was self-imposed from dim feelings of dignity, depending chiefly on the popularity of any officer concerned. The returning envoys shouted back their message to anyone who stopped them in the street to ask. While Meleager was still reading Perdikkas' letter, the troops were pouring into the hall of audience, having called their own Assembly.

Eumenes in his business room listened to the rumble of conflicting voices, and the scrape of boot-nails continuing the ruin of the marble floor. A stair in the thickness of the wall had a window which overlooked the hall. He saw that the soldiers had not come armed only with token weapons; despite the heat, they had on their corselets; helmets were worn, not held. A visible division was starting; on one side the men who were for accepting the conditions; on the other, alarmed and angry, those who had committed themselves irretrievably to Meleager. The rest were waiting to have their minds made up for them. This, Eumenes thought, is how civil wars begin. He made his way to the royal rooms.

Meleager was there, standing over Philip and coaching him in a speech. Philip, more aware of his sweating desperation than of anything he said, was fidgeting, not taking in a word. "What," asked Eumenes bluntly, "are you telling him to say?"

Meleager's light-blue eyes, always prominent, were now bloodshot too. "To say no, of course."

In the level voice to which even Alexander in anger had paid attention, Eumenes said, "If he says that, swords will be out before you can take breath. Have you looked in the hall? Look now."

A big, heavy hand clutched Eumenes' shoulder. He turned, startled. It had never occurred to him that Philip would be strong.

"I don't want to say it. I can't remember it. Tell him I've forgotten."

"Never mind," said Eumenes quietly. "We will think of something else."

The royal fanfare made a brief silence in the hall. Philip came forward, Eumenes just behind him.

"Macedonians!" He paused, reminding himself of the words the kind, calm man had taught him. "There is no need for strife. The peacemakers will be the victors here." He almost turned round for approval; but the kind man had told him not to.

A pleased murmur went round the hall. The King had sounded just like anyone else.

"Do not condemn free citizens . . ." prompted Eumenes softly.

"Do not condemn free citizens, unless you wish for civil war." He paused again; Eumenes, screening his lips with his hand, gave him his lines. "Let us try again for reconcilement. Let us send another embassy." He drew a breath of triumph. Eumenes whispered, "Don't look round."

There was no serious opposition. All welcomed a breathing-space, and argued only the ways and means; but as the voices grew louder, they brought back to Philip that dreadful day when he had run away from the hall, and they had given him a robe to make him come back again, and then . . . Alexander had been lying dead, as if he were carved in marble. Alexander had told him . . .

He felt at his head, at the gold diadem they always made him wear when he came out here. He took it off, and, holding it out, walked forward.

Behind him, Meleager and Eumenes gave a united gasp of dismay. He extended, confidingly, the crown to the staring soldiers. "Is it because I'm King? It doesn't matter. I'd sooner not be King. Here, look; you can give it to someone else."

It was a curious moment. Everyone had been at stretch, till the half-relief of borrowed time. Now this.

Always prone to emotion—a trait which Alexander had used with unfailing skill—the Macedonians were borne on a flood of sentiment. What a decent, good fellow; what a law-abiding King. Living under his brother's shadow had made him over-modest. No one laughed as he looked about for someone to take the crown. There were reassuring cries of "Long live Philip, Philip for King!"

With happy surprise, Philip resumed his crown. He had

got everything right, and the kind man would be pleased with him. He was still beaming when they shepherded him inside.

Perdikkas' tent was pitched in the shade of a tall palm-grove. He was settled back into surroundings so familiar that he seemed never to have left them; the light bed and folding chair, the armor-stand, the chest (there had been a pile of chests in the days of victorious loot, but that was over), the trestle table.

His brother Alketas and his cousin Leonnatos were with him when the new envoys came. Leonnatos was a long-boned auburn-haired man, who reminded the world of his connections with the royal house by copying Alexander's leonine haircut, even, said his enemies, reproducing its wave with the tongs. His ambitions, though high, were as yet inchoate; meantime he supported Perdikkas.

The envoys had been sent out while their message was considered. Peace was offered in King Philip's name, if his claim was recognized, and his deputy, Meleager, was appointed to share the supreme command with Perdikkas.

Leonnatos tossed back his hair; a gesture rarely used by Alexander, which in his pupil had become a mannerism. "Insolence! Do we need to disturb the others?"

Perdikkas glanced up from the letter. "Here," he said easily, "I see the hand of Eumenes."

"No doubt," said Alketas, surprised. "Who else would write it?"

"We will accept. Nothing could be better."

"*What?*" said Leonnatos, staring. "You can't take that brigand into the command!"

"I told you, I see the hand of Eumenes." Perdikkas

stroked the dark stubble on his chin. "He knew what bait
would draw the beast from his lair. Yes, let us have him out.
Then we shall see."

The barge on the Tigris was nearing the bend where the
ladies must disembark, to join their caravan and proceed by
land.

Dusk was falling. Their tent had been pitched on grass,
away from the river-damp and the mosquitoes. They
stepped ashore as the first torches were kindled about the
camp; there was a smell of burnt fat as the lamb for supper sizzled over the fire.

The chief eunuch of the escort, as he handed Stateira off
the gangplank, said softly, "Madam. The villagers who
came selling fruit are saying that the Great King is dead."

"He warned me of it," she answered calmly. "He said
there was this rumor among the peasants. It is in his letter;
he said we should not heed it."

Holding up her gown from the rushes heavy with dew,
she swept on towards the lamplit tent.

To a spirited music of trumpets and double flutes, the
foot-soldiers marched out under the towers of the Ishtar
Gate, watched by the relieved Babylonians, to seal their
peace with the Companions.

At their head rode Meleager, the King beside him. Philip
made a cheerful and seemly figure, wearing the scarlet
shoulder-cloak that Alexander had once given him, sitting
a well-trained, solid horse that would walk half a length
ahead of Konon with the leading-rein. He hummed to
himself the tune that the pipes were playing. The air was

still fresh with morning. All would be well, everyone was
to be friends again. It would be no trouble, now, to go on
being King.

The Companions waited on their glossy horses, restive
from leisure; their bridles sparkling with gold pendants and
silver cheek-rosettes, a fashion set by Alexander for Boukephalas. Dressed in the workmanlike panoply of campaign,
plain Thracian helmet and stamped leather cuirass, Perdikkas watched with grim satisfaction the marching phalanx,
the gaudy rider leading it. Meleager had had his parade
armor adorned with a large gold lion-mask, and his cloak
was edged with bullion. So! The beast was drawn.

They accorded Philip the royal salute. Well coached, he
acknowledged it and reached out his arm; Perdikkas bore,
with resolute affability, the crushing of his huge paw. But
Meleager, with a look offensively familiar, had pushed up
after, his own hand ready for the clasp of reconciliation. It
was with far greater reluctance that Perdikkas returned that
grip. He told himself that Alexander had once had to break
bread with the traitor Philotas, biding his time; and if he
had balked at it, few of his advance force, including Perdikkas probably, would be alive today. "It was necessary," was
what Alexander had said.

It was settled that the absent Krateros, considering his
high rank and royal lineage, should be appointed Philip's
guardian. Antipatros should keep the regency of Macedon.
Perdikkas should be Chiliarch of all the Asian conquests,
and, if Roxane bore a boy, should be joint guardian with
Leonnatos. They were Alexander's kinsmen, which
Meleager could not claim; but since he was to share the high
command, the distinction did not trouble him. He had
begun already to give them his views on the management
of the empire.

When all this business was done, Perdikkas made a last proposal. It was the ancient custom of Macedon, after civil war (another ancient custom) to exorcise discord with a sacrifice to Hekate. He proposed that all the troops in Babylon, horse and foot, should assemble on the plain for the Purification.

Meleager willingly agreed. He planned an impressive appearance, proper to his new rank. He would have his helmet topped with a double crest, like Alexander's at Gaugamela. Conspicuous; and a lucky omen.

Shortly before the rite, Perdikkas asked the Bodyguard to a private supper. He was back, now, at his house in the royal park. The generals rode or strolled over in the falling twilight, under the ornamental trees brought from far and wide by the Persian kings to adorn the paradise. A simple occasion, a meeting of old friends.

When the servants had left them with the wine, Perdikkas said, "I have chosen the men and briefed them. I think that Philip—I suppose we must get used to calling him that —will have learned his part."

Till Krateros, his new guardian, could take charge of him, Perdikkas was doing so. Since he lived in his accustomed rooms, with his accustomed comforts, he had scarcely noticed the change, except for the welcome absence of Meleager. He was getting new lessons; but that was to be expected.

"He has taken to Eumenes," Ptolemy said. "Eumenes doesn't bully him."

"Good. He can help to coach him. Let us hope the noise and spectacle won't confuse him . . . There will be the elephants."

"Surely," said Leonnatos, "he has seen elephants by now?"

"Of course he has," Ptolemy said impatiently. "He traveled from India with them, in Krateros' convoy."

"Yes, true." Perdikkas paused. There was a silence, a sense of more to come. Seleukos, to whose command the elephant corps belonged, said, "Well?"

"King Omphis," said Perdikkas slowly, "had a certain use for them in India."

There were sharply drawn breaths all round the suppercouches. It was Niarchos who said distastefully, "Omphis maybe. Never Alexander."

"Alexander was never in our dilemma," said Leonnatos unwisely. "No," returned Ptolemy. "Nor like to be."

Perdikkas cut in, with brusque authority. "No matter. Alexander knew very well the power of fear."

The men were astir at cockcrow, to march to the Field of Purgation at break of day, and get the rite finished before the crushing heat of noon.

The rich wheatfields, which bore three crops a year, had been lately harvested. The sun, floating up from the flat horizon, slanted its first beams over miles of stubble, gleaming like golden fur. Here and there, scarlet pennants marked the limits of the parade ground, which were significant to the rite.

Thick and squat, their ancient Assyrian brick mortared with black bitumen, jagged and crumbling with the centuries and with the lassitude of a long-conquered race, the walls of Babylon, impassive, overlooked the plain. They had seen many deeds of men, and looked incapable of amazement. A wide stretch of their battlements had been flattened down into a new, smooth platform. Its smoke-blackened bricks still smelled of burning; streams of molten pitch had hardened down its sides. In the ditch below was a great pile of debris; half-charred timber with broken carvings of lions and ships and wings and trophies, still dimly picked out with gilding. It was the remains of the two-hundred-foot pyre on which, not long before his death, Alexander had burned the body of Hephaistion.

Long before dawn, the crowds had started to gather along the walls. They had not forgotten the splendors of Alexander's entry into Babylon; a free show, for it had surrendered peacefully, and he had forbidden his men to plunder it. They remembered the streets flower-strewn and wafted with frankincense; the procession of exotic gifts, gold-bedizened horses, lions and leopards in gilded cages; the Persian cavalry, the Macedonian cavalry; and the gold-plated state chariot with the slight, glittering figure of the victor like a transfigured boy. He had been twenty-five, then. They had hoped for more splendors when he came back from India; but he had given them only that stupendous funeral.

Now they waited, to see the Macedonian men of war march out in their pride, and offer their gods appeasement; the citizens, the soldiers' women and children, the smiths and tentmakers and sutlers and wagoners and whores, the shipwrights and seamen from the galley-slips. They loved a show; but under expectation was a deep unease. A time had gone, a time was coming; and they did not like the auspices of its birth.

Most of the army had crossed the river overnight, by Queen Nitokris' Bridge, or by the innumerable ferryboats of reed and pitch. They slept in the open, and polished their gear for the morrow. The watchers on the walls saw them getting up by torchlight, the sound of their stirring like a murmuring sea. Further away, the Companions' horses whinnied.

Hooves drummed on the timbers of Nitokris' Bridge. The

leaders arrived, to direct the sacrifice which would cleanse men's hearts from evil.

The rite was very old. The victim must be dedicated, killed and disemboweled, its four quarters and its entrails carried to the boundaries of the field. The army would march into the space thus purified, would parade, and sing a paean.

The sacrifice was, as it had always been, a dog. The finest and tallest wolfhound had been chosen from the royal kennels; pure white, handsomely feathered. Its docility, as the huntsman led it forward to the altar, promised the good omen of a consenting sacrifice; but when its leash was handed to the sacrificer, it growled and flew at him. Even for its size, it was immensely strong. It took four men to overpower it and get the knife to its throat; they finished with more of their own blood on them than the victim's. To make things worse, in the midst of the struggle the King had rushed up shouting, and only with trouble had been coaxed away.

Hastily, before there could be brooding on the augury, the four horsemen, appointed to asperse the plain, galloped to its four corners with their bloody offerings. The lumps of white and scarlet were flung outward with averting invocations to Triple Hekate and the infernal gods; and the exorcised field was ready to receive the army of Alexander.

The squadrons and the phalanxes were ready. The burnished helmets of the horsemen gleamed; their crests of red or white horsehair, the pennants on their lances, stirred in the morning breeze. Their short sturdy Greek ponies whinnied at the tall horses of the Persian troops. Most of the Persian foot had melted away, trudging dusty caravan trails to their distant villages. The Macedonian foot was present to a man. They stood in close order, their whetted speartips making a glitter about them.

A square had formed on the wide stubbled plain. Its base was the wall of Babylon; its left side was the infantry; its right, the cavalry. Between them, making the fourth side, were the royal elephants.

Their mahouts, who had come with them from India, and knew them as a mother knows her child, had worked on them all yesterday in the high thatched elephant-sheds among the palm-trees; crooning and clucking and slapping, washing them in the canal; painting on their foreheads, in ochre or scarlet or green, sacred symbols enlaced with elaborate scrollwork; draping their wrinkled flanks with tasseled nets brilliantly dyed and threaded with gold bullion; fastening jeweled rosettes through slits in their leather ears; grooming their tails and toes.

It was a year since the mahouts had had a chance to make their children fine. They had had their schooling on the royal maidan at Taxila; their children also. They had talked to them softly, reminding them of old days beside the Indus, while they reddened their feet with henna, as the custom had always been for such occasions. Now in the pink early light they sat proudly on their necks, wearing their ceremonial silks and turbans with peacock feathers, their beards freshly dyed blue or green or crimson; each holding the gold-bound ivory goad, studded with gems, which King Omphis in his magnificence had presented with each elephant to King Iskandar. They had served two famous kings; the world should see that they and their children knew how things were done.

The generals, who had been pouring their libations at the bloody altar, went off to join their detachments. As Ptolemy and Niarchos rode side by side towards the ranks of the Companions, Niarchos rubbed a spash of blood from his bridle-arm, saying, "The gods below don't seem disposed to cleanse us."

"Are you surprised?" said Ptolemy. His craggy face was set in creases of disgust. "Well, God willing, I shall be far away before long."

"And I, God willing . . . Do the dead watch us, as poets say?"

"Homer says the unburied dead do . . . He never did let go easily." He added, not altogether to Niarchos, "I shall make him what amends I can."

It was time for the King to take his time-honored place at the right of the Companions. His horse was ready. He had been well rehearsed. Eager to produce him and get to business, Perdikkas was grinding his teeth in the effort to keep his temper.

"Sir, the army awaits you. The men are watching. You cannot let them see you cry. You are the King! Sir, compose yourself. What is a dog?"

"He was Eos!" Philip was scarlet-faced, tears running into his beard. "He knew me! We used to play tug-of-war. Alexander said he was strong enough to look after himself. He knew me!"

"Yes, yes," said Perdikkas. Ptolemy was right, Alexander should have had him smothered. Most of the crowd had thought he was assisting in the sacrifice; but all the omens had been disquieting. "The gods required him. It is done now. Come."

Obedient to authority and to a voice far more impressive than Meleager's, Philip wiped his eyes and nose with the corner of his scarlet cloak, and let a groom hoist him up on his embroidered saddle-cloth. His horse, a seasoned veteran of parades, followed each maneuver of the one beside it. Philip felt the leading-rein must still be there.

The troops awaited the final ceremony; the sound of the trumpet, giving the note of the paean for them to sing.

Perdikkas, the King beside him, turned to the officers

strung out behind him, leading their squadrons. "Forward!" he barked. "Slow—march!"

The pipers struck up, instead of the paean, the cavalry walk familiar at parades. The sleek and glittering lines paced smoothly forward, rank upon rank, stepping delicately as they had done on triumphant days in the years of miracle, at Memphis, at Tyre, at Taxila, at Persepolis, and here on this very field. At their head rode Perdikkas, and, carried by his wise charger, the King.

The infantry, taken unawares by this maneuver, stood in their ranks and muttered. The decay of discipline showed; spears dipped or leaned askew. They were light parade spears, not the tall sarissas; suddenly their bearers felt half-armed. The advancing cavalry looked formal and ceremonious; had there been some muddle in the briefing? Such doubts, once unthinkable, were common nowadays. Under Meleager their morale was low, their bonding shaky.

Perdikkas gave an order. The left and center wings reined to a halt; the right, the royal squadron, still advanced. He said to Philip, "When we stop, sir, make your speech. You remember?"

"Yes!" said Philip eagerly, "I'm to say—"

"Hush, sir, not now. When I have said 'Halt!' "

Neatly, stylishly, the royal squadron advanced till it was fifty feet from the phalanx. Perdikkas halted it.

Philip lifted his arm. He was used by now to his comfortable horse. Set firmly on the embroidered saddle-cloth, in a loud and unexpectedly deep voice, surprising even to himself, he shouted, "Surrender the mutineers!"

There was a moment of absolute, stunned silence. This was their own, their chosen Macedonian King. The front ranks, staring across incredulous, saw his face strained in the simple effort of a child getting his lesson right; and knew at last what they had done.

Voices broke out among the lines, suddenly raised, appealing for support. They came from Meleager's ringleaders. Among uncertain undertones, their own noise isolated them; it could be heard how few they were.

Slightly at first, looking almost accidental, spaces began to open around them. It was coming home to their former comrades that they themselves were not precisely threatened. And who, after all, had been to blame? Who had foisted on them this hollow King, the tool of anyone who, for the moment, owned him? They forgot the peasant spearman who had first called for Philip's son; remembering only how Meleager had dressed the fool in Alexander's robe, and tried to profane Alexander's body. What did anyone owe his creatures?

Perdikkas beckoned the herald, who rode up with a paper in his hand. In his trained, carrying voice, he read out the names of Meleager's thirty. Meleager's own name was not called.

In his station of honor before the right-wing phalanx, he felt, around him, the last lees of loyalty ebb away, leaving him high and dry. If he stepped forward, challenged Perdikkas' perfidy—that was the signal they were waiting for over there. He froze, the statue of a soldier, sweating cold under the brazen Babylonian sun.

Sixty men dismounted from Perdikkas' squadron. On foot they formed pairs; one holding a set of fetters, the other a coil of rope.

There was a crucial pause. The thirty turned here and there, protesting. Some spears were waved, some voices urged resistance. In the confusion, the trumpet spoke again. Quietly, seeming only to confer with him, Perdikkas had been rehearsing Philip in his next speech.

"Deliver them up!" he shouted. "Or we will ride against you!" He began, unprompted, to gather up his reins.

"Not now!" hissed Perdikkas, to his relief. He had no wish to go any nearer the spears. They used to point all one way, when Alexander was there.

The spaces widened around the thirty as the fetter-men approached them. Some gave up and submitted; some struggled, but their captors had been picked for strength. All were soon standing, with fettered feet, in the space between the lines. They awaited they knew not what. There had been something odd in the faces of their captors, who had not met their eyes.

"Bind them," said Perdikkas.

Their arms were trussed to their sides. The cavalry fell back to its first line, leaving once more a hollow square. The fetter-bearers pushed the bound men over; they fell forward helplessly, twisting in their bonds, alone under the sky in the field hallowed to Hekate.

From the far side came the shrilling of an eastern pipe and a roll of drums.

The hot sun flashed on the goads of gold and ivory, King Omphis' gifts. Gently the mahouts pricked the necks of their good children, shouting the old command.

Rising like one, fifty trunks curled backward. The troops heard with awe the high blare of their war-cry. Slowly, then at a steady thudding roll, their tread felt through the ground, the huge bedizened beasts moved forward.

The mahouts in their gleaming silks flung off their well-trained silence. They drummed with their heels, hallooing, slapping the necks of their mounts with their jeweled hands or the butts of the goads. They sounded like boys let out of school. The elephants fanned out their great ears, and, squealing with excitement, began to run.

A kind of groan, of horror and a dreadful fascination, ran through the watching lines. Hearing it, the men on the ground writhed to their knees, staring about them. At first they looked at the goads; then one man, still struggling, saw the hennaed feet as they drummed closer, and understood. He screamed. Others tried to roll away in the thick grey dust. They had only time to move a yard or two.

With drawn hissing breath, the army of Alexander saw the treading of the human vintage; the bursting of the rind, the scarlet juices running from the pounded flattened flesh. The elephants moved with well-trained intelligence, catching the rolling bodies with their trunks, and steadying them while the feet came down, trumpeting as the war-smell steamed up from the ground.

From his station besides Perdikkas, Philip uttered little breathless cheers. This was not like the killing of Eos. He was fond of elephants—Alexander had let him ride one—but nobody was hurting them. His eye was filled with their splendid trappings, his ear with their proud brayings. He hardly noticed the bloody mash below them. In any case, Perdikkas had told him that those were all wicked men.

The mahouts, seeing the work well done, calmed and praised their children, who willingly came away. They had done such things in battle, and several still bore the scars. This had been painless and quick. Following their leader, an elephant of great age and wisdom, they formed in line, red to the knees; paraded past Perdikkas and the King, touching brow with trunk in a grave salute; then went their way to the shady elephant-houses, the reward of palm-kernels and melons, the cool pleasant bathe which would sluice off the scent of war.

As indrawn breaths escaped, and the silence in the ranks was breaking, Perdikkas signed to the herald to blow again, and rode forward, a length ahead of the King.

"Macedonians!" he said. "With the death of these traitors the army is truly cleansed, and fit again to defend the empire. If there is anyone among you who, deserving these men's fate, has today escaped it, let him thank his fortune and learn loyalty. Trumpeter! The paean."

The stirring air sang out; the cavalry took it up. After a dragging moment, the infantry came in. Its ancient fierceness was reassuring as a lullaby. It took them back to days when they knew who and what they were.

It was over. Meleager left the ground, alone. His confederates were dead; out of all his hangers-on, not one came near him. He might have had the plague.

The servant who had held his horse seemed to look at him not with meant insolence, but with an inquisitiveness which was worse. Behind, in the vacant square, two covered wagons had appeared, and men with pitchforks were heaving the corpses into them. Two cousins and a nephew of his were there; he ought to arrange their funerals, there was no one else. The thought of searching that trampled meat for shreds of identity revived his nausea; dismounting, he vomited till he was cold with emptiness. As he rode on, he was aware of two men behind him. When he stopped they had drawn rein while one adjusted his saddle-cloth. Now they moved on.

He had fought in many battles. Ambition, comradeship, the bright fierce certainty radiated by Alexander, enemies on whom one could revenge and redeem one's fear, all these had carried him along and made him brave. Never before had he faced a lonely end. His mind began to run, like a hunted fox's, upon likely refuge. Above him, thick and ragged and pitch-black, sullen with the blood of worked-out slaves, loomed the walls of Babylon and the crumbling ziggurat of Bel.

He rode through the tunneled gateway. The men were following. He turned off into narrow streets where women crushed themselves into doorways to give him room; filthy deep courts between eyeless houses, where huddles of

thievish men stared at him dangerously. The pursuit was
no longer in sight. Suddenly he came out into the wide
Marduk Way, the temple just before him. A hallowed
place, to Greeks as well as to barbarians. Everyone knew
that Alexander had sacrificed there to Zeus and Herakles.
Sanctuary!

He hitched his horse to a fig-tree in the weed-grown
outer precinct. Through rank greenery a trodden path led
to the ruined entry; from the gloom beyond came the uni-
versal temple smell of incense, burnt meat and wood-ash,
the Babylonian smell of foreign unguents and foreign flesh.
As he walked towards it in the dazzling heat, someone stood
in the sunlight facing him. It was Alexander.

His heart stopped. Next moment he knew what he was
looking at, but still he could not move. The statue was
marble, tinted like life; a dedication eight years old from the
first Babylonian triumph. It stood at ground-level, the plinth
as yet unbuilt. Nude but for a red chlamys across one
shoulder, grasping a spear of gilded bronze, Alexander
calmly awaited the new temple he had endowed. His deep-
set eyes, with their smoke-grey enamel irises, gazed out at
Meleager, saying "Well?"

He stared back, attempting defiance, at the searching
face, the smooth young body. You were lean and sinewy
and hacked about with scars. Your forehead was creased,
you were drawn about the eyes, your hair was fading. What
is that idol? An idea . . . But memory, once invoked, con-
jured all too potently the real presence. He had seen the
living anger . . . He strode on into the temple.

At first the gloom almost blinded him after the harsh
sun. Presently, by the light of a smoke-shaft high above, he
saw looming in shadow the colossal image of Bel, Great
King of Gods, enthroned with fists on knees. His towering
miter almost touched the roof; he was flanked by winged

lions with the heads of bearded men. His scepter was tall as a man; his robe, from which the gold leaf was peeling, glimmered dimly. His face was blackened with age and smoke, but his ivory-inlaid eyes glared fiercely yellow. Before him was the fire-altar, covered with dead ash. No one, it seemed, had told him there was a new King in Babylon.

No matter, an altar was an altar. Here he was safe. Content at first to get back his breath and enjoy the cool from the thick high walls, soon he started to peer about for signs of life. The place seemed deserted; yet he felt a sense of being observed, assessed, considered.

In the wall behind Bel, there was a door set in the dark-glazed tiles. He felt, rather than heard, stirrings of life behind it; but he dared not knock. Authority had drained from him. Time dragged by. He was a temple suppliant, someone should attend to him. He had not eaten since daybreak; behind the ebony door were men, food, wine. But he did not go to tell them he was there. He knew they knew it.

A rusty sunset light lowered in the courtyard. The shadows deepened round frowning Bel, drowning all but his yellow eye-whites. With the dark, he came into possession. The temple seemed peopled with the ghosts of men like stone, treading with stony feet the necks of their conquered enemies, offering their blood to this stone demon. More than for food, Meleager craved for the open skies of a mountain shrine in Macedon, the color and light of a Greek temple, the gracious and human countenance of its god.

The last light-ray left the courtyard; there was only a square of dusk, and, within, thick dark. Behind the door, low voices sounded and went away.

His horse stamped and snorted outside. He could not stay here and rot; under cover of dark he could be gone.

Someone would take him in . . . but those who were safe
were dead. Better to leave the city now, go west, hire out his
sword to some satrap in nearer Asia. But he must get first
to his rooms; he would need gold, he had taken bribes from
scores of petitioners to the King . . . The dusk in the courtyard moved.

Two shadows showed in the glimmering square. They
came on, into the broken entry. They were not the shadows
of Babylonians. He heard the rasp of drawn swords. "Sanctuary!" he shouted. "Sanctuary!"

The door beyond Bel's image opened a crack, lamplight
bright in the darkness. He shouted again. The crack closed.
The shadows approached, vanishing into blackness. He set
his back to the unlit altar and drew his sword. As they
came close, it seemed to him he knew them; but it was
only the familiar smell and outline of men from home. He
called their names aloud, recalling old friendships in the
army of Alexander. But the names were wrong; and when
they dragged back his head across the altar, it was remembering Alexander that they cut his throat.

Stripped of its banners and plumes, wreathed with cypress
and weeping willow, the lamenting caravan paced slowly
under the Ishtar Gate. Perdikkas and Leonnatos, warned
by the forerunners of its coming, had ridden to meet the
wife of Alexander and tell her that she was widowed. Bareheaded, their hair still cropped in mourning, they rode
beside the wagon train, which had now the air of a cortege.
The princesses sobbed, their women keened and chanted
ritual threnodies. The keepers of the gate heard wondering
these new tears, so long after the days prescribed.

In the harem, the rooms of the chief wife waited, perfumed and immaculate, as ordained by Bagoas two months

before. The Warden had feared that after Alexander's death Roxane would demand them; but to his deep relief she seemed settled where she was. No doubt her pregnancy had quietened her. So far, thought the Warden, so good.

Perdikkas escorted Stateira there, concealing his surprise at her arrival; he had supposed her established in Susa to bear her child in quiet. Alexander, she said, had summoned her. He must have done so without informing anyone. He had done some very odd things, after Hephaistion's death.

Handing her down the wagon steps to the Warden, he thought her more beautiful than at the Susa wedding. Her features had purity of line, the Persian delicacy, fined down by pregnancy and fatigue, which had put smudges of faint cobalt under her large dark eyes; their lids with their long silky lashes looked almost transparent. The Persian kings had always bred for looks. Her hand on the curtain was long-fingered and smooth as cream. She had been wasted on Alexander; he himself, a good inch taller, could have stepped out with her very well. (His own Susa bride, a swarthy Median chosen for exalted birth, had greatly disappointed him.) At least, Alexander had finally had the sense to get a child on her. It should be certain of beauty, if nothing else.

Leonnatos, assisting Drypetis, noted that her face, though still immature, held distinguished promise. He too had a Persian wife; but this need not keep him from looking higher. He rode off in thought.

An obsequious train of eunuchs and waiting-women led the princesses through Nebuchadrezzar's devious corridors to the once-familiar rooms. As in childhood, they felt after the space and light of the Susa palace the frowning Babylonian strength. But then they came through to the sunny courtyard, the fishpool where they had floated their boats of split bamboo in lily-leaf archipelagos, or reached shoulder-

deep after the carp. In the room that had been their
mother's they were bathed and scented and fed. Nothing
seemed changed since that summer eight years before, that
watershed of time, when their father had brought them
here before marching to meet the King of Macedon. Even
the Warden had remembered them.

Their meal done, their attendants dismissed to be settled
in their own quarters, they explored their mother's clothes-
chest. The scarves and veils still released their memory-
stirring scent. Sharing a divan, looking out on the sunlit
pool, they recollected that other life; Stateira, who had
been twelve when it ended, reminding Drypetis, who had
been only nine. They talked of their father whom Grandmother would never name, remembering him in their
mountain home before he had been King, laughing as he
tossed them eight feet in the air. They thought of their
mother's perfect face, framed in the scarf with the seed-
pearls and gold beads. Everyone gone—even Alexander—
except for Grandmother.

They were growing sleepy when a shadow crossed the
doorway. A child came in, with two silver cups on a silver
tray. She was about seven years old, enchantingly pretty,
with a blend of Persian and Indian looks, cream-skinned,
dark-eyed. She dipped a knee without spilling a drop. "Honored ladies," she said carefully. This, clearly, was all her
Persian, learned by heart. They kissed and thanked her; she
dimpled at them, said something in Babylonian, and
trotted away.

The silver cups were misted with coolness, pleasant to
touch. Drypetis said, "She had beautiful clothes, and gold
earrings. She wasn't a servant's child."

"No," said Stateira, worldly-wise. "And if not, you know,
she must be our half-sister. I remember, Father brought
most of the harem here."

"I'd forgotten." Drypetis, a little shocked, looked around

her mother's room. Stateira had gone out into the court-yard, to call back the child again. But she had gone, and no one was in sight; they had told their women they wished to rest undisturbed.

Even the palms seemed bleached in the dazzling heat. They lifted the cups, admiring their chased birds and flowers. The drink tasted of wine and citron, with a deli-cate bitter-sweet tang.

"Delicious," said Stateira. "One of the concubines must have sent it to make us welcome; she was too shy to come herself. Tomorrow we might invite her."

The heavy air was still perfumed with their mother's clothes. It felt homely, secure. Her grief for her parents, for Alexander, grew dim and drowsy. This would be a com-forting place to bear his child in. Her eyelids closed.

The shadow of the palms had barely slanted when pain awoke her. She thought at first that her child must be mis-carrying, till Drypetis clasped her belly and screamed aloud.

Perdikkas, as Regent of Asia, had moved into the palace. He was seeing petitioners in the small audience room when the Warden of the harem appeared, unheralded, his clay-grey face and evident terror having passed him through the guards. Perdikkas, after one look, had the room cleared and heard him.

When the princesses began to cry for help no one had dared go near them; everyone in hearing had guessed the cause. The Warden, desperate to exculpate himself (he had in fact had no hand in it) had not waited for them to breathe their last. Perdikkas ran with him to the harem.

Stateira lay sprawled on the divan, Drypetis on the floor where she had rolled in her death-throes. Stateira drew her last gasp as Perdikkas entered. At first, transfixed with horror, he was aware of no one else in the room. Then he perceived that in the ivory chair before the toilet-table a woman was sitting.

He strode across and stared down at her, silent, hardly able to keep his hands from her throat. She smiled at him.

"You did this!" he said.

Roxane raised her brows. "I? It was the new King. Both of them said so." She did not add that, before the end, she had taken pleasure in undeceiving them.

"The King?" said Perdikkas furiously. "Who will believe that, you accursed barbarian bitch?"

"All your enemies. They will believe it because they wish. I shall say that he sent the draught to me too; but when these fell sick I had not yet drunk it."

"You . . ." For a while he vented his rage in curses. She listened calmly. When he paused, for sufficient answer she laid her hand over her womb.

He looked away at the dead girl. "The child of Alexander."

"*Here*," she said, "is the child of Alexander. His only child . . . Say nothing, and so will I. She came here without ceremony. Very few will know."

"It was *you* who sent for her!"

"Oh, yes. Alexander did not care for her. I did as he would have wished."

For a moment she felt real fear; his hand had dropped to his sword-hilt. Still gripping it, he said, "Alexander is dead. But if ever again you say that of him, when your brat is born I will kill you with these hands. And if I knew it would take after you, I would kill you now."

Growing cool again, she said, "There is an old well in the back court. No one draws from it, they say the water is foul. Let us take them there. No one will come."

He followed her. The well-cover had lately been loosened from its seal of grime. As he lifted it a smell of ancient mold came out.

He had no choice and knew it. Proud as he was, ambitious and fond of power, he was loyal to Alexander, dead as alive. His son should not, if Perdikkas could prevent it, enter the world branded as a poisoner's child.

He returned in silence, going first to Drypetis. Her face was soiled with vomit; he wiped it with a towel before he carried her to the dark hole of the well. When she had slipped from his hands, he heard her clothes brushing the brick till, about twenty feet down, she reached the bottom. He could tell, then, that the well was dry.

Stateira's eyes were staring open, her fingers clutched the stuff of the divan. The eyes would not close; while Roxane waited impatiently, he went to the chest for something to cover her face, a veil stitched with scarab-wings. When he began to move her, he felt wet blood.

"What have you done to her?" He drew back in revulsion, wiping his hand on the coverlet.

Roxane shrugged. Stooping, she lifted the robe of embroidered linen. It could be seen that Alexander's wife in her death-pangs had brought forth his heir.

He stared down at it, the four-month manikin, already human, the sex defined, even the nails beginning. One of the fists was clenched as if in anger, the face with its sealed eyes seemed to frown. It was still tied to its mother; she had died before she could pass the afterbirth. He drew his dagger and cut it free.

"Come, hurry," said Roxane. "You can see that the thing is dead."

"Yes," said Perdikkas. It hardly filled his hands, the son of Alexander, the grandson of Philip and Darius, carrying in its threadlike veins the blood of Achilles and of Kyros the Great.

He went again to the chest. A scarf trailed out, stitched with seed-pearls and gold beads. Carefully, like a woman, he wrapped the creature in its royal shroud, and gave it its

own journey to the burial-place, before returning to send
its mother after it.

Queen Sisygambis sat playing chess with the Head Chamberlain. He was an elderly eunuch with a distinguished past
going back to King Ochos' reign. An expert survivor of
countless court intrigues, he played a canny game, and
offered more challenge than the waiting-ladies. She had
invited him to relieve her boredom, and mere courtesy
demanded that she should attend to him. She brooded over
the ivory armies on the board. Now that the girls were
gone with their young attendants, the harem seemed to have
been left behind by time. Everyone here was old.

The Chamberlain saw her lethargy and guessed the
cause. He fell into one or two of her traps and rescued
himself, to enliven the game. In a pause, he said, "Did you
find, when the King was here, that he had remembered
your instruction? You said, before he marched east, that
he had promise if he would apply his mind."

She said smiling, "I did not test him. I knew he would
have forgotten." For a moment, reflected from the distance, rays of vitality seemed to surge through the muted
room. "I used to tell him it was called the royal war-game,
and for my sake he pretended to care who won. But when
I scolded him and told him he could do better, he said,
'But, Mother, these are *things*.' "

"He is not a man for sitting still, indeed."

"He needed more rest. It was not the time to go down
to Babylon. Babylon has always been to winter in."

"It seems he means to winter in Arabia. We shall scarcely
see him this year. But when he marches, for sure he will
send Their Highnesses back to you, as soon as the child is
born and the lady Stateira can travel."

"Yes," she said a little wistfully. "He will want me to see the child." She returned to the board, and moved an elephant to threaten his vizier. A pity, he thought, that the boy had not sent for her; she doted on him still. But, as she had said, it was no time to go down to Babylon, and she was turned eighty.

They had finished the game, and were drinking citron, when the Chamberlain was summoned, urgently, by the commander of the garrison. When he came back, she looked at his face, and grasped the arms of her chair.

"Madam . . ."

"It is the King," she said. "He is dead."

He bowed his head. It was as if her body had known already; at his first word the chill had reached her heart. He came up quickly, in case she was going to fall; but after a moment she motioned him to his chair, and waited for him to speak.

He told her as much as he had learned, still watching her; her face was the color of old parchment. But she was not grieving only; she was thinking. Presently she turned to a table near her chair, opened an ivory casket, and took out a letter.

"Please read me this. Not the substance only. Word for word."

His sight was not what it had been; but by bringing it close he could see quite clearly. He translated scrupulously. At *I have been sick, and there is ignorant talk that I am dead*, he looked up and met her eyes.

"Tell me," she said, "is that his seal?"

He peered at it; at a few inches, the detail was sharp enough. "It is his likeness, and a good one. But it is not the royal seal. Has he used this before?"

Without speaking, she put the casket into his hands. He looked at the letters, written in elegant Persian by a scribe; his eye caught one ending: *I commend you, dear Mother, both to your gods and mine, if indeed they are not the same, as I think they are.* There were five or six letters. All had the royal seal, Olympian Zeus enthroned, his eagle perched on his hand. She read the answer in his face.

"When he did not write to me . . ." She took the casket and set it down beside her. Her face was pinched as if with cold, but without astonishment. All her middle years had been passed in the dangerous reign of Ochos. Her husband had had royal blood enough to be in danger whenever the King felt insecure. Trusting almost no one, he had trusted her and told her everything. Intrigue, revenge and treachery had been daily weather. In the end, Ochos had killed him. She had believed that he lived again in her tall son; his flight from Issos had almost killed her with shame. In the desolate tent, the young conquerer was announced, to visit the family his enemy had abandoned. For the children's sake, performing dignity like a well-trained animal its trick, she had knelt to the tall handsome man before her. He stepped back; everyone's dismay made her aware of a frightful error; she began to bow to the smaller man she had overlooked. He had taken her hands and raised her, and for the first time she saw his eyes. "Never mind, Mother . . ." She had had Greek enough for that.

The Chamberlain, the old survivor, almost as pale as she, was trying not to look at her. Just so someone had looked away when her husband had had his last summons to the court.

"They have murdered him." She said it as something evident.

"This man says the marsh-fever. It is common at Babylon in summer."

"No, they have poisoned him. And there is no word of my granddaughters?"

He shook his head. There was a pause while they sat

silent, feeling disaster strike on their old age, a mortal illness, not to be shaken off.

She said, "He married Stateira for policy. It was my doing
he got her with child."

"They may still be safe. Perhaps in hiding."

She shook her head. Suddenly she sat up in her chair,
like a woman thinking, Why am I idling like this, when
I have work to do?

"My friend, a time is over. I shall go to my room now.
Farewell. Thank you for your good service in all these
years."

She read new fear in his face. She understood it; they had
both known Ochos' reign. "No one will suffer. No one will
be charged with anything. At my age, to die is easy. When
you go, will you send my women?"

The women found her composed and busy, laying out
her jewels. She talked to them of their families, advised
them, embraced them and divided her jewels among them,
all but King Poros' rubies, which she kept on.

When she had bidden them all farewell, she lay down on
her bed in the inner room, and closed her eyes. They did
not try, after her first refusals, to get her to eat or drink. It
was no kindness to trouble her, still less to save her alive
for the coming vengeance. For the first few days, they left
her alone as she had ordered. On the fourth, seeing her begin to sink, one or other kept watch beside her; if she knew
of them, she did not turn them away. On the fifth day at
nightfall, they became aware that she was dead; her breathing had been so quiet, no one could be sure when it had
ended.

Galloping day and night, by dromedary, by horse, by mountain mule as the terrain needed, man throwing to man the
brief startling news, the King's Messengers had carried

their tidings of death from Babylon to Susa, Susa to Sardis, Sardis to Smyrna, along the Royal Road which Alexander had extended to reach the Middle Sea. At Smyrna, all through the sailing season, a despatch-boat was ready to carry his letters to Macedon.

The last courier of the long relay had arrived at Pella, and given Perdikkas' letter to Antipatros.

The tall old man read in silence. Whenever Philip had gone to war he had ruled Macedon; since Alexander crossed to Asia he had ruled all Greece. The honor which had kept him loyal had also stiffened his pride; he looked far more regal than had Alexander, who had looked only like himself. It had been a joke of his among close friends that Antipatros was all white outside, with a purple lining.

Now, reading the letter, knowing he would not after all be replaced by Krateros (Perdikkas had made that clear) his first thought was that all south Greece would rise as soon as the news had broken. The news itself, though shocking, was a shock long half-expected. He had known Alexander from his cradle; it had always been inconceivable that he would make old bones. Antipatros had almost told him so outright, while he was preparing to march to Asia without begetting an heir.

It had been a false move to hint at his own daughter; the boy could hardly have done better, but it had made him feel trapped, or used. "Do you think I've time now to hold wedding feasts and wait about for children?" he had said. He could have had a half-grown son, thought Antipatros, with our good blood in him. And now? Two unborn half-breeds; and meantime, a pride of young lions, slipped off the leash. He remembered, not without misgivings, his own eldest son.

He remembered, too, a scrap of gossip from the first year of the young King's reign. He had told someone, "I don't want a son of mine reared here while I'm away."

And that was behind it all. That accursed woman! All through his boyhood she had made him hate his father, whom he might have admired if let alone; she'd shown him marriage as the poisoned shirt of Herakles (that, too, a woman's doing!), then, when he'd reached the age for girls and could have had his pick, she was outraged that he'd taken refuge with another boy. He could have done far worse than Hephaistion—his father had, and got his death by it—but she could not live with what she'd brought about, had made an enemy where she could have had an ally; and all she'd achieved was to come second instead of first. No doubt she'd rejoiced to hear of Hephaistion's death. Well, she had another to hear of now, and let her make the best of it.

He checked himself. It was unseemly to mock a mother's grief for her only son. He would have to send her the news. He sat down at his writing-table with the wax before him, seeking some decent and kindly word for his old enemy, some fitting eulogy of the dead. A man, he reflected, whom he had not seen for more than a decade, whom he thought of still as a brilliantly precocious boy. What had he looked like, after those prodigious years? Perhaps one might still see, or guess. It would be something suitable with which to end his letter, that the body of the King had been embalmed to the likeness of life, and only awaited a worthy bier to begin its journey to the royal burial ground at Aigai.

TO QUEEN OLYMPIAS, HEALTH AND PROS-PERITY . . .

It was full summer in Epiros. The high valley on its mountain shoulder was green and gold, watered from the deep winter snows which Homer had remembered. The calves were fattening, the sheep had yielded their fine soft wool, the trees bent, heavy with fruit. Though it was against all custom, the Molossians had prospered under a woman's rule.

The widowed Queen Kleopatra, daughter of Philip and sister of Alexander, stood with the letter of Antipatros in her hand, looking out from the upper room of the royal house to the further mountains. The world had changed, it was too soon to know how. For Alexander's death she felt awe without grief, as for his life she had felt awe without love. He had entered the world before her, to steal her mother's care, her father's notice. Their fights had stopped early, in the nursery; after that they had not been close enough. Her wedding day, the day of their father's murder, had made her a pawn of state; him it had made a king. Soon he had become a phenomenon, growing with distance more dazzling and more strange.

Now for a while, the paper in her hand, she remembered the days when, boy and girl with only two years between them, their parents' ceaseless strife had brought them together in defensive collusion; remembered, too, how if their mother had to be braved in one of her dreadful weeping rages, it had been he who would always go and face the storm.

She laid Antipatros' letter down. The one for Olympias was on the table beside it. He would not face her now; she herself must do it.

She knew where she would find her; in the ground-floor state guest-room where she had been first received to attend the funeral of Kleopatra's husband, and where she had since remained. The dead King had been her brother; more and more she had encroached on the kingdom's business, while she pursued through a horde of agents the feud with Antipatros which had made her position in Macedon impossible.

Kleopatra set resolutely the square chin she had inherited from Philip, and, taking the letter, went down to her mother's room.

The door was ajar. Olympias was dictating to her secretary. Kleopatra, pausing, could hear that she was drawing up a long indictment against Antipatros, going back ten years, a summary of old scores. *"Question him on this, when he appears before you, and do not be deceived if he claims that . . ."* She paced about impatiently while the scribe caught up.

Kleopatra had meant to behave, on so traditional an occasion, as a daughter should; to show the warning of a grave sad face, to utter the usual preparations. Just then her eleven-year-old son came in from a game of ball with his companion pages; a big-boned auburn boy with his father's face. Seeing her hesitating at the door, he looked at her with an air of anxious complicity, as if sharing her caution before the seat of power.

She dismissed him gently, wanting to hug him to her and cry, *"You* are the King!" Through the door she saw the secretary busily scratching the wax. He was a man she hated, a creature of her mother's from long ago in Macedon. There was no knowing what he had known.

Olympias was a few years over fifty. Straight as a spear, and slender still, she had begun to use cosmetics as a woman does who means only to be seen, not touched. Her greying hair had been washed with camomile and henna; her lashes and brows were lined in with antimony. Her face was whitened, her lips, not her cheeks, were faintly reddened. She had painted her own image of herself, not enticing Aphrodite but commanding Hera. When, catching sight of her daughter in the doorway, she swept round to rebuke the interruption, she was majestic, even formidable.

Suddenly, Kleopatra was swept by a red surge of anger.

Stepping forward into the room, her face like stone, making no gesture to dismiss the scribe, she said harshly, "You need not write to him. He is dead."

The perfect silence seemed deepened by each slight intrusive sound; the click of the man's dropped stylus, a dove in a nearby tree, the voices of children playing a long way off. The white cream on Olympias' face stood out like chalk. She looked straight before her. Kleopatra, nerved for she could not tell what elemental furies, waited till she could no longer bear it. Quiet with remorse, she said, "It was not in war. He died of fever."

Olympias motioned to the scribe. He made off, leaving his papers in disorder. She turned towards Kleopatra.

"Is that the letter? Give it to me."

Kleopatra put it into her hand. She held it, unopened, waiting, dismissive. Kleopatra shut the thick door behind her. No sound came from the room. His death was something between the two of them, as his life had been. She herself was excluded. That, too, was an old story.

Olympias grasped the stone mullion of the window, its carvings biting, unfelt, into her palms. A passing servant saw the staring face and thought, for a moment, that a tragic theater mask had been propped there. He hurried on lest her sightless gaze should light on him. She stared at the eastern sky.

It had been foretold her before his birth. Perhaps as she slept he had stirred within her—he had been restless, impatient for life—and it had made her dream. Billowing wings of fire had sprung from her body, beating and spreading till they were great enough to waft her into the sky. Still the fire had streamed from her, an ecstasy, flowing over mountains and seas till it filled the earth. Like a god she had surveyed it, floating on the flames. Then, in a moment, they were gone. From some desolate crag where they had abandoned her, she had seen the land black and smoking, sparked with hot embers like a burned-out hillside. She had started wide awake, and put out her hand for her husband. But she was eight months gone, he had long since found other bedfellows. She had lain till morning, remembering the dream.

When, later, the fire was running over the wondering world, she had said to herself that all life must die, the time was far off and she would not live to see it. Now all was fulfilled; she could only clench her hands upon the stone and affirm that it must not be. It had never been in her to accept necessity.

Down on the coast, where the waters of Acheron and Kokytos met, was the Nekromanteion, the Oracle of the Dead. She had gone there long ago, when for her sake Alexander had defied his father, and they had both come here in exile for a time. She remembered the dark and winding labyrinth, the sacred drink, the blood-libation which gave the shades strength to speak. Her father's spirit had stirred in the gloom and spoken faintly, saying her troubles would soon end and fortune shine on her.

It would be a long day's ride, she must set out at dawn. She would make the offering and take the draught and go into the dark, and her son would come to her. Even from Babylon, from the world's end, he would come . . . Her mind paused. What if the first-comers were those who had died at home? Philip, with Pausanias' dagger in his ribs? His new young wife, to whom she had offered poison or the rope? Even for a spirit, even for Alexander, it was two thousand miles from Babylon.

No; she would wait till his body came; that, surely, would bring his spirit nearer. When she had seen his body, his

spirit would seem less strange. For she knew that she feared
its strangeness. When he left, he had been still a boy to
her; she would receive the body of a man nearing middle
age. Would his shade obey her? He had loved her, but
seldom obeyed.

The man, the ghost, slipped from her grasp. She stood
there empty. Then, uninvoked, vivid to sight and touch,
came the child. The scent of his hair, nuzzled into her
neck; the light scratches on his fine skin, his grazed dirty
knees; his laughter, his anger, his wide listening eyes. Her
dry eyes filled; tears streaked her cheeks with eye-paint; she
bit on her arm to muffle her crying.

By the evening fire, she had told him the old family
tales of Achilles handed down by word of mouth, always
reminding him that it was from her side that the hero's
blood came down to him. When schooldays began he had
come eagerly to the *Iliad*, coloring it with the Achilles of
the tales. Reaching the *Odyssey*, he came upon Odysseus'
visit to the land of shades. ("It was in my country, in
Epiros, that he spoke with them.") Slowly and solemnly,
looking out past her at a reddening sunset sky, he had
spoken the words.

> "Achilleus,
> *no man before has been more blessed than you, nor ever*
> *will be. Before, when you were alive, we Argives honored you*
> *as we did the gods, and now in this place you have great authority*
> *over the dead. Do not grieve, even in death, Achilleus."*
> *So I spoke, and he in turn said to me in answer,*
> *"O shining Odysseus, never try to console me for dying.*
> *I would rather follow the plow as thrall to another*
> *man, one with no land allotted him and not much to live on,*
> *than be a king over all the perished dead."*

Because he did not cry when he was hurt, he was never ashamed of tears. She saw his eyes glitter, fixed on the glowing clouds, and knew that his grief was innocent; only for Achilles, parted from hope and expectation, the mere shadow of his glorious past, ruling over shadows of past men. He had not yet believed in his own mortality.

He said, as if it were her he was reassuring, "But Odysseus did console him for dying, after all, it says so."

So I spoke, and the soul of the swift-footed scion of Aiakos
stalked away in long strides across the meadow of asphodel,
happy for what I had said of his son, and how he was famous.

"Yes," she had said. "And after the war his son came to Epiros, and we are both descended from him."

He had considered it. Then: "Would Achilles be happy if I were famous too?"

She had bent and ruffled his hair. "Of course he would. He would stride through the asphodel and sing."

She let go of the window-column. She felt faint and ill; going to her inner room she lay down and wept fiercely. It left her almost too weak to stand, and at last she slept. At dawn, she woke to the recollection of great grief, but her strength was almost recovered. She bathed and dressed and painted her face, and went to her writing-table. *TO PERDIKKAS, REGENT OF THE ASIAN KINGDOMS, PROSPERITY . . .*

On the roof of their house, a few miles inland from Pella, Kynna and Eurydike were practicing with the javelin.

Kynna, like Kleopatra, was one of Philip's daughters, but by a minor marriage. Her mother had been an Illyrian princess, and a noted warrior, as the customs of her race allowed. After a border war against her formidable old father Bardelys, Philip had sealed the peace treaty with a wedding, as he had done several times before. The lady Audata would not have been his choice for her own sake; she was comely, but he had trouble remembering which sex he was in bed with. He had paid her attention enough to get one daughter on her, given them a house, maintained them, but seldom called on them till Kynna was of marriageable age. Then he had given her in wedlock to his nephew Amyntas, his elder brother's child, the same whom the Macedonians had passed over in his infancy, to make Philip King.

Amyntas, obedient to the people's will expressed in the Assembly, had lived peaceably through Philip's reign. Only when conspirators were planning the King's murder had he fallen to temptation, and agreed when the deed was done to accept the throne. For this, when it came to light, Alexander had put him on trial for treason, and the Assembly had condemned him.

Kynna, his wife, had withdrawn from the capital to his country estate. She had lived there ever since, rearing her daughter in the martial skills her Illyrian mother had taught her. It was her natural bent; it was an occupation; and she felt, instinctively, that one day it would be of use. She had never forgiven Amyntas' death. Her daughter Eurydike, only child of an only child, had known as long as she could remember that she should have been a boy.

The core of the house was a rugged old fort going back to the civil wars; later the thatched house had been built beside it. It was on the flat roof of the fort that the woman and the girl were standing, throwing at a straw man propped on a pole.

A stranger could have taken them for sisters; Kynna was only just thirty, Eurydike was fifteen. They both took after the Illyrian side, tall, fresh-faced, athletic. In the short men's tunics they wore for exercise, their brown hair plaited back out of their way, they looked like girls of Sparta, a land of which they knew almost nothing.

Eurydike's javelin had left a splinter in her palm. She pulled it out, and called in slave-Thracian to the tattooed boy who was bringing back the spears from the target, and who should have seen they were rubbed smooth. As he worked they sat to rest on a block of stone set for an archer, stretched and took deep breaths of the mountain air.

"I hate the plains," said Eurydike. "I shall mind that more than anything."

Her mother did not hear; she had been looking out at the hill-road that led between the village huts to their gate. "A courier is coming. Come down and change your clothes."

They climbed down the wooden steps to the floor below, and put on their second-best dresses. A courier was a rare event, and such people reported what they saw.

His gravity and sense of drama almost made Kynna ask his errand before she broke the seal. But it would be undignified; she sent him off to be fed before she read Antipatros' letter.

"Who is dead?" asked Eurydike. "Is it Arridaios?" Her voice was eager.

Her mother looked up. "No. It is Alexander."

"*Alexander!*" She spoke with disappointment more than grief. Then her face lightened. "If the King is dead, I needn't marry Arridaios."

"Be quiet!" said her mother. "Let me read." Her face had changed; it held defiance, resolution, triumph. The girl said anxiously, "I needn't marry him, Mother? Need I? Need I?"

Kynna turned to her with glowing eyes. "Yes! Now indeed you must. The Macedonians have made him King."

"*King?* How can they? Is he better, have his wits come back?"

"He is Alexander's brother, that is all. He is to keep the throne warm for Alexander's son by the barbarian. If she has a son."

"And Antipatros says I am to marry him?"

"No, he does not. He says that Alexander had changed his mind. He may be lying, or not. It's no matter which."

Eurydike's thick brows drew together. "But if it's true, it might mean Arridaios is worse."

"No, Alexander would have sent word; the man is lying, I know it. We must wait to hear from Perdikkas in Babylon."

"Oh, Mother, let us not go. I don't want to marry the fool."

"Don't call him the fool, he is King Philip, they have named him after your grandfather . . . Don't you see? The gods have sent you this. They mean you to right the wrong that was done your father."

Eurydike looked away. She had been barely two when Amyntas was executed, and did not remember him. He had been a burden on her all her life.

"Eurydike!" The voice of authority brought her to attention. Kynna had set herself to be father as well as mother, and done it well. "Listen to me. You were meant for great things, not to grow old in a village like a peasant. When Alexander offered you his brother's hand to make peace between our houses, I knew that it was destiny. You are a true-born Macedonian and royal on both sides. Your father should have been King. If you were a man, they would have chosen you in Assembly."

The girl listened in a growing quiet. Her face lost its sullenness; aspiration began to kindle in her eyes.

"If I die for it," said Kynna, "you shall be reigning Queen."

⊙   ⊙   ⊙

Peukestes, Satrap of Persia, had withdrawn from his audience chamber to his private room. It was furnished in the
manner of the province, except for the Macedonian panoply
on the armor-stand. He had changed from his formal robe
to loose trousers and embroidered slippers. A tall fair man,
with features of lean refinement, he had curled his hair
Persian-style; but at Alexander's death, conforming to Persian custom, had shaved it to the scalp, instead of cropping
it as he would in Macedon. When exposed it still felt chilly;
to warm his head he had put on his cap of office, the helmet-
shaped kyrbasia. This gave him an unintended look of state;
the man he had summoned approached him with down-
cast eyes, and prepared to go down in the prostration.

Peukestes looked at him startled, at first not knowing
him; then he put out his hand. "No, Bagoas. Get up, be
seated."

Bagoas rose and obeyed, acknowledging, with some gesture of the face, Peukestes' smile. His dark-circled eyes
looked enormous; there was just enough flesh on him to
display the elegance of his skull. His scalp was naked of
hair; when it began to grow he must have shaved again. He
looked like an ivory mask. Yes, something must be done
for him, Peukestes thought.

"You know," he said, "that Alexander died leaving no
will?"

The young eunuch made an assenting gesture. After a
pause he said, "Yes. He would not surrender."

"True. And when he understood that the common fate
of man had overtaken him, his voice had gone. Or he would
not have forgotten his faithful servants . . . You know, I kept
vigil for him at the shrine of Sarapis. It was a long night,
and a man had time to think."

"Yes," said Bagoas. "That was a long night."

"He told me once that your father had an estate near Susa, but was unjustly dispossessed and killed while you were young." No need to add that the boy had been castrated and enslaved, and sold to pleasure Darius. "If Alexander could have spoken, I think he would have bequeathed you your father's land. So I shall buy out the man who has it, and give it you."

"The bounty of my lord is like rain on a dry river-bed." A beautiful movement of the hand went with it, like an absent-minded reflex; he had been a courtier since he was thirteen. "But my parents are both dead; so are my sisters, at least if they were fortunate. I had no brother; and I shall have no son. Our house was burned to the ground; and for whom should I rebuild it?"

He has made a grave-offering of his beauty, Peukestes thought; now he is waiting to die. "And yet, it might please your father's shade to see his son restore his name with honor in the ancestral place."

Bagoas' hollow eyes seemed to consider it, like something infinitely distant. "If my lord, in his magnanimity, would give me a little time . . . ?"

He wants only to be rid of me, Peukestes thought. Well, I can do no more.

That evening Ptolemy, on the eve of departing to the satrapy of Egypt, was his guest at supper. Since it seemed they might never meet again, their talk grew reminiscent. Presently it turned upon Bagoas.

"He could make Alexander laugh," Ptolemy said. "I have heard them often."

"You would not think so now." Peukestes related the morning's interview. The talk passed to other things; but Ptolemy, who had a mind that wasted nothing, pleaded tomorrow's press of business and left the party early.

Bagoas' house stood in the paradise a little way from the

palace. It was small but elegant; often Alexander had spent an evening there. Ptolemy remembered the torches in their sconces by the door, the sound of harps and flutes and laughter, and, sometimes, the eunuch's sweet alto singing.

At first sight all was dark. Nearer, he saw a dim single lamp yellowing a window. A small dog barked; after a while, a sleepy servant peered through the grille, and said the master had retired. These courtesies over, Ptolemy went round towards the window.

"Bagoas," he said softly, "it's Ptolemy. I am going away forever. Won't you bid me goodbye?"

There was only a short silence. The light voice said, "Let the lord Ptolemy in. Light the lamps. Bring wine."

Ptolemy entered, politely disclaiming ceremony, Bagoas politely insisting. A taper was brought, light shone on his ivory head. He was dressed, in the formal clothes he must have worn to call on Peukestes. They looked now as if he had slept in them; he was buttoning the jacket up. On the table was a tablet covered with score-marks; what was erased looked like an attempt to draw a face. He pushed them aside to make room for the wine-tray, and thanked Ptolemy for the honor of his visit with impeccable civility; peering at him blankly from deep hollow eyes, as the slave kindled the lamps, like an owl revealed in daylight. He looked a little mad. Ptolemy thought, Am I too late already?

He said, "You have truly mourned for him. I too. He was a good brother."

Bagoas' face remained inexpressive; but tears ran from his eyes in silence, like blood from an open wound. He brushed them absently away, as one might a lock of hair which has a habit of straying, and turned to pour the wine.

"We owed him tears," Ptolemy said. "He would have wept for us." He paused. "But, if the dead care for what

concerned them in life, he may be needing more from his
friends than that."

The ivory mask under the lamp turned to a face; the
eyes, in which desperation was tempered by older habits of
gentle irony, riveted themselves on Ptolemy's. "Yes?" he
said.

"We both know what he valued most. While he lived,
honor and love; and, after, undying fame."

"Yes," Bagoas. "So . . . ?"

With his new attention had come a profound and weary
skepticism. Why not, thought Ptolemy; three years among
the labyrinthine intrigues of Darius' court before he was
sixteen—and, lately, why not indeed?

"What have you seen since he died? How long have you
been shut up here?"

Raising his large dark disillusioned eyes, Bagoas said with
a vicious quiet, "Since the day of the elephants."

For a moment Ptolemy was silenced; the wraith had
hardened, dauntingly. Presently he said, "Yes, that would
have sickened him. Niarchos said so, and so did I. But we
were overborne."

Bagoas said, answering the unspoken words, "The ring
would have gone to Krateros, if he had been there."

There was a pause. Ptolemy considered his next move;
Bagoas looked like a man just waked from sleep, considering his thoughts. Suddenly he looked up sharply. "Has anyone gone to Susa?"

"Bad news travels fast."

"News?" said Bagoas with unconcealed impatience. "It
is protection they will need."

Suddenly, Ptolemy remembered something said by his
Persian wife, Artakama, a lady of royal blood bestowed by
Alexander. He was leaving her with her family till, as he
had said, the affairs of Egypt were settled. He had been

uneasy with a harem, its claustral and stifling femininity, after the free-and-easy Greek hetairas. He meant his heir to be a pure-bred Macedonian, and had, in fact, offered for one of Antipatros' many daughters. But there had been some piece of gossip . . . Bagoas' eyes were boring into his.

"I have heard a rumor—worth nothing I daresay—that a Persian lady came from Susa to the harem here, and was taken sick and died. But—"

Bagoas' breath hissed through his teeth. "If Stateira has come to Babylon," he said in a soft deadly voice, "of course she has been taken sick and died. When first the Bactrian knew of me, I would have died of the same sickness, if I had not given some sweetmeats to a dog."

Ptolemy felt a sickening conviction. He had been with Alexander on that last visit to Susa, been brought once to dine with Sisygambis and the family. Pity and disgust contended with the thought that if this had happened, and Perdikkas had condoned it, his own design was justified.

"Alexander's fame," he said, "has not been very well served since the gods received him. Men who cannot match his greatness of soul should try at least to honor it."

Bagoas brooded on him, thoughtful, in a grey calm; as if he stood on the threshold of a door he had been going out of, and could not be sure it was worth while to turn back. "Why have you come?" he said.

The dead are not respectful, Ptolemy reflected. Good, it saves time.

"I will tell you why. I am concerned for the fate of Alexander's body."

Bagoas hardly stirred, but his whole frame seemed to change, losing its lethargy, becoming wiry and tense. "They took their oath!" he said. "They took it on the Styx."

"Oath . . . ? Oh, all that is over. I'm not talking of Babylon."

He looked up. His hearer had come in from the threshold; the door of life had swung to behind him. He listened, rigidly.

"They are making him a golden bier; nothing less is due to him. It will take the craftsmen a year to finish. Then, Perdikkas will have it sent to Macedon."

"To *Macedon!*" The look of stunned shock quite startled Ptolemy, his homeland customs taken for granted. Well, so much the better.

"That is the custom. Did he not tell you how he buried his father?"

"Yes. But it was *here* they . . ."

"Meleager? A rogue and a halfwit, and the rogue is dead. But in Macedon, that is different. The Regent is nearly eighty; he may be gone before the bier arrives. And his heir is Kassandros, whom you know of."

Bagoas' slender hand closed in a sinewy fist. "Why did Alexander let him live? If he had only given me leave. No one would have been the wiser."

I don't doubt it, thought Ptolemy, glancing at his face. "Well, in Macedon the King is entombed by his rightful heir; it confirms his succession. So, Kassandros will be waiting. So will Perdikkas; he will claim it in the name of Roxane's son—and, if there is no son, maybe for himself. There is also Olympias, who is no mean fighter either. It will be a bitter war. Sooner or later, whoever holds the coffin and the bier will need the gold."

Ptolemy looked for a moment, and looked away. He had come remembering the elegant, epicene favorite; devoted certainly, he had not doubted that, but still, a frivolity, the plaything of two kings' leisure. He had not foreseen this profound and private grief in its priestlike austerity. What memories moved behind those guarded eyes?

"This, then," he said inexpressively, "is why you came?"

"Yes. I can prevent it, if I have help that I can trust."

Bagoas said, half to himself, "I never thought they would be taking him away." His face changed and grew wary. "What do you mean to do?"

"If I have word of when the bier sets out, I will march from Egypt to meet it. Then, if I can treat with the escort —and I think I can—I will take him to his own city, and entomb him in Alexandria."

Ptolemy waited. He saw himself being weighed. At least there were no old scores between them. Less than delighted when Alexander took a Persian to his heart and bed, he had been distant to the boy, but never insolent. Later, when it was clear the youth was neither venal nor ambitious, simply a tactful and well-mannered concubine, their chance meetings had been unstrained and easy. However, one did not sleep with two kings and remain naive. One could see the assessment he was making now.

"You are thinking of what I stand to gain; and why not? A great deal, of course. It may even make me a king. But —and this I swear before the gods—never a king of Macedon and Asia. No man alive can wear the mantle of Alexander, and those who grasp at it will destroy themselves. Egypt I can hold, and rule it as he wanted. You were not there, it was before your time; but he was proud of Alexandria."

"Yes," said Bagoas. "I know."

"I was with him," said Ptolemy, "when he went to Ammon's oracle at Siwah in the desert, to learn his destiny."

He began to tell of it. Almost at once the worldly alertness in his hearer's face had faded; he saw the single-minded absorption of a listening child. How often, he thought, must that look have drawn the tale from Alexander! The boy's memory must read like a written scroll. But to hear it from someone else would give some new and precious detail, some new sight-line.

He took trouble, therefore, describing the desert march,

the rescuing rain, the guiding ravens, the serpents pointing as they lay, the sands' mysterious voices; the great oasis with its pools and palm-glades and wondering white-robed people; the rocky acropolis where the temple was, with its famous courtyard where the sign of the god was given.

"There is a spring in a basin of red rock; we had to wash our gold and silver offerings in it, to cleanse them for the god, and ourselves as well. It was icy cold in the hot dry air. Alexander of course they did not purify. He was Pharaoh. He carried his own divinity. They led him into the sanctuary. Outside, the light was all shimmering white, and everything seemed to ripple in it. The entrance looked black as night, you'd have thought it would have blinded him. But he went in as though his eyes were on distant mountains."

Bagoas nodded, as if to say, "Of course; go on."

"Presently we heard singing, and harps and cymbals and sistra, and the oracle came out. There is not room for it inside the sanctuary. He stood there to watch it, somewhere in the dark.

"The priests came out, forty pairs of them, twenty before and twenty behind the god. They carried the oracle like a litter, with long shoulder-poles. The oracle is a boat. I don't know why the god should speak through a boat on land. Ammon has a very old shrine at Thebes. Alexander used to say it must have come first from the river."

"Tell me about the boat." He spoke like a child who prompts an old bedtime story.

"It was long and light, like the bird-hunters' punts on the Nile. But sheathed all over with gold, and hung with gold and silver votives, all kinds of little precious things swinging and glittering and tinkling. In the middle was the Presence of the god. Just a simple sphere.

"The priest came out into the court with Alexander's

question. He had written it on a strip of gold and folded
the gold together. He laid it on the pavement before the
god, and prayed in his own tongue. Then the boat began
to live. It stayed where it was, but you could see it quicken."

"You saw it," said Bagoas suddenly. "Alexander said he
was too far."

"Yes, I saw. The carriers stood with empty faces, waiting;
but they were like flotsam on a still river-pool, before the
flow of the river lifts it. It does not stir yet; but you know
the river is under all.

"The question lay shining in the sun. The cymbals
sounded a slow beat and the flutes played louder. Then the
carriers began to sway a little where they stood, just as
flotsam sways. You know how the god answers: back for no,
forward for yes. They moved forward like all one thing, a
skein of water-weed, a drift of leaves, till before the question
they stopped, and the prow dipped. Then the trumpets
sounded, and we waved our hands and cheered.

"We waited, then, for Alexander to come out from the
sanctuary. It was hot; or we thought so, not having yet
been in Gedrosia." A shadowy smile replied to him. They
were both survivors of that dreadful march.

"At last he came out with the high priest. I think more
had happened than he had come to ask. He came out with
the awe still in him. Then, I remember, he blinked in the
sudden brightness, and shaded his eyes with his hand. He
saw us all, and looked across and smiled."

He had looked across at Hephaistion and smiled; but
there was no need to say so.

"Egypt loved him. They welcomed him with hymns as
their savior from the Persians. He honored all their temples
that Ochos had profaned. I wish you had seen him laying
out Alexandria. I don't know how far it has gone up now,
I don't trust the governor; but I know what he wanted, and

when I am there I shall see it done. There is only one thing he left no mark for: the tomb where we shall honor him. But I know the place, by the sea. I remember him standing there."

Bagoas' eyes had been fixed upon a light-point on his silver cup. He raised them. "What is it you want done?"

Silently, Ptolemy caught his breath. He had been in time.

"Stay here in Babylon. You refused Peukestes' offer; no one else will make you his concern. Bear with it if they take your house for some creature of Perdikkas'. Stay till the bier is ready and you know when it will set out. Then come to me. You shall have a house in Alexandria near where he lies. You know that in Macedon that could not be."

In Macedon, he thought, the children would stone you in the street. But you have guessed that; there is no need to be cruel.

"Will you take my hand on it?" he said.

He held out his big-boned right hand, calloused from the spear-shaft and the sword, its seams picked out by the lamp as he held it open. Pale, slender and icy cold, Bagoas' hand took it in a precise and steady grip. Ptolemy remembered that he had been a dancer.

In a last fierce spasm, Roxane felt her infant's head thrust out of her. More gently, with swift relief, turned by a skillful midwife, the moist body slid after. She stretched her legs out, dripping with sweat and panting; then heard the child's thin angry cry.

Shrill with exhaustion, she cried out, "A boy, is it a boy?"

Acclamation and praise and good-luck invocations rose in chorus. She gave a great groan of triumph. The midwife lifted the child to view, still on its blue-white cord. From

the half-screened corner where he had vigilantly watched
the birth, Perdikkas came forward, confirmed the sex, uttered a conventional phrase of good omen, and left the
room.

The cord was tied, the afterbirth delivered; mother and
child were washed with warm rose-water, dried, anointed.
Alexander the Fourth, joint King of Macedon and Asia,
was laid in his mother's arms.

He nuzzled for warmth, but she held him at arms' length
to look at him. He was dark-haired.

The midwife, touching the fine fluff, said it was birth-
hair that would fall away. He was still red and crumpled,
his face closed up in the indignation of the newly born; but
she could see through the flush an olive, not a rosy coloring.
He would be dark, a Bactrian. And why not? Alone in a
harsh alien element, missing the womb's blind comfort,
he began to cry.

She lowered him to her body, to take the weight from
her arms. He hushed; the slave-girl with the feather fan
had come back to the bedside; after the bustle, the women
with silence and soft feet were setting to rights the rooms
of the Royal Wife. Beyond the door, the courtyard with
its fishpool lay under the mild winter sun. Reflected light
fell on the dressing-table, and on the gold and silver toilet-
set that had been Queen Stateira's; her jewel-box stood
beside it. All was triumph and tranquillity.

The nurse came fussing up with the antique royal cradle,
plated with gold and time-yellowed ivory. Roxane drew the
coverlet over the sleeping child. Under her fingers, almost
disguised by the elaborate embroidery, was a smear of
blood.

Her stomach heaved. When she had moved into this
room it had all been refurbished and redraped. But the bed
was a fine one and they had not changed it.

She had stood by while Stateira writhed and tried to

clutch at her and moaned "Help me! Help me!" and fumbled blindly with her clothes. Roxane had flung them back to see her beaten enemy, her son's rival, come naked into the world he would never rule. Could it be true that the thing had opened its mouth and cried? Disturbed by her tightened fingers, the infant wailed.

"Shall I take him, madam?" said the nurse timidly by her side. "Would madam like to sleep?"

"Later." She softened her grip; the child quietened and curled itself against her. He was a king and she was a king's mother; no one could take it from her. "Where is Amestrin? Amestrin, who put this filthy cover on my bed? It stinks, it is disgusting, give me something clean. If I see it again, your back will know it."

After panic scurryings, another cover was found; the state one, a year's work in Artaxerxes' day, was whisked out of sight. The baby slept. Roxane, her body loosening into comfort from its labor, sank into drowsiness. In a dream she saw a half-made child with the face of Alexander, lying in blood, its grey eyes staring with anger. Fear woke her. But all was well; he was dead and could do nothing, it was her son who would rule the world. She slept again.

3 2 2 B. C.

THE ARMY OF KING PHILIP was encamped in the Pisidian hills. Perdikkas, blood-spattered and smeared with ash, was picking his way down a stony path strewn with dead men and abandoned weapons. Above him, circling a cloud of stinking smoke, vultures and kites made exploring swoops, their numbers thickening as news of the banquet spread. The Macedonians, prompter than the birds, scavenged the charred ruins of Isaura.

Spared by Alexander because they had surrendered without a fight, the Isaurians had been left with orders to pull down the robber fort from which they had plagued their neighbors, and to live peaceably. In his long absence they had murdered his satrap and fallen back into old ways. This time, from bad consciences or from having less trust in Perdikkas than in Alexander, they had defended their craggy nest to the bitter end. When their outworks fell, they had locked into their houses their goods, their wives and children, set timber and thatch alight, and to the hellish music of the fires had hurled themselves on the Macedonian spears.

Some fifteen years of war had made Perdikkas almost nightmare-proof; in a few days he would be dining out on the story; but with the stench of burnt flesh still hanging in the air he had had enough for today, and had welcomed the news that a courier awaited him in his camp below.

His brother Alketas, a hard man and his second in command, would oversee the raking of the cinders for half-melted silver and gold. His helmet was scorching hot; he took it off and wiped his sweating forehead.

From the royal tent of dyed and emblazoned leather, Philip came out and ran towards him. "Did we win?" he asked.

He was armed in cuirass and greaves, a thing he had insisted on. In Alexander's day, when he had followed the army much as now, he had worn civil dress; but now that he was King, he knew what was due to him. He had in fact been eager to fight; but, used to obedience, had not insisted, since Alexander had never let him do it. "You're all bleeding," he said. "You ought to see a doctor."

"It's a bath I need." When alone with his sovereign, Perdikkas dispensed with formality. He told him as much as it was good for him to know, went to his own tent, cleaned himself, put on a robe, and ordered the courier brought.

This person was a surprise. The letter he brought was reticent and formal; he himself had much to say. A hardy grizzled man in his early sixties, with a missing thumb lost at Gaugamela, he was a minor Macedonian nobleman, and not so much a messenger as an envoy.

With elation, tinged by well-founded misgiving, Perdikkas reread the letter to gain time for thought. *TO PERDIKKAS, REGENT OF THE ASIAN KINGDOMS, FROM KLEOPATRA, DAUGHTER OF PHILIP AND SISTER OF ALEXANDER, GREETING.* After the usual well-wishings, the letter glanced at their cousinship, recalled his distinguished services to Alexander, and proposed a conference, to discuss *matters concerning the well-being of all the Macedonians.* These matters were not specified. The last sentence disclosed that the Queen had set out already from Dodona.

The envoy, affecting negligence, was toying with his wine-cup. Perdikkas coughed. "Am I to hope that if I should beg the honor of the lady Kleopatra's hand, my suit would be graciously received?"

The envoy gave a reassuring smile. "So far, the Kings have been elected only by the Macedonians in Asia. Those in the homeland might like their own chance to choose."

Perdikkas had had a grueling and hideous, even though successful, day. He had come back for a bath, a rest and a drink, not to be offered at short notice the throne of Macedon. Presently he said, with a certain dryness, "Such happiness was beyond my hopes. I feared she might still be mourning Leonnatos."

The veteran, whom Perdikkas' steward had refreshed while he was waiting, settled into his chair. The wine was strong, with no more than a splash of water, Perdikkas having felt he needed it. The diplomat gave way visibly to the soldier.

"I can tell you, sir, why he was her first choice, for what it's worth. She remembered him from her childhood at home. He climbed a tree once, to get down her cat for her, when he was a boy. You know what women are."

"And in the end I believe they did not meet?"

"No. When he crossed from Asia to fight the southern Greeks, he'd only time to raise his troops in Macedon and ride on down. Bad luck that he fell before our victory."

"A pity that his troops were so cut up. I hear he fought while he could stand. A brave man; but hardly the stuff of kings?"

"She was well out of it," said the soldier bluntly. "All her friends tell her so. It was a fancy; she soon got over grieving. Lucky for her she has the chance to think better now." He tipped back his cup; Perdikkas refilled it. "If she had seen *you*, sir, at Gaugamela . . ."

This word of power diverted them into reminiscence.

When they came back to business, Perdikkas said, "I suppose the truth is, she wants to get away from Olympias."

The envoy, flushed and relaxed, planked down his cup and leaned his arm on the table. "Sir. Let me tell you, between ourselves, that woman is a Gorgon. She's eaten that poor girl piece by piece, till she's hardly mistress of her house, let alone the kingdom. Not that she lacks spirit; but left as she is, without a man to stand by her, there's no fighting Olympias. She has the Molossians treating her like a queen. She *is* a queen. She looks like a queen; she has the will of a king. And she's Alexander's mother."

"Ah. Yes . . . So Kleopatra has a mind to leave her Dodona, and make a bid for Macedon?"

"She's Philip's daughter."

Perdikkas, who had been thinking quickly, said, "She has a son by the late King." He had no wish to be caretaker for a stepson.

"*He'll* inherit at home, his granddam will see to that. Now Macedon . . . No woman has ever reigned in Macedon. But Philip's daughter, married to a royal kinsman who's ruled like a king already . . ." Abruptly, remembering something, he hitched at his belt-purse, and brought out a flat package wrapped in embroidered wool. "She sent you this, seeing it's a long time since you had a sight of her."

The portrait was painted with skill, in encaustic wax on wood. Even allowing for convention, which smoothed away personality like a blemish, it could be seen that she was Philip's daughter. The strong hair, the thick upswept eyebrows, the resolute square face, had defeated the artist's well-meant insipidity. Perdikkas thought, Two years younger than Alexander—about thirty-one, now. "A queenly and gracious lady," he said aloud. "A dowry in herself, kingdom or no." He found more of this kind to say, while he played for time. Danger was great; ambition also. Alexander had taught him long ago to assess, decide, and act.

"Well," he said, "this is serious business. She needs something more than a yes. Let me sleep on this. When you dine with us tonight, I'll tell them all you brought a letter from Olympias. She's forever writing."

"I have brought one. She approves, as you may well suppose."

Perdikkas set the thick roll aside, summoned the steward to find his guest a lodging, and, left alone, sat with his elbows on the rough camp-table and his head between his hands.

Here he was found by his brother Alketas, whose servants carried two rattling sacks filled with stained, smoked gold, cups and arm-rings and necklaces and coin; the Isaurians had been successful robbers. The slaves gone, he showed Perdikkas the loot, and was annoyed by his abstraction. "Not squeamish?" he said. "You were there in India, when the men thought the Mallians had killed Alexander. You should have a strong stomach after that."

Perdikkas looked at him in irritation. "We'll talk later. Is Eumenes back in camp? Find him, he can bath and eat later, I have to see him now."

Eumenes appeared quite shortly, washed, combed and changed. He had been in his tent, dictating his memoir of the day's events to Hieronymos, a young scholar who, under his patronage, was writing a chronicle of the times. His light compact body was toughened and tanned from the campaign; soon he would be riding north to get his satrapy of Kappadokia in order. He greeted Perdikkas with a calm alert expectancy, sat down, and read the letter Perdikkas handed him. At the end, he allowed himself a slight lift of the brows.

Looking up from the scroll, he said, "What is she offering? The regency or the throne?" Perdikkas understood him perfectly. He meant, Which do you plan to take?

"The regency. Or would I be talking to you now?"

"Leonnatos did," Eumenes reminded him. "And then decided that I knew too much." He had, in fact, barely escaped with his life, having affirmed his loyalty to Alexander's son.

"Leonnatos was a fool. The Macedonians would have cut his throat; and they'd cut mine if I disinherited Alexander's boy. If they elect him when he comes of age, so be it. But he's the Bactrian's son; by that time, they may not be so fond of him. Then we'll see. Meantime, I'll have been King in all but name for fifteen years or so, and I shan't complain."

"No," said Eumenes grimly. "But Antipatros will."

Perdikkas sat back in his leather-slung camp-chair, and stretched out his long legs. "That's the crux. Advise me. What shall I do with Nikaia?"

"A pity indeed," said the Greek, "that Kleopatra didn't write a few months sooner." He sat reflecting, like a mathematician before a theorem. "You won't need her now. But you've sent her the betrothal gifts. She's the Regent's daughter. And she's on her way."

"I offered for her too soon. Everything seemed in chaos; I thought I should make sure of an ally while I could . . . Alexander would never have tied his hands like that. *He* always made alliances when he could dictate the terms." It was rarely, now, that he was self-critical; he must be disturbed, Eumenes thought. He tapped absently at the letter. Perdikkas noted that even his nails were clean.

"Antipatros puts out his daughters as a fisherman puts out lines."

"Well, I took the bait. What now?"

"You've bitten at the bait. The hook's not yet in your belly. Let us think." His neat thin lips came together. Even on campaign, he shaved every day. Presently, looking up, he said crisply, "Take Kleopatra. Take her now. Send an escort to meet Nikaia; tell her you're sick, wounded; be civil, but have her taken home. Act at once, before Antipatros is ready. Or he'll hear of it, you won't know how or when; and he'll act before *you're* ready."

Perdikkas bit his lip. It sounded prompt and decisive; probably it was what Alexander would have done. Except that he would never have put himself in need of it. Among these doubts, a disturbing thought intruded: Eumenes hated Antipatros. The Regent had been snubbing him ever since he had been a junior secretary, advanced by Philip because of his quick mind. The old man had all the prejudices of his race against the effete, fickle, subtle men of the south. Eumenes' loyalty, his distinguished war record, had never made any difference. Even when he was in Asia as Chief Secretary to Alexander, Antipatros had tried often to go over his head. Alexander, whom it irritated, had made a point of replying through Eumenes.

Now that Perdikkas had been counseled to burn his boats, he felt a certain flinching. He said to himself that here was an old enmity, of the kind that warps a man's better judgment.

"Yes," he said, affecting gratitude. "You are right. I'll write by her envoy tomorrow."

"Better use word of mouth. Letters can go astray."

". . . But I'll tell her, I think, that I've already married Nikaia. It will be true by the time it reaches her. I'll ask her to wait till I can decently get free. I'll put the palace of Sardis at her disposal, and ask her to consider us betrothed in secret. That will give me room to maneuver."

Seeing Eumenes looking at him in silence, he felt the need to justify himself. "If there were only Antipatros to consider . . . But I don't like what I hear of Ptolemy. He's raising too big an army down in Egypt. It only needs one satrap to make a kingdom of his province, and the empire will fall apart. We must wait a little and see what he means to do."

A bland winter sun shone down through the columned window into Ptolemy's small audience room. It was a handsome house, almost a small palace, built for himself by the previous administrator, whom Ptolemy had executed for oppression. The slight rise commanded a view of new straight streets and handsome public buildings, their pale unweathered stone touched up with paint and gilding. New wharves and quays fringed the harbor; hoists and scaffolding surrounded a couple of nearly finished temples ordered by Alexander. Another temple, less advanced, but promising to be the most imposing, stood near the waterfront, where it would dominate the prospect for incoming ships.

Ptolemy had had a busy but congenial morning. He had seen the chief architect, Deinokrates, about the sculpture on the temples; some engineers, who were replacing insanitary canals with covered drains; and the heads of several nomes, to whom he had restored the right to collect taxes. This, to the Egyptians who had suffered under his predecessor, meant something like a fifty percent tax reduction. A rapacious man, resolved to execute his commission and enrich himself as well, he had imposed forced levies and forced labor, extorted fortunes by threats to kill the sacred crocodiles, or to pull down villages for building-sites (which he would do in the end, when he had squeezed them dry). Moreover, he had done all this in the name of Alexander, which had so enraged Ptolemy that he had gone through the administration like a consuming fire. It had made him extremely popular, and he had remained so.

He was now busy recruiting. Perdikkas had only allowed him two thousand men when he took over the satrapy. He had found, when he got there, its garrison almost mutinous, the men's pay in arrears while the interest was being skimmed off it. Things were different now. Ptolemy had not been the most brilliant of Alexander's commanders; but he was reliable, resourceful, brave and loyal, all things Alexander valued; and, above all, he was good at looking after his men. He had fought under Philip before Alexander had his first command; the pupil of two great masters, he had learned from both. Trusted, sufficiently feared, and liked, he was apt with small touches of personal concern. Before his first year was out, thousands of active veterans settled in Alexandria were begging to re-enlist; by now, volunteers were arriving by land and sea.

He had not allowed this to inflate ambition. He knew his limits, and had no wish for the stresses of boundless power. He had what he had wanted, was content with it and meant to keep it; with luck, to add a little more. His men were well paid and fed; they were also well trained.

"Why, Menandros!" he said warmly as the last applicant came in. "I thought you were in Syria. Well, this is an easier climb than the Birdless Rock. You got here without a rope."

The veteran, recognized at sight as a hero of that renowned assault, grinned with delight, feeling that after an uncertain year he had arrived where he belonged. The interview was happy. Ptolemy decided to take a break in his inner sanctum. His chamberlain, an Egyptian of great discretion, scratched at the door.

"My lord," he murmured, "the eunuch of whom you spoke has come from Babylon."

The broken nose in Ptolemy's craggy face pointed like a hound's at a breast-high scent. "I'll see him here," he said.

He waited in the pleasant, cool, Greek-furnished room. Bagoas was shown in.

Ptolemy saw a Persian gentleman, soberly suited in grey, equipped for travel with a businesslike sword-belt, its slots well stretched by the weapons left outside. He had grown his hair; a modest length of it fringed his round felt hat. He looked handsome, lean, distinguished and of no particular age. Ptolemy supposed he must be twenty-four.

He made the graceful genuflection due to a satrap, was invited to sit, and offered the wine which had awaited the morning's leisure. Ptolemy made the proper inquiries about his health and journey; he knew better than to be precipitate with a Persian. It was clear that the midnight encounter in the paradise was to be remembered in substance only; etiquette was to be preserved. He remembered from old days Bagoas' infinite resources of tact.

The courtesies fully observed, he asked, "What news?"

Bagoas set aside his wine-cup. "They will be bringing him out from Babylon two months from now."

"And the convoy? Who's in command?"

"Arybbas. No one has questioned it."

Ptolemy sighed audibly with relief. Before marching south, he had proposed this officer to design and supervise the bier, citing his expertise; he had devised several important shrines for Alexander, and could handle craftsmen. Not cited was that he had served in India under Ptolemy's command, and been on excellent terms with his commander.

"I waited," said Bagoas, "till I was sure of it. They would need him, in case of mishap, to see the bier repaired."

"You have made good time, then."

"I came up the Euphrates, and then by camel to Tyre. The rest by sea. Forty days in all."

"You will be able to rest awhile, and still be in Babylon before they start."

"If God permits. As for the bier, in a hundred days it could hardly reach the coast. The roadmakers are out al-

ready, smoothing the way. Arybbas reckons it will travel
ten miles a day on level ground, or five over hills, if sixty-
four mules pull it. To bring it from Asia into Thrace, they
plan to bridge the Hellespont."

The quiet madness of the house in the park was gone.
He spoke with the concentration of a man going about
his chosen calling. He looked lean and fit after his long
journey.

"You have seen it then?" Ptolemy asked. "Is it worthy
of Alexander?"

Bagoas considered. "Yes, they have done all that men
can."

Arybbas must have excelled himself, Ptolemy thought.
"Come to the window. There is something you must see."

He pointed to the temple rising on the waterfront, the
sea, pale blue under the mild sky, shining between the
unfinished columns.

"There is his shrine."

For a moment, the reticent face beside him lit and
glowed. Just so, Ptolemy remembered from another life,
the boy had looked when Alexander rode past in a victory
parade.

"It should be ready in another year. The priests of Ammon would like him to go to Siwah; they say it would have
been his wish. I have considered it, but I think this is his
place."

"When you have seen the bier, sir, you will know it
could never go to Siwah. If once its wheels sank into sand,
a team of elephants could not drag it free . . . That is a
fine temple. They have worked quickly to get so far."

Ptolemy had known that this must sometime be met. He
said gently, "It was begun before I came. Alexander approved the plan himself. It is the temple he ordered for
Hephaistion . . . He did not know how soon he himself
would need it."

Bagoas' face returned to agelessness. He gazed in silence
at the sunlit shafts of stone. Presently he said calmly, "Hephaistion would give it him. He would have given him
anything."

Except his pride, thought Ptolemy; that was his secret,
it was why Alexander felt him as a second self. But it was
only possible because they were boys together. Aloud he
said, "Most men would welcome Alexander as a guest, even
in death. Well, let us come to ways and means."

At the table he unlocked a silver-clasped document-box.
"This letter I shall give you when you leave, along with
funds for your journey. Do not deliver it in Babylon. When
the bier sets out, no one will wonder that you wish to follow
it. Do nothing till it reaches Thapsakos—the Syrian border
will be soon enough—and give it to Arybbas then. It com-
mits him to nothing. It says I shall meet him at Issos, to
do honor to Alexander. He will hardly suppose, I think, that
I shall come alone."

"I will see," said Bagoas coolly, "that he is prepared."

"Don't lose the letter in Babylon. Perdikkas would send
an army corps for escort." Wasting no words, Bagoas
smiled.

"You have done well. Tell me, have you heard anything
of Roxane's child? He must be walking now. Does he favor
Alexander?"

One of Bagoas' fine brows moved upward a very little.
"I myself have not seen him. But the harem people say he
takes after his mother."

"I see. And King Philip, how is he?"

"Very well in health. He has been allowed a ride on an
elephant, which made him happy."

"So. Well, Bagoas, you have earned my gratitude; trust
in it from now on. When you are rested, see the city; it will
be your home."

Bagoas made the elegant half-prostration of the gentleman to the satrap, learned at Darius' court, and took his
leave.

Later, as the sun declined towards the western desert, he
walked down to the temple. This was the evening prome-
nade of the Alexandrians, who would pause to notice the
progress of the work; off-duty soldiers of Macedon and
Egypt, merchants and craftsmen from Greece and Lydia
and Tyre and Cyprus and Judaea; wives and children, and
hetairas looking for trade. The crowd was not yet oppressive; the city was still young.

The workmen on the site were packing their tools in
their straw bags; the nightwatchmen were coming with their
cloaks and food-baskets. From the ships tied to the waterfront men were going ashore; the ship-guards on board
kindled torches whose tarry smell hung over the water. As
dusk fell, on the temple terrace a burning cresset was
hoisted on a tall pole. It was not unlike the one Alexander
used to have by his tent in central Asia, to show where his
headquarters was.

The strollers drifted towards home; soon no one was
about but the watchmen and the silent traveler from
Babylon. Bagoas looked at Hephaistion's house, where
Alexander would be his guest forever. It was fitting, it was
what he would have wished, and after all it made no difference. What was, was, as it had always been. When
Alexander breathed his last, Bagoas had known who would
be awaiting him beyond the River. That was why he had
not killed himself; the thought was not to be borne of
intruding on that reunion. But Alexander had never been
ungrateful, he had never turned love away. One day, after
faithful service done, there would be, as there had always
been, a welcome.

He turned back towards the palace guest-house, where

they were lighting the lamps. Alexander would be served worthily here. Nothing else had ever mattered.

In the manor-house of the late Prince Amyntas, Kynna and Eurydike were trimming each other's hair. They were preparing for their journey. Till they were out of Macedon, they planned to travel as men.

The Regent, Antipatros, was besieging stubborn forts in the mountains of Aitolia, where the last of the Greek revolt still smoldered on. He had taken most of his troops. This was their chance.

"There," said Kynna, standing back with the shears. "Many young men wear it as long as that, since Alexander set the fashion."

Neither of them had had to sacrifice much hair; it was strong and wavy, not long. A maid was called to sweep up the clippings. Eurydike, who had already prepared her mule-packs, went to the stack of spears in the corner, and chose out her favorite javelins.

"We shan't have much chance to practice on the road."

"Let us hope," said Kynna, "that we may not need them in earnest."

"Oh, robbers won't attack ten men." They were taking an escort of eight retainers. She glanced at her mother's face, and added, "You're not afraid of Olympias?"

"No, she is too far away, we shall be in Asia before she hears."

Eurydike looked again. "Mother, what is it?"

Kynna was pacing the room. On stands and tables and shelves were the family treasures, her dead husband's heritage from his royal father, and pieces from her dowry; her own father, King Philip, had given her a handsome wedding. She was wondering how much she dared entrust to such a journey. Her daughter could not go empty-handed, but ...

"Mother, there is something . . . Is it because we've heard nothing from Perdikkas?"

"Yes. I don't like it."

"How long since you wrote to him?"

"I did not. It was proper for him to write." She turned to a shelf and picked up a silver cup.

"There is something else you've not told me. I know there is. Why is Antipatros against our going? Have they betrothed the King to someone else? . . . Mother, don't pretend you don't hear me. I'm not a child. If you don't tell me, I won't go."

Kynna turned round, with a face that would have meant a whipping a few years back. The tall girl, implacable, stood her ground.

Kynna put down the cup with its boar-hunt chasing. She bit her lip.

"Very well, since you will have it; I daresay it's better. Alexander said frankly it was an empty marriage. He offered you wealth and rank; I daresay you could have gone home after, for all he cared."

"You never told me so!"

"No, because you were not meant to grow old in a village. Be quiet and listen. He never looked further than the reconcilement of our houses. That was because he believed what his mother told him. He believed that his brother was born a fool."

"So are all fools. I don't understand."

"Don't you remember Straton the mason?"

"But that was because a stone fell on his head."

"Yes. He was not born stumbling in his speech, or asking for a tree when he wanted bread. That was done by the stone."

"But all my life, I've heard Arridaios was a fool."

"All your life he has been one. You are fifteen, and he is thirty. When your father was hoping to be King, he told me a good deal about Philip's house. He said that when Arridaios was born, he was a fine strong child, and forward. It is true your father was still a child himself, and it was servants' talk; but he listened, because it concerned another child. They said that Philip was pleased with the boy, and Olympias knew it. She swore Philinna's bastard should not disinherit her son. The child was born in the palace. Maybe she gave him something, maybe she saw to it that something should hit his head. So your father heard them say."

"What a wicked woman! Poor baby, I would not do it to a dog. But it's done; where is the difference now?"

"Only born fools beget fools. Straton's children are all sound."

Eurydike drew a sharp, shocked breath. Her hands gripped defensively the javelin she was holding. "No! They said I need not. Even Alexander said so. You promised me!"

"Hush, hush. No one is asking it. That is what I'm telling you. That is why Antipatros is against it and Perdikkas doesn't write. It is not what they want. It is what they fear."

Eurydike stood still, absently passing her hand up and down the shaft of the javelin; it was a good one, of smooth hard cornel-wood. "You mean, they are afraid I could found a royal line, to displace Alexander's?"

"So I think."

The girl's hand tightened on the shaft so that the knuckles paled. "If that is what I must do to avenge my father, then I will. Because he left no son."

Kynna was appalled. She had only wanted to explain their dangers. Quickly she said that it had been only slaves' talk; there had always been gossip about Olympias, that she coupled with serpents, and had conceived Alexander by the fire from heaven. It might well be true that Philinna had borne a fool, and it had not shown till the child was growing.

Eurydike looked carefully at the javelin, and put it aside with the few she meant to take. "Don't be afraid, Mother. Let's wait till we are there, and I can see what I ought to do. Then I will do it."

What have I made, thought Kynna; what have I done? Next moment she reminded herself that she had made what she had planned, and done what she had long resolved. She sent word to the herdsman to bring an unblemished kid, for a sacrifice to dedicate their enterprise.

Arybbas, the creator of Alexander's bier, made his way to the workshop for his daily visit. He was a dandified but not effeminate man, soldier and aesthete, a remote kinsman of the royal house, and of course too aristocratic ever to have worked for hire. Alexander had made him lavish presents whenever he had created a shrine, a royal barge, or a public spectacle, but that had been just between friends. Alexander, who loved to give money away, took offense when it was stolen, and had valued his probity as well as his gifts. Ptolemy, when recommending him to Perdikkas, had stressed this virtue, so necessary in a man handling a great deal of gold.

He had in fact watched it jealously; not a grain had stuck to his fingers, nor anyone else's. Weighing was a daily rite. A sumptuous designer, used by Alexander when notable splendor was required, he had used with gusto the whole treasure entrusted to him, for Alexander's honor and his own. As the magnificent structure he had inspired took shape under the hammers and gouges and graving-tools of his hand-picked craftsmen, exultation mingled with solemnity; he pictured Alexander surveying it with approval. *He* had appreciated such things. Arybbas had never cared much for Perdikkas.

Outside the workshop he noticed that Bagoas the eunuch was loitering about again, and, smiling graciously, beckoned him up. Though hardly a person whose company one would seek in public, he had shown impeccable taste, and an eye for the finer points. His devotion to the dead was touching; it was a pleasure to let him view the work.

"You will find a change," he said. "Yesterday they mounted it on the wheel-base. So now you can see it whole."

He rapped with his staff. Bolts grated; the little postern opened in the great door. They stepped into shadow surrounding a blaze of glory.

The broad matting on the roof, which kept out bad weather and thieves at night, had been rolled back to open the great working skylight. The spring sun shafted down dazzlingly on a miniature temple, sheathed all over with gold.

It was some eighteen feet long; its vaulted roof was of gold scales set with gems, glowing balas rubies, emerald and crystal, sapphire and amethyst. On its ridge like a banner stood a laurel wreath with leaves of shimmering sheet-gold; on its corners victories leaned out, holding triumphant crowns. It was upheld by eight golden columns; around the cornice was festooned a flower-garland in fine enamels. On the frieze were pictured the exploits of Alexander. The floor was of beaten gold; the wheels were sheathed with it, their axles capped with lion-heads. A net of gold wire half hid the inner sanctuary on three sides; on the fourth, two couchant gold lions guarded the entry.

"See, they have hung the bells."

Those too were of gold; they hung from the tassels of the

garland. He lifted his staff and struck one; a clear musical
sound, of surprising resonance, throbbed through the shed.
"They will know of his coming."

Bagoas swept his hand across his eyes. Now he had entered the world again he was ashamed of tears; but he could
hardly bear that Alexander would not see it.

Arybbas did not notice; he was talking to the overseer
about making good the dents and scratches caused by the
hoisting. Perfection must be restored.

In a far corner of the shed gleamed, dimly, the sarcophagos, blazoned with the royal sunburst of Macedon. Six
men could scarcely lift it; it was solid gold. Only at last, at
the outset of his journey, would Alexander be brought out
in his cedar coffin where, hollow and light, he lay in a bed
of spices and sweet herbs, to be laid among more spices in
his final resting place. Satisfied that it was undamaged,
Arybbas left.

Outside, Bagoas offered unstinted praise, the price of
admission, willingly paid. "It will be counted among the
wonders of the world." He added deliberately, "The Egyptians are proud of their funeral arts; but even there I saw
nothing to compare with it."

"You have been to Egypt?" Arybbas asked, surprised.

"Since my service with Alexander ended, I have traveled
a little to pass my time. He spoke so much of Alexandria,
I wished to see it for myself . . . You, sir, of course, were
there at its foundation."

He said no more, leaving Arybbas to ask questions. To
these he replied obligingly, leaving loose ends which
prompted further questions. These led to a modest confes-
sion that he had been granted an audience with the Satrap.

"As it happened, though officers and friends of Alexander had come from most of nearer Asia to join his army, I
was the only one from Babylon, so he asked for news. He

had heard, he said, that Alexander's bier was to be a marvel, and asked who had been charged with it. When he knew, he exclaimed that Alexander himself could wish for no one better. 'If only,' he said, 'Arybbas could be here to adorn the Founder's temple.' . . . Perhaps, sir, that is indiscreet of me." Fleetingly, like a reflection upon water, appeared the smile which had entranced two kings. "But I don't think that he would mind."

They talked for some time, Arybbas having found his curiosity about Alexandria sharpened. Riding back to his house, he was aware he had been delicately probed; but he did not pursue this thought. If he knew what Ptolemy wanted, it might be his duty to divulge it; and this, he suspected, might be to his disadvantage.

In the thick-walled palace of red stone on the red-rock citadel of Sardis, Kleopatra and her women were settled in modest comfort by the standards of nearer Asia; in luxury by those of Epiros. Perdikkas had had the royal apartments refurbished and redraped, and staffed with well-trained slaves.

To Nikaia his bride, during their brief honeymoon, he had explained the arrival of the Molossian Queen by saying she was in flight from her mother, who had usurped her power and threatened her life; a daughter of Antipatros would believe anything of Olympias. After some ceremonious festivities suited to her rank, he had despatched the lady to an estate of his nearby, on the grounds that war continued and he would soon be taking the field. Returning to Sardis, he resumed his courtship of Kleopatra. His visits and costly gifts had all the conventions of betrothal.

Kleopatra had enjoyed her journey; the family restlessness had not passed her by. The sight of new horizons had con-

soled her even for leaving her son behind. His grandmother
would treat him like a son of her own whom she could train
for kingship. When she herself was married and living in
Macedon, she could see him often.

She had assessed Perdikkas more as a colleague than a
husband. He was a dominating man, and she had sounded
him for signs that he would overrule and bully her. It
seemed, however, he had the sense to know that without
her support he could neither get nor keep the regency.
Later, depending on how he behaved, she might help him
to the throne. He would be a hard king; but after Antipatros a soft one would be despised.

With a certain detachment, she imagined him in bed
with her, but doubted it would be of much importance to
either of them once she had produced an heir. Clearly, it
would be more valuable and more lasting to make a friend
of him than a lover; this she was already doing with some
success.

On this day of early spring he was to take the midday
meal with her. Both preferred the informality of noon and
the chance of undisturbed talk. The single dish would be
good; he had found her a Karian cook. She studied his
tastes against the time when they would be married. She
did not mean to deal hardly with Antipatros' poor plain
little girl, as her mother had done with rivals; Nikaia could
go back safe to her family. The Persian wife from Susa had
done so long ago.

He arrived on foot from his quarters at the other end of
the rambling palace, whose buildings clambered about the
rock. He had dressed for her with a jeweled shoulder-brooch
and a splendid arm-ring clasped with gold gryphon heads.
His sword-belt was set with plaques of Persian cloisonné.
Yes, she thought, he would make a convincing king.

He liked to talk of his wars under Alexander, and she to

listen; only fragmented news had reached Epiros, and he had seen the whole. But before they had reached the wine, her eunuch chamberlain coughed at the door. A despatch had arrived for His Excellency's urgent attention.

"From Eumenes," he said as he broke the seal. He spoke rather too easily, aware that Eumenes called nothing urgent without good cause.

As he read, she saw his weathered tan go sallow, and sent out the slave who was serving them. Like most men of his time, he sounded the words he read (it was thought remarkable in Alexander to have suppressed this reflex); but his jaw had set; she heard only an angry mutter. Seeing his face at the end, she guessed that he would look like this in war. "What is it?" she said.

"Antigonos has fled to Greece."

Antigonos . . . while he stared before him, she remembered that this was the Satrap of Phrygia, nicknamed One-Eye. "Was he not under arrest for treason? I suppose he was afraid."

He gave a snort like a horse's. "He, afraid? He has gone to betray me to Antipatros."

She saw that he wanted only to be thinking ahead; but there was more here than she had been told, and she had a right to know. "What was the treason? Why was he being held?"

He answered savagely, "To stop his mouth. I found out that he knew."

She took this in without trouble; she was not a daughter of Macedon for nothing. My father, she thought, would not have done it; nor Alexander. In the old days . . . must we go back to that? She only said, "How did he come to know?"

"Ask the rats in the wall. He was the last man I'd have confided in. He was always close with Antipatros. He must have smelled something and sent a spy. It's all one now, the harm's done."

She nodded; there was no need to spell it out. They must be married with royal ceremony before attempting Macedon. There was no time now; Antipatros would be marching north from Aitolia the moment he got the news. A scrambled wedding would bring them nothing but scandal. She thought, This will mean war.

He swung himself down from his dining-couch and began to stride the room; she had a stray thought that they might as well be married already. Wheeling round, he said, "And I still have to deal with those accursed women."

"What women?" She let her voice sharpen; he was keeping too much, lately, to himself. "You've said nothing of women; who are they?"

He made a sound, compounded of impatience and embarrassment. "No. It was hardly fitting; but I should have told you. Philip, your brother . . ."

"Pray, don't call that wittol my brother!" She had never shared Alexander's tolerance of Philinna's son. Her only passage of arms with Perdikkas had taken place when he had wanted to install the King in the palace, as became his rank. "If he comes, I go." He had seen in her face a flash of Alexander's will. Philip had stayed in the royal tent; he was used to it, and had no thought of any other arrangement. "What has *he* to do with women, in God's name?"

"Alexander betrothed him to Adeia, your cousin Amyntas' daughter. He even granted her the royal name of Eurydike, which she's made a point of using. I don't know what he meant by it. Shortly before he died, Philip took a turn for the better. Alexander seemed pleased. You'd not know, it's too long since you saw either of them. Alexander took him along in the first place to keep him safe out of the way, in case someone should use him in Macedon. Also, as he told me one night when he was drunk, because Olympias might have killed him if he was left behind. But he got a kind of fondness for him, after taking care of him all those years. He was glad to see him looking more like a man, and let him be seen with him, helping at the sacrifices and so on. Half the army saw it, that's why we've the trouble we have today. But there were no plans for any wedding. If he'd not fallen ill, he'd have marched to Arabia within the month. In the end, I expect, the marriage would have been by proxy."

"He never told me!" For a moment her face was an injured child's; a long story was there, if Perdikkas had cared to read it.

"That was on account of your mother. He was afraid, if she knew, she'd do the girl an injury."

"I see," said Olympias' daughter, without surprise. "But he should never have done it. Of course we must free her now, poor child." He did not answer. In a new voice of authority, she said, "Perdikkas, these are my kin. It is for me to say."

"Madam, I know." He spoke with studied respect; he could well afford it. "But you have misunderstood. Antipatros canceled the contract with my agreement, some months ago. In his absence, without his leave, her mother Kynna has brought the girl to Asia. They are demanding that the marriage shall proceed."

His exasperation spoke for his truth. "Shameless!" she cried. "There you see the barbarian blood!" It might almost have been Olympias speaking.

"Indeed. They are true Illyrians. I hear that they traveled as far as Abdera dressed as men, and carrying arms."

"What will you do with them? I can have no dealings with such creatures."

"They will be dealt with. I have no time; I must meet

with Eumenes, before Antipatros crosses to Asia. Krateros will be sure to join him, which is much worse. The men love Krateros . . . My brother will have to meet them, and keep them from making mischief."

Presently he left to make his dispositions. One of these was to send to Ephesos, summoning Roxane and her child. He had known better than to quarter the Bactrian on the daughter of Philip and Olympias; besides, if she knew of their plans she would probably have him poisoned. But now it was time to move, and she must follow the army. At least, he thought, she was used to that.

On the high road to the Syrian coast, flashing in the sun and ringing all its bells, the bier of Alexander trundled towards Issos. The sixty-four mules drew it, four yoke-poles hitching each four teams of four. The mules wore gold wreaths, and little gold bells on their cheeks. Their tinkling, and the deep clear chime of the bells upon the bier, mingled with the shouts of the muleteers.

In the shrine, between the gold columns and the shimmering golden nets, the sarcophagos lay draped with its purple pall. On it was displayed Alexander's panoply of arms, his helmet of white iron, his jeweled sword-belt, his sword and shield and greaves. The cuirass was the parade one; the one he had used in battle was too worn and hacked to match the splendors around.

When the iron-bound felloes of the gold-sheathed wheels jolted on rough ground, the bier only swayed gently; there were hidden springs above the axles. Alexander would come whole to his tomb. Veterans in the escort said to each other that if he had been anywhere near as careful of his body while he was alive, he would be with them yet.

All along the road sightseers stood in expectant clusters,

awaiting the sound of the distant bells. The fame of the
bier had far outstripped its progress. Peasants had walked
a day from mountain hamlets, and slept in the open to
await it; riders on horses or mules or asses kept along by it
for miles, unwilling to relinquish it. Boys ran themselves to
a standstill, dropping like spent dogs when the escort struck
camp at night, creeping to the cook-fires to beg a crust,
and listening half in dreams to the soldiers' tales.

At each town on the way, sacrifices were offered to the
deified Alexander; the local bard would extol his deeds,
inventing marvels when his store of history failed. Arybbas
presided calmly over these solemnities. He had had Ptolemy's letter, and knew what he would do.

Save for his one visit to Arybbas' tent, Bagoas made himself imperceptible. By day he rode among the changing
sightseers; at night he slept among the Persian soldiers
who formed the rear guard. They all knew who he was, and
no one troubled him. He was keeping faith with his lord,
as a true follower of Mithra ought. They respected his
pious pilgrimage, and thought no more of it.

Kynna and her daughter had traveled as armed men,
sleeping in their baggage-cart with their retainers in the
open round them, till they could take ship from Abdera.
There the people were Greek, there was plenty of mer-
chant shipping, and the only question asked was whether
they could pay. Kynna, who could deceive no one at close
quarters, resumed female dress; Eurydike traveled as her
son.

The ship carried hides on deck; the retainers found them
a grateful bed at night, but their smell made Eurydike sick
at the first flurry of wind. At last, they sailed into the
green sheltering arms of the long gulf of Smyrna. From
now on, their progress must be very different.

Smyrna consisted of ancient ruins, an old village, and a brand-new town refounded by Alexander, whom the harbor had impressed. The traffic had grown with his conquests, and it was now a busy port. Here they would be seen and spoken of; though Babylon was still far off, they must think about appearances. The old man who acted as their major-domo—he remembered Amyntas' father—went before them to seek good lodgings, and hire transport for the long journey overland.

He returned with startling news. The journey to the east was not required of them. Perdikkas, and King Philip with him, were no further off than Sardis, some fifty miles.

They felt a shock, as people do when a distant crisis leaps up close; then told each other that luck was speeding them. Eurydike went ashore with a long cloak over her tunic, and, in the lodging, assumed himation and robe.

They must travel at once with public consequence, a king's betrothed traveling to her bridal. They should of course have been met at the port by a kinsman or friend of the groom; but the greater their state, the less they would be questioned. They could afford lavishness for so short a journey; Amyntas' estates had never been confiscated, their quiet life had not been due to poverty.

When, two days later, they set out, their train was an imposing one. Thoas the major-domo, who had purchased them maids and porters, reported that according to people here they should have a eunuch chamberlain. Kynna, much outraged, replied that they were Greek, as was her daughter's bridegroom, and they had not crossed to Asia to adopt the disgusting customs of the barbarians. Alexander, she had heard, had been given too much that way.

The faithful Thoas, transacting all this business, made no secret of his ladies' rank, or of their purpose. It was no spy, but the eternal gossip of travelers on the road, that ran ahead of them with the news to Sardis.

⊙   ⊙   ⊙

The field of Issos still yielded up old weapons and old
bones. Here, where Darius had first fled from Alexander's
spear leaving mother and wife and children to await the
victor, two armies sacrificed a milk-white bull before the
golden bier. Ptolemy and Arybbas poured incense side by
side. The escort had been much moved by Ptolemy's address, affirming the divine hero's wish that his body return
to his father Ammon.

Each of Arybbas' men had been given a hundred drachmas, a bounty worthy even of Alexander. Arybbas himself
had received, in private, a talent of silver, and in public the
rank of general in the Satrap's army, whither all his Macedonian troops had agreed to follow him. There was a feast
at night in Alexander's honor; a whole spit-roast sheep and
an amphora of wine to each campfire. Next morning, satrap and general riding either side the bier, the funeral
cortege turned south towards the Nile.

Bagoas, whose name had been proclaimed in no citation,
followed behind the rear guard. The other Persians had
gone home; but the troops from Egypt made the column
a very long one, and he was far, now, from the bier. When
he topped a rise, he could just see its glittering crest. But he
rode contented. His task was done, his god was served; and
there would still be his fame to tend in his chosen city. A
Greek might have seen in him the serenity of the initiate,
fresh from a celebration of his mystery.

Kynna's caravan was within a day's journey from Sardis.
They were not hurrying; they meant to arrive there next
morning before the heat began. Its fame had reached even
Macedon for wealth and luxury; the bride of a king must

not be outshone by his subjects. Overnight they would prepare their entry.

Along the road, the stony heights were topped with old forts, newly repaired by Alexander to command the passes. They passed rock-slabs carved with symbols, and inscriptions in unknown writing. The travelers who passed them making for the port were all barbarians, strange to sight and smell; Phoenicians with blue-dyed beards, Karians with heavy earrings dragging down their lobes; a train of Negro carriers bare to the waist, their blackness strange and terrible to a northern eye used only to the red-haired slaves from Thrace; sometimes a trousered Persian, the legendary ogre of Greek children, with embroidered hat and curved sword.

To Eurydike all was adventure and delight. She thought with envy of world-wandering Alexander and his men. Kynna, beside her under the striped awning, kept a cheerful countenance, but felt her spirits flag. The alien speech of the passers-by, the inscrutable monuments, the unknown landscape, the vanishing of all she had pictured in advance, were draining her of certainty. Those black-veiled women, carrying burdens beside the donkeys their menfolk rode, if they knew her purpose would think her mad. The two-wheeled cart jolted over stones, her head was aching. She had known that the world was vast, that Alexander in ten years had never reached the end of it; but at home in her native hills it had no meaning. Now, on the mere threshold of the illimitable east, she felt like a desolation its indifferent strangeness.

Eurydike, who had been admiring the defenses of the forts and pointing out their chain of beacons, said, "Is it true, do you think, that Sardis is three times as big as Pella?"

"I daresay. Pella is only two generations old; Sardis ten

maybe, or even more." The thought oppressed her. She looked at the girl in her careless confidence, and thought, I brought her here from home, where she could have lived out her life in quiet. She has no one but me to turn to. Well, I am healthy and still young.

Night would soon fall. An outrider brought news that they were within ten miles of Sardis. Soon they must find a camping-place. A rocky turn shut off the westering sun, and the road grew dusky. The slope above them, dark against a reddening sky, was scattered with great boulders. Somewhere among them a man's voice called, "Now!"

Stones and shale fell rattling on the road, dislodged by scrambling men. Thoas at the escort's head shouted out, "Ware thieves!"

The men reached the road, thirty or forty or them, on foot, with spears. Among them the escort looked what it was, a troop of willing, confused old men. Those who had ever fought had done it in Philip's wars. But they were true Macedonians, with the archaic virtues of the liegeman. They shouted defiance, and thrust at the bandits with their spears.

The squeal of a wounded horse echoed against the rocks. Old Thoas fell with his mount; a huddle of men closed stabbing over him.

There was a high shout, a wordless "Hi-yi!" of challenge. Kynna leaped down from the cart, Eurydike beside her. Their spears had been at hand; with practiced speed they had kilted their skirts into their girdles. With their backs to the cart, which rocked with the shifting of the frightened mules, they stood to face the enemy.

Eurydike felt a shiver of exultation. Here at last was war, real war. Though she could guess the consequence of defeat if they were taken alive, it was mainly a good reason for fighting well. A man reached out at her, fair-skinned, with a week's red stubble on his chin. He had on a hide cuirass, so she went for his arm. The spear sunk in; he leaped back crying out, "You hell-cat!" grasping the wound. She laughed at him; then realized with a sudden shock that here, in Lydia, a bandit had spoken Macedonian.

One of the lead mules, hurt by a spear, suddenly squealed and leaped forward. The whole team bolted, the cart bucking and bouncing behind. It struck her, but she just kept her feet. There was a cry beside her. Kynna had fallen; she had been braced against the cart when it moved off. A soldier was leaning over her with a spear.

A man came forward with upheld hand. The men around her withdrew. It grew quiet, except for the struggling mules which had been pulled up by the soldiers, and the groans of three of the escort on the ground. The rest had been overpowered, save for old Thoas, who was dead.

Kynna moaned; the almost animal sound of a warm-blooded creature struggling in pain to breathe. Her breast was stained with red.

Eurydike's first impulse was to run to her, take her in her arms, entreat the bandits for mercy. But Kynna had trained her well. This too was war; there would be no mercy for asking, only for winning. She looked at the chief who had been at once obeyed, a tall dark man with a lean cold face. Knowledge was instant: not bandits, soldiers.

Kynna groaned again; the sound was fainter now. Pity and rage and grief lit like one flame in Eurydike, as they did in Achilles, shouting for dead Patroklos on the wall. She leaped to her mother's body and stood across it.

"You traitors! Are you men of Macedon? This is Kynna, King Philip's daughter, the sister of Alexander."

There was a startled pause. The men all turned towards the officer. He looked angry and disconcerted. He had not told them.

A thought came to her. She spoke this time in the language of the soldiers, the peasant dialect of the countryside she had known before she was taught court Greek. "I am Philip's grandchild, look at me! I am Amyntas' daughter, the grandchild of King Philip and King Perdikkas." She pointed at the lowering officer. "Ask him. *He* knows!"

The oldest soldier, a man in his fifties, walked across to him. "Alketas." He used the name without honorific, as a freeman of Macedon could do to kings. "Is what she says true?"

"No! Obey your orders."

The soldier looked from him to the girl, and from her to the other men. "I reckon it's true," he said.

The men drew together; one of them said, "They're no Sarmatians, like he said. They're as Macedonian as I am."

"My mother . . ." Eurydike looked down. Kynna stirred, but blood was running from her mouth. "She brought me here from Macedon. I am betrothed to Philip, your King, the brother of Alexander."

Kynna stirred. She rose a little on one arm. Chokingly she said, "It is true. I swear by . . ." She coughed. A rush of blood came out, and she fell back. Eurydike dropped her spear and knelt beside her. Her eyes fixed, showing the whites.

The old soldier who had faced Alketas came over and stood before her, confronting the rest. "Let them alone!" he said. Another and another joined him; the rest leaned on their spears in a confused and sullen shame. Eurydike flung herself on her mother's body and wept aloud.

Presently, through the sound of her own crying, she heard voices raised. It was the sound of mutiny. Had she known, it was one with which Macedonian generals were growing over-familiar. Ptolemy had confided to close friends in Egypt that he was glad to hand-pick his men, and be rid of the standing army. It put one in mind of Alexander's old horse Boukephalas, liable to kick anyone else who tried to mount him. Like the horse, it had been too long used to a rider with clever hands.

More urgently now, Eurydike thought of throwing herself upon their mercy, begging them to burn her mother's body decently, give her the ashes to bury in the homeland, and take her back to the sea. But, as she wiped the blood from Kynna's face, she knew it for the face of a warrior steadfast to the death. Her shade must not find that she had borne a coward.

Under her hand was the gold pendant her mother always wore. It was bloodstained, but she slipped it over the lifeless head, and stood erect.

"See. Here is my grandfather King Philip's likeness. He gave it to my grandmother Audata on her wedding day, and she to my mother when she married Amyntas, King Perdikkas' son. Look for yourself."

She put it in the veteran's cracked horny hand; they crowded round him, poring over the gold roundel with the square-boned, bearded profile. "Aye, Philip it is," the veteran said. "I saw him many a time." He rubbed it clean on a fold of his homespun kilt and gave it back to her. "You should take care of that," he said.

He spoke as if to a young niece; and it struck a chord in all of them. She was their foundling, the orphan of their rescue and adoption. They would take her to Sardis, they told Alketas; she had Philip's blood in her as any fool could see; and if Alexander had promised her his brother, wed they should be, or the army would know why.

"Very well," said Alketas. He knew by now that discipline hung by a thread, and maybe his life. "Then get the road cleared, and look alive."

With rough competence the soldiers laid Kynna out in

the cart, and covered her with a blanket; brought their own transport-cart for the dead and wounded guards, picked up the baggage which the porters had dropped when with the maids they fled to the hills. They settled the cushions for Eurydike, to ride beside her dead.

One of them rode off willingly with Alketas' despatch to his brother Perdikkas. On his way would be the main camp of Perdikkas' and Eumenes' armies, where he could spread the news.

So, when the last turn of the road showed her the red-rock citadel with the city around its feet, it showed her also a great throng of soldiers, crowding the road, and parting to make an avenue of honor, as if for a king.

As she came they cheered her. Close to her by the road she heard gruff murmurs: "Poor maid." "Forgive them, lady, he told them wrong." The strangeness, the dreamlike consummation of their long intent, made her mother's death dreamlike too, though she could have reached out and touched the body.

From her high window, Kleopatra looked down with Perdikkas, fuming, beside her. She saw his impotence, and struck her hand in anger on the sill. "You are permitting this?"

"No choice. If I arrest her, we shall have a mutiny. Now of all times . . . They know that she's Philip's grand-child."

"And a traitor's daughter! Her father plotted my father's murder. Will you let her marry his son?"

"Not if I can help it." The cart was coming nearer. He tried to descry the face of Amyntas' daughter, but it was too far. He must go down and make some gesture which would preserve his dignity and, with luck, gain time. Just then new movement below, from a new direction, caught his eye. He leaned out, stared, and, cursing, swung back into the room.

"What is it?" His rage and dismay had startled her.

"Hades take them! They are bringing Philip out to her."

"What? How can—"

"They know where his tent is. You wouldn't have him here. I must go." He flung out, without even the curtest apology. For a very little, she thought, he would have cursed her, too.

Down below in the thick outer walls the huge gates stood wide. The cart halted. A group of soldiers, pulling something, came running out of the gateway.

"Lady, if you'll please to step down, we've something here more fit for you."

It was an old and splendid chariot, its front and sides plated with silver gryphons and gold lions. Lined with tooled red leather, it had been built for Kroisos, that legend for uncounted riches, the last Lydian King. Alexander had made a progress in it, to impress the people.

This moving throne made her sense of dream grow deeper. She came to herself to say that she could not leave her mother's body untended.

"She'll be watched with, lady, like she ought, we've seen to that." Worn black-clad women came forward with eager pride; veterans' wives, looking from work and weather old enough to be their mothers. A soldier approached to hand Eurydike down. At the last moment Alketas, making a virtue of necessity, came up to do the office. For a moment she flinched; but that was not the way to take an enemy's surrender. She inclined her head graciously and took his offered arm. A team of soldiers grasped the chariot-pole, and pulled it forward. She sat like a king on Kroisos' chair.

Suddenly, the sound of the cheering altered. She heard

the ancient Macedonian cries: "Io Hymen! Euoi! Joy to the bride! Hail to the groom!"

The groom was coming towards her.

Her heart gave a lurch. This part of the dream had been blurred.

The man came riding, on a beautiful, slow-pacing dapple-grey. A grizzled old soldier led it by the rein. The face of the bearded rider was not unlike the one on the gold medallion. He was looking about him, blinking a little. The old soldier pointed towards her. When he looked straight at her, she saw that he was frightened, scared to death. Among all she had thought of, so far as she had allowed herself to think at all, she had not thought of this.

Urged by the soldiers, he dismounted and walked up to the chariot, his blue eyes, filled with the liveliest apprehension, fixed on her face. She smiled at him.

"How are you, Arridaios? I am your cousin Eurydike, your uncle Amyntas' daughter. I have just come from home. Alexander sent for me."

The soldiers all around murmured approval, admiring her quick address, and cried, "Long live the King"

Philip's face had brightened at the sound of his old name. When he was Arridaios he had had no duties, no bullying rehearsals with impatient men. Alexander had never bullied, only made one pleased to get things right. This girl reminded him, somehow, of Alexander. Cautiously, less frightened now, he said, "Are you going to marry me?"

A soldier burst into a guffaw, but was manhandled by indignant comrades. The rest listened eagerly to the scene.

"If you would like it, Arridaios. Alexander wanted us to marry."

He bit his lip in a crisis of irresolution. Suddenly he turned to the old soldier who led his horse. "Shall I marry her, Konon? Did Alexander tell me to?"

One or two soldiers clapped hands over their mouths. In

the muttering pause, she was aware of the old servant subjecting her to a searching scrutiny. She recognized a resolute protector. Ignoring the voices, some of them growing ribald, which were urging the King to speak up for the girl before she changed her mind, she looked straight at Konon, and said, "I will be kind to him."

The wariness in his faded eyes relaxed. He gave her a little nod, and turned to Philip, still eyeing him anxiously. "Yes, sir. This is the lady you're betrothed to, the maid Alexander chose for you. She's a fine, brave lady. Reach out your hand to her, and ask her nicely to be your wife."

Eurydike took the obedient hand. Large, warm and soft, it clung to hers appealingly. She gave it a reassuring pressure.

"Please, Cousin Eurydike, will you marry me? The soldiers want you to."

Keeping his hand, she said, "Yes, Arridaios. Yes, King Philip, I will."

The cheers began in earnest. Soldiers who were wearing their broad-brimmed hats flung them into the air. The cries of "Hymen!" redoubled. They were trying to coax Philip into the chariot beside her, when Perdikkas, red and panting from his race down the steep and winding steps of the ancient city, arrived upon the scene.

Alketas met him, speaking with his eyes. Both knew too well the mood in which Macedonians grew dangerous. They had seen it in the time of Alexander, who had dealt with it at Opis by leaping from his dais and arresting the ringleaders with his bare hands. But such things had been Alexander's mystery; anyone else would have been lynched. Alketas met with a shrug of the shoulders his brother's furious stare.

Eurydike in the chariot guessed at once who Perdikkas was. For a moment she felt like a child before a formidable adult. But she stood her ground, sustained by strengths she was largely unaware of. She knew she was the grandchild of Philip and King Perdikkas, great-grandchild of Illyrian Bardelys, the old terror of the border; but she did not know they had bequeathed her more than pride in them; she had some of their nature, too. Her sequestered youth, fed upon legends, let her see in her situation nothing absurd or obscene. All she knew was that these men who had cheered her should not see her afraid.

Philip had been standing with one hand upon the chariot, arguing with the men who had been trying to hoist him into it. Now he grabbed her arm.

"Look out!" he said. "Here comes Perdikkas."

She put her hand over his. "Yes, I see him. Come up here, and stand by me."

He scrambled up; encouraging soldiers steadied the chariot as his weight rocked it. Grasping the rail, he stood rigid with scared defiance; she rose to her feet beside him, summoning her nerve. Briefly, they presented an uncanny semblance of a triumphant pair, remote in pride and power. Tauntingly, the soldiers flung at Perdikkas the marriage-cry.

He reached the chariot; there was a moment of held breath. Then he raised his hand in salute.

"Greeting, King. Greeting, daughter of Amyntas. I am glad that the King has been prompt to welcome you."

"The soldiers made me," mumbled Philip anxiously. Eurydike's clear voice cut in: "The King has been very gracious."

Philip gazed anxiously at these two protagonists. No vengeance from Perdikkas happened. The soldiers were pleased, too. He gave a conniving grin. Hiding with care her almost incredulous amazement, Eurydike knew that, for the present, she had won.

"Perdikkas," she said, "the King has asked for my hand with the goodwill of the Macedonians. But my mother, the sister of Alexander, is lying here murdered, as you know. First of all I must have leave to direct her funeral."

Loud, respectful sounds of approval greeted this. Perdikkas agreed with as good a grace as he could. Scanning the sullen faces, thinking of Antipatros' forces making for the Hellespont, he added that the death of her noble mother had been a shocking error, due to ignorance and to the valor of her defense. The matter would of course be searched to the bottom shortly.

Eurydike bowed her head, aware that she would never know what Alketas' orders had really been. Kynna would at least meet the flame with all the honors of war; one day her ashes must return to Aigai. Meantime, her funeral offerings must be courage and resolve. As for her blood-price, that would be with the gods.

The funeral was barely over, when news reached Perdikkas that Alexander's bier was proceeding in state to Egypt.

It struck him like a thunderbolt. All his plans had been directed against the threat from the north, the outraged father-in-law to whom he had already despatched Nikaia. Now, from the south, came a clear declaration of war.

Eumenes was still in Sardis, summoned when danger came from the north alone. It had come, as they both knew, from neglect of his advice to marry Kleopatra openly, to send Nikaia still virgin home, and advance at once on Macedon. This was not spoken of. Like Kassandra, Eumenes was fated never to reap much good from being right. A Greek among Macedonians had no business to know best. He refrained, therefore, from pointing out that Perdikkas could now have been Regent of Macedon with a royal bride, a power against which Ptolemy could have attempted nothing; and merely voiced a doubt that he was planning war.

"All he has done so far in Egypt has been to dig in and make himself snug. He's ambitious, yes; but what are his ambitions? It was a fine piece of insolence to steal the body; but even that may be only to glorify Alexandria. Will he trouble us if he's let alone?"

"He's already annexed Kyrene. And he's raising a bigger army than he needs."

"How does he know? If you march against him he'll need it."

Perdikkas said with sudden venom, "I hate the man."

Eumenes offered no comment. He remembered Ptolemy as a gangling youth, hoisting the child Alexander up on his horse for a ride. Perdikkas had been a friend of the King's manhood, but it had never been quite the same. Alexander promoted on merit—even Hephaistion had started at the bottom—and Perdikkas had outstripped Ptolemy in the end. But it was Ptolemy who had suited Alexander like a well-worn, comfortable shoe; the trusted Perdikkas had never quite matched that ease. Ptolemy, by instinct and from watching Alexander, had a way with men; he knew when to relax discipline as well as when to tighten it; when to give, when to listen, when to laugh. Perdikkas felt the absence of that sixth sense as a man might feel short sight; and envy ate at him.

"He's like a vicious dog, that eats the flock it should be guarding. If he's not whipped back, the rest will be at it too."

"Maybe; but not yet. Antipatros and Krateros will be marching *now*."

Perdikkas' dark jaw set stubbornly. He has changed, thought Eumenes, since Alexander died. His desires have changed. They grow hubristic, and he knows it. Alexander contained us all.

Perdikkas said, "No, Ptolemy can't wait. That asp of Egypt must be stepped upon in the egg."

"Then we divide the army?" His voice was neutral; a Greek among Macedonians had said enough.

"Needs must. You shall go north, and refuse Antipatros the Hellespont. I will settle with Ptolemy, and settle for good . . . But before we march, we must have this accursed wedding. The men won't move else. I know them too well."

Later that day, Perdikkas spent an hour reasoning with Kleopatra. In the end, with flattery, cold logic, appeal, and as much charm as he could conjure, he persuaded her to act as Eurydike's matron of honor. The troops were set on the marriage; it must be done with a good grace. Any grudging would be remembered against them both, which they could not afford.

"The girl was a child at nurse," he said, "when they murdered Philip. I doubt even Amyntas was more than on the fringe of it. I was there when he was tried."

"Yes, I daresay. But it is all disgusting. Has she no shame at all? Well, you have dangers enough without my making more for you. If Alexander was willing to give it countenance, I suppose I can do the same."

Eumenes did not await the feast. He marched at once to meet the forces of Antipatros and Krateros (another of his sons-in-law); leading the Macedonians with their loose and dubious loyalty to the alien Greek. For Eumenes, that was an old story. Perdikkas, whose business was less urgent, stayed on another week to give his troops their show.

Two days before the wedding, a flustered maid announced to Eurydike in her inner room—built for the chief wife of old Kroisos—that the Queen of the Epirotes had come to visit her.

Kleopatra arrived in state. Olympias had not stinted her since she left home; meanness had never been one of her sins. Her daughter came dressed like a queen, and with queenly gifts: a broad gold necklace, a roll of Karian embroidery stitched with lapis and gold. For a moment, Eurydike was overwhelmed. But Kynna had trained her in manners as well as war; she achieved a kind of naive dignity which moved Kleopatra against her will. She remembered her own wedding, to an uncle old enough to be her father, at seventeen.

The compliments paid, the formal sweet cakes tasted, she went dutifully over the wedding ritual. It was a dry business, since there could be no question of the sly feminine jokes traditional at such a conference. Careful correctness resulted. Kleopatra's sense of duty nagged at her. This grave guarded girl, left alone in the world at fifteen; what did she know? Kleopatra smoothed her gown over her knees, and looked up from her ringed fingers.

"When you met the King"—how allude to so disgraceful an occasion?—"did you have time to talk with him? Perhaps you saw he is a little young for his years?"

Eurydike's straight eyes met hers, deciding that she meant well and must be answered civilly. "Yes. Alexander told my mother so; and I see it is so."

This was promising. "Then, when you are married, what do you mean to do? Perdikkas would give you an escort to your kin in Macedon."

Eurydike thought, It is not quite a command, because it cannot be one. She answered quietly, "The King has a right that I should be his friend, if he needs a friend. I will stay for a while and see."

Next day, such ladies of standing as Sardis could supply—wives of senior officers and administrators, with a few timid ornate Lydians—paid their respects. Later, in the quiet afternoon, sacred since Kroisos' day to the siesta, came a different caller. A twittering maid announced a messenger from the household of the bridegroom.

Old Konon, when shown in, eyed the attendants meaningly. She sent them out, and asked what message he brought.

"Well, madam . . . to wish you health and joy, and God speed the happy day." Delivered of this set speech, he swallowed audibly. What could be coming? Eurydike, dreading the unknown, looked withdrawn and sullen. Konon, his nervousness increased, marshaled his words. "Madam, he's taken a real liking to you, that's sure. He's forever talking of Cousin Eurydike, and setting out his pretty things to show you . . . But, madam, I've cared for him man and boy, and I know his ways, which he sets store by, seeing he was ill-used before I came. If you please, madam, don't turn me off. You'll not find me taking liberties or putting myself forward. If you'll just keep me on trial, to see if I suit; I won't ask more."

So that was all! In her relief she could have embraced him; but of course one must not show it. "Did I not see you with the King? Your name is Konon, is it not? Yes, you will be welcome to stay on. Please tell the King so, if he should ask."

"He's never thought to ask, madam. It would have put him in a terrible taking." They eyed each other, a little relaxed, still cautious. Konon was reaching for words, even for the little that could be said at all. "Madam, he's not used to big feasts, not without Alexander giving him the lead and seeing him through it. I daresay they told you, he has a bad turn sometimes. Don't be afraid, if you just leave him to me, he'll soon be right again."

Eurydike said she would. Echoing silence engulfed them. Konon swallowed again. The poor girl would give anything

to know what he didn't know how to tell her—her groom
had no notion that the act of sex could be performed with
a second party. At length, turning crimson, he managed,
"Madam, he thinks the world of you. But he'll not trouble
you. It wouldn't be his way."

She was not too naive to understand him. With as much
dignity as she could summon, she said, "Thank you, Konon. I am sure the King and I will agree together. You
have leave to go."

Philip woke early on his wedding morning. Konon had
promised that he could wear the purple robe with the great
red star. Besides, he was going to be married to Cousin
Eurydike. She would be allowed to stay with him, and he
could see her whenever he liked. Perdikkas himself had said
so.

That morning, the bath-water came in a big silver ewer,
carried by two well-dressed young men who stayed to pour
it over him, wishing him good luck. This, Konon explained,
was because he was a bridegroom. He saw the young men
exchange a grin across him; but such things often happened.

A good many people were singing and laughing outside
the door. He was no longer in his familiar tent, but had a
room in the palace; he did not mind, he had been allowed
to bring all his stones. Konon explained that there was
no room in the tent for a lady, while here she could stay
next door.

The young men helped him put on the beautiful robe;
then he was taken by Perdikkas to sacrifice at the little
temple of Zeus at the top of the hill. Alexander had built
it there, where fire had fallen from heaven. Perdikkas told
him when to throw incense on the burning meat, and what
to say to the god. He got everything right, and the people

sang for him; but nobody praised him afterwards, as Alexander used to do.

Perdikkas, indeed, had had trouble enough to plan a convincing ceremony. Thanks to Alketas, the bride had no family to give the marriage feast. He was grateful to Kleopatra for consenting to hold the torch of welcome in the bridal chamber. But what mattered most, because the troops would see it, was the wedding procession.

Then, to compound his troubles, at midday two forerunners announced the approach of the lady Roxane. Since this affair, he had entirely forgotten having sent for her, and had not even asked her to the wedding.

Lodgings were hastily prepared; her closed litter was carried up through the city. The Sardians crowded to see; the soldiers gave a few restrained greetings. They had never approved of Alexander's foreign marriages; but now he was dead, a kind of aura clung to her. Besides, she was the mother of his son. The child was with her. A Macedonian queen would have held him up for them to see; but Bactrian ladies did not show themselves in public. The child was teething and fretful, and could be heard whimpering as the litter passed.

Dressed in his wedding robe, and putting a good face on it, Perdikkas greeted her and invited her to the feast; prepared, he said, at short notice owing to the imminence of war.

"You told me nothing of it!" she said angrily. "Who is this peasant girl you have found for him? If the King is to marry, he should have married me."

"Among Macedonians," said Perdikkas frostily, "a dead king's heir does not inherit his harem. And the lady is granddaughter to two kings."

A crisis of precedence new arose. Alexander and his officers had married their foreign wives by the local rites; Roxane, ignorant of Macedonian custom, could not be brought to see that Kleopatra was taking a mother's place and could not be removed from it. "But I," she cried, "am the mother of Alexander's son!"

"So," said Perdikkas, very nearly shouting, "you are the kinswoman of the *bridegroom*. I will send someone to explain the rite to you. See to it that your part is properly done, if you want your son accepted by the soldiers. Don't forget they have the right to disinherit him."

This sobered her. He had changed, she thought; grown colder, harsher, more overbearing. He had not forgiven Stateira's death, it seemed. She was unaware that others had noticed a change as well.

Philip had looked forward all day to the wedding ride. It did not disappoint him. Not since the time he rode an elephant had he enjoyed himself so much.

He wore the purple robe, and a gold diadem. Eurydike beside him had a yellow dress, and a yellow veil flung back from a wreath of gold flowers. He had thought they would have the car all to themselves, and had been displeased when Perdikkas got up on the other side. Eurydike was married to *him*, and Perdikkas could not marry her as well. Hastily people had explained that Perdikkas was best man; but it was Cousin Eurydike he listened to. Now he was married, he felt much less frightened of Perdikkas; he had been on the point of pushing him out of the car.

Drawn by white mules, they drove along the processional Sacred Way, which bent and turned to bring it downhill without stairs. It was adorned with old statues and shrines, Lydian, Persian, Greek. Flags and garlands were everywhere; as the sun sank they were starting to light the torches. People were standing and cheering all the way, climbing up on the house-roofs.

The tasseled, sequin-netted mules were led by soldiers wearing scarlet cloaks and wreaths. Behind and in front, musicians played Lydian airs on flutes and pipes, shook sistra with their little tinkling bells, and clanged great cymbals. Auspicious cries in mingled tongues rose like waves. The sunset glow faded, the torches came out like stars.

Full of it all, Philip turned and said, "Are you happy, Cousin Eurydike?"

"Very happy." Indeed, she had imagined nothing to compare with it. Unlike her groom, she had never before tasted the pomps of Asia. The music, the shouts of acclamation, elated her like wine. This was her element, and till now she had never known it. Not for nothing was she the daugh-ter of Amyntas, a king's son who, when a crown was offered him, could not forbear to reach for it. And now," she said, "you must not call me cousin any more. A wife is more important than a cousin."

The wedding feast was set out in the great hall, with a dais for the women in their chairs of honor, a flower-decked throne for the bride. Her gifts and her dowry were displayed on stands around her. With wondering and distanced eyes, she saw again the jewels and cups and vases, the bolts of fine dyed wool, which Kynna had brought with cherishing care from Macedon. Only one piece was missing, the silver casket which now held her calcined bones.

Kleopatra led her to the King's high table to take her piece of the bride-loaf, sliced with his sword. It was clear that he had never handled a sword before; but he hacked a piece off bravely, broke it in two when told, and, as she tasted hers—the central rite of the wedding—asked her if it was nice, because his own piece was not sweet enough.

Back on her dais, she listened to a hymn by a choir of maidens; Lydians mostly, mangling the words, a few Greek daughters trying hard to be heard. Then she became aware that the women round her were murmuring together, stir-

ring with little fidgets of preparation. With a sudden clutch
in her midriff, she knew that when the song ended, they
would lead her to the nuptial chamber.

All through the ride, nearly all through the feast, she had
overleaped this moment, throwing her mind ahead to next
month, next year, or living in the present only.

"Have you had instruction?"

She looked round with a start. The voice, with a strong
foreign accent, came from just beside her. Not till this
morning had she met the widow of Alexander. She had
bowed to a small jeweled woman, stiff with embroideries
of gold and pearl, rubies like pigeons' eggs hanging from her
ears. Her surface had been so stunning that she had seemed
hardly human, a kind of splendid adornment for the feast.
Now, Eurydike met the gaze of two large black eyes, their
whites brilliantly clear between eyelids dark with kohl,
fixed on her in concentrated malice.

"Yes," she said quietly.

"So, truly? I had heard your mother was a man, as well
as your father. To look at you, one might think so."

Eurydike gazed back, fascinated as the prey by the preda-
tor. Roxane, bright as a little shrike, leaned out from her
chair of honor. "If you know all you should, you will be
able to teach your husband." Her rubies flashed; the song,
rising to its climax, did not cover her rising voice. "To Alexander he was like a dog under his table. He trained him to
heel, then sent him back to the kennel. It is *my* son who is
King."

The song was over. Along the dais there were agitated
rustlings.

Kleopatra rose to her feet, as she had seen Olympias do
it. The others stood up with her. After a moment Roxane
followed, staring defiantly. In the formal, studied Greek of
her father's court, looking down from her Macedonian

height at the little Bactrian, she said, "Let us remember
where we are. And who we are, if we can. Ladies, come.
The torches. Io, Hymen! Joy to the bride!"

"Look!" said Philip to Perdikkas, who had the place of
honor beside him. "Cousin Eurydike is going away!" He
scrambled anxiously to his feet.

"Not now!" Grabbing him by his purple robe, Perdikkas
thumped him back on his supper-couch. With savage
geniality he added, "She is changing her dress. We will
take you to see her presently."

The guests in hearing, even the elegant young Lydian
servers who had picked up a bit of Greek, made stifled
noises. Perdikkas, lowering his voice, said, "Now listen to
the speeches, and when they look at you, smile. We are
going to drink your health."

Philip pushed forward his wine-cup, an engraved gold
Achaemenid treasure from the Persian occupation. Konon,
standing behind his chair, got it quickly back from a too-
zealous server, and filled it from a jug of watered wine, in
the strength given to Greek children. He looked incongru-
ous among the graceful Lydians and well-born Macedonian
pages waiting at table.

Perdikkas rose to make the best man's speech, recalling
the groom's heroic ancestry, the exploits of his grandfather
whose name he had auspiciously assumed; the lineage of
his mother, the noble lady of horse-loving Larissa. His
compliments to the bride were adequate, though rather
vague. Philip, who had been occupied in feeding someone's
curly white poodle which had been sitting under the table,
looked up in time to acknowledge the cheers with an obedient grin.

A harmless person, a distant royal connection, responded

for the bride, uttering bland platitudes about her beauty, virtue and high descent. Once more the health was given, and honored with ritual shouts. It was the time for serious drinking.

Goblets were emptied and briskly filled, faces reddened under tilting wreaths, voices grew louder. Captains still in their thirties argued and bragged about past wars and women; Alexander had died young with young men all about him. For the older men, a real Macedonian wedding brought back the feasts of their youth. Nostalgically, they roared out the time-honored phallic jokes remembered from their family bridals.

The noble pages had slipped out to get their share. Presently one said, "Poor fellow. Old Konon might let him have a mouthful he can taste, at his own wedding. It might put heart in him." He and a friend came up behind Philip's couch. "Konon, Ariston over there told me to say he pledges you." Konon beamed, and looked about for his well-wisher; Perdikkas was talking to the guest on his other side. The second page filled up the royal cup with neat wine. Philip tasted his new drink, liked it, and tilted back his cup. By the time Konon noticed and angrily diluted it, he had had more than half.

Some of the men started to sing a skolion. It was not yet lewder than a wedding feast allowed, but Perdikkas pulled himself together. He had known all along that this could not be a long drinking-bout. A little time yet could be allowed for hospitality, but soon he must break it up. He stopped drinking, to keep alert.

Philip felt a surge of well-being, strength and gaiety. He banged the table in time with the skolion, singing loudly, "I'm married, married, married to Eurydike!" The white poodle pawed at his leg; he picked it up and put it on the table, where it ran about, scattering cups, fruit and flowers,

till someone hurled it off, when it fled yelping. Everyone
laughed; some men far gone in drink bawled ancient en-
couragements to first-night prowess.

Philip gazed at them with blurred eyes, in which lurked
a dim anxiety and suspicion. His purple robe felt too hot,
in the stew of torch-warmed humanity. He heaved at it,
trying to take it off.

Perdikkas saw that it was high time. He called for a
torch, and gave the signal to conduct the bridegroom.

Eurydike lay in the great perfumed bed, in her night-robe
of fine mussel-silk, the brideswomen gathered round her.
They talked among themselves; at first they had dutifully
included her, but none of them knew her, and the wait for
the men was always tedious; the more since coy jokes were
barred. Mostly the floor was held by Roxane, who described
the far more splendid ceremonies of Alexander's day, and
patronized Kleopatra.

Solitary in the little crowd, with its warm smell of female
flesh, of the herbs and cedar-wood of clothes-chests, essence
of orange and of rose, Eurydike heard the rising sounds of
the men's revelry. It was warm, but her feet felt icy cold in
the linen sheets. They had slept in wool at home. The room
was huge, it had been King Kroisos' bedchamber; the walls
were patterned in colored marbles, and the floor was porphyry. A Persian lamp-cluster of gilt lotuses hung over the
bed, bathing her in light; would anyone put it out? She
had an overpowering memory of Philip's physical presence,
his strong stocky limbs, his rather sweetish smell. The little
she had eaten lay in her like lead. Supposing she was sick
on the bed. If her mother were only here! The full sense
of her loss came home to her; she felt, terrified, a surge of
approaching tears. But if Kynna were here, she would be

ashamed to see her cry in the presence of an enemy. She pulled in her stomach muscles, and forced back the first sob in silence.

Behind the matrons the bridesmaids clustered whispering. Their song sung, their small rite done of turning back the bride-bed and sprinkling it with perfume, they had nothing to do. Among a little set of sisters and cousins and friends, the tittering began; dying away if one of the great ladies looked round, rustling like a faint breeze in leaves. Eurydike heard it; she too had nothing to do. Then suddenly she knew that the sounds from the hall had altered. Supper-couches scraped along the floor, the slurred singing stopped. They were getting up.

Like a tense soldier released by the call to onset, she summoned up her courage. Soon all these people must go, and leave her alone to deal with him. She would talk to him, tell him stories. Old Konon had said he would not trouble her.

Roxane too had heard the sounds. She turned, clashing her intricate ruby earrings. "Joy to the bride!" she said.

Surrounded and pushed on by laughing, drunken, torch-bearing men, stumbling over his robe on the shallow stately stairs with their painted murals, Philip made his way towards the royal bedchamber.

His head swam, he sweated in his purple robe; he was angry about the dog being chased away. He was angry with Perdikkas for fetching him from the table, and with all the men for mocking him, as he knew they were; they had stopped even pretending. They were laughing at him because they knew he was scared. He had heard the jokes in the hall; there was something he was expected to do with Eurydike, so bad that one must not do it even by oneself, if anyone could see. He had been beaten long ago for being seen. Now, he believed—no one had thought to tell him otherwise—they would all stand and watch him. He didn't know how, and was sure Cousin Eurydike would not like it. Perdikkas was holding him by the arm, or he would have run away.

He said, despairingly, "It's my bedtime. I want to go to bed."

"*We'll* put you to bed," they chorused. "That's why we're here." They roared with laughter. It was like the bad old days at home, before Alexander had taken him away.

"Be quiet." Perdikkas' voice, suddenly unfestal, an angry martinet's, sobered everyone down. They led Philip to an anteroom, and started to undress him.

He let them take off the hot purple robe; but when they undid the girdle of his sweat-soaked tunic, he fought them, and knocked two flying. The rest all laughed; but Perdikkas, looming and awful, commanded him to remember he was King. So he let them strip him, and put him into a long white robe with a gold-embroidered hem. They let him use the chamber-pot (where was Konon?); then there was no more to stay for. They led him to the door. He could hear inside a murmur of women's voices. *They* would be watching, too!

The wide doors opened. There was Eurydike, sitting up in the great bed. A little brown slave-girl, laughing, ran before him with a long snuffer, ready to quench the hanging lamps. A great wave of anger and misery and fear built up in him. It hummed and boomed in his head, booom, booom, booom. He remembered, he knew that soon the white flash would come. Oh, where was Konon? He shouted, "The light! The light!" and it flashed, a lightning that struck all through him.

Konon, who had been standing in shadow along the

passage, ran in. Without apology he shoved aside the horrified group, shocked sober, which bent over the rigid figure
on the floor; pulled from his belt-pouch a wooden wedge;
prised Philip's jaws apart, so that his tongue should not
fall back and choke him. For a moment, he looked up at
the men with bitter reproach and anger; then his face
settled back into the blank mask of the soldier confronted
with stupid officers. He said to Perdikkas, "Sir, I can see to
him. I know what to do. If the ladies could leave, sir."

Disgusted and ashamed, the men stood aside to let the
women go first. In panic disregard for precedence, the
bridesmaids ran at once, their slippers pattering on the
stairs. The matrons of middle rank, obsessed all day with
etiquette and protocol, clustered helplessly, waiting for the
queens.

Eurydike sat in the bed, grasping around her the crimson
gold-fringed coverlet, looking for help. She had on only
her thin wedding shift; how could she get up in the presence
of men; of Konon, who was staying? Her clothes were on an
ivory stool, at the far end of this great room. Would none
of them remember her, stand to shield her, put something
round her?

She heard a sound from the floor. Philip, stiff as a board
till now, had begun to twitch. In a moment he was in the
throes of the clonic spasm, his whole frame jerking and
thrashing, his robe flung up by his kicking legs.

"Joy to the bride!" It was Roxane, looking down over
her shoulder as she swept towards the door.

"Come, ladies." Kleopatra gathered in a glance the
huddled matrons, averting her face from scandal. Making
for the door she paused, and turned back to the bed. Eurydike saw the long look of contempt, the unwilling pity.
"Will you come? We will find you something to wear."
Her eye moved to the clothes-stool; an officious matron
bustled over.

Eurydike looked after the widow of Alexander, whose gold embroideries gleamed beyond the door; she looked up at Alexander's sister, to whom she was like a beaten whore, whose shame must be covered for the house's honor. She thought, What do I know even of *him*, except that he killed my father? May the gods curse them all. If I die for it, I will make them kneel at my feet.

The matron brought her himation of dyed saffron, the lucky color of fertility and joy. She took it in silence, and wrapped it round her as she rose. Philip's tremor was growing weaker; Konon was holding his head, to keep it from striking the floor. Standing between him and the watching faces, she said, "No, lady, I will not come. The King is sick, and my place is with my husband. Please leave us and go away."

She fetched a pillow from the bed, and laid Philip's head on it. He was hers now, they were both victims together. He had made her a queen, and she would be a king for both of them. Meantime, he must be put into bed and covered warmly. Konon would find her a place to sleep.

3 2 1 B. C.

SOUTH DOWN THE ANCIENT COAST ROAD that followed the eastern shore of the Middle Sea, the army of Perdikkas marched with its long following train: grooms and chandlers, smiths and carpenters and harness-makers, the elephants, the endless wagons, the soldiers' women, the slaves. At Sidon, at Tyre, at Gaza, the people looked down from the mended walls. It was eleven years since Alexander had passed that way alive, whom they had just seen on his last progress, going to Egypt with a chime of bells. This army was no business of theirs; but it meant a war, and war has a way of spreading.

Flanked by its guard of armed Bactrian and Persian eunuchs, Roxane's wagon followed the march, as it had followed from Bactria to India, to Drangiana, to Susa, to Persepolis, to Babylon. Each part had been many times renewed as its journeys lengthened, but it seemed the same, smelling as before of the stamped dyed leather that roofed it, of the essences which at each new city her eunuchs had brought for her approval; even now, a drift of scent on a cushion could bring back the heat of Taxila. Here were the heavy turquoise-studded bowls and trinkets of her dowry, the vessels of chased gold from Susa, a censer from Babylon. It might all have been the same, except for the child.

He was nearly two, and seen to be small for his age; but,

as she said, his father must have been so. Otherwise, it was clearly her looks he favored; the soft dark hair, the bright dark eyes. He was lively, and seldom ill; curious and exploring; a terror to his nurses who must watch his safety at peril of their lives. Though he must be protected, she did not like him thwarted; he must learn from the beginning that he was a king.

Perdikkas called on her every few days; he was the King's guardian, as he reminded her whenever they fell out, which happened often. He was offended that the child shrank from him; it came, he said, of never seeing any other man. "His father, you should remember, was not reared among eunuchs."

"Among *my* people they leave the harem at five, and still make warriors."

"However, he beat them. That is why you are here."

"How dare you," she cried, "call me a captive of the spear! You who were our wedding guest! Oh, if he were here!"

"You may well wish that," Perdikkas said, and left to visit his other ward.

When the army made camp, Philip had his tent just as before. Eurydike, as became a lady of rank, had her wagon; and in this she slept. It lacked Roxane's splendors; but, as she had not seen them, she found it comfortable, and even handsome when her dowry things were set out. It had a roomy locker; and in this, disguised in a roll of blankets, at the hour of departure she had concealed her arms.

Philip was quite happy with these arrangements. He would have been gravely disconcerted by her presence in his tent at night; she might even have wanted Konon to go. In the daytime he was delighted to have her company;

would often ride beside her wagon, and point out the sights
they passed. He had traversed this whole route in the train
of Alexander, and from time to time something would jog
an inconsequent flash of memory. He had been encamped
for months before the huge walls of Tyre.

In the evening, she dined with him in his tent. She hated
at first to watch him eat, but with instruction he improved
a little. Sometimes at sunset, if the camp was near the shore,
she would walk with him, guarded by Konon, helping him
to look for stones and shells; and then she talked to him,
telling the legends of the royal house of Macedon she had
heard fom Kynna, right back to the boy who took the sun-
beam for his wages. "You and I," she said, "will be King
and Queen there soon."

A dim anxiety stirred in his eyes. "But Alexander told
me . . ."

"That was because he was King himself. All that is
over. You *are* the King. You must listen to me, now that
we are married. I will tell you what we can do."

They had passed the Sinai, and in the lands of Egypt made
camp by the flat green coast. A few miles ahead was the
ancient port of Pelusion; beyond that, the spread-fingered
Delta of the Nile, webbed with its intricate veins of canal
and stream. Beyond the Nile was Alexandria.

Among the date-palms and little black irrigation canals
and clumps of tall papyrus, the army spread itself restlessly. The warm dry wind from the southern sand was just
beginning; the Nile was low, the crops stood deep in the
rich silt, the patient oxen toiled at the wooden water-
wheels. By the elephant-lines, the mahouts stripped off
their dhotis to wash their children in the canal, gaily splash-
ing them as they showered themselves with their trunks

after the hot trudge across Sinai. The camels, drinking prodigiously, refilled their secret storage tanks; the soldiers' women washed their clothes and their children. The sutlers went out to find supplies. The soldiers prepared for war.

Perdikkas and his staff scanned the terrain. He had been here with Alexander; but that was eleven years back, and for the last two, Ptolemy had been making himself at home. The land's long vistas showed where, at vital points of access, where a mound or a rocky outcrop offered foundation, stout forts of brick or timber had appeared. He could get no further coastwise; Pelusion was well defended by the salt-marsh between. He must strike south, below the meshes of the Delta.

The main camp must stay here. He would take a mobile force, light and unencumbered. Alexander had taught him that. He rode back to his tent in the quick-falling dusk which the breath of the desert reddened, to make his plans.

Through the wide straggling camp, the cook-fires budded and bloomed; little fires of the women, big ones—for the nights were cold still—where twenty or thirty men would share their bean-soup and porridge, their bread and olives, with a relish of dates and cheese, washed down with rough wine.

It was in the hour between food and sleep, when men talked idly, told tales or sang, that the voices began to sound around the camp, just beyond the reach of the firelight. They called softly, speaking good Macedonian; uttering familiar names, recalling old battles under Alexander, old fallen friends, old jokes. First unrebuffed, then hesitantly welcomed, the speaker would come up to the fire. Just a jar together for old times' sake, seeing he'd brought one. Tomorrow, who could say, they might have to kill each other, but meantime, good health and no hard feelings. As for himself, he could only speak as he'd found; now Alex-

ander was gone, Ptolemy was next best. He was a soldier
and no one's fool; but he looked after you, he had time for
your troubles, and where else would you find that today?
What wage, by the way, was Perdikkas paying veterans?
What? (A shake of the head, a long contemptuous whistle.)

"He promised you loot, I suppose? Oh, yes, it's *there*; but
not so you'll ever get to it. This country's murder to those
who don't know the waterways. Look out for the crocodiles;
they're bigger than in India, *and* cunning."

To a growing audience, he would go on to the comforts
and pleasures of Alexandria, the shipping from everywhere,
the good fresh food, the wineshops and the girls, the good
air all the year round; and Alexander to bring the city luck.

The wine-jar emptied, his mission done, the visitor would
slip away, his footfalls merging into the uncanny noises of
the Egyptian night. As he threaded his way back to his fort,
he would reflect comfortably that he'd not given them a
word of a lie, and doing old friends a kindness was a very
good way of earning a hundred drachmas.

Perdikkas made his last camp a little above the wrist of
the Nile, from which the fingers of the Delta spread north-
wards. The noncombatants he had brought thus far would
await him; among them the Kings, whom he wanted under
his eye. From here he would make his march towards the
river.

They watched him and his soldiers go into the shimmer
of morning mist, horse and foot, the pack-mules with the
rations, the camel-train with the parts for the catapults, the
elephants plodding after. For a long time they grew smaller
in the flat distance, vanishing at last into a low horizon of
tamarisk and palm.

Pacing the royal tent, Eurydike waited restlessly for news.
Konon had found an escort, and taken Philip riding. She

too had liked to ride, free on the hills of Macedon, sitting astride; but she had to remember, now, what would be acceptable in a queen. Perdikkas had told her so.

Now that for the first time she was with an amy in the field, all her training and her nature rebelled at being laid aside with slaves and women. Her marriage she had felt as a grotesque necessity, something to be managed, altering nothing of herself; even more, now, she felt women an alien species, imposing no laws upon her.

Over by her wagon, her two maids sat in its shade, chattering softly in Lydian. Both were slaves. She had been offered ladies-in-waiting, but had refused, telling Perdikkas she would not ask softly nurtured women to endure the hardships of the march. The truth was that she would not endure the tedium of female talk. To sex she was indifferent; in this respect she needed women even less than men. Her wedding night had killed the last of that. In adolescent dreams she had fought, like Hippolyta, at a hero's side. Since then she had become ambitious, and her dreams were otherwise.

By the third morning she was impatient even of ambition, which had no outlet. The day stretched before her, empty and flat as the land. Why should she endure it? She remembered the locker in the wagon which contained her arms. Her man's tunic was there as well.

She was the Queen; Perdikkas should have sent reports to her. If no one would bring her news, she would go and see.

All she knew of the expedition she had heard from Konon, who had many friends in the camp. Perdikkas, he had said, had started out without telling anyone his objective, neither the camp commandant nor the senior officers who were going with him. He had heard there had been spies about the camp. The officers had not liked it; Seleukos, who commanded the elephants, liked to know how they would be used. Konon kept to himself much more than he had told; they were saying in camp that Perdikkas was far higher-handed these days than Alexander ever was; Alexander had known how to talk you round.

He had confided, however, to Eurydike that with the stores and remounts they'd taken, he reckoned they would not be marching above thirty miles. And that was the distance to the Nile.

Eurydike changed into her tunic, clasped on her tooled-hide corselet, laced down the shoulder-pieces, put on riding-boots and greaves. Her breasts were small and the corselet hid their curve. Her helmet was a simple, unplumed Illyrian war-cap; her grandmother, Audata, had worn it on the border. The drowsy servants never saw her go. Down at the horse-lines the grooms took her for one of the royal squires, and at her imperious order led a sound horse out.

Even after three days, the spoor of the troops was plain: the plowed-up grass, the bared dust, the horse and camel droppings, the trampled banks of the irrigation canals, the leaked water caking in the little fields. The peasants laboring to mend the dikes looked up with sullen hatred of all destructive soldiers.

She was only a few miles out when she met the messenger.

He was riding a camel; a dusty, drawn-faced man, who stared at her angrily for not making way for him. But he was a soldier; so she wheeled round and overtook him. Her horse shied from the camel; she called, "What news? Has there been a battle?"

He leaned over to spit; but his mouth was dry, and only the sound came out. "Get out of my way, boy, I've no time for you. I've despatches for the camp. They must get ready to take the wounded . . . what are left of them." He switched his mount; it bobbed its scornful head and left her in its dust.

An hour or two later, she met the wagons. As they came nearer, she guessed their freight from the groaning, from the water-carriers on their donkeys, and the doctor leaning under one of the awnings. She rode down the line, hearing the humming flies, a curse or a cry when a wagon jolted.

The fourth of them had men talking and looking out; men with disabled limbs, not too weak to be alert. She saw inside a familiar face; it was the veteran who had first taken her part on the Sardis road, when her mother died.

"Thaulos!" she called, riding up to the tailboard. "I am sorry to see you hurt."

She was hailed with amazement and delight. Queen Eurydike! And they had taken her for some young blood in cavalry! What was she doing here? Had she meant to lead them into battle? A daughter of the house—her granddad would have been proud of her. Ah well, lucky she had been too late for yesterday's work. It did one good to see her.

She did not understand that it was her youth they found endearing; that had she been thirty instead of fifteen they would have made a barrack-room joke of her for a mannish termagant. She looked like a charming boy without having lost her girlishness; she was their friend and ally. As she walked her horse beside the cart, they poured out their discontents to her.

Perdikkas had marched them to a place on the Nile called Camelford. But of course the ford was guarded by a fort across the stream, with a palisade, a scarp, and the wall of the fort on top. Perdikkas' scouts had reported it lightly manned.

A younger veteran said resentfully, "But what he forgot was that Ptolemy learned his trade from Alexander."

"Perdikkas hates him," said another, "so he underrates him. You can't afford that in war. Alexander knew better."

"That's it; of course the fort was undermanned. Ptolemy

was keeping mobile, till he knew where the stroke would
be. Once he did know, he came like the wind; I doubt
Alexander would have been much quicker. By the time
we were half across, he was in the fort with a regiment."

"And another thing I'll tell you," Thaulos said. "He
didn't want to shed Macedonian blood. He could have lain
low, and fallen on us as we crossed; for he'd come up out
of sight. But up he stood on the walls, with a herald, and
his men all shouting, trying to scare us back. He's a gentleman, Ptolemy. Alexander thought the world of him."

With a grunt of pain, he eased himself over on the
straw to favor his wounded leg. She asked if he needed
water; but they were all in need of talk. The desperately
wounded were in other carts.

Perdikkas, they said, had made a speech calling upon
their loyalty. It was he who was guardian of the Kings, who
had his appointment direct from Alexander. This they
could not deny; moreover he was paying them, and their
pay was not in arrears.

Scaling-ladders had been carried by the elephants; and it
was they, too, who had torn down the palisades on the riverbank, as their mahouts directed them, plucking out the
stakes like the saplings whose leaves they fed on, their thick
hides making little of javelins from above. But the defenders had been well trained; the glacis was steep; the men dislodged from the ladders had rolled down the broken palisade into the river, where the weight of their armor drowned
them. It was then that Perdikkas had ordered the elephants
to assault the walls.

"Seleukos didn't like it. He said they'd done their stint.
He said there was no sense in a beast carrying two men up
where they'd be level with a dozen, and exposing its head
as well. But he was told pretty sharply who was in command. And he didn't like that either."

The elephants were ordered to give their war-cry. "But it didn't scare Ptolemy. We could see him up on the wall with a long sarissa, poking back our men as they came up. An elephant can scare any man down on the ground; but not when he's on a wall above it."

The elephants had labored up the scarp, digging their heavy feet into the earth, till Old Pluto, the one the others followed, started to pull at the wall-timbers. Old Pluto could shift a battering-ram. But Ptolemy stood his ground, threw off the missiles with his shield, reached out his long spear and got Old Pluto's eyes. The next elephant up, some-one picked off the mahout. So there were these two great beasts, one blind and the other unguided, pounding and blundering down the scarp, trampling anyone in their way.

"And that," said one man, "is how I got a broken foot. Not from the enemy. And if I never walk straight again, it's not Ptolemy I'll blame for it."

There was a growl of anger from every man in the cart. They had seen little more of the action, having been wounded about this time; they thought it had gone on all day. She rode by them a little longer, offering sympathy, then asked them the way to Camelford. They urged her to take care, to do nothing rash, they could not spare their Queen.

As she rode on, a dark moving bulk appeared in the middle distance, coming slowly from a palm-grove that fringed a pool. As it drew near, she saw two elephants in single file, the smaller going first, the bigger one holding it by the tail. Old Pluto was going home, led as he had been by his mother forty years ago in his native jungle, to keep him safe from tigers. His mahout sat weeping on his neck; his wounded eyes, dropping bloody serum, seemed to be weeping too.

Eurydike noted him, as proof of Ptolemy's prowess. At

home her chief diversion had been the hunt; she took for granted that animals were put into the world for men to use. Questioning the other mahout, who seemed to have his wits about him, she learned that Perdikkas had abandoned the assault at evening, and marched after dark, the man did not know where. Clearly, if she rode on she risked falling among the enemy; so she turned back to the camp.

No one had missed her but old Konon, who recognized her as she came back; but, as she warned him with her eyes, it was not his place to rebuke her. He would not dare give her away. For the rest, Philip's wedding had been a nine days' wonder, and just now they had other concerns. It was she herself who began, dimly and gropingly, to see her way ahead.

The army of Perdikkas, what was left of it, came back next day.

Stragglers came first, unofficered, undisciplined, unkempt. Clothes, armor and skin were plastered with dried Nile mud; they were black men, but for their light angry eyes. They went about the camp, seeking water to drink and clean themselves, spreading each his tale of confusion and disaster. The main force followed, a sullen, scowling mass, led by Perdikkas with a face of stone, its tight-lipped officers keeping their thoughts to themselves. Her female dress and seclusion resumed, she sent out Konon to learn the news.

While he was gone, she became aware that round the small circle of the royal quarters a ring of men was gathering. They settled down in groups, not talking much, but with the air of men agreed upon their business. Puzzled and disturbed, she looked for the sentries who should have been somewhere near; but they had joined the silent watchers.

Some instinct dispelled her fear. She went to the entry of

the royal tent, and let herself be seen. Arms went up in salute; it was all quiet, it had an air of reassurance, almost of complicity.

"Philip," she said, "stand in the opening there, and let those men see you. Smile at them and greet them as Perdikkas taught you. Show me; yes, like that. Say nothing, just salute them."

He came in, pleased, to say, "They waved to me."

"They said, 'Long live Philip.' Remember, when people say that, you must always smile."

"Yes, Eurydike." He went to lay out with his shells some beads of red glass she had bought him from a peddler.

A shadow darkened the tent-mouth. Konon paused for leave to enter. When she saw his face, her eyes moved to the corner, where they kept Philip's ceremonial spear. She said, "Is the enemy coming?"

"Enemy?" He made it sound like an irrelevance. "No, madam . . . Don't be in a worry about the lads out there. They've taken it on themselves, just in case of trouble. I know them all."

"Trouble? What trouble?"

She saw his old soldier's stone-wall face. "I can't say, madam. They say one thing and another in the camp. They were cut up badly, trying to cross the Nile."

"I've seen the Nile." Philip looked up. "When Alexander . . ."

"Be quiet and listen. Yes, Konon. Go on."

Perdikkas, it seemed, had given his men a few hours' rest after the assault upon the fort. Then he had ordered them to strike camp and be ready for a night march.

"Konon," said Philip suddenly, "why are all those men shouting?"

Konon too had heard; his narrative had been flagging. "They're angry, sir. But not with you or the Queen. Don't

fret about it, they won't come here." He took up his tale
again.

Perdikkas' men had fought through the heat of the day
and on till evening. They were discouraged and dog-tired;
but he had promised them an easy crossing, further south
at Memphis, down the east bank of the river.

"Memphis," said Philip brightening. Long ago, from a
window, he had watched the tremendous pageant of Alexander's enthronement as Pharaoh, Son of Ra. He had
seemed to be made all of gold.

Konon was saying, "Alexander, now; *he* knew how to
make a man throw his heart into it."

Outside, the voices of the encircling soldiers rose a tone
or two, as if receiving news. The sound sank again.

In the dark before dawn, Konon went on, they had come
to the crossing-place. Here the river was split by a mile-
long island, breaking its force, and the forks were shallower.
They were to cross in two stages, assembling on the island
in between.

"But it was deeper than he'd thought. Half over from
this side, they were chest-deep. With the current pulling
at their shields, some of them keeled over; the rest had all
they could do to keep their feet. So then Perdikkas remembered how Alexander crossed the Tigris."

He paused, to see if she knew about this famous exploit.
But she had encouraged no one to talk about Alexander.

"It's a fast stream, the Tigris. Before he sent the infantry across, he stood two columns of cavalry in the river,
upstream and down of them. Upstream to break the current, downstream to catch any man carried away. He was
the first man in on foot, feeling out the shoals with his
spear."

"Yes," said Eurydike coolly. "But what did Perdikkas
do?"

"What *he* did was to use the elephants."

"They didn't get drowned?" said Philip anxiously.

"No, sir. It was the men that drowned . . . Where's that idle loafing Sinis? Trust a Karian to go off at a time like this. A moment, madam." He took a taper to the little clay day-lamp which kept a source of fire, and kindled the cluster on the big branched lamp-stand. Outside, a red glow showed that the soldiers were making a cook-fire. Konon's shadow, made huge by the light behind him, loomed dark and manifold on the worn linen hangings of the tent.

"He put the elephants upstream, in line across, and the cavalry downstream; then he told the phalanx to advance. They went in, the phalanx leaders each with his men. And when they got to the middle, it was as if the Nile had come up in flood. It was over their heads; the horses downstream had to swim for it. It was the weight of the elephants did it; it stirred up the muddy bottom, which the Tigris didn't have. But the worst of all, they all say, was to see their mates being taken by crocodiles."

"I've seen a crocodile," said Philip eagerly.

"Yes, sir, I know . . . Well, before it deepened too much, a good few men had scrambled up on the island. Perdikkas saw there was no going ahead; so he hailed them, and ordered them to come back."

"Come *back*?" said Eurydike. She listened with new ears to the sounds outside; the muttering that rose and fell, a long keening from the bivouacs of the soldiers' women. "He ordered them back?"

"It was that or leave them there. It meant throwing away their arms, which no Macedonian did as long as Alexander led them, and they don't forget it. Some of them shouted out they'd as soon take their chance in the west channel, and give themselves up to Ptolemy. No one knows what became of them. The rest went back in the water, which was deeper than ever, full of blood and crocodiles.

A few got out. I've talked with them. One of them left his hand in a crocodile's mouth. The rest of his arm's in ribbons, he'll never live . . . They lost two thousand men."

She thought of the groaning hospital carts, a mere drop now in the ocean of disaster. A sweeping impulse, compounded of anger, pity, contempt, and ambition grasping at opportunity, lifted her out of herself. She turned to Philip.

"Listen to me." He waited, attentive; recognizing as a dog would do the note of imperative command. "We are going out to see the soldiers. They have been treated badly, but they know we are their friends. This time, *you* must speak to them. First return their salute; then say—now, listen very carefully—'Men of Macedon. My brother's spirit would grieve to see this day.' Don't say anything more, even if they answer you. I will talk to them then."

He repeated it after her; they went out into the falling dark, lit from behind by the lamps inside the tent, and from before by the soldiers' fire.

An instant cheer greeted them; the word ran round, men ran up crowding to hear. Philip did not falter; she had not charged him with more than he could retain. She saw him pleased with himself, and, lest he should be tempted to improvise, turned to him quickly with a show of wifely assent. Then she spoke.

They were all ears. The King's sense of their wrongs had amazed and pleased them; he could not be as slow as people said. A man of few words. No matter, the Queen would be worth hearing.

Roxane, near by in her wagon, had supposed the troop to have been posted for her own protection. Her eunuchs had told her there was trouble in the camp; but their Greek was poor, and no soldier had had time for them. Now with bewildered anger she heard the young ringing voice crying out against the waste of the gallant dead; promising that when the time came for the King himself to rule them, he would see to it that good men's lives were not thrown away.

Roxane heard the cheers. All her five years of marriage had been told with cheers; shouts of acclamation, the rhythmic roar as the victory parade went by. This sound was different; starting with indulgent affection, but ending with a chorus of revolt.

There, thought Roxane, was an unsexed virago! That bastard and fool the husband should never share *her* child's throne. Just then the child, who had been on edge all day, bumped into something and began to cry. Eurydike, the cheering over, heard the sound, and said to herself that the barbarian's brat should never reign in Macedon.

Perdikkas sat in his tent at his trestle table, stylus in hand, a wax diptych blank before him. He was alone. Before this he should have called his staff to a war council, to decide on his next move; but, he thought, he must give them time to cool. Seleukos had answered him in monosyllables; Peithon had looked foxily under his reddish brows and down his pointed nose, saying this or that, but none of what he thought; Archias, though known to be in camp, had not reported at all. Once more he regretted having sent Alketas north with Eumenes; there was nothing like a kinsman in treacherous times.

Round the double bowl of his tall-stemmed table-lamp, brittle bronze beetles and papery moths fluttered and fell in a ring of ephemeral death. Outside the tent, the squires on duty were talking softly together. It was a breach of discipline, but he was strangely reluctant to go out and deal with it. All he could hear was, now and then, a name. Through the slit of his tent-flap, like a fiery crack, shone the flame of the fire at which the rest were sitting. He had not—yet—the royal right to choose fresh boys from the noble houses of Macedon. One or two had died of fever, or fallen in war; the rest were all here still, his inheritance from the death-chamber in Babylon. He had not had much time for them lately, just taken for granted that they would be there at call. They had been with him at the Nile, ready with spare horses, waiting till he was ready to cross.

The soft voices buzzed, a little nearer now, or a little less careful. "Alexander always used to . . ." "Alexander would no more have . . ." "Never! Remember how he . . ." The voices sank; voices not of protest but of intimate, private judgment. He got to his feet, then sat down again, staring at the tiny holocaust around the lamp. Well, he trusted me with his ring; do they forget that? But as if he had spoken aloud, he seemed to hear a murmur: "But Krateros was in Syria. And Hephaistion was dead."

Seeking warmth and comfort, his memory groped back to the days of youth and glory; further yet, to the moment of exultation when, the blood of Philip's assassin red on his sword, he had first looked into those searching intent grey eyes. "Well done, Perdikkas." (He knew my name!) "When my father has had his rites, you will hear from me." The long pageant of the short years unrolled. He rode in triumph through Persepolis.

There was a break in the sounds outside. The squires had fallen silent. New voices now; older, terser, more purposeful. "You may dismiss." A single, uncertain "Sir?" Then, a little louder—Peithon surely—"I said, dismiss. Go to your quarters."

He heard the click of weapons and armor, the fall of departing feet. Not one had come in, to ask for orders, to give a warning. Two years ago, they had cheered him for defying Meleager. But then, they had only just come from the room in Babylon.

His tent-flap opened. For a moment he saw the bright leap of the fire, before the press of men blotted it out. Peithon; Seleukos; Peukestes with his Persian scimitar. And more behind them.

Nobody spoke; there was no need. He fought while he could, grimly, in silence. He had his pride; he had been, even though not for long, second to Alexander. His pride chose for him, when it was too late to think, not to die calling for help that would not come.

From the royal tent, Eurydike heard the rising confusion of rumor and counter-rumor, contention and savage cheers. Their protectors grew restless, seeking news. There was a sudden stir; a young man ran up, helmetless, red and sweating with excitement and the heat of the fire.

"King, lady. Perdikkas is dead."

She was silent, more shocked than she would have supposed. Before she could speak, Philip said with simple satisfaction, "Good. That's good. Did you kill him?"

"No, sir." (Just as if, she thought subconsciously, a real man had asked.) "It was the generals, as I understand. They . . ."

He paused. A new sound had pierced the vague fluctuant din: the roar of a lynch-mob for its prey. Soon it was mingled with the shrieks of women. For the first time she was afraid. A mindless thing was abroad, a thing that could not be spoken with. She said, "What is it?"

He frowned and bit his lip. "There's always some will go too far once they begin. They'll be after Perdikkas' people. Don't be afraid, lady; they won't harm the Kings'."

She was startled by a strong voice just beside her. "If they come here, I'll kill them."

Philip had found his ceremonial spear, and was fiercely

grasping it. The ornate blade was pointed. It took her a little time to coax it from his hands.

Ptolemy arrived in the camp next day.

He had been informed of Perdikkas' death as soon as it took place—some said before—and arrived with a cavalcade which, though impressive, had no appearance of threat. Relying on his informants, he chose to present himself as a man of honor trusting in his peers.

He was warmly welcomed, even cheered. The soldiers saw in this intrepid confidence a touch of Alexander. Peithon, Seleukos and Peukestes met and escorted him.

He had brought Arybbas, riding at his right hand. The bier of Alexander had been installed at Memphis, to await the completion of his tomb; Perdikkas from across the fatal river might almost have caught the gleam of its gold crest. Its architect now gave the generals a friendly salute. After the briefest pause they returned it; things had to be lived with as they were.

Ptolemy's terms had been agreed beforehand. The first of them was that he should address the army, to answer Perdikkas' accusation of treason. The generals had little choice. He had offered a gentleman's undertaking not to incite their own troops against them. The need for this reassurance spoke, after all, for itself.

The engineers, working at speed, had run up a rostrum. As Alexander had accustomed them to do, they put it near the royal quarters. Eurydike took it at first for a scaffold, and asked who was being put to death. They told her that Ptolemy was to make a speech.

Philip, who had been arranging his stones in an elaborate spiral, looked up alertly. "Is Ptolemy coming? Has he brought me a present?"

"No, he is only coming to talk to the

"He always brings me a present." He

able lump of yellow crystal from central

Eurydike was staring at the tall dais,

Now Perdikkas was dead, the only appo

the Kings was the distant Krateros, campa

in Syria against Eumenes. There was no

either. Was this the moment destiny had appointed? "Men

of Macedon, I claim the right to govern in my own name."

She could teach him that, and afterwards speak herself, as

she had done last night. Why not?

"Philip. Put that away now." Carefully she gave him his

words. He was not to interrupt Ptolemy's speech; she would

tell him when to begin.

A ring of soldiers cordoned the royal quarters. It was only

to protect them from the crush of the Assembly; but it

gave space, one could step out and be heard. She rehearsed

her speech in her head.

Ptolemy, flanked by Peithon and Arybbas, mounted the

steps to the rostrum, welcomed with cheers.

Eurydike was astounded. She had heard cheers already

that day, but it had never occurred to her that they could

be in honor of the recent enemy. She had heard of Ptolemy

—he was, after all, a kind of left-handed kinsman—but had

never seen him. She was young, still, in the history of Alex-

ander's army.

However often told by Perdikkas that he was a traitor,

the troops knew Ptolemy as a well-liked man, and one who

led from the front. From the start, none of them had

really wanted to go to war with him; when they met dis-

asters, there had been no bracing hatred of the enemy to

stiffen their morale. Now they hailed him as a revenant

from better days, and heard him eagerly.

He began with an epitaphion for the dead. He mourned

ey did the loss of brave former comrades, against whom would have grieved him to lift his spear. Many had been cast up on his side of the river, whom, had they lived, he would have been proud to enroll under his command. They had had their due rites and he had brought their ashes. Not a few, he was glad to say, had reached shore alive. He had brought them back; they were here now at Assembly.

The rescued men led the cheering. All had been freed without ransom; all had enlisted with Ptolemy.

And now, he said, he would speak of him who, while he lived, had united all Macedonians in pride, victory and glory. Moving many to tears, he told them of Alexander's wish to return to the land of Ammon. (Surely, thought Ptolemy, he would have said so if he could have spoken at the last.) For doing Alexander right, he had been accused of treason, though he had never lifted sword against the Kings; and this by a man who had himself been reaching for the throne. He had come here to submit himself to the judgment of the Macedonians. Here he stood. What was their verdict to be?

The verdict was unanimous; it verged on the ecstatic. He waited, without anxiety or unbecoming confidence, till it had spent itself.

He was glad, he said, that the soldiers of Alexander held him in remembrance. He would subvert no man's loyalty; the army of the Kings could march north with his goodwill. Meantime, he had heard that through the late misadventures the camp was short of supplies. Egypt had had a good harvest; it would be his pleasure to send some victuals in.

Rations were indeed disorganized, stale and scanty; some men had not eaten since yesterday. There was a furor of acclamation. Seleukos mounted the dais. He proposed to the Assembly that Ptolemy, whose magnanimity in victory had equaled even Alexander's, should be appointed Regent in Asia, and guardian of the Kings.

Cries of assent were hearty and unanimous. Hands and hats waved. No Assembly had ever spoken with a clearer voice.

For a moment—all the time he had—he stood like Homer's Achilles, this way and that dividing the swift mind. But he had made his choice, and nothing had really happened to change it. As Regent, he would have had to leave prospering friendly Egypt, where he was as good as King already; to lead his troops, who liked and trusted him, into a cutthroat scrimmage where one could trust no one —look at Perdikkas, his body hardly cold! No. He would keep his own good land, husband it, and leave it to his sons.

Gracefully but firmly, he made his speech of refusal; the satrapy of Egypt, and the building of Alexandria, were a great enough charge for such a man as himself. But since he had been honored with their vote, he would take it on himself to name two former friends of Alexander to share the office of guardian. He gestured to Peithon and Arybbas.

In the royal tent, Eurydike heard it all. Macedonian generals learned how to make their voices carry, and Ptolemy's soundbox was resonant. She heard him end his speech with some homespun army anecdote, mysterious to her, delightful to the soldiers. With a sense of hopeless defeat she observed his height, his presence, his air of relaxed authority; an ugly, impressive man, talking to men. Philip said, "Does your face hurt you?" and she found she had covered it with her hands. "Shall I make my speech now?" he said. He began to step forward.

"No," she said. "Another day you shall make it. There are too many strangers here."

He went back happily to play with his toys. She turned to find Konon just behind her. He must have been standing there quietly for some time. "Thank you, madam," he said. "I think it's better."

⊙   ⊙   ⊙

Later that day, an aide announced that Ptolemy would shortly pay his respects to the King.

He arrived soon after, saluted Eurydike briskly, and clapped Philip's shoulders in a fraternal embrace, to his beaming pleasure. It was almost as good as Alexander coming. "Have you brought me a present?" he asked.

His face scarcely flickering, Ptolemy said heartily, "Of course I have. Not here; I had to talk to all these soldiers. You'll get it tomorrow . . . Why, Konon! It's a long time, eh? But I see you take good care of him; he looks as fit as a warhorse. Alexander used to say, 'That was a good posting.' "

Konon saluted with glistening eyes; no one since Alexander had commended him. Ptolemy turned to go, before remembering his manners. "Cousin Eurydike, I hope that all goes well with you. Philip's been fortunate, I see." He paused, and took a long second look at her. In a pleasant, but different voice, he added, "A sensible wife like you will keep him out of mischief. He's had enough in his life of people trying to use him. Even his father, if Alexander hadn't . . . well, never mind. Now Alexander's gone, he needs someone to watch out for him. Well—health and prosperity, cousin. Farewell."

He was gone, leaving her to ask herself what had possessed her, a queen, to bow to a mere governor. He had meant to warn, not praise her. Another of Alexander's arrogant kindred. At least she would never see *him* again.

Roxane received him with more formality. She still took him for her son's new guardian, and offered the sweetmeats kept for important guests, warning him against the intrigues

of the Macedonian vixen. He disillusioned her, praising
Peithon and Arybbas. Where, he wondered as he nibbled
his candied apricot, would she be today if Alexander were
alive? Once Stateira had borne a boy, would he have put
up with the Bactrian's tantrums?

The child was clambering over him, clutching his clean
robe with sticky hands. He had grabbed at the sweets,
thrown down his first choice on the rug, and helped himself to more, with only the fondest of maternal chiding.
None the less, Ptolemy took him on his knee, to see Alexander's son who bore his name. His dark eyes were bright
and quick; he knew better than his mother did that he was
being appraised, and put on a little performance, bouncing
and singing. His father was always a showman, thought
Ptolemy; but he had a good deal to show. What will this
one have?

He said, "I saw his father when he was as young as this."

"He takes after both our houses," said Roxane proudly.
"No, Alexander, don't offer a guest a sweet after you have
bitten it . . . He means it for a compliment, you know."
He tried another, this time throwing it down.

Ptolemy lifted him firmly down and set him on his feet.
He resented it (That's his father, Ptolemy thought) and
started to howl (And that's his mother). It dismayed
rather than surprised him to see Roxane picking him out
his favorites from the dish, and feeding him in her lap.
"Ah, he will have his way. Such a little king as he is already."

Ptolemy got to his feet and looked down at the child; who
looked up, from the cosseting lap, with a strange uneasy
gravity, pushing his mother's hands away.

"Yes," he said. "He is the son of Alexander. Do not forget that his father could rule men because he had first
learned to rule himself."

Roxane caught the child to her breast and stared at him resentfully. He bowed and saw himself out. At the entrance of the tent with its precious rugs and gem-studded hanging lamps, he turned to see the boy gazing after him with wide dark eyes.

In the palace of Sardis, seated in the same room where she had entertained Perdikkas, Kleopatra confronted Antipatros, the Regent of Macedon.

Perdikkas' death had shocked her to her roots. She had not loved him; but she had committed her life to him, and founded on him her future. Now she looked into a void. She was still trying to come to terms with her desolation when Antipatros arrived from his campaign in Kilikia.

She had known him all her life. He had been fifty when she was born. Except that his hair and beard and brows had turned from grizzle to white, he seemed unchanged, and as formidable as ever. He sat in the chair Perdikkas had often used, spear-straight, fixing her with a faded but fierce blue eye of inflexible authority.

It was his fault, she said to herself, that Olympias had come from Macedon to Dodona to make her life intolerable. It was his fault she was here. But the habit of youth still held; he was the Regent. It was she who felt in his presence like a child who has wickedly broken something old and precious, and awaits a well-earned chastisement.

He had not rebuked her; simply addressed her as someone whose deep disgrace could be taken for granted. What was there to say? It was she who had set the landslide moving. Through her, Perdikkas had rejected the Regent's daughter, after marrying her for policy; had planned to usurp his power, loyally wielded through two kings' reigns. She sat silent, twisting a ring on her finger, Perdikkas' betrothal gift.

After all, she thought, trying to summon up defiance, he is not the rightful Regent. Alexander said he was too oppressive, Perdikkas told me so. By rights, Krateros should be Regent now.

Antipatros said in his slow harsh voice, "Did they tell you that Krateros is dead?"

"Krateros?" She stared, almost too dulled to feel it. "No, I had not heard." Handsome commanding Krateros, the soldiers' idol next to Alexander; never Persianized, Macedonian dyed in grain. She had adored him at twelve years old when he was one of her father's squires; she had treasured a strand of horsehair left in a tree by his helmet crest. "Who killed him?"

"It would be hard to say." He stared back under his white thatched brows. "Perhaps he might think that you did. As you know, Perdikkas sent Eumenes north to hold the straits against us. He was too late for that; we crossed, and divided our forces, and it was he who met with Eumenes. The Greek is clever. He guessed that if his own Macedonians knew whom they were to fight, they would mutiny and go over; so he kept it from them. When the cavalry met, Krateros' horse went down. His helmet was closed, he was not recognized; the horses trampled him. When it was over they found him dying. I am told that even Eumenes wept."

She was past tears. Hopelessness and humiliation and grief lay on her like black stones. It was grey winter with her; in silence she bore the cold.

He said drily, "Perdikkas was unfortunate." Was it possible, she thought, that there was more to come? He sat there like a judge counting the hangman's lashes. "Eumenes' victory was complete. He sent a courier south to Egypt, to tell Perdikkas. If he had heard in time, he might have persuaded his men that his cause was still worth following. When it reached the camp he was dead."

What did we do, she thought, to make the gods so angry?

But she knew the annals of the throne of Macedon. She had the answer: We failed.

"And so," Antipatros was saying, "all Eumenes got for his trouble—and he is wounded too, I hear—was to be condemned in his absence, for treason and for the death of Krateros. Perdikkas' army condemned him in Assembly . . . also, when they mutinied, a mob of them murdered Atalante, Perdikkas' sister. Perhaps you knew her."

She had sat in this room, tall and dark like her brother; rather grave, because of his other marriage, but civilly planning for the wedding; a woman with dignity. For a moment Kleopatra shut her eyes. Then she straightened. She was Philip's daughter. "I am sorry for it. But they say, Fate rules all."

He said only, "And now? Will you go back to Epiros?"

It was the final stroke, and he must know it. He knew why she had left her dead husband's land, which she had governed well. He knew that she had offered herself to Leonnatos and then Perdikkas, not in ambition but in flight. No one knew more than he about Olympias. His wronged daughter was in his house in Macedon; and Olympias' daughter was wholly in his power. If he chose, he could pack her off like a runaway child, in custody to her mother. Rather than that she would die; or even beg.

"My mother is governing in Epiros till my son succeeds. It is her country; she is Molossian. There is no place for me in Epiros any more. If you will grant it me"—the words almost scorched her throat—"I will stay here in Sardis and live privately. You have my word I shall do nothing more to trouble you."

He kept her waiting, not to punish her but to think. She was still worth, to any well-born adventurer, what she had been to two dead pretenders. In Epiros she would be restless and resentful. It would be wisest to have her killed. He

looked, and saw her father in her face. For two reigns he
had kept his oath of loyalty to absent kings; now his pride
was invested in his honor. He could not do it.

"These are uncertain times. Sardis has been fought for
time out of mind, and we are still at war. If I do as you
ask, I cannot ensure your safety."

"Who is safe in this world?" she said, and smiled. It was
her smile that for the first time made him pity her.

The army of the Kings had struck camp in Egypt. Gener-
ously victualed and politely seen off by Ptolemy, it was
marching north to its rendezvous with Antipatros.

The guardians of the Kings, appointed after Alexander's
death, were now both dead within two years of it. Their
office was held, at present, by Peithon and Arybbas.

In the two royal households, only Roxane had known the
fallen Krateros. He had convoyed her back from India with
the noncombatants, while Alexander was shortening his
life in the Gedrosian desert. She had greatly preferred him
to Perdikkas, and looked forward to being in his charge
again. She had had a new gown made to receive him in;
her mourning for Krateros had been sincere. The new
guardians were both unpromising. Peithon, fiercely devoted
to Alexander, had always regarded her as a campaign wife
who ought to know her place. Arybbas she suspected of
preferring boys. Besides, they had only visited her both
together; a precaution privately agreed between them.

To Eurydike, Krateros had been only a name. She had
heard of his death with relief; his fame had threatened a
powerful force; more powerful, she had been quick to sense,
than the present guardians could command.

Soon after the mutiny she had felt the change of air.
Morale had altered. These were now men who had success-

fully defied their leaders; some were men who had shed
blood. They had won; but their inward certainty was
wounded, not strengthened, by their victory. They had been
led disastrously and did not repent rebellion; but a navel-
cord that had nourished them had been broken, a common
trust. Without it they felt restless and bereaved.

Peithon and Arybbas had not filled up their emptiness.
Peithon they knew by repute, as all the eight Bodyguards
were known; but few, as it happened, had ever served with
him. His quality was untested, and in the meantime they
found him uninspiring. As for Arybbas, his record under
Alexander had been undistinguished except in the field of
art, which did not interest them.

If either one had given signs of hidden fire, the army
would have been his own; it was like a pack of powerful dogs
missing a master's voice. But on both alike their office sat
uneasily; both alike were anxious to avoid all occasion for
disorder, all look of rivalry or of forming factions. Both
went about their duties with sober competence.

Thus the drama dragged, the action sagged; the audience
fidgeted, coughed and yawned, began fingering its apple-
cores and half-bitten onions and crusts, but was not quite
ready yet to throw them at the actors. The play was a gift
to any talented supporting player who had the wit to steal it.
Eurydike, waiting in the wings, felt the theater pausing
and knew that her cue had come.

Had Peithon had about him the wily veterans of his old
command, some gnarled and canny phalanx-leader would
have come to his tent and said, "Sir, with respect. That
young wife of King Philip's is going about among the men
and making trouble . . . Oh, not that kind of trouble, she's
a lady and knows it too; but . . ." But Peithon's crafty old
veterans had marched with Krateros, carrying the gold with
which Alexander had paid them off. It was Eurydike who
had her allies and her faithful spies.

Her chief problem was Philip. On the one hand he was indispensable; on the other, he could not safely be produced for more than minutes. To receive men without him would invite scandal; with him, disaster.

And yet, she thought, my blood is as good and better. What is he but the bastard of a younger son, even if his father did seize the throne? *My* father was the rightful King; what's more, I was born in wedlock. Why should I hold back?

She picked up her faction first from soldiers who already knew her; her saviors on the Sardis road, the men who had guarded the tent in Egypt; some of the walking wounded who had survived the battle on the Nile. Soon many found pretexts to approach her wagon on the march, give a respectful greeting, and ask if she or the King had need of anything. She had taught Philip, if he was riding beside her, to smile and salute and go a short way ahead. Thus sanctioned by her husband, the ensuing talk was relieved of any awkwardness.

Soon, by devious ways known to soldiers not keenly scrutinized, the King had his own unofficial guard, and his wife commanded it. It was proud of itself, and its unrostered numbers grew.

The march dragged on, at foot-pace with all its followers. A young officer of her troop, remembering Alexander (they were all prone to this, and she had learned better than to check them), told how he used to leave the sluggish column and go hunting with his friends. The idea delighted her. One or other of them would ask leave to ride out for the day and join the column at sunset, taking a few comrades; a common indulgence in a peaceful area. She would get into her men's clothes and, asking no one's leave, go with them.

Of course the news got round; but it did her no harm. She was played into her role by now, fed by her audience. A confiding gallant boy, a girl receiving gratefully their protection and support, a queen who was wholly Macedonian; in all these parts they loved her.

In upland pastures, sharing a breakfast of barley-cake and thin wine, she would tell them stories of the royal house, from her great-grandfather Amyntas down; of his gallant sons, Perdikkas and Philip, both kings and both her grandfathers, fighting the Illyrians on the border when Perdikkas fell. "And because of Philip's valor they made him King. My father was a child and could not help them; so they passed him by. He never questioned the people's will, he was always loyal; but when Philip was murdered, false friends accused him falsely, and the Assembly put him to death."

They hung on her words. All of them in their youth had heard old garbled tales around the family fire; but now they were getting the real truth, straight from a queen of the royal line; they were proud, impressed and deeply grateful. Her chastity, so evident to them, so natural to her as to be unconsidered, awed them. Each one of them would boast of her notice to a dozen envious comrades when the wine-skin went round at night.

She talked, too, of Philip. He had been delicate, she said, in youth; when he grew strong, Alexander was in the full tide of his victories, and his brother felt abashed beside him. Now, he would be glad no longer to be ruled by guardians, but himself to be the guardian of the Macedonians, whose good he had at heart. But because of his modesty, Perdikkas had usurped his rights; and the new guardians did not know him, or care to know.

Philip was pleased, when he rode through the camp, to be so often and so warmly greeted. He would salute and smile; soon she advanced his instruction. He learned to say, "Thank you for your loyalty," and was happy to see how much the soldiers liked it.

Arybbas, going about, once or twice noticed these greetings, but saw no harm in them and did not report them to Peithon. Peithon for his part was paying the price for his own resentment of Perdikkas' overbearing ways. On the march to Egypt he had shrugged his shoulders and lost interest in administration. By the time catastrophe had prompted them to kill Perdikkas, Peithon was out of touch with the men. Mutiny had made them truculent; all he wanted was to get the army in one piece to the rendezvous with Antipatros. Once an Assembly could be mustered there, a permanent guardian could be elected. He would stand down with relief.

Discipline, meantime, he left to the junior officers, who in turn thought it wiser to take things easily. Eurydike's faction grew and fermented. When the army made camp at Triparadisos, the brew was ready.

Triparadisos—Three Parks—was in north Syria, the creation of some past Persian satrap who must have wished to emulate the Great King himself. Its small river had been channeled into pools and cascades and fountains, with marble bridges and whimsical stepping-stones of obsidian and porphyry. Rhododendron and azalea jeweled the gentle hills; specimen trees of great rarity and beauty, brought here by ox-train in a solid bed of their native earth, made laced or spreading patterns against a springlike sky. There were glades starred with lilies, whose green perspectives were overlooked by summerhouses with fretted screens, designed for harem ladies; and hunting-lodges of cedar-wood for the satrap and his guests.

During the years of war, the deer had been mostly poached, the peacocks eaten, and a good deal of timber felled; but to restless weary soldiers it was Elysium. Here was the ideal rest-camp in which to await Antipatros, reported a few days' march away.

The generals ensconced themselves in the chief hunting-lodge, built on a central eminence and commanding long man-made vistas. In the glades and clearings the army camped, bathing in the sparkling streams, cutting the trees for cook-fires, snaring conies and liming birds for the pot.

Arybbas found it delightful, and went off on long rambling rides with a dear friend. Peithon so much outranked him that it seemed more graceful, as well as much more pleasant, to leave discipline to him.

Peithon, who thought him a lightweight, scarcely missed him, but thought uneasily that Alexander would have found the men something to do. Games very likely, with prizes big enough to keep them on their toes for a few days' practice . . . He considered talking to Seleukos; but Seleukos, who thought he had a better claim to the guardianship than Arybbas, had been sulking lately. Well, thought Peithon, better leave it alone.

Philip and Eurydike were lodged in the summerhouse of the old satrap's chief wife. By now she had the remount officer among her partisans; a good horse was always hers for the asking. She rode about her business, wearing her man's tunic now all day. Peithon and Arybbas saw from their knoll, if they happened to look out, only a distant horseman like any other.

By now, most of the camp knew what was going on. Not everyone approved; but Philip was King, there was no getting past that; and no one loved either guardian well enough to risk the dangerous task of talebearing. No matter, the doubtful thought; any day now Antipatros would arrive.

As it happened, however, an inland cloudburst had brought the river Orontes down in flood, across Antipatros' line of march. Seeing no pressing need for haste in peaceful

country, and preferring to keep his eighty-year-old bones
dry, he made camp on rising ground and awaited the sinking of the waters.

In Triparadisos the weather was fresh and fine. Bright
and early one day, when the dew lay on the spring lilies in
crystal globes, and the birds were singing high in the fifty-
year-old trees, Peithon was wakened by an aide who rushed
into his room half dressed, still tying his girdle. "Sir, the
men . . ."

His voice was drowned by a trumpet-call which brought
Peithon to his feet, naked and staring. It was the royal
fanfare which announced a king.

Arybbas came running in, a robe thrown around him.
"It must be Antipatros. Some fool of a herald . . ."

"No," said Peithon. "Listen." He peered through the
little window. "What in the Furies' name . . . ? Get
dressed! Get armed!"

It was quick work for Alexander's veterans. They came
out on the verandah from which the satrap had aimed his
arrows at driven game. The broad glade before them was
filled with soldiers. At their head, mounted, were Philip
and Eurydike. The trumpeter stood by them, looking defiant, and full of the importance of a man who is making
history.

Eurydike spoke. She was wearing her man's tunic, and
all her armor except her helmet. She was uplifted, glowing;
her skin was clear and transparent; her hair shone; the
vitality of great daring flowed through her and rayed out
of her. She did not know, nor would have wished to know,
that Alexander had glowed like this on his great days; but
her followers knew it.

Young, clear and hard, her voice carried as far as Ptolemy's bass had done in Egypt. "In the name of King
Philip son of Philip! Perdikkas his guardian is dead. He

has no need of new guardians. He is of age, thirty years old, and able to reign for himself. He claims his throne!"

Beside her, Philip threw up his hand. His shout, startlingly loud, unfamiliar to all his hearers, boomed out. "Macedonians! Do you take me for your King?"

The cheers came crashing back, making the birds beat up from the tree-tops. "Long live King Philip! Long Live Queen Eurydike!"

A galloping horse thudded over to the lodge. The rider threw his bridle to a scared slave and strode up to the verandah. Seleukos, whose courage was legendary and who knew it, was having no one say he had skulked in his quarters during a mutiny. He was a well-liked general. In his presence, incipient shouts of "Death to the guardians!" sank away. The cheers for Philip went on.

Through the din, Seleukos bawled in Peithon's ear, "They're not all here. Play for time. Call for a full Assembly."

It was true that about a third of the men looked to have stayed away. Peithon stepped forward; shouts sank to muttering. "Very well. You're free Macedonians, you have your rights. But remember, Antipatros' men are only a few miles off, and they have *their* rights. This touches all the citizens."

There was a surge of discontent. They were keyed-up, impatient. It needed only Eurydike's "No! Now!" to set them off again.

Something made her look around. Philip was drawing his sword.

She had had to let him wear it if he was to look like a man, let alone a king. In another moment, by the look of his eyes, he would be charging at the lodge. For an instant she hesitated. Would they follow him . . . ? But he would be helpless in combat, all would be lost. "Let's kill them!" he said eagerly. "We can kill them, look."

"No. Put it back." He did so, obedient though regretful. "Now call out to the men, 'Let Peithon speak.' "

He was at once obeyed. Never before had he so impressed the soldiers. Peithon knew he could do no more. "I hear you," he said. "Yes, you can call Assembly. Don't blame me when the Regent comes and it's all to be done again. Herald, you down there. Come up here and sound."

The Assembly was held in the glade before the hunting-lodge. The men who had stayed aloof answered the summons; there were rather more than Eurydike had thought. But the glow of success was on her when, with Philip, she mounted the verandah which was to serve as rostrum. Smiling she looked around the cheering faces. The silent ones she could do without well enough.

At the far end of the platform, Peithon was talking quietly to Seleukos. She ran over in her mind what she meant to say.

Peithon came up to her. "You shall have the last word. A woman's privilege." He was sure of himself, she thought. Well, let him learn.

He stepped forward briskly to the front of the platform. He got a few boos, but soon the sound died down. This was Assembly, and ancient custom held.

"Macedonians!" His crisp bark cut through the last murmurs. "In Egypt, in full Assembly, you appointed me and Arybbas as guardians of the Kings. It seems that you've changed your minds, never mind why. So be it. We accept. No need to put it to the vote; we are both agreed. We resign the guardianship."

There was complete, stunned silence. They were like men in a tug-of-war when the other team lets go. Peithon made the most of it.

"Yes, we resign. *But*, the office of guardian stands. That

office was decreed in full Assembly when Alexander died. Remember, you have two kings, one of them too young yet to speak for himself. If you vote Philip to rule in his own right, you appoint him guardian of Alexander's son, till he comes of age. Before you vote, consider all these things."

"Yes! Yes!" They were like the audience at a play when the actors are slow to enter. Eurydike saw it. It was for her that they were waiting; and she was ready.

"Here, then," said Peithon, "is Philip son of Philip, who claims his right to rule. King Philip, come here." Meekly, with a look of faint surprise, Philip joined him at the head of the central steps. "The King," said Peithon, falling back a pace, "will now address you and state his case."

Eurydike stood frozen. The sky had fallen on her, and she had not seen that it was inevitable from the first.

She was crushed by the shock of her own folly. She sought no excuse, did not remind herself that she was only just turned sixteen. In her own mind she was a king, a warrior. She had blundered, and that was all.

Philip gazed around him, smiling vaguely. He was greeted with friendly, encouraging cheers. They all knew he was a man of few words, and over-modest. "Long live Philip!" they called. "Philip for King!"

Philip's head went up. He knew quite well what the meeting was about, Eurydike had told him. But she had told him, too, never to say a word she had not taught him first. He shot an anxious look at her, to see if she would talk instead; but she was looking straight before her. Instead, the voice of Arybbas just behind him, smooth and insistent, said, "Sir, speak to the soldiers. They are all waiting."

"Come on, Philip!" they shouted. "Silence for the King!" He waved his hand at them; they hushed each other to hear.

"Thank you for your loyalty." That was safe, he knew;

yes, they all liked it. Good. "I want to be King. I'm old enough to be King. Alexander told me not to, but he's dead." He paused, collecting his thoughts. "Alexander let me hold the incense. He told Hephaistion, I heard him, he said I'm not as slow as I'm made out to be." There were indeterminate noises. He added, reassuringly, "If I don't know what to do, Eurydike will tell me."

There was a moment's stupefied pause, then confused uproar. They turned on one another, abusive, expostulating, wrangling. "I told you, now you see." "He spoke to me like any man, only yesterday." "He has the falling sickness, it takes men so." "Well, he told us the truth, you can give him that."

Eurydike stood as if bound to the execution post. Gladly she would have been dispersed in air. Everywhere, repeated as the joke was relished, she heard, "Eurydike will tell me what to do." Encouraged by his reception, Philip was still speaking. "When I'm King, I shall always ride an elephant."

Behind him, Peithon and Arybbas looked complacently at each other.

Something in the laughter began to give Philip doubts. It reminded him of the dreadful wedding night. He remembered the magic phrase, "Thank you for your loyalty"; but they did not cheer, only laughed louder. Should he run away, would he be caught? He turned on Eurydike a face of panic appeal.

At first she moved like an automaton, carried by her pride. She gave the smug guardians a single look of scorn. Without a glance at the buzzing crowd below, she went on to Philip and took him by the hand. With ineffable relief and trust he turned to her. "Was the speech right?" he said.

Holding up her head, for a moment she faced the crowd before she answered him. "Yes, Philip. But it is finished now. Come, we can sit down."

She led him to the benches by the wall, where once the satrap and his guests had sat with their wine to await the huntsman's call.

The Assembly continued without them.

It was involved and fretful. The factions had collapsed into absurdity. A few hundred voices urged Peithon and Arybbas to resume their charge, meeting a vigorous refusal. Seleukos in turn declined. While lesser names were being tossed about, a courier rode in. He announced that Antipatros with his army was crossing the Orontes, and would arrive within two days.

Peithon, giving out this news, reminded the men that ever since Perdikkas' death both the Kings had been on their way to Macedon, where they belonged. Who, then, was more fitted than the Regent to be their guardian, now Krateros was dead? Sullenly they settled for this solution, since no one had a better one.

Quietly, during the debate, Eurydike had led her husband away. Over their midday meal he repeated his speech to Konon, who praised it and avoided meeting her eyes.

She hardly heard them. Beaten to her knees, faced with surrender, she felt her blood remembering its sources. The shade of Alexander taunted her; he, at sixteen, had held Macedon as Regent, and fought a victorious war. The fire of her ambition smoldered still under its embers. Why had she been humbled? Not for reaching too high, but too low. I was mocked, she thought, because I did not dare enough. From now on, I will claim my rights for myself.

At evening, when the sun sank over Asia and the first smoke rose, she put on her man's tunic, called for her horse, and rode out among the watch-fires.

Two days later, riding ahead of the Regent and his army, Antigonos One-Eye reached the camp at Triparadisos.

He was the man who had escaped to Macedon to reveal Perdikkas' plot. Alexander had made him Satrap of Phrygia; the grateful Regent had appointed him Commander-in-Chief of all the troops in Asia. He was now on the way to take up his new command.

He rode a Persian "great horse," being so tall that no Greek horse could carry him far. But for his eye-patch—he had lost the eye winning Phrygia for Alexander—he was still a handsome man. His even handsomer young son Demetrios, who went with him everywhere, worshipped him. Riding side by side, they made an impressive pair.

With the small column of his entourage, he entered the woodland fringes of the park. Soon, cocking his ear, he motioned his train to halt.

"What is it, Father? Is it a battle?" The boy's eyes kindled. He was fifteen, and had never yet fought in war.

"No," said his father, listening. "It's a brawl. Or mutiny. High time I came, by the sound. Forward." To his son he said, "What's Peithon about? He did well enough under Alexander. Never think you know a man whom you've only seen acting under orders. Well, he's a stopgap here. We'll see."

The prospect did not displease him. His own ambitions were great.

Eurydike had rallied to her cause about four-fifths of the army. At the head of her troops, she had appeared before the generals' lodge, announced with the royal fanfare, demanding, this time, joint rule for Philip and herself.

The three generals gazed down with revulsion, not unmixed with fear, at the mob below. It looked worse than mutinous; it looked anarchic. Eurydike herself was half aware of this. Her training in weaponry had not included military drill, and she had not considered in advance that her following would be more manageable, as well as more impressive, if she drew it up in some kind of formation. A year ago, the junior officers (the seniors had held aloof) would have managed for her; but much had happened in a year, and most of it bad for discipline. So now an armed rabble followed her; men shouldered each other to get in front, and hurled insults at the generals.

It was as boos and jeers were drowning Peithon's voice that Antigonos and his suite had come into earshot.

After his first distant glimpse, he sent Demetrios to scout ahead; it was good training for the boy. He cantered gaily into the trees, coming back to report that there was a horde of men gathered in front of what looked like headquarters, but no one to speak of at the back.

Meantime, Eurydike felt, behind her, the mass begin to seethe. She must lead them on, now, or somehow hold them back. Inherited instinct told her she would not lead them long. They would surge past her and lynch the generals. After that, her frail authority would be swept away.

"Herald, blow halt!" She faced them with lifted arms; they swayed restlessly, but came no further. She turned again to confront the generals.

The verandah was empty.

During the uproar of the last few minutes, the generals had learned that their new commander-in-chief had arrived in camp. He was in the lodge behind them.

The room inside, with its dark wood and little windows, had an air of dangerous gloom, in which, peering, they made out the towering form of Antigonos, seated in the satrap's chair; glaring at them, like a Cyclops, with his single eye. The young Demetrios, a splinter of light picking out his dazzling profile, stood like a fierce attendant spirit behind him.

Antigonos said nothing. He pierced them with his eye, and waited.

As he heard out their lamentable tale, his face changed slowly from grimness to sheer incredulity. After a disturbing pause, he said, "How old *is* this girl?"

Shouting against the impatient roar from outside, Seleukos told him.

Antigonos swiveled his head to sweep them with his eye, ending at Peithon. "Thundering Zeus!" he said. "Are you soldiers or pedagogues? Not even pedagogues, by God! Stay here." He strode out on the verandah.

The apparition from nowhere of this huge, formidable and famous man, instead of the expected victims, startled the crowd into almost total silence. Eurydike, who had no idea who he was, stared at him blankly. Philip, whom she had forgotten, began, "That's Antigonos. He . . ."

He was drowned by a boom from Antigonos' great chest. Soldiers in the front, despite themselves, straightened up and made vain shuffling efforts to dress their line.

"*Stand* back there, you sons of fifty fathers!" Antigonos roared. "*Get* back, Hades and the Furies take you! What do you think you are, a horde of naked savages? Stand up and let me look at you. Soldiers, are you? I've seen better soldiers robbing caravans. Macedonians, are you? Alexander wouldn't know you. Your own mothers wouldn't know you, not if they could help. If you want to hold Assembly, you'd better look like Macedonians, before some real ones come here and see you. That will be this afternoon. Then you can hold Assembly, if the rest agree. Clean yourselves up, curse you, you stink like goats."

Eurydike heard, dismayed, defiant shouts change to an indeterminate grumbling. Antigonos, who had ignored her, seemed to see her for the first time.

"Young lady," he said, "take your husband back to his quarters, and look after him. It's a wife he needs, not a female general. Go about your work, and leave me to mine. I learned it from your grandfather before ever you were born."

There was a wavering pause; the edges of the press began to fall away, the center to loosen. Eurydike cried out, "We will have our rights!" and some voices took it up, but not enough. The hateful giant had beaten her, and she did not know even his name.

Back in the tent, Konon told her. While she considered her next move, the smell of food reminded her that her young stomach was hungry. She waited till Philip had done —she hated to see him eating—and sat down to her meal.

Somewhere outside, a high imperious voice was arguing with the guard. Konon, who was pouring her wine, looked up. A youth came in; stunningly handsome, and hardly as old as herself. With his perfect features and clustering short gold curls, he could have posed for a Hermes to any sculptor. Like Hermes he entered lightly, and stood poised before her, fixing her with the gaze of a scornful god.

"I am Demetrios, son of Antigonos." He sounded, too, like a deity announcing himself at the opening of a play. "I am here to warn you, Eurydike. It is not my custom to make war on women. But if you harm a hair of my father's head, your life shall pay for it. That is all. Farewell."

He was gone, as he had come, through the disorganized army; his speed, his youth and arrogance cleaving his way.

She stared after this first antagonist of her own age. Konon snorted. "The insolent young dog! Who let him in? 'Not my custom to make war on women'! Who is *he* used to make war on, I'd like to know? His father should take a strap to him."

Eurydike ate quickly and went out. The visitation had spurred her flagging purpose. Antigonos was a force of nature with which she could not contend; but he was one man alone. The troops were still mutinous and ripe for

revolt. She dared not assemble them, which would bring
him down on her again; but she went among them, reminding them that Antipatros, who was coming, was not the
rightful Regent, that he feared being displaced by a rightful
King. If he was allowed, he would seek out Philip and herself and all the best of their followers, to be put to death.

Antigonos, meanwhile, had sent one of his suite to meet
the Regent and warn him to prepare for trouble. But the
Regent and his escort had come by short-cuts over the hills;
the messenger missed his way, arriving late at the tail-end
of the column. There he was told that the old man had
gone ahead with his bodyguard, long before noon.

Sitting straight on his easy-pacing charger, his stiff legs
aching on the saddle-cloth, his face set in the harsh stare
which was his mask for the pains and infirmities of age, the
Regent rode to Triparadisos. His doctor had urged him to
go by litter. But so had his son Kassandros, back in Macedon; who was only waiting to insist that his failing strength
called for a deputy—naturally, himself. Antipatros neither
trusted nor much liked his eldest son. Here in Syria, since
Perdikkas' death anything might have happened; and he
meant to arrive, the gods and physic helping him, looking
like a man to be obeyed.

The main gate into the park was dignified with great
columns topped with stone lotuses. Antipatros took the
good road which duly led him there.

Noises came from beyond; but to his annoyed surprise no
escort was there to meet him. He told his herald to an-
nounce him with a trumpet blast.

In the lodge, the generals knew, with dismay, that his
main force could not have come so quickly. Their envoy
had missed him. Almost at once a rising commotion was
heard; and a squadron leader, who had not joined the revolt,

came galloping up. "Sir! The Regent's here with no more than fifty horse, and the rebels are mobbing him."

They ran for their helmets—the rest of their armor was on—and shouted for their horses. Neither Peithon nor Arybbas had ever lacked personal courage; they reached for their javelins briskly. Antigonos said, "No, not you two. If you come they'll fall on all of us. Stay here, get anyone you can find and hold the lodge. Come, Seleukos. We'll go and talk to them."

As Seleukos mounted, vaulting upon his spear, Antigonos on his tall horse beside him, he felt for a moment the old elation of the golden years. It was welcome after the squalid affair in Egypt, from which he did not yet feel clean. When, though, in those years had he ever felt in danger from his own men?

The Regent had reached an age when discomfort and fatigue bothered him more than danger. Expecting nothing worse than disaffection, he had come in a light riding tunic and straw sun-hat, armed only with his sword. Seleukos and Antigonos, galloping down between huge cedars and deodars and spreading planes, saw the tight knot of the bodyguard sway in the press around it, the broad-brimmed hat fly off among the helmets, the vulnerable gleam of silver hair.

"Try not to draw blood," called Antigonos to Seleukos. "They'll kill us then." With a bellow of "Halt, there!" he shoved down into the press.

Their firmness, their fame, Antigonos' great height and overwhelming presence, got them through to the Regent, glaring under his white brows like an ancient eagle beset by crows, and grasping his old sword. "What's this, what's this?" he said. Antigonos gave him a brief salute (did he think there was time to chat? the old man must be failing at last) and addressed the soldiers.

Had they no shame? They claimed to respect the King; had they no respect for Philip his great father, the maker of their nation, who had appointed this man and trusted him? He had never been deposed by Alexander, only summoned for a conference while a deputy relieved him . . . Antigonos when he chose could persuade as well as dominate. The crowd sullenly parted; the Regent and his rescuers rode up to the lodge.

Eurydike had been preparing her speech for the coming Assembly, and knew nothing of the fracas till it was over. It shocked her that followers of hers might have butchered this ancient man. It offended her poetic image of war. Besides, they should be under her control and seen to be so. Only Athenian demagogues made speeches while others fought.

An hour before sunset, Antipatros' main force arrived. She heard, rumbling on into the dusk, the horse and foot filing into the parks, the shouting and creaking of the supply trains, the bustle of camp slaves pitching tents, the rattle of stacked arms, the whinnying of horses scenting their kind; and, lasting long after, the hubbub of men in animated talk, exchanging news and rumors and opinions. It was the sound of the agora, the wineshop, the gymnasium, the forum; age-long leitmotif of the lands by the Middle Sea.

After sundown, a few of her following came, to say they had been arguing her cause with Antipatros' men; one or two had cuts and bruises. But these had been little fights, stopped quickly by authority. She read the omens of discipline restored, and not wholly unwelcome. When a senior officer of the Regent's staff came to the tent, they all, to a man, saluted.

He announced that a full Assembly would be held next day, to decide the kingdom's affairs. King Philip would no doubt wish to attend it.

Philip had been building himself a little fort on the floor, and trying to man it with some ants who persisted in deserting. Hearing the message, he said anxiously, "Must I make a speech?"

"That, sir, is as you wish," the envoy said impassively. He turned to Eurydike. "Daughter of Amyntas, Antipatros sends you greeting. He says that though it is not the custom of the Macedonians for women to address Assembly, you have his leave to do so. When he himself has spoken, they will decide if they wish to hear you."

"Tell him I shall be there."

When he had gone, Philip said eagerly, "He promised I needn't make a speech if I didn't want to. Please don't make me."

She felt she could have struck him; but she held back, fearing to lose her hold on him. Indeed, she had some fear of his strength.

The Assembly was held next day with ancient procedure. Foreign soldiers, the legacies of Alexander's catholic racial mix, were barred. An impressive rostrum was raised in the biggest clearing, with seats of honor below it. As Eurydike took her place, whispering to Philip a last order to keep still, she felt in the huge throng a new, impalpable change. Something was different, and yet somehow familiar. It was the feel of the homeland, the native hills.

Antigonos spoke first. Here, at Assembly, the angry general was gone. A statesman spoke, not without the skills of oratory. With dignity he reminded them of their heroic past under Alexander, urged them not to disgrace it, and introduced the Regent.

The old man stepped briskly up to the rostrum. His own

army cheered him; no hostile sound was heard. As he looked about him, as with perfect timing he signed for silence, an unwanted voice said within Eurydike, This man is a king.

He had reigned over Macedon and Greece throughout Alexander's wars. He had crushed the sporadic risings of the south, imposed on its cities the rulers of his choice, exiled his opponents. He had defeated even Olympias. Now he was old and brittle, his height had begun to shrink, his deep voice to crack; but still, given off from his inner core, the aura of power and command surrounded him.

He told them of their forefathers, he told them of Philip who had rescued their fathers from invasion and civil war, and begotten Alexander who had made them masters of the world. They had become a tree with wide and spreading branches—he gestured to the noble timber standing round—but the greatest tree will die if its roots are sundered from its native earth. Could they bear to sink down among the barbarians they had conquered?

He told them of the birth of Arridaios, the lackwit they had honored with Philip's name; he told what Philip had thought of him, ignoring his presence in the seats below. He reminded them that in all their history, they had never had a woman ruler. Would they now choose a woman and a fool?

Philip, who had followed this peroration, nodded sagely. He found it somehow reassuring. Alexander had told him he ought not to be King, and now this forceful old man agreed. Perhaps they would tell him, now, that he could be Arridaios again.

Antipatros' own men had been for him from the start. For the rebels, it was like a slow awakening from restless dreams. All round her, like the sough of shingle on an ebb-tide beach, Eurydike felt the lapse of the withdrawing sea.

She would not, could not admit defeat. She would speak, it was her right; she had won them once and would again. Soon this old man would finish talking, and she must be ready.

Her hands had clenched, her back and her shoulders tightened; her stomach contracted, achingly. The aching turned to a cramp, a low heavy drag which, with dismay, she tried at first not to recognize. In vain; it was true. Her menses, not due for four days, had started.

She had always counted carefully, always been regular. How could it happen now? It would come on quickly, once begun, and she had not put on a towel.

She had been strung-up this morning; what had she failed to notice in all the stress? Already she felt a warning moisture. If she stood on the rostrum, everyone would see.

The Regent's speech approached its climax. He was talking of Alexander; she hardly heard. She looked at the thousands of faces round her, on the slopes, in the trees. Why, among all these humans made by the gods, was she alone subject to this betrayal, she only who could be cheated by her body at a great turn of fate?

Beside her sat Philip, with his useless gift of a strong man's frame. If she had owned it, it would have carried her up to the rostrum and given her a voice of bronze. Now she must creep from the field without a battle; and even her well-wishers would think, Poor girl!

Antipatros had finished. When the applause subsided, he said, "Will the Assembly now hear Eurydike, daughter of Amyntas, the wife of Arridaios?"

No one dissented. Antipatros' men were curious; her partisans were ashamed to vote against her. Their minds were made up, but they were prepared at least to listen. Now was the moment for a true leader to compel their hearts . . . She had come, the morning being fresh, with a himation round her shoulders. Now, carefully, she slipped it down to her elbows, to drape in a curve over her buttocks, as elegant ladies wore it in fresco paintings. Getting to her feet, taking care over her draperies, she said, "I do not wish to address the Macedonians."

Roxane had kept her tent in a good deal of alarm, among scared eunuchs and terrified women; sure that if the mutiny succeeded, Eurydike's first action would be to kill her and her child; it was, as Roxane saw it, the natural thing to do.

It took her some time to learn the Assembly's decision, since only Macedonians had attended. At length her wagoner, a Greek-speaking Sidonian, came back to report that the wife of Philip had been quite put down without a word to say; that Antipatros the Regent had been made guardian of both the Kings; and that, as soon as the great lords had agreed to divide the satrapies, he would take both royal households back to Macedon.

"Ah!" she cried, and threw off fear like a cloak. "All will be well, then. It is my husband's kingdom. They know the fool Philip from his childhood days; of course they will have none of him. It is my child they will wish to see. Alexander's mother will be waiting."

Alexander had never read her the letter Olympias had sent him when he had informed her of his marriage. She had advised him, if the barbarian girl should bear a boy, to have it smothered lest it should someday pretend to the throne. It was high time for him to visit the homeland and beget a Macedonian, as she had begged him to do before he crossed to Asia. This letter had not been placed in the royal archives. He had shown it to Hephaistion, and then burned it.

3 1 9 B. C.

BESIDE THE GREAT PALACE of Archelaos at Pella stood Antipatros' house. It was solid but unpretentious; scrupulously correct, he had always avoided a regal style. Its only adornments were a columned portico and a terrace.

The house was hushed and closed. Straw and rushes were laid on the terrace paving. Small groups of people stood at decent distances, to watch the comings and goings of the doctors and the kin: townspeople drawn by curiosity and the sense of drama; guest-friends awaiting the signal for condolence and funeral plans; dealers in mourning-wreaths and grave-goods. Hovering more discreetly, or represented by spies, were the consuls of client cities, who had the most at stake.

Nobody knew who would inherit power when the old man unclenched at last his grasp of life, or whether his policies would be continued. His last action, before he took to his bed, had been to hang two envoys bringing a petition from Athens, a father and son who he found had corresponded with Perdikkas. Neither age nor his wasting sickness had softened Antipatros. Now the watchers scanned, whenever it appeared, the set frowning face of his son Kassandros, trying to read the omens.

Near by in the palace, that famous wonder of the north, where both the Kings maintained their separate households, the tension was like the string of a drawn bow.

Roxane stood in her window, looking from behind a curtain at the silent crowd. She had never felt at home in Macedon. The mother of Alexander had not been there to receive her or admire her son, having vowed, it seemed, never to set foot in Macedon while Antipatros lived. She was still in Dodona. To Roxane the Regent had behaved with formal courtesy; but before they had crossed the Hellespont he had sent her eunuchs home. They would cause her, he told her, to be taken for a barbarian, and people would ill-use them. She was now fluent in Greek, and could be attended by Macedonian ladies. The ladies had instructed her, politely, in the local customs. Politely, they had dressed her suitably; and, very politely, made it clear that she spoiled her son. In Macedon, boys were made ready to be men.

He was now four, and in this foreign place inclined to cling to her; she in her loneliness could hardly bear him out of her sight. Soon Antipatros had reappeared—no doubt the women were his spies—and declared himself amazed that Alexander's son should have only a few words of Greek. It was time that he had a pedagogue. This person arrived next day.

The customary sober slave, Antipatros had decided, was not enough. He had chosen a vigorous young patrician, already at twenty-five a veteran of the Greek rebellion. Antipatros had noticed the strictness of his army discipline. He had had no occasion to notice that he was fond of children.

It had been the dream of Kebes' life to fight under Alexander; he had been drafted to go with the contingent Antipatros would have brought to Babylon. He had borne in silence his shattered hopes, and performed his distasteful duty of fighting fellow-Greeks instead, though his men thought him rather dour. From habit rather than intent he

Mary Renault

had accepted his appointment dourly, betraying nothing to
the Regent of the elation within.

The first sight of the dark-haired, soft-skinned, plump
child had disappointed him; but he had not expected an
Alexander in little. For the mother he had been prepared.
She clearly supposed that once out of her care her son
would be bullied and beaten; the child, seeing he was expected to be frightened, struggled and whined. Taken out
firmly without fuss, he displayed a lively curiosity and
swiftly forgot his tears.

Kebes knew the maxim of the famous Spartan nurses:
never expose a small child to fear, let him enter confidently
on boyhood. By small safe stages, he introduced his charge
to horses, to large dogs, to the noise of soldiers drilling.
Roxane, waiting at home to comfort her ill-used child,
found him full of himself, trying to describe the delights
of his morning, for which he knew only Greek.

He picked up the language quickly. Soon he was talking
incessantly of his father. Roxane had told him he was the
son of the world's most powerful king; Kebes related the
legendary exploits. He himself had been a boy of ten when
Alexander crossed to Asia; he had seen him in the height
of his glowing youth, and imagined the rest. If the child
was still too small to emulate, he could already learn to
aspire.

Kebes had been happy in his work. Now, waiting with the
rest before the straw-strewn terrace, he felt the uncertain
future shadowing his achievement. Had the child, after all,
any more in him than boys at home whom he had known
at the same age? Had the great days gone forever? What
world would he and his like inherit?

He was brooding on this when the ritual wails began.

⊙   ⊙   ⊙

Roxane heard them from her window, saw the waiting people turning to one another, and went in to pace her room, pausing sometimes to clutch the child to her breast. Alarmed, he asked what was the matter, getting no answer but, "What will become of us now?"

Five years before, in the summer palace of Ekbatana, Alexander had told her of Kassandros, the Regent's heir, whom he had left behind in Macedon from fear of treachery. When Alexander died he had been in Babylon; very likely he had had him poisoned. In Pella he had come to pay his respects to her, professedly on behalf of his sick father; really, no doubt, to look at Alexander's son. He had been civil, but unmeaningly, merely accounting for his presence; she had hated and feared his reddish freckled face, his harsh pale eyes, his look of undisclosed purpose. Today she was more frightened than during the mutiny in Syria. If only she could have stayed in Babylon, in a world she knew, among people she could understand!

Kassandros in the death-chamber stared with embittered anger at his father's shrunken corpse. He could not bring himself to lean and close his eyes; an old aunt, looking reproach, pressed down the withered lids and pulled up the blanket.

Across the bed from him stood stolid, fifty-year-old Polyperchon, his grey stubbled chin unshaven from the nightwatch; making a matter-of-fact gesture of respectful grief, his mind already on his new responsibilities. To him, not to Kassandros, Antipatros had bequeathed the guardianship of the Kings. Thorough to the last, before he drifted into coma he had sent for all the chief noblemen to witness his intent, and elicited their oath to vote for it at Assembly.

He had been senseless since yesterday; the ceasing of the

breath was a mere formality. Polyperchon, who had respected him, was glad to end the tiring vigil and get to business, which was in arrears. He had not sought his new charge; Antipatros had had to plead with him. It had been shocking and terrible, like seeing his own stern father groveling at his feet.

"Do this for me," he had wheezed. "Old friend, I beg you." Polyperchon was not even an old friend; he had been in Asia with Alexander until he rode back with Krateros. He had been in Macedon when Alexander died, and made himself useful in the southern rebellion. While the Regent had been away in nearer Asia fetching home the Kings, Polyperchon had been left as deputy. That had been the start of it.

"I took my oath to Philip." The dying man had cleared his throat, even that an effort. His voice rustled like dry reeds. "And to his heirs. I will *not*"—he choked, and paused —"be forsworn by my son. I know him. I know what . . . Promise me, friend. Swear by the Styx. I beg you, Polyperchon." In the end he had sworn, only to stop it and escape. Now he was bound.

As Antipatros' last gasps tainted the air, he could feel Kassandros' hatred flowing out at him across the body. Well, he had faced hard men under Philip at Chaironeia, under Alexander at Issos and Gaugamela. He had not risen above brigade commander, yet Alexander had picked him for the Bodyguard, and trust went no higher than that. Polyperchon, he had said, holds on.

Soon he must make himself known to the royal households, taking his eldest son; an Alexandros, he liked to think, who would bring no discredit on the name. Kassandros, who cared greatly what people thought of him, could at least be trusted to put on a handsome funeral.

◉   ◉   ◉

Eurydike had been out riding when the Regent died. She had known the news was near; when she had had it, she would be pent in the dreary, stifling rites of mourning, which it would be indecent to neglect.

For company on her ride she had a couple of grooms, and a strapping young lady of her household, chosen only because she was a hill-woman and rode well. The days of her cavalry escorts were over; Antipatros had had her vigilantly watched for conspiracy with soldiers. Only Philip himself, by bursting into tears, had persuaded him to leave old Konon. Even so, she sometimes got salutes, and still acknowledged them.

Turning back towards Pella with a westering sun behind her, the hill-shadows creeping out over the lagoon, she felt a stirring of destiny, a change of pace in the wheel of fortune. It was not without hope that she had awaited the cries of mourning.

To her, as well as to Roxane, Kassandros had paid his respects during his father's illness. Formally speaking, he had paid them to the King her husband; but with some finesse had conversed respectfully with Philip, while making it clear that his words were meant for her. The looks which, to Roxane, had seemed fierce and savage, were to Eurydike those of a fellow-countryman; not notable for beauty, but engraved with resolution and strength. He would have, no doubt, his father's hardness; but also his father's competence.

She had assumed, since he clearly did so, that he would succeed his father. She had known what he meant when he said that the Macedonians were fortunate in having *one* king of the true blood, and a queen who was no less so. He had hated Alexander, he would never allow the barbarian's child to rule. It had seemed to her that they understood each other.

The news of Polyperchon's election had disconcerted her.

She had never met him, barely knew him by sight. Now, when she came back from her ride, she found him in the royal rooms, talking with Philip.

He must have been there some time. Philip seemed quite at ease with him, and was telling him a rambling story about snakes in India. "Konon found it under my bath. He killed it with a stick. He said the little ones were the worst."

"Quite right, sir. They could get into a boot, a man of mine died of it." He turned to Eurydike, complimented her on her husband's health, begged her to call on him if he could be of service, and took his leave. Clearly it was too soon, with the Regent still unburied, to ask him about his plans; but she was angry that he had told her nothing, and presented himself to Philip without regard for her absence.

All through the long pompous funeral rites, walking in the procession with shorn hair and ash on her black dress, adding her wail to the chant of lamentation, she scanned Kassandros' face, whenever he came in sight, for some hint of purpose. It was only solid, correct, shaped for the occasion.

Later, when the men went to the pyre to burn the body, and she stood apart with the women, she heard a loud cry, and saw some kind of stir beside the fire. Then Konon was running through all the men of rank towards it. Soon he came out, with a couple of the guard of honor, carrying Philip, with flaccid limbs and open mouth. Lagging, ashamed, she went over and walked with them towards the palace.

"Madam," Konon muttered, "if you could speak to the General. He's not used to the King, he doesn't know what upsets him. I had a word with him, but he told me to remember my place."

"I will tell him." With the back of her head, she could feel scornful Roxane looking after her. One day, she thought, you will not make light of me.

In the palace, Konon undressed Philip, washed him—in the fit he had wetted his robe—and put him to bed. Eurydike in her room took off her mourning dress and combed the soft wood-ash from her ritually disheveled hair. She thought, He is my husband. I knew what he was before I took him. I did it from free choice; so I am bound to him in honor. My mother would tell me so.

She called for a warm egg posset with a splash of wine, and took it in to him. Konon had gone off with the dirty clothes. He looked up at her pleading, like a sick dog at a hard master. "See," she said, "I have brought you something nice. Never mind that you were taken ill, you couldn't help it. Many people don't like to watch a funeral pyre."

He looked at her thankfully and put his face to the bowl. He was glad that she asked no questions. The last thing he remembered, before the drumbeat in his head and the terrible white light, was the beard of the corpse blackening and stinking in the fire. It had brought back to him a day a long time ago, before he went journeying with Alexander. That had been the funeral of the King, so they had told him, but he had not known whom they meant. They had cut short his hair and put a black robe on him and dirtied his face, and made him walk with a lot of people crying. And there was his frightening father, whom he had not seen for years, lying on a bed of logs and brushwood, with a grand bedspread, grim-faced and dead. He had never seen a dead man before. Alexander was there. He too had had a haircut, the fair crop shone in the sun. He had made a speech, quite a long one, about what the King had done for the Macedonians; then, suddenly, he had taken a torch from someone who had been holding it, and stuck it in among the brushwood. Horrified, Philip had watched as the flames rushed up, roaring and crackling, running along the edges of the embroidered pall, then bursting through it; then the hair and the beard . . . For a long time afterwards, he would wake with a scream in the night, and could tell no one that he had dreamed of his burning father.

The polished marble doors closed on Antipatros' tomb, and an uneasy calm fell upon Macedon.

Polyperchon gave out that he had no wish for arbitrary powers. Antipatros had governed for an absent ruler. It was now proper that the chief men should share his counsels. Many Macedonians approved this sign of antique virtue. Some others said that Polyperchon was incapable of decision and wished to avoid too much responsibility.

The calm became easier. Every eye was upon Kassandros.

His father had not wholly passed him over. He had been appointed Chiliarch, Polyperchon's second in command, a rank to which Alexander had given high prestige. Would he be content with it? Men watched his rufous impassive face as he came and went in Pella, and said to each other that he had never been a man to swallow slights.

However, having buried his father he went quietly about his business through the mourning month. When it was up, he paid his respects to Philip and Eurydike.

"Greet him," she said to her husband when he was announced, "and then don't talk. It may be important."

Kassandros' greetings to the King were brief. He addressed himself to the Queen. "I shall be gone for a time; I am going to our country place. I have had a good deal to try me; now I mean to make up a hunting party of old friends, and forget public affairs."

She wished him well with it. He did not miss the questioning in her eyes.

"Your goodwill," he said, "has been a solace and support to me. You and the King may count on me in these troubled times. You, sir"—he turned to Philip—"are your father's undoubted son. *Your* mother's life was never a public scandal." To Eurydike he said, "As no doubt you know, there have always been doubts about the birth of Alexander."

When he had gone, Philip said, "What did he mean about Alexander?"

"Never mind. I am not sure what he meant. We shall find out later."

Antipatros' country place was an old run-down hill-fort, overlooking a well-managed rich estate. He had lived at Pella, and run the land with a bailiff. His sons had used the place for hunting parties, such as this one had, till now, appeared to be.

In the upper room of the rude keep a fire was burning on the round hearth under the smoke-hole; autumn nights were sharp in the hills. Around it, on old benches or sheepskin-covered stools, sat a dozen or so of youngish men, dressed in the day's leather and tough-woven wool, smelling of the horses which could be heard stirring and champing on the floor below, where grooms speaking Thracian were mending and waxing tack.

Kassandros, a red man in the red firelight, sat by his brother Nikanor. Iollas had died soon after he got home from Asia, of a quartan fever picked up in the Babylonian swamps; he had gone down quickly, showing little fight. The fourth brother, Alexarchos, had not been invited. He was learned, slightly mad, and mainly employed in inventing a new language for a utopian state he had seen in visions. Besides his uselessness, he could not be trusted to hold his tongue.

Kassandros said, "We've been here three days and no

one's come spying. We can begin to move. Derdas, Atheas, can you start early tomorrow?"

"Yes," said the two men across the hearth.

"Get fresh horses at Abdera, Ainos; Amphipolis if you must. Take care at Amphipolis, keep away from the garrison, someone might know you. Simas and Antiphon can start next day. Keep a day between you on the road. Two men aren't noticed, four make people look."

Derdas said, "And the message for Antigonos?"

"I'll give you a letter. You'll be safe enough if you don't draw notice. Polyperchon's a blockhead. I'm hunting, good, he can go to sleep again. When Antigonos reads the letter, tell him anything he wants to know."

They had been hunting boar in the woods all day, to keep up appearances; soon afterwards the party went off to bed, at the far end of the big room behind a dressed hide curtain. Kassandros and Nikanor lingered by the hearth, their soft voices muted by the stable sounds below.

Nikanor was a tall, lean, sandy-colored man; a capable soldier, who stood by the family loyalties and feuds and looked no further. He said, "Are you sure you can trust Antigonos? He wants more than he has, that's plain."

"That's why I can trust him. While he's stretching out in Asia, he'll be glad to have Polyperchon kept busy in Greece. He'll leave me Macedon; he knows Asia will take him all his time."

Nikanor scratched at his head; one seemed always to pick up lice on a hunting party. He caught one and dropped it in the fire. "Are you sure of the girl? She'd be as dangerous as Antigonos, if she knew how. She made trouble enough for Father, and for Perdikkas before that. But for her, Philip would be a nothing."

"M-m," said Kassandros reflectively. "That's why I asked you to watch her while I'm gone. I told her nothing, of course. She'll take our side, to keep out the barbarian's child. She showed me that."

"Good so far. But she's the King's wife and she means to be reigning Queen."

"Yes. With her descent, I daresay I shall need to marry her."

Nikanor's pale eyebrows rose. "And Philip?"

Kassandros made a simple gesture.

"I wonder," said Nikanor thoughtfully, "if she'd consent to that."

"Oh, I daresay not. But when it's done, she won't settle down with the loom and the needle, it's not in her. She'll marry me sure enough. Then she can behave herself. Or . . ." He made the gesture again.

Nikanor shrugged. "Then what about Thessalonike? I thought you'd settled for her. *She's* Philip's daughter, not his granddaughter."

"Yes, but the blood's only on the father's side. Eurydike first. When I'm King I can marry both. Old Philip would have made nothing of that."

"You're sure of your luck," Nikanor said uneasily.

"Yes. Ever since Babylon, I've known that my time has come."

A half-month later, towards evening on a day of mist and rain, Polyperchon came to the palace, urgently demanding to see the King.

He barely waited to be announced. Philip, with Konon's help, was still gathering up an arrangement of his stones which he had been elaborating all day. Eurydike, who had been waxing the leather of her cuirass, had no time to hide that either. She looked resentfully at Polyperchon, who bowed formally, having first saluted the King.

"I've nearly put it away," said Philip apologetically. "It was a Persian paradise."

"Sir. I must ask your presence at a council of state tomorrow."

Philip looked at him in horror. "I won't make a speech. I don't want to make a speech."

"You need not, sir; only assent when the rest have voted."

"On what?" asked Eurydike sharply.

Polyperchon, a Macedonian in the old tradition, thought, A pity Amyntas lived long enough to beget this meddlesome bitch. "Madam. We have news that Kassandros has crossed to Asia, and that Antigonos has welcomed him."

"What?" she said, startled. "I understood he was hunting on his estate."

"That," said Polyperchon grimly, "is what he wished us to understand. We may now understand that we are at war. Sir, please be ready at sunup; I will come and escort you. Madam.'" He bowed, about to depart.

"Wait!" she said angrily. "With whom is Kassandros at war?"

He turned on the threshold. "With the Macedonians. They voted to obey his father, who had thought him unfit to govern them."

"I wish to attend the council."

Polyperchon jutted at her his grizzled beard. "I regret, madam. That is not the custom of the Macedonians. I wish you good night." He strode out. He was furious with himself for not having had Kassandros watched; but at least he need not put up with insolence from a woman.

The council of state considered the country's dangers and found them grave. Kassandros, it was clear, would only stay in Asia to get the forces he needed. Then he would make for Greece.

Since the last years of Philip's reign, and all through Alexander's, the Greek states had been governed as Macedon ordained. Democrat leaders had been exiled, the franchise confined to men of property, whose oligarch leaders had to be pro-Macedonian. Alexander had been a long way off, and Antipatros had had a free hand. Since his supporters had enriched themselves at the expense of the many exiles, there had been violent consternation when Alexander, returning from the wilderness, had ordered them brought home and their lands restored. He had summoned the Regent to report to him in Babylon; Kassandros had gone instead. When Alexander died, the Greeks had risen, but Antipatros had crushed them. The cities, therefore, were still governed by his satellites, whose support for his son would be a matter of course.

All this time, the Greek envoys were hanging about in Pella, waiting, as they had done since the funeral, to learn the policy of the new regime towards their various states. They were now hastily summoned, and handed a royal proclamation. Much had been done in Greece, it said, which Alexander had never sanctioned. They could now with the goodwill of the Kings, his heirs, restore their democratic constitutions, expel their oligarchs, or execute them if desired. All their citizen rights would be defended, in return for loyalty to the Kings.

Polyperchon, escorting Philip from the council chamber, explained these decisions to Eurydike with punctilious care. Like Nikanor, he had reflected that she had a great capacity for mischief. She should not be idly provoked.

She listened without much comment. While the council deliberated, she too had had time for thought.

"A dog came in," said Philip as soon as his mentor had

gone. "He had a great bone, a raw one. I said to them, he must have stolen it from the kitchen."

"Yes, Philip. Quiet now, I must think."

She had guessed right, then; when Kassandros came to see her, he had been offering her alliance. If he won this war, he would depose the child of the barbarian, assume the guardianship, enthrone Philip and herself. *He* had spoken to her as an equal. He would make her a queen.

"Why," asked Philip plaintively, "do you keep walking about?"

"You must change your good robe, you will get it dirty. Konon, are you there? Please help the King."

She paced the room with its carved windows and great painted inner wall, covered with a life-sized mural of the sack of Troy. Agamemnon was carrying off Kassandra, shrieking, from the sanctuary; the wooden horse loomed between the gate-towers; in the foreground, at the household altar, Priam was lying in his blood; Andromache clasped to her bosom her dead child. All the background was fighting, flames and blood. It was an antique piece, the work of Zeuxis, commissioned by Archelaos when he built the palace.

About the hearth with its worn old stones clung faded aromatic odors, a fume of ancient burnings, and curious stains. It had been, for many years, the room of Queen Olympias. Much magic, people used to say, had been worked in it. Her sacred snakes had had their basket by this hearth, her spells their hiding-places. One or two were indeed still where she had left them, for she meant to return. Eurydike only knew that the room had a presence of its own.

Striding about it, she pondered her unspoken bargain with Kassandros, and for the first time thought, What then?

Only the child of the barbarian could beget a new generation. When he had been driven out, she and Philip would reign alone. Who would succeed them?

Who fitter than the grandchild of Philip and Perdikkas to carry on their line? To do that, she could put up with childbirth. For a moment she thought shrinkingly of teaching Philip; after all, there were women in every city who for a drachma put up with worse. But no, she could not. Besides, what if he should sire a fool?

If I were a man! she thought. On the hearth a bright fire of dry lichened apple-wood was burning, for winter was drawing on. The blackened stones under the fire-basket released drifts of old tainted incense in the heat. If I were a king, I could marry twice if I chose, our kings have often done so. A vivid recollection came to her of Kassandros' powerful presence. He had offered to be her friend . . . But then, there was Philip.

For a moment, recalling that moment of silent speech, she was on the edge of comprehension. To the last tenant of this room it would have been a simple thing, a matter of ways and means. Eurydike felt it loom, and flinched away from it. To see it must be to choose, yes or no, and she would not. She only said to herself that she must be able to depend upon Kassandros, and it was useless to think too far ahead. But the smell of the old myrrh in the stones was like the smoke of the hidden thought, buried under the smoldering embers, waiting its time.

3 1 8 B. C.

Eumenes sat in his tent on the kindly coastland of Kilikia, looking across the sea towards Cyprus' distant hills. The warm fruitful plain was a paradise after the cramped fort, perched on the high Tauros, where Antigonos had kept him invested all through last winter in the bitter mountain wind. A spring of good water, plenty of grain, and precious little else. The men's gums had started to rot from the lack of greenstuff; he had had hard work to stop them from eating the horses, on which their lives might yet depend; he had kept the beasts exercised by having their forequarters hoisted up once a day in slings, and making the grooms shout and hit at them, so that they thrashed about and got into a sweat. He had almost made up his mind to slaughter them when, of a sudden, Antigonos sent an envoy to offer terms. The Regent was dead, it was every man for himself, and Antigonos wanted an ally.

He had demanded an oath of loyalty before he lifted the siege. To Antigonos and the Kings, the envoy said. Eumenes had changed it, in the act of swearing, to Olympias and the Kings. The envoy had let it pass. Antigonos had not liked it; but by the time he knew of it, they had all got out. This was as well; Eumenes had heard from Polyperchon, appointing him in the Kings' name to Antigonos' command; which, since Antigonos would certainly not resign it, he would have to get by force. Meantime, he was to take over the provincial treasury of Kilikia, and the command of its garrison regiment, the Silver Shields.

He was now in camp with them, while they made themselves snug with stolen comforts, won by every devious ruse known to campaigners who had been, many of them, fifty years under arms. None of them had been serving for less than forty; tough, wicked old sweats whom Alexander had thought himself well shot of, and whom even he had not rid himself of without a mutiny. They had been his legacy from his father Philip, men of the phalanx, wielders of the long sarissa, all of them hand-picked fighters. They had been young men along with Philip; many were older than he would have been if he were still alive. Now, when they should be living with their loot and Alexander's bounty on their homeland farms, here they still were, hard as their boot-nails, their discharge held up by the death of Krateros and their own obdurate resistance; never yet beaten, and ready to march again.

Not a man was under sixty; most of them were past seventy; their arrogance was a proverb; and Eumenes, a generation younger, and an alien Greek, had to take them over.

He had almost refused; but while, after the siege, he was salvaging his scattered forces, he had a letter brought by land and sea from Epiros. It was from Olympias.

> I beg you to help us. Only you, Eumenes, are left, most loyal of all my friends, and best able to rescue our forsaken house. I entreat you, do not fail me. Let me hear from you; shall I entrust myself and my grandson to men who claim, one after another, to be his guardians, and then are found planning to steal his heritage? Roxane his mother sends me word that she fears for his life, once Polyperchon leaves Macedon

*to fight the traitor Kassandros. Is it best she flies to me
here, bringing the boy; or shall I raise troops and go to
Macedon?*

The letter had deeply moved him. He had been still
young when first he had met Olympias, and so had she.
Often in Philip's absences the Regent, who loathed her,
had sent Eumenes with messages to her, partly to slight
her with his lower rank, partly to keep out of her way. During many domestic quarrels Philip had done the same. To
the young Greek, she had a quality of archaic myth; a
Bacchic Ariadne, waiting the embrace of a Dionysos who
never came. He had seen her in tears, in savage mirth, in
blazing anger and sometimes in regal grace. He had no more
desired her than one desires a splendid play of lightning
over the sea; but he had adored her. Even when he had
known well that she was in the wrong, and that he had to
tell her so, he had never gone to face her without a thrill
at the heart. In fact, she had often unbent to him. He had
been a handsome young man; though she had never been
able to make him her partisan or subvert his faith to
Philip, she had enjoyed his admiration.

He knew she had harassed Alexander all through Asia,
pursuing her feud with the Regent; he remembered how,
handing him one such letter, her son had said, "By God,
she charges high rent for the nine-months' lodging she
gave me!" But he had said it half laughing; he, too, had
loved her through everything. He had left her still beautiful; and, like Eumenes, was never to see her old.

One thing he now knew at once: on no account must she
go to Macedon, with or without an army. She knew modera-
tion no more than a hunting leopardess; she would not be
there a month before she destroyed her cause. He had
written to her exhorting her to stay in Epiros till the present

war was settled; meantime, she could count on his fidelity, to her and to Alexander's son.

He did not refer to Roxane and her fears. Who would say what fancies might scare the Bactrian? During his long campaign, followed by the winter siege, he had had little news from Europe. Since the wedding at Sardis, he had barely heard of Eurydike.

Soon Antigonos would be after him—clearly the man meant to make a kingdom for himself in Asia—and he must be moving, with his native levies and their stiffening, the battle-hardened Silver Shields. From his tent-opening, he could see them now, sitting in their groupings established over half a century, while their women made their break-fasts; Lydian women, Tyrian women, Bactrians and Parthians and Medes and Indians, the spoils of their long wanderings, with a few old hardy Macedonians who had come with them from home and somehow survived. The surviving children—a third, perhaps, of those begotten along the way—chattered softly round the cook-fires, wary of a clout from their fathers; brown and honey-colored and fair, speaking their lingua franca. When camp broke, the women would pack the wagon train with all its world-wide pickings, and march once more.

On the next knoll, Eumenes could see the tents of the two commanders, Antigenes and Teutamos; crafty and stubborn old war-dogs, each old enough to be his father. Today he must call them to a war council; and would they defer to him without resentment? From wounded pride, he knew too well, comes treachery. He sighed wearily, his mind going back to the days when he and they had not been flotsam on the stream of history, but had proudly shaped its course. Those old sinners over there, he thought, even they must remember.

His mind had been suppled by years of precarious sur-

vival; now it took one of those leaps which had saved him
in places tighter than this. The day was still young, the
sunlight upon Cyprus fresh and tender. He shaved, dressed
himself neatly without ostentation, and called the herald.

"Sound," he said, "for the officers to assemble."

He had his slaves set out the stools and camp-chairs
casually, without precedence, on the grass. As the leathery
ancients, taking their time, approached, he waved them
affably to be seated. From the chair they left for him, he
rose and addressed them standing.

"Gentlemen, I have called you together to give you serious news. I have received an omen."

As he had foreseen, dead silence fell. Old soldiers were
as superstitious as sailors. They all knew what chance can
do to a man in war.

"If ever the gods gave a man a powerful dream, they
gave one to me at cockcrow. A dream more real than waking. My name was called. I knew the voice, it was Alexander's. He was in my tent, in that very chair that you,
Teutamos, are sitting on. 'Eumenes!' he said."

They sat forward in their chairs. Teutamos' gnarled
hands stroked the pinewood arms as if he touched a talis-
man.

"I begged his pardon for sleeping in his presence, as if
he had been alive. He had on his white robe edged with
purple, and a gold diadem. 'I am holding a council of
state,' he said. 'Are you all here?' And he looked about him.
Then it seemed the tent was not mine but his, the tent he
took from Darius. He was there on his throne, with the
Bodyguard around him; and you too were there, with the
other generals, waiting for his words. He leaned forward
to address us; but as he began, I woke."

Skilled in the arts of rhetoric, he had tried none here.
He had looked and spoken like a man remembering some-

thing momentous. It had worked. They were looking at one
another, but not in distrust, only wondering what it meant.

"I believe," he said, "that I divined Alexander's wish.
He' is concerned for us. He wants to be present at our
councils. If we appeal to him, he will guide us in our decisions." He paused for questions; but they hardly murmured.

"So let us not receive him meanly. Here we have the gold
of Koyinda which you, gentlemen, have guarded for him
faithfully. Let us send for craftsmen to make him a golden
throne, a scepter and a diadem, let us dedicate a tent to
him, and lay the insignia on the throne, and offer incense
to his spirit. Then we will confer before him, making him
our supreme commander."

Their shrewd, scarred faces considered him. He was not,
it seemed, setting himself above them; he was not planning to steal the treasure; if Alexander had appeared only
to him, after all he had known him well. And Alexander
liked his orders obeyed.

The tent, the throne and the insignia were ready within
a week. Even some purple was found, to dye a canopy.
When it was time to march towards Phoenicia, they met
in the tent to discuss the coming campaign. Before they
sat down, each offered his pinch of incense at the little
portable altar, saying, "Divine Alexander, favor us." All of
them deferred to Eumenes, whose divination was manifest
around them.

It did not matter that scarcely any of them had seen Alexander enthroned. They remembered him in old leather
cuirass and burnished greaves, his helmet off for them to
see him, riding along the line before an action, reminding
them of their past victories and telling them how to win
another. They did not care that the local goldsmith was
not of the highest skill. The shining of the gold, the smoke
of frankincense, wakened a memory long silted over by the

weather and war and weariness of thirteen years; of a golden chariot driving in triumph through the flower-strewn streets of Babylon; the trumpets, the paean, the censers and the cheers. For a little while, standing before the empty throne, it seemed to them that they might become what they once had been.

3 1 7 B. C.

THE SPRING SUN WARMED THE HILLS, melting the snows; first filling, then tempering the streams. Roads deep in mud and silted with scree grew firm again. The land opened to war.

Kassandros, with the fleet and army Antigonos had lent him, crossed the Aegean and landed at Piraeus, the port of Athens. Before his father was dead, he had sent a man of his own to take command of the Macedonian garrison in the harbor fort. While the Athenians were still discussing the royal decree and the offer of their ancient liberties, they found that the garrison had come down and occupied the harbor. Kassandros had sailed in unopposed.

Polyperchon, getting this news, despatched advance troops under his son Alexandros. The campaign hung fire; he prepared to set out himself. When he began to mobilize, he came to the palace to see King Philip.

Eurydike received him with the offerings of formal hospitality; she was resolved to have her presence recognized. Polyperchon, as formally, asked after both their health, listened to Philip's account of a cockfight to which Konon had lately taken him, and then said, "Sir. I have come to tell you that we shall soon be marching south together. The traitor Kassandros must be dealt with. We shall start in seven days. Please tell your people to have your baggage ready. I will see your man about your horses."

Philip nodded cheerfully. He had been on the march for

nearly half his life, and took it as a matter of course. He did not understand what the war was about; but Alexander had seldom told him. "I shall ride Whitefoot," he said. "Eurydike, which horse will you ride?"

Polyperchon cleared his throat. "Sir, this is a campaign. The lady Eurydike will of course remain at Pella."

"But I *can* take Konon?" said Philip anxiously.

"By all means, sir." Polyperchon did not look that way.

There was a pause. He awaited the storm. But in fact Eurydike said nothing.

It had never occurred to her that she could be left behind. She had looked forward to the escape from the tedium of the palace to the freedom of the camp. In the first moment of learning that she had been relegated to the women's rooms she had been as angry as Polyperchon had expected, and had been on the point of protest, when there came into her mind Kassandros' unspoken message. How could she influence affairs, trailing along with the army, watched at every turn? But here at home, with the guardian away at war . . .

She swallowed her anger at being so belittled, and held her peace. Afterwards, she found a lingering hurt that Philip had found Konon more necessary than her. After all I have done for him, she thought.

Polyperchon meantime was at the other end of the palace. Here were the quarters where the elder Philip had moved, when he ceased to share the great bedchamber with Olympias. They were handsome enough to satisfy Roxane, and her son did not complain of them. They opened onto an old orchard where he liked to play now that the days grew warmer. The plum-trees were already budding, and the grass smelled of hidden violets.

"Considering his tender years and need of his mother,"

Polyperchon said, "I shall not expose the King to the hardships of the march. In any treaties I may sign or edicts I may issue, his name will of course appear with King Philip's, as if he were present too."

"So," said Roxane, "Philip will go with you?"

"Yes; he is a grown man, it will be expected."

"Then his wife will go to care for him?" Her voice had sharpened.

"No, madam. War is not women's business."

She opened her black eyes till the clear white showed all round. "Then," she cried, "who will protect my son and me?"

What could the foolish woman mean? He brought down his brows in irritation, and answered that Macedon would be left well garrisoned.

"Macedon? Here, in this house, who will protect us from that she-wolf? She will only wait to see you gone before she murders us."

"Madam," he said testily, "we are not now in the wilds of Asia. The Queen Eurydike is a Macedonian and will obey the law. Even if she wished otherwise, she would not dare touch the son of Alexander. The people would have her blood."

He left, thinking, Women! They make war seem a holiday. The thought consoled him among his cares. Since the new decree, nearly all the Greek cities were in a state of civil war, or on the verge of it; the coming campaign promised every kind of confusion and uncertainty. Roxane's notion that he would add to his troubles by taking that termagant girl along was enough to make a man laugh.

A week later the army marched. From the balcony of the great bedchamber, Eurydike had watched the troops assemble on the great drill-field where Philip and Alexander

had trained their men; had seen the long column wind
slowly down alongside the lagoon, making for the coast
road to the south.

As the lumbering baggage train began to follow the soldiers, she looked about her at the horizons of the land she
still meant to rule. Over the near hills was her father's
house where Kynna had taught her war. She would keep
it for her hunting-lodge, her private place, when she was
Queen.

She looked down idly at the grandiose front of the palace
with its painted pediment and columns of colored marble.
On the broad steps the tutor Kebes came down, the child
Alexander beside him, trailing a wooden hobby-horse by its
scarlet bridle. The child of the barbarian, who must not
reign. How would Kassandros deal with that? She frowned.

Roxane behind her curtains grew weary of watching
wagons, a sight too long familiar. Her eyes wandered. There
on a balcony, brazenly showing herself to the world like a
harlot looking for trade, stood Philip's mannish wife. What
was she staring at so fiercely? Roxane's ear caught the
sound of her own child's piping chatter. Yes, it was at him
that she was looking! Swiftly, Roxane made the sign
against the evil eye, and ran to her casket. Where was the
silver charm her mother had given her against the malice
of harem rivals? He must put it on. A letter was beside it,
with the royal seal of Epiros. She reread it, and knew what
she must do.

Kebes proved easy to persuade. The times were doubtful;
so was his own future. He could well believe that the son
of Alexander was in danger, and not only from his mother's
spoiling. He had softened to Roxane; she might need protection too. It was eleven years since her beauty had hit
Alexander like a fiery arrow across a torchlit hall; but her
looks had been tended, her legend lived in them still. It

seemed to the young man that he too could enter the legend, rescuing the woman Alexander had loved, and his only child.

It was he who chose the litter-bearers and the armed escort of four; who swore them to secrecy, who bought the mules, who found a messenger to ride ahead with news of their coming. Two days later, just before dawn, they were on the mountain road making for Dodona.

The royal house had a steep-pitched roof to throw off the winter snows. Roofs in Molossia gave no platform for watchers. Olympias stood in the window of the King's bed-chamber, which she had taken when her daugher left it. Her eyes were fixed on a curl of smoke from the nearest hilltop. On three heights in an eastward line she had had beacons laid, to signal the approach of her daughter-in-law and grandson. Now she sent for the captain of the palace guard, and ordered him to meet them with an escort.

Olympias had assented to her age. In the month of mourning for Alexander she had washed the paint from her face, and covered her hair with a dark veil. When the month was over, and she put the veil away, her hair was silky white. She was sixty, and lean where she had been slim. Her fine redhead's skin was brittle like pressed petals; but lacking color the proud bone showed more. Under their white brows, the smoky grey eyes could still pale dangerously.

She had waited long for this day. As the emptiness of loss came home to her, she had craved to touch this last living vestige of him; but the child was unborn, there was no remedy for waiting. With the wars' delays, her longing dulled and earlier doubts returned. The mother was a barbarian, a campaign wife, whose son he had meant to pass over—in a secret letter he had told her so—if the Great King's daughter had borne a boy. Would anything remain of him in this stranger?

When the child reached Macedon, her feud with Antipatros had left her only two ways to go back there, submission or war. The first was unthinkable; against the second Eumenes, on whom she must depend, had warned her. Then Roxane had written begging for a refuge, and she had answered, "Come."

Next day the cavalcade arrived; the tough Molossian troopers on their shaggy ponies, two disheveled waiting-women on stumbling donkeys, a covered litter with its mules. Her eyes on the litter, she did not see at first the young man who carried across his horse's withers a six-year-old boy. He lifted him down and spoke to him quietly, pointing. Resolutely, on legs more a boy's than a child's, he walked up the steps, gave her a soldier's salute, and said, "May you live, Grandmother. I am Alexander."

She took him between her hands while the company made respectful gestures, and kissed his brow, dirty with travel, and looked again. Kebes had fulfilled his trust. Alexander's son was no longer the podgy nursling of the harem tent. Olympias saw a beautiful young Persian, fine-boned and dark-eyed. The hair was cut sloping to the nape, as Alexander used to wear it, but it was straight, heavy, and raven-black. He looked up at her from under his fine dark brows and his blue-brown, thick-lashed eyelids; and though there was nothing of him anywhere that was Macedonian, she saw Alexander in his upward, deep-set gaze. It was too much, it took her a few moments to gather herself together. Then she took his pale slender hand. "Welcome, my child. Come, bring me to your mother."

◉   ◉   ◉

The roads from Pella down into Greece had been smoothed since old Philip's reign for the swift march of armies. The roads to the west were rough. Despite the difference in distance, therefore, it was at about the same time that Polyperchon in the Peloponnese, and Olympias in Dodona, got news from Macedon that Eurydike had assumed the regency.

Polyperchon got, in addition, an order signed by her, directing him to hand over to Kassandros the Macedonian forces in the south.

Speechless for a while, the old soldier kept his head, offered the courier wine without disclosing the message, and asked for news. It seemed that the Queen had called Assembly, and addressed it with great spirit. The barbarian woman, she told them, had fled the land with her child, fearing the anger of the Macedonians; she would do well not to return. All who had known Alexander would testify that the child looked nothing like him. He had died before the birth, had never acknowledged the infant; there was no proof that he was the father. Whereas she herself had on both sides the Macedonian royal blood.

For a time, Assembly had been in doubt. But Nikanor, Kassandros' brother, had given her his voice and the whole clan had come in with him. That had carried the vote. She was now giving audiences, receiving envoys and petitioners, and in all ways acting as reigning Queen.

Polyperchon thanked the man, rewarded and dismissed him, cursed to relieve his feelings, and sat down to think. He quickly decided what he himself would do; and, soon afterwards, what to do with Philip.

He had had hopes of him, if he could be removed from his wife's control; but had soon learned better. At first, he had been so docile that it had seemed safe to produce him, set up impressively on a gold-canopied throne, for a delegation from Athens. In the midst of a speech he had guffawed at a rhetorical trope which, like a child, he had taken literally. Later, when Polyperchon had rebuked a speaker, the King had grabbed at his ceremonial spear; if Polyperchon had not grappled with him in front of everyone, the man would have been run through. "You said," he had protested, "that he told lies." The delegation had been dismissed too hastily, causing a political disaster and some lives.

It was now clear to Polyperchon that all Philip was good for was to hold the throne for Alexander's son, who had better come of age quickly. As for Eurydike, her claim was plain usurpation.

Konon came when sent for, saluting woodenly. His silent "I told you so" had irked Polyperchon after the incident of the spear and several others. Good riddance to both of them. "I have decided," he said, "to send back the King to Macedon."

"Sir." The general felt, reverberating from this blank surface, knowledge that the campaign had gone badly, that he had had to raise the important siege of Megalopolis, that Kassandros still held the Piraeus and might well get Athens, in which event the Greek cities would join him. But that was irrelevant now.

"I will give you an escort. Tell the Queen that I am sending back the King in obedience to her wishes. That is all."

"Sir." Konon left, relieved. He could have told them all beforehand, if he had been asked. Now, he thought, they would all have a chance to live in peace.

At a massive table of inlaid hardstone with lion-feet of gilded bronze, Eurydike sat in the royal study. King Archelaos, nearly a century ago, had designed this splendid sanctum when he built the palace to stun foreigners with its magnificence. From it, whenever they were at home, Philip the Second had ruled Macedon and his spreading conquests, and Alexander had ruled all Greece. Since Alexander had gone to rule the world from a moving tent, no king had sat at the table under Zeuxis' mural of Apollo and the Muses. Antipatros, rigidly correct, had governed from his own house. She had found everything swept, polished, scrupulously neat, and empty.

It had awaited a tenant for seventeen years, as long as she had lived. Now it was hers.

When she called Assembly to claim the regency, she had not told Nikanor of what she meant to do. She had guessed he would think it rash, but that confronted with the fact he would support her, sooner than hurt his brother's cause. She had thanked him afterwards, but had fended off his efforts to advise her. She meant to rule for herself.

Awaiting news from the south, she had spent most of her time on what she most enjoyed, exercising the army. She felt, at last, that she was fulfilling her true destiny when she rode along a line of cavalry, or took the salute of the phalanx presenting their great sarissas. She had seen a good deal of army drill and talked to many soldiers; she knew all the procedure. They were amused and delighted with her. After all, they thought, they were just a garrison army; if there was action the generals would of course resume command. Taking this for granted, they performed for her indulgently.

Her fame was spreading, Eurydike, the warrior Queen of Macedon. One day she would strike her own coinage. She was tired of seeing the eager long-nosed face of Alexander hooded in his lion-skin. Let Herakles give place to Athene, Lady of Citadels.

Each day she waited to hear whether Polyperchon had surrendered his command to Kassandros as she had ordered. So far she had heard from neither. Instead, unheralded, Philip returned to Pella. He carried no despatches and did not know where his guardian was going next.

He was delighted to be home, and ran on at length about his adventures on campaign, though all he knew of the debacle at Megalopolis was that the wicked people in the fort had put down spikes to hurt the elephants' feet. Even so, had she had patience to listen to his ramblings she might have learned something of value. He had been present, as a matter of form, at several councils from which Konon was excluded. But she was busy, and answered him with half her mind. She seldom asked where he was; Konon took him about and amused him. She had ceased to issue orders in his name, and used only her own.

Until just lately, everything had gone smoothly. She understood the disputes of Macedon, nearly all brought by petitioners in person. But suddenly, all at once, a flood of business was coming in from the south, even from Asia. It had not yet occurred to her that all these matters had been going to Polyperchon, who had dealt with them in Philip's name. Now, Philip was here; and Polyperchon, for good reasons, was no longer accessible.

She looked with dismay at petitions from towns and provinces she had never heard of, seeking judgments on land claims; reports on delinquent, distant officials; long obscure letters from priests of temples founded by Alexander, seeking guidance about rituals; reports from Asian satraps on the encroachments of Antigonos; passionate protests from pro-Macedonians of Greek cities, exiled or dispossessed under the new decree. Often she had trouble even in reading the script with its many contractions. Turning over in helpless bewilderment this heap of documents, she reflected unwillingly that it must be a fraction of what Alexander had dealt with in an army camp, in the rest-breaks of conquering an empire.

The chief secretary, who knew all this business, had gone south with Polyperchon, leaving only a subordinate at Pella. She would have to send for this underling and try to hide her ignorance. She rang the silver bell with which, long ago, her grandfather had summoned Eumenes.

She waited. Where was the man? She rang again. Urgent muttering voices sounded outside the door. The secretary came in, shaken, without apology for delay, without asking her what she wanted. She saw fear in his face, and the resentment of a frightened man towards someone who cannot help.

"Madam. There is an army on the western border."

She sat up with brightening eyes. The border wars were the ancient proving-ground of the Macedonian kings. Already she saw herself in arms, leading the cavalry. "The Illyrians? Where have they crossed?"

"Madam, no. From the southwest. From Epiros. Won't you see the messenger? He says Polyperchon is leading them."

She straightened in her chair, her pride answering his fear. "Yes, I will see him. Bring him in."

It was a soldier, anxious and dusty, from a garrison fort on the Orestid hills. He begged pardon, his horse had gone lame, he had had to come on by mule, a poor beast, all he could get. It had lost him a day. He gave her the despatch from his commander, shocked to discover how young she was.

Polyperchon was on the border, announcing by heralds that he had come to restore Alexander's son. He was in the country of his clan and kindred, and many of them had joined him. From the fort itself there had, unhappily, been some desertions, and the post was gravely undermanned. Between the lines, she read the intention to surrender.

She sent the man out, and sat looking before her. On the far side of the room stood a bronze youth looking back, a Hermes, holding a lyre. He stood on a plinth of green marble, Attic, poised; his gravity seeming stern to an eye used to modern prettiness. A subtle melancholy in his face had once made her ask an old palace steward who he was. Some athlete, said the man, done by Polykleitos the Athenian; he had heard it was during the great siege when the Spartans won the war, and Athens was broken. No doubt King Archelaos' agents had picked it up cheaply afterwards; there was a great deal, then, to be had for very little.

The bronze face gazed at her with eyes of dark-blue lapis laid into white glass, between lashes of fine bronze wire. They seemed to say, "Listen. I heard the footsteps of Fate."

She got to her feet, confronting him. "You lost. But I am going to win." Presently she would give orders to raise the army and prepare to march. But first she must write to Kassandros and call him to her aid.

Travel to the south was quick. Her letter reached him in three days.

He was camped before a stubborn fort in Arkadia. That dealt with, he planned to reduce the Spartans, those relics of an outworn past. They had come down to walling their city, that proud open town whose only bulwark had been its warriors' shields. Their soul was cowed, they would soon be under his hand.

Athens had made terms and had let him appoint its governor. The officer who had taken the Piraeus for him had expected the post; but he had been looking too ambitious, and Kassandros had had him disposed of in a dark alley.

The new governor was a harmless, obedient client. Soon, thought Kassandros, he must visit the Lyceum. There was a great deal to be done there.

Eurydike's appointment of him as supreme commander, though too precipitate, had helped to sway many wavering Greek allegiances. Even some who had killed their oligarchs and restored democracy were now thinking again. He would be glad to finish with the south; he was interested in war only as an instrument of policy. He was not a coward, he could get his orders obeyed, he was a competent strategist, and that was all. Deep in his being, burned there since his youth, was a bitter envy of Alexander's magic. No one would cheer himself hoarse for Kassandros, no one be proud to die for him; his men would do what they were paid to do. That vain tragedian, he thought; let us see how he looks to the new age.

The news that Polyperchon was withdrawing his forces and heading north had been no great surprise. He was old and tired and a loser; let him go home with his tail between his legs, and bed down in his kennel.

Eurydike's despatch, therefore, had been a rude shock to him. The stupid, reckless girl, he thought. Had this been the time to denounce Alexander's brat? He fully intended, once Philip was out of the way, to govern at first as the boy's regent. There would be plenty of time before he came of age. Now, instead of biding the hour, as anyone would who had the beginning of statecraft, she had flung the country into a succession war. Did she know no history? One of her family should have remembered better than that.

Kassandros reached a decision. He had made a bad bargain and must get it off his hands, quickly, like an unsound horse. Afterwards, everything would be simpler.

He sat down to write a letter to his brother Nikanor.

◉   ◉   ◉

With banners and standards streaming, with shrill flutes and the deep-toned aulos giving the time, the royal army of Macedon marched through the high western hills towards Epiros.

Summer had come. The thyme and sage bruised by the tramping feet censed them with aromatics; the uncurled bracken stood waist-high; heather and sorrel purpled the moors. The burnished helmets, the dyed horsehair plumes, the little bright pennants on the tall sarissas, glittered and glowed in long streams of moving color, winding down through the passes. Herd-boys on the crags cried the warning that soldiers were coming, and called their little brothers to help drive in the sheep.

Eurydike in burnished armor rode at the head of the cavalry. The heady air of the hills exalted her; the wide prospects from the heights stretched before her like worlds to conquer. She had always known that this was her nature and her fate, to ride to victory like a king, her land behind her and her horsemen at her side. She had her Companions as a ruler of Macedon should. Before she marched she had made it known that when the war was won the lands of the western traitors would reward her loyal followers. Not far off, led by Nikanor, rode the clan of the Antipatrids, a hearteningly solid force.

Their chief had not appeared, nor sent her word. Clearly, as Nikanor said, some misadventure had overtaken her messenger. It would be better to send again, and she had done so. Then, too, the troops in the Peloponnese were often on the move, and that might have caused delay. At all events, said Nikanor, he himself was doing as he knew Kassandros would wish.

Philip on his big steady horse was riding near by; he, also, panoplied for war. He was still the King, and the troops would expect to see him. Soon, when they came near the enemy, he must be settled in a base-camp out of the way.

He was placid and cheerful, traveling with an army; he could hardly remember when this had not been his life. Konon was with him, riding as usual half a length behind. Philip had wanted him alongside, the better to talk about the sights upon the way; but Konon, as usual, had said it would not be proper before the men. Dimly, after the years, Philip still missed the days of strangeness and changing marvels, when his life had moved with the journeys of Alexander.

Konon had withdrawn into his thoughts. He, too, could have wished for Alexander, and for more urgent reasons. Ever since his young master Arridaios had become King Philip, he had known that the time would come which was coming now, had felt it in his bones. Well, he thought, it was an old proverb, not to look back at the end. He was nearly sixty, and few men lived longer.

A rider showed briefly on the crest of the ridge ahead. A scout, he thought; had the girl seen? He looked at Philip ambling along, a half-smile on his broad face, enjoying some pleasant fantasy. She ought to take more thought for him. Supposing . . .

Eurydike had seen. She too, long before this, had sent out scouts. They were overdue; she sent off two more. The army moved on, bright, burnished, the flutes giving the time.

Presently, when they reached the next ridge, she herself would ride up and survey the terrain. That, she knew, was the duty of a general. If the enemy was in sight she would study his dispositions, then hold a war council and dispose her troops.

Derdas, her second in command—a new promotion, so many of the higher ranks had marched with Polyperchon —rode up to her, young, lank-limbed, frowning with re- sponsibility. "Eurydike, the scouts ought to be back; they may have been taken. Shouldn't we make sure of the high ground? We may be needing it."

"Yes." It had seemed that the gallant march in the fresh morning would go on till she herself chose to end it. "We will lead with the cavalry, and hold it till the infantry comes up. Form them up, Derdas; you take the left wing, and of course I shall take the right."

She was issuing further orders, when a harsh, peremptory cough sounded at her elbow. She turned, startled and put out. "Madam," said Konon. "What about the King?"

She clicked her tongue impatiently; far better to have left him behind at Pella. "Oh, take him back to the wagon train. Have a tent set up there."

"Will there be a battle?" Philip had come up, looking interested and eager.

"Yes," she said quietly, mastering her irritation before the onlookers. "Go to the camp now, and wait till we come back."

"Must I, Eurydike?" A sudden urgency disturbed Philip's placid face. "I've never been in a battle. Alexander never let me. None of them let me. Please let me fight in this one. Look, here's my sword."

"No, Philip, not today." She motioned to Konon; but he did not move. He had been watching his master's face; now he looked into hers. There was a short silence. He said, "Madam. If the King wishes. Maybe it would be best."

She stared at him, at his sorrowful and sober eyes. Understanding, she caught her breath. "How dare you? If there were time I would have you flogged for insolence. I will see you later. Now obey your orders."

Philip hung his head. He saw that he had misbehaved, and everyone was angry. They would not beat him; but the memory of ancient beatings moved in his mind. "I'm sorry," he said. "I hope you win the battle. Alexander always did. Goodbye." She did not look after him as he went.

Her favorite horse was led up, snorting and tossing its

head, full of high spirits. She patted the strong neck, grasped the tough mane on the withers, and vaulted with her spear onto the scarlet saddle-cloth. The herald stood near, his trumpet at the ready, waiting to sound the advance.

"Wait!" she said. "First I will address the men."

He gave the brief flourish for attention. One of the officers, who had been watching the ridge ahead, began to speak; but the trumpet drowned it.

"Men of Macedon!" Her clear voice carried as it had on the march from Egypt, at Triparadisos, at the Assembly where they had voted her the regency. Battle was near; let them only be worthy of their fame. "If you were brave fighting against foreign enemies, how much more gloriously you will fight now, defending your land, your wives, your . . ."

Something was wrong. They were not hostile; they were simply not attending, staring past her, speaking to one another. Suddenly, young Derdas, gravity changed to urgency, grasped her horse's headstall, wheeled it round to face forward, and shouted, "Look!"

All along the crest of the ridge ahead, a dark dense bristle had sprouted. It was thick with spears.

The armies faced each other across the valley. Down at the bottom was a stream, low now in summer, but with a wide bed of stones and boulders bared by winter scour. The horsemen on both sides looked at it with distaste.

The western rise which the Epirote army commanded was higher than the Macedonian position. If their full strength was on view, however, they were outnumbered three to two on foot, though somewhat stronger in cavalry.

Eurydike, standing on an outcrop to survey the field, pointed this out to Derdas. The enemy flanks were on

278 [Mary Renault

broken, brushy ground which would favor infantry. "Yes," he said, "if they let our infantry get there. Polyperchon may be no"—he just stopped himself from saying Alexander—"but he knows better than that."

The old man could be clearly seen on the opposite slope, in a clump of horsemen, conferring. Eurydike's men pointed him out to one another, not feeling him a great menace in himself, but bringing the comfortless thought that they were about to fight old comrades.

"Nikanor." (He had left his contingent to join the council of war.) "There is still no signal from the beacon?"

He shook his head. The beacon had been laid on a peak behind them, commanding a view of the southern pass. "Without a doubt Kassandros would be here, if something had not prevented him. Perhaps he has been attacked upon the march. You know the confusion in the Greek states, thanks to Polyperchon."

Derdas made no comment. He did not like Nikanor's disposition of his men, but this was no time to say so.

Eurydike stood on the tall flat rock, shading her eyes to look across at the enemy. In her bright helmet and gold-studded cuirass, her knee-high kilt of scarlet wool above her shining greaves, she looked a gallant figure. Derdas thought to himself that she looked like a boy actor in a play, masked to enact the young Achilles at Aulis. It was she, however, who first saw the herald.

He emerged from the knot around Polyperchon, and rode down towards them; unarmed, bareheaded, with a white wool fillet round his grey hair, carrying a white rod bound with olive; a man with presence.

At the stream-bed he dismounted, to let his horse pick its way over the stones. Having crossed, he walked a few paces forward and waited. Eurydike and Derdas came down to meet him. She turned to Nikanor to join them, but he had disappeared into the mass.

The herald had voice as well as presence, and the curve of the slope threw up his words like the hollow bowl of a theater.

"To Philip son of Philip, to Eurydike his wife, and to all the Macedonians!" He sat at ease on his strong stocky horse, a ward of the gods, protected by immemorial custom. "In the name of Polyperchon, guardian of both the Kings." He paused, just long enough for suspense. "Also," he added slowly, "in the name of Queen Olympias, daughter of King Neoptolemos of Molossia; wife of Philip, King of the Macedonians; and mother of Alexander."

In the silence, a dog could be heard to bark in a village half a mile away.

"I am charged to say this to the Macedonians. Philip found you pressed by enemies and torn with civil wars. He gave you peace, reconciled your factions, and made you masters of all Greece. And by Queen Olympias herself he was the father of Alexander, who made the Macedonians masters of the world. She asks you, have you forgotten all these benefits, that you will drive out Alexander's only son? Will you take up arms against Alexander's mother?"

He had thrown his voice past Eurydike and her staff, to the silent ranks of men. When he ceased, he wheeled round his mount, and pointed.

Another rider was coming from the group above. On a black horse, in a black robe and veil, Olympias paced slowly down towards the stream.

She rode astride, in a wide skirt that fell to the tops of her crimson riding-boots. The headstall of her horse glittered with gold rosettes and silver plaques, the spoils of Susa and Persepolis. She herself wore no ornaments. A little way above the stream, where she could be seen by everyone, and where Eurydike had to look up to her, she drew rein and threw back the dark veil from her white hair. She said nothing. Her deep-set grey eyes swept the hushed murmuring ranks.

Eurydike was aware of the distant gaze pausing upon her. A light breeze floated back the black veil, stirred the horse's long mane and ruffled the snowy hair. The face was still. Eurydike felt a shiver go through her. It was like being glanced at by Atropos, the third Fate, who cuts the thread.

The herald, who had been forgotten, now suddenly raised his loud voice again. "Macedonians! There before you is the mother of Alexander. Will you fight against her?"

There was a pause, like the pause of a rearing wave before it topples to break. Then a new sound began. It was a slight rapping, at first, of wood on metal. Then it was a spreading rattle, a mounting beat; then, echoing back from along the hillside, a thunderous drumming, the banging of thousands of spear-shafts upon shields. With a united roar the royal army cried, "No!"

Eurydike had heard it before, though never so loudly. It had greeted her when she was voted Regent. For many long seconds, she thought they were defying the enemy, that the shouting was for her.

Across the stream, Olympias raised her arm in a regal gesture of acknowledgment. Then, with a beckoning movement, she turned her horse. She moved up the hill like a leader of warriors, who need not look back to be sure that they will follow.

As she went up in triumph, the whole prospect on the opposite slope fragmented. The royal army drawn up in its formations, the phalanx, the cavalry, the light-armed skirmishers, ceased to be an army, as a village struck by an earthquake ceases to be a street. There was just a mass of men, with horses heaving about among them; shouting to each other, gravitating to groups of friends or clansmen; the whole united only in a single disordered movement, going like landslide pebbles down towards the stream.

Eurydike was overwhelmed in it. When she began to shout orders, to exhort them, she was scarcely heard. Men jostled her unnoticing; those who saw her did not meet her eyes. Her horse grew restive in the crush and reared, she was afraid of being thrown and trampled.

An officer thrust through to her, held the horse and quieted it. She knew him, he was one of her partisans from the very first days in Egypt, a man about thirty, light-haired, with a skin still yellowed from some Indian fever. He looked at her with concern. Here at last, she thought, was a man in his right mind. "How can we rally them?" she cried. "Can you find me a trumpeter? We must call them back!"

He ran his hand over the horse's sweating neck. Slowly, like a man explaining something simple to a child, which even a child must see, he said, "But, madam. That is Alexander's mother."

"Traitor!" She knew it was unjust, her anger belonged elsewhere. She had seen, at last, her real enemy. Not the terrible old woman on the black horse; she could be terrible only because of him, the glowing ghost, the lion-maned head on the silver drachmas, directing her fate from his golden bier.

"There's no help for it," said the man, forbearingly, but with little time to spare for her. "You don't understand. You see, you never knew him."

For a moment she grasped her sword; but one cannot kill a ghost. The jostling press below was beginning to cross the stream. Names were shouted, as the soldiers of Polyperchon welcomed back old friends.

He sighted a brother in the crush, and gave an urgent

wave, before turning back to her. "Madam, you were too young, that's all. You made a good try of it, but . . . There's not a man wishes you harm. You've a fresh horse there. Make for the hills before her people cross over."

"No!" she said. "Nikanor and the Antipatrids are over there on the left. Come, we'll join them and fall back and hold Black Pass. *They'll* never make peace with Olympias."

He followed her eyes. "They won't do that. But they're off, you see."

She saw, then, that the force on the heathery rise was moving. Its shining shields were facing the other way. Its head was dipping already over the skyline.

She looked round. The man had sought his brother, and vanished down the hill.

Dismounting, she held her horse, the only living thing that would still obey her. As the man had said, she was young. The despair she felt was not the grim resignation of Perdikkas, paying the price of failure. Both had played for power and lost; but Perdikkas had never put his stake upon love. She stood by the fretting horse, her throat choking, her eyes blinded with tears.

"Eurydike, come, hurry." A little group, some of her court, had found its way to her. Wiping her eyes, she saw they were not defiant but afraid; marked men all of them, old allies of Antipatros, who had thwarted Olympias' intrigues, had intrigued against her, had crossed her will and wounded her pride and helped drive her out of Macedon. "Quickly," they said. "Look, that cavalry there, those are Molossians, they're heading this way, it is you they will be looking for. Quickly, come."

She galloped with them cross-country, cutting the corners of the rutted road, letting her horse pick its line over the heath; thinking how Nikanor had said that he was doing as he knew his brother would wish; remembering

Kassandros' red hair and inflexible pale eyes. No messenger
from her had fallen among thieves; he had had her cry for
help, and decided she was expendable.

On the shoulder of the next hill they stopped to breathe
their horses, and looked back. "Ah!" said one of them.
"That was what they were after, to loot the baggage train.
There they are at it; so much the better for us." They
looked again; and there was a silence which no one liked
to break. In the distance they saw, among the wagons, a
single tent with men surrounding it. A small far-off figure
was being led outside. Eurydike realized that from the
moment when Olympias had appeared and her army
melted, she had forgotten Philip entirely.

They made their way east towards Pella, avoiding the look
of fugitives as best they could, using for hospitality the
mesh of guest-friendship that webbed every Greek land,
excusing by their haste their lack of servants. They kept
ahead of the news, pretending that a treaty had been signed
upon the border, that they were hurrying to Pella to call
Assembly and confirm the terms which the army in the
west had agreed to. In this way they lodged for several
nights, and left each morning aware of a cloud of doubt.

Nearing Pella, she glimpsed the tall keep of her father's
house. With unbearable longing she remembered the quiet
years with Kynna, the small boyish adventures and heroic
dreams, before she entered the great theater of history, to
enact a tragedy in which no god came down at last from
the machine to vindicate Zeus' justice. From her childhood
on she had been given her role and taught her lines and
shown the mask she must wear. But the poet was dead,
and the audience had booed the play.

At Mieza, they passed an old manor whose overgrown

gardens scented the warm air with roses. Someone said that
this was the schoolhouse where Aristotle had taught many
years ago. Yes, she thought bitterly; and now his boys were
ranging the earth to pick up the leavings of their school-
fellow, who, grasping at power to serve a use beyond it, had
put his stake upon love and swept the board.

They dared not enter Pella. They had only traveled at
their own horses' pace; a courier with remounts on the way
could have been there long before them, and they could
not be sure of the garrison after the news from the western
army. One of her suite, a certain Polykles, was brother to
the commandant of Amphipolis, an old stronghold near
the Thracian border. He would help them to get away by
sea.

Henceforward they must try not to be seen. Their arms
discarded, wearing homespun bartered for with peasants,
they nursed their weary horses, skirting the great timeworn
road that had carried Darius the Great towards Marathon,
Xerxes to Salamis, Philip to the Hellespont and Alexander
to Babylon. One by one, pleading sickness, or just disap-
pearing in the night, her small company fell away. On the
third day, there was only Polykles.

From a long way off they saw the great keep of Amphipolis, commanding the mouth of the Strymon River. There
was a ferry there; troops were there also. They turned inland to seek the nearest ford. But at the ford, too, they
were awaited.

When they brought her into Pella, she asked them to untie
her feet, which were bound under the mule she rode, to let
her wash and comb her hair. They replied that Queen
Olympias had ordered her brought just as she was.

On the low hill above the town stood what looked at
first like a thicket of stunted trees, laden with birds. When

they came near, ravens and crows and kites rose, angrily cawing, from the branches. It was Gallows Hill, where the corpses of criminals were nailed up after execution, like vermin in a gamekeeper's larder. Philip's murderer had hung there once. The present corpses were no longer to be recognized—the scavengers had fed well—but their names had been painted on boards nailed at their feet. NIKANOR SON OF ANTIPATROS, one board said. There were more than a hundred crosses; the reek almost reached the town.

In the audience hall, on the throne where Eurydike had heard petitioners and envoys, Olympias was seated. She had changed her black robes and was dressed in crimson, with a gold diadem on her head. Beside her on a chair of state sat Roxane, the young Alexander on a stool at her knee. He stared with round dark eyes at Eurydike when she was led in, unkempt and dirty, with fetters on her legs and wrists.

The irons had been forged to restrain strong men. Her wrists with their dead weight hung down before her. She could only walk by sliding each foot in turn along the floor, and every step chafed her ankles. To keep the fetters from tripping her, she had to walk with an ungainly straddle. But she held her head high as she shuffled towards the throne.

Olympias nodded to one of the guards. He gave Eurydike a hard shove in the back; she toppled forward, bruising her chained hands. Struggling to her knees she looked up at the faces. Some had laughed; the child had laughed with them, but was suddenly grave. Roxane was still smiling. Olympias watched under dropped lids, intently, like the cat that waits for the caught mouse to move.

She said to the guard, "Is this slut the woman who claims to be Queen of Macedon?" He assented, woodenly. "I do not believe you. You must have found her in the harbor stews. You, woman. What is your name?"

Eurydike thought, I am alone. No one wishes me courage or will praise it. Any courage I have is for me, alone. She said, "I am Eurydike, the daughter of Amyntas son of Perdikkas."

Olympias turned to Roxane, and said conversationally, "The father a traitor, the mother a barbarian's bastard."

She stayed on her knees; if she tried to rise, her weighted wrists would pull her over. "And yet, your son the King chose me to marry his brother."

Olympias' face tautened with an old anger; the flesh seemed to grow dense. "I see he did well. The trull is well matched with the fool. We will keep you apart no longer." She turned to the guards and for the first time smiled. Eurydike could see why she did it seldom; one of her front teeth was black. The guards seemed to blink before they saluted. "Go," she said. "Take her to the marriage chamber."

When she had toppled twice trying to rise, the guards set her on her feet. She was led to the rear courts of the palace. Dragging her fetters, she passed the stables, and heard her horses whinny; the kennels, where the deep-voiced hounds she had hunted with barked at the foreign sound of her weighted footsteps. The guards did not hustle or harry her. They walked awkwardly at her dragging pace; once, when she tripped over a rut, one of them caught her to keep her from falling; but they did not look at her or speak to one another.

Today or tomorrow, or soon, she thought; what matter? She felt death present in her flesh, its certainty like a sickness.

Ahead was a low-walled stone hut with a pointed roof of thatch. A stink came from it; a privy, she thought, or perhaps a sty. They steered her towards it. A muffled sobbing sounded from within.

They lifted the crossbar from the rough timber door. One of them peered into the fetid gloom. "Here's your wife, then." The sobbing ceased. They waited to see if she would go in without being forced. She stooped under the low lintel; the roof inside was hardly higher, the thatch pricked her head. The door closed behind her, the crossbar clattered back.

"Oh, Eurydike! I will be good! I promise I'll be good. Please make them let me out now."

By the light of a foot-square window under the eaves she saw Philip, in fetters, hunched sideways against the wall. The whites of his eyes glittered in the tear-stained dirt of his face. He gazed at her pleadingly and held out his hands. The wrists were rubbed raw.

The room was furnished with a wooden stool, and a litter of straw like a horse's. At the further end was a shallow pit, reeking with excrement and buzzing with great blue flies.

She moved to the space under the high roof-peak, and he saw her fetters. He wept again, wiping his running nose. The smell of unwashed flesh repelled her as much as the privy. Involuntarily she drew back against the far wall; her head met the roof again and she had to crouch on the filthy floor.

"Please, please, Eurydike, don't let them beat me again."

She saw then why he did not sit with his back to the wall. His tunic was stuck to his skin with dark stripes of clotted blood; when she came near he cried, "Don't touch it, it hurts." Flies were clustering on the yellow serum.

Fighting back her nausea she said, "Why did they do it?"

He gulped back a sob. "I hit them when they killed Konon."

A great shame filled her. She covered her eyes with her chained hands.

He eased his shoulder against the wall, and scratched his side. She had felt already the tickle of insects around her legs. "I shouldn't have been King," he said. "Alexander told me I shouldn't be. He said if they made me King someone would kill me. Will they kill me?"

"I don't know." Having brought him here, she could not refuse him hope. "We may be rescued. You remember Kassandros? He didn't help us in the war; but now Olympias has killed his brother and all his kin. Now he must come. If he wins, he will let us out." She sat down on the stool, holding her wrist-chains in her lap to ease their weight, and looking at the window-square, whose patch of sky was edged by a distant tree. A gull, seeking the pickings of the kitchen-midden, floated across from the wide free waters of the lagoon.

He asked her unhappily for permission to use the pit. When necessity drove her there, the flies flew up and she saw their crawling maggots.

Time passed. At length he sat up eagerly. "Suppertime," he said, and licked his lips. It was not only squalor that had changed him; he had lost several stone. A tuneless whistling was coming towards the hut.

A grimy, broken-nailed hand appeared in the window-hole, grasping a hunk of black bread smeared with greasy dripping. Another followed, then a crock of water. She could see nothing of the face but the end of a coarse black beard. The whistling receded.

Philip seized his bread and tore at it like a starving dog. It seemed to her she would never eat again; but her captors had fed her that morning. She had no need to ask if he had eaten that day. She said, "You can have my piece today; I will eat tomorrow."

He looked at her, his face illuminated, radiant. "Oh, Eurydike, I'm so glad you've come."

Afterwards he told her, rambling, the tale of his cap-

tivity. His sufferings had confused his mind, he was often
hardly coherent. She listened dully. Far off and muted, as
they might reach a sickroom, came the sounds of early
evening, the lowing of cattle, horses returning from the
stables, dogs barking, peasants hailing each other after
work, the stamp and rattle of the changing guard. A cart
lumbered near with a heavy load; she could hear the oxen
straining, the driver cursing and beating them. It did not
pass by, but creaked to a halt, and, rumbling and rattling,
tipped its load. She listened dully, aware that she was
exhausted, thinking of the crawling straw. She propped
her back to the wall and fell into an unsleeping doze.

Footsteps approached. Is it now? she thought. Philip
was stretched out and snoring. She waited to hear the bar
withdrawn. But there came only the indistinct sounds of
peasants at heavy work. She called, "What is it? What do
you want?"

The mutterings died into silence. Then, as if a stealthy
sign had been made, the stirrings began again. There was a
kind of patting and scraping against the door, then a thud,
and another.

She went to the little window, but it did not overlook
the door. All she could see was part of a heap of rough-
dressed stone. She was tired, and slow to understand, but
suddenly the sound came clearly: the slap of wet mortar,
and the scraping of a trowel.

Kassandros was walking his siege-lines on the damp Arka-
dian plateau under the walls of Tegea; thick, dark, mossy,
impacted brick, stuff that would only dent under a ram
that could have loosened ashlar. The town had a perpetual
spring inside; it was a slow business to starve them out.
They had told his heralds that they were under the special
patronage of Athene, who had promised in some oracle of

remote antiquity that their city would never be taken by force of arms. He was resolved to make Athene eat her words.

He did not hurry to meet the courier from Macedon; it was sure to be another appeal from Eurydike. Then as he came near he saw the face of disaster, and took the man to his tent.

He was a servant who had escaped the massacre of the Antipatrids. To the tale of death he added that Olympias had had the tomb of his brother Iollas battered down and his bones scattered for beasts to eat, claiming that he had poisoned her son in Babylon.

Kassandros, who had listened in rigid silence, leaped from his chair. There would be a time for grief; all he could feel was a blazing hate and rage. "That wolf-bitch! That Gorgon! How did they let her set foot in Macedon? My father warned them against her with his dying breath. Why did they not kill her on the border?"

The messenger said, without expression, "They would not fight the mother of Alexander."

For a moment, Kassandros felt that his head would burst. The man looked with alarm at his staring eyes. Aware of it, he fought for composure. "Go, rest, eat. We will speak again later." The rider went off, not wondering that a man should be moved by such a slaughter of his kin.

When he had come to himself, he sent an envoy to make terms with the Tegeans. He excused them from allegiance to himself, if they would merely agree not to help his enemies. Face-saving formulae were exchanged; the siege was lifted; the Tegeans went in procession to the old wooden temple of Athene, to bring her thank-offerings for keeping her ancient promise.

⊙   ⊙   ⊙

Behind the walled-up door, time passed like the days of a slow fatal illness, bringing misery by small additions; more stink, more flies and lice and fleas, more festering of their sores, weakness and hunger. But still the bread and water came every day to the window-hole.

At first Eurydike had counted the days, scratching with a pebble on the wall. After seven or eight she missed one and lost count, and ceased to make the effort. She would have sunk into blank apathy, broken only by fighting with the insects, but for Philip.

His mind could not hold the sum of disaster long enough to be capable of despair. He lived from day to day. Often he would complain to the man who brought the food, and he would sometimes answer, not cruelly but like a sulky servant unjustly blamed, saying he had his orders and that was the end of it. She scorned to utter a word to him; but as time passed he grew a little more forthcoming, bringing out old saws about the ways of fortune. One day he even asked Philip how his wife was. He looked at her and answered, "She says I'm not to tell."

She drowsed away half the day but could not sleep at night. Philip's snores were noisy, the vermin as tormenting as her thoughts. One morning early, when they were awake and already hungry, she said to him, "Philip. I made you claim the throne. It was for myself I wanted it. It is my fault you are shut up here, my fault that you were beaten. Do you want to kill me? I do not mind. If you like I will show you how." But he only said with a whine like a sick child's, "The soldiers made me. Alexander told me not to."

She thought, I need only give up my bread to him. He would take it gladly if I gave it, though he will not rob me. I would surely die quickly, now. But when the time came she could not bear her hunger, and ate her share. To her surprise, she was aware that the portion had grown larger.

Next day there was still more, enough to save for a frugal breakfast.

At the same time, they began to hear the voices of the guard outside. They must have been told to keep their distance—her record of subversion was well known—their comings and goings had been only measures of time. But discipline was relaxing, they talked and gossiped carelessly, weary perhaps of guarding a place without an exit. Then one night, as she lay watching through the window-hole a single star, there was a soft approach, the click of leather and metal; the opening was darkened for a moment, and when it lightened, there were two apples on the sill. The mere smell was ambrosia.

After that something came every night, and with less stealth, as if the officer of the watch were himself conniving. No one stayed to talk at the window, no doubt a hanging matter; but they talked to their relief, as if they meant to be heard. "Well, we've our orders, like it or not." "Rebels or no, enough's enough." "And too much is hubris, which the gods don't like." "Aye, and by the look of it they won't wait long."

Well versed in the tones of mutiny, she sensed something else. These men were not plotting; they were talking openly the common talk of the streets. She thought, We are not that woman's only victims; the people have sickened of her. What did they mean by the gods not waiting long? Can it be that Kassandros is marching north?

There had been cheese and figs in the night, and the jug had had watered wine in it. With better food her listlessness had left her. She dreamed of rescue, of the Macedonians staring with pity at their filth and wretchedness, clamoring for retribution; of her hour of triumph when, washed and robed and crowned, she resumed her throne in the audience chamber.

⊙   ⊙   ⊙

Kassandros' sudden departure for the north had left confusion behind him; his forsaken allies in the Peloponnese
had to face alone the Macedonians led by Polyperchon's
son. When their desperate envoys overtook his column, he
only said he had business that would not wait.

Democrat Aitolians had manned Thermopylai against
his passage. Such challenges had no romance for him. More
practical than Xerxes, he commandeered everything that
would float in the busy strait between Euboia and the main-
land, and bypassed the Hot Gates by sea.

In Thessaly, Polyperchon himself awaited him, still faithful, despite Olympias, to Alexander's son. He too was side-
stepped; some troops were detached to tie him up, while
the main force pressed on northeast. Skirting Olympos,
they were soon on the borders of Macedon.

The coastal fortress of Dion lay ahead. Kassandros' envoys
promised an end to the unlawful tyranny of women and a
return to the ancient customs. After a short conclave
within, the gates were opened. Here he held court, receiving all who offered support or brought him intelligence.
Many kinsmen of Olympias' victims, or men whom she had
proscribed, came to join him, full of their wrongs and
clamoring for vengeance. But others came by stealth who
till lately would not have come; men who had refused to
fight the mother of Alexander, and who said now that no
one but Alexander could have held such a woman in check.
These would go back, spreading news of Kassandros'
pledges, and his claim to the regency on behalf of Roxane's
son.

One day, he remembered to ask of such a visitor, "And
when they took Amyntas' daughter, how did she die?"

The man's face lightened. "There at least I have good

news for you. She was alive when I left, and Philip too.
They are treated shockingly, walled up in a wretched sty;
there is a great deal of anger among the people. I'm told
they were in a very poor way, till even the guards took pity
on them and gave them a little comfort. If you hurry, you
can save them still."

Kassandros' face had set in a moment's stillness. "Shame-
ful!" he said. "Olympias should have borne her good fortune more becomingly. Can they have lived so long?"

"You can count on that, Kassandros. I had it from one
of the guard."

"Thank you for the news." He leaned forward in his
chair, and spoke with sudden animation. "Let it be known
I mean to right their wrongs. They shall be restored to all
their dignities. As for Olympias, I shall hand over her person to Queen Eurydike, to punish as she sees fit. Tell the
people."

"Indeed I will; they will be glad to hear. I'll get word, if I
can, to the prison. It will cheer them to have hope at last."

He left, big with his mission. Kassandros sent for his
officers, and told them he would delay his march for a few
days more. It would give his friends time, he said, to gather
more support.

Three mornings later, Eurydike said, "How quiet it is. I
don't even hear the guard."

The first dawn was glimmering in the window-hole. The
night had been cool, the flies were not yet awake. They
had eaten well on what the night-guard had brought. The
watch had changed just before dawn as usual; but the relief
had been quiet, and now there was no sound of their move-
ments. Had they deserted, mutinied? Or been called to

help defend the city, which would mean Kassandros had come?

She said to Philip, "Soon we shall be free, I feel it."

Scratching at his groin, he said, "Can I have a bath?"

"Yes, we shall have baths and good clean clothes, and beds to sleep in."

"And I can have my stones back?"

"Yes, and some new ones too." Often in their close quarters his nearness, his smell, the way he ate and belched and relieved himself, had been barely endurable; she would gladly have exchanged him for a dog; but she knew that she owed him justice. She must care for her mind, if she was to be fit again for ruling. So she seldom scolded him, and, if she did, gave him a kind word after. He never sulked, always forgave, or perhaps simply forgot.

"When will they let us out?" he said.

"As soon as Kassandros wins."

"Listen. People are coming now."

It was true, there were footsteps; three or four men by the sound. They were on the door side, where the window did not look. Their voices muttered but she could not make out their words. Then, suddenly, came a sound there was no mistaking—a blow of a pick on the wall that closed the door.

"Philip!" she cried. "They have come to rescue us!"

He whooped like a child, and peered vainly through the window. She stood up in the space under the roof-point, listening to the fall of rubble and thud of stones. The work went quickly; the wall had been a shoddy job, by men without their hearts in it. She called out, "Are you Kassandros' men?"

There was a pause in the pick-strokes; then a thick foreign voice said, "Yes, Kassans men," but she could tell he had not understood her. His next words, to his workmates, were not in Greek, and now she recognized the sound.

"They are Thracians," she said to Philip. "They are slaves sent to knock down the wall. When that's done, someone will come to unbar the door."

Philip's face had altered. He withdrew as far from the door as he could without falling into the privy. Old days, before the benevolent reign of Konon, were coming back to him. "Don't let them come in," he said.

She had begun to reassure him, when there was a laugh outside.

She stiffened. It was not the laughter of slaves, complaisant or discreet. She knew, with a crawling of the flesh, the nature of this archetypal mirth.

The last stones fell. The crossbar clattered from the door. It creaked open; the sunrise burst dazzling in.

Four Thracians stood on the threshold, staring across the rubble.

They choked, clapping hands to their mouths and noses; men bred in the clean hill air, with hundred-foot cliffs to receive the ordure of their villages. In this pause, she saw on their cheeks and foreheads their warrior tattoos, saw their pectorals of engraved bronze etched with silver, their cloaks with bands of tribal colors, the daggers in their hands.

Sickly she thought, The Macedonians would not do it. She stood straight, in the center where the roof was high.

The leading Thracian confronted her. He wore an armbracelet of a triple-coiled snake, and greaves with women's faces embossed upon the kneecaps. Spiral blue tattoos on his brow, and on his cheeks to his dark-red beard, made his expression impenetrable. "Kill me then!" she cried, lifting her head. "You can boast that you killed a queen."

He put out his arm—not the right, with the dagger, but

the left with the coiled bronze snake—and swept her out of his way. She lost her footing and fell.

"You slave, don't you dare hit my wife!" In a moment, the cowering form by the privy had hurled itself straight forward from a bent-kneed crouch. The Thracian, taken unawares with a butted midriff, had the breath knocked out of him. Philip, fighting like an ape enraged, using feet and knees and nails, struggled to get the dagger. He had sunk his teeth in the Thracian's wrist when the others fell on him.

Between his roars of pain as the knives went in, she thought that he called for Konon; then he gave a guttural choke, his head arched back gaping, he clawed at the dirt floor and lay still. One of the men shoved at him with a foot, but he did not move.

They turned to each other, like men whose task is done.

She rose on her hands and knees. A booted foot had trodden on her leg; she wondered that she could still move it. They were staring down at the body, comparing the bites and scratches Philip had given them. She caught in their unknown jargon a note of admiration; they had found, after all, a king.

They saw her movement and turned to look at her. One of them laughed. A new horror gripped her; till now she had thought only of the knives.

The man who had laughed had a round, smooth-skinned face and a pale scanty beard. He came towards her smiling. The leader who wore the greaves called something out, and the man turned away with a gesture which said he could do better for himself than this stinking drab. They looked at their red blades and wiped them on Philip's tunic. One of them threw it back to show the groin; the leader, rebukingly, pulled it down again. They went out, picking their way over the scattered stones.

She tottered to her feet, shaking and dazed and cold with shock. It had all taken, perhaps, two minutes from the time when the door gave way.

Clear early sun streaming through the doorway picked out the stale filth, the fresh scarlet blood on the body. She blinked in the unaccustomed light. Two shadows fell across it.

They were Macedonians, and unarmed, the second attendant on the first, for he stood half a pace behind and carried a bundle. The first came forward, a thickset middle-aged man in a decent drab tunic and shoulder-cloak. He gazed a few moments in silence at the scene, clicking his tongue in disapproval. Turning to the other he said, "Mere butchery. A disgrace."

He stepped into the entry, confronting the haggard, mat-haired woman with her grimy feet and black nails, and spoke in the flat, rather pompous voice of a minor functionary doing his office with regard for his own importance.

"Eurydike, daughter of Amyntas. I act under command, do you therefore hold me guiltless before the gods. Olympias, Queen of the Macedonians, says this by me. Because your father was born lawfully of royal blood, she does not condemn you to execution like the bastard your husband. She gives you leave to end your own life, and offers you a choice of means."

The second man came forward, and looked for somewhere to put his bundle down. Seeming disconcerted to find no table, he opened it on the ground, and, like a peddler, set out the contents on the cloth: a short fine dagger, a stoppered flask, and a cord of plaited flax with a running noose.

Silently she considered them, then looked from them to the sprawling corpse beside her. If she had joined him as he fought, perhaps it would all be over. Kneeling she picked up the phial; she had heard that the Athenian hemlock killed with a creeping cold, giving no pain. But this came from Olympias, and if she asked what it was they might lie. The dagger was sharp; but she knew she was too weak to strike it home; half dead, what would they do to her? She fingered the rope. It was smooth, well made and clean. She looked up at the peak of the hut where the roof stood eight feet high, and said, "This will do."

The man gave a businesslike nod. "A good choice, lady, and quickly over. We'll soon have it fixed, you've a stool there, I see." When the servant mounted it, she saw there was even an iron hook, fixed to a little crossbeam, such as is found in places where tools or tackle are kept. No, they would not be long.

So, she thought, nothing at all remained. Not even style; she had seen hanged men. She looked down at Philip, left tumbled like a slaughtered beast. Yes, after all, something was still left. Piety remained to her. This was the King her husband, who had made her a queen, who had fought and died for her. As the executioner, his task done, stepped down from the stool, she said, "You must wait awhile."

The jug of watered wine, left by the night-guard for their comfort, stood untouched in the window. She knelt beside him, and wetting a corner of her tunic hem, washed his wounds as well as she could, and cleaned his face. She straightened his legs, laid his left arm on his breast and his right beside him, closed his eyes and mouth and smoothed his hair. Set in the gravity of death he looked a comely man. She saw the executioners looking at him with a new respect; she had done that at least for him. Scraping her hand along the earth floor, she strewed on him the ritual pinch of dust which would free him to cross the River.

There was one thing still, she thought; something for herself. It was not for nothing that her blood came down from the warring Macedonian kings and the chieftains of Illyria. She had her blood-feud; and if she could not pursue it, the powers whose work it was must do it for her. She stood up from the body, stretching her hands palms downwards over the trampled and bloodstained earth.

"Witness, you gods below," she cried aloud, "that I received these gifts from Olympias. I call upon you, by the waters of Styx, and by the power of Hades, and by this blood, to give her in her turn such gifts as these." She turned to the men, saying, "I am ready."

She kicked the stool away for herself, not flinching or leaving them to take it, as they had seen strong men do many a time. All in all they thought she had shown a good deal of spirit, not unworthy of her ancestry; and when it seemed that her struggle might last longer than was needful, they dragged her down by the knees, to pull the noose tight and help her die.

Olympias, these needful things attended to, summoned her council. Few of the men about her were bound, now, by loyalty to her person. Some had blood-feuds with the Antipatrids; many knew they had given Kassandros cause for vengeance; others, she guessed, were loyal only to the son of Alexander. She sat at the great table of gilt and hardstone where her husband Philip had sat, a young king, in the old days of the civil wars which men of no more than sixty could still remember, and men of seventy had fought in. She did not ask them for advice. Her own will sufficed for her. The old men and soldiers sitting before her saw her impenetrable solitude, her enclosure in her will.

She did not mean, she told them, to sit at ease in Pella while rebels and traitors overran her frontiers. She would go south to Pydna; it was only some fifteen miles north of

Dion where Kassandros had insolently set up his standard. Pydna had a harbor; it was well fortified; from there she would direct the war.

The soldiers approved. They thought of the bloodless victory in the west.

"Good," she said. "In two days I shall move the court to Pydna."

The soldiers stared. This was another thing entirely. It meant a horde of women, servants and noncombatants taking up room, getting under the feet of the garrison, having to be fed. After a pause in which everyone waited for someone else to speak first, they told her so.

She said, unmoved, "Our allies can join us by sea, without losses from fighting on the march. When we are in full strength, when Polyperchon has joined us, we will meet Kassandros."

Agenor, a veteran of the east who had been given the chief command, cleared his throat and said, "No one questions the honor of Polyperchon. But it is said he has had desertions." He paused; everyone wondered if he would dare go on. "And, as you know, we can expect nothing now from Epiros."

She stiffened in her ivory-inlaid chair. The Epirotes who had followed her to the border had mutinied when ordered to fight in Macedon, and gone home. Only a handful of Molossians was left. She had shut herself up for two days to nurse her pride, and Kassandros' secret partisans had made the most of them. The councilors looked angrily at Agenor; they had seen her face harden. She fixed on him her inflexible dangerous eyes, looking out from her mask of will. She said, "The court will move to Pydna. This session is closed."

The men left, looking at one another, not speaking till they were in the open. Agenor said, "Let her have her way. But she must be out before the winter."

⊙   ⊙   ⊙

Kassandros had had good news from the officer he had sent
to deal with Polyperchon. Avoiding battle, he had infil-
trated the straggling camp with men who had a clansman
or kinsman there. They spread the news that Olympias had
shed the royal blood of Macedon, herself a foreigner and
a usurper; and offered a bounty of fifty drachmas to any
good Macedonian who would join Kassandros' force. Every
morning the numbers in Polyperchon's camp were fewer;
soon he and his faithful remnant were too few to consider
more than their own defense. They dug themselves into
the best of the local hill-forts, mended its walls, provisioned
it, and waited upon events.

The corn and the olives ripened, the grapes were trodden,
the women took to the mountains to honor Dionysos; in
the dark before dawn the shrill Bacchic cry answered the
first cockcrow. In Pydna, the watchers on the harbor walls
scanned the sea, which the first autumn winds were ruffling.
No sails appeared but those of the fisher-boats, already running for home.

Before the first gales began, Kassandros appeared from
the passes he now commanded, and surrounded Pydna with
a palisade.

3 1 6 B. C.

IT WAS SPRING IN THE VALLEYS. The peaks of Olympos still dazzled with winter snow under a clear pale sky. A single wreath of cloud hid the Throne of Zeus. His eagles had forsaken its lifeless purity to fend for themselves on the lower crags. Around the summits, only sheer cliffs that would not hold a snowflake slashed the white cloak with black.

In the foothills, the waters of the thaw scoured ravines and gullies in torrents that ground the boulders like thunder. Below, under the walls of Pydna, a mild sun warmed the corpses which the cold had stiffened, releasing their carrion reek, and the kites returned to them.

Olympias, pacing the walls, looked out beyond the siege-lines to the wild mountain ranges where the lynxes and wolves ran free, where the pines were shrugging the snow from their furry shoulders like awakening bears.

Her gaunt face looked out from a shapeless mass of clothing, layer upon layer. She had come in mild autumn weather, resolved that the war would be over in a month and Kassandros dead. Alexander had always done what he resolved, that she knew. He had seldom discussed with her the complex calculations which had preceded action. There was a sharp wind today; she was wearing even her state robe heaped over her shoulders like a wrap. With hunger one felt the cold.

The other women were huddled indoors over their tiny fire. The men upon the ramparts, skull-faced, glanced dully at her as she passed, their vitality too low to nourish a hot hate. All through the winter there had been no assault upon the walls; the corpses in the ditch were all dead of starvation. They had been flung there not from callousness but necessity; there was no room left in the fort to dig more graves.

Scattered among them were the huge bones of the elephants. The horses and mules had soon been eaten; but elephants were instruments of war, and, besides, no one had dared to slaughter them. They had tried to keep them alive on sawdust; for a time their complaining moans and forlorn trumpetings had disturbed the night, then one by one they had sunk down in their stalls, and what meat was left on them, all sinew, had been something to chew on for a while. The mahouts, who were useless now, had been taken off the ration list; they too were below the walls.

Somewhere in the fort a camp-woman's child was crying; new born, soon gone. The young Alexander was too old to cry. She had seen to it that he still had enough; he was a king and must not have the strength of his manhood crippled in his youth. Though the food was wretched he had been unexpectedly good, telling her that his father had gone hungry with his men. But often she would find herself looking through him, seeing the tall grandson she could have had if her son had obeyed her, and married before he rode to war. Why, she asked herself; why?

On the rampart that faced the sea the air was cleaner, with a sharp scent of spring. The Olympian massif with its snowy crests called to her like the trees to a captive bird. Last autumn's Dionysia was the first for forty years that she had not spent with her maenads in the mountains. Never again, said the caw from the kite-haunted bones.

She refused it angrily. Soon, when it was sailing weather, Eumenes, whose loyalty had never failed, would cross with his troops from Asia.

There was a stirring along the ramparts. A little crowd was gathering and growing, coming towards her. She drew back from the brink and waited.

The band of emaciated men approached without sign of violence. Few looked to have strength for it. Their clothes hung on them like half-empty sacks; several leaned on a comrade's shoulder to keep their feet. Men of thirty could have been sixty. Their skin was blotched with scurvy and many had toothless gums. Their hair was falling. One, to whom still clung vestiges of command, came forward and spoke, lisping a little because his front teeth had gone.

"Madam. We request permission to leave."

She looked at them, speechless. Anger surfaced in her eyes and fell away into their depths. The old, thin voice seemed not a man's but a Fate's.

Answering her silence, he said, "If the enemy attacked he could lay us out barehanded. All we can do here now is share the last of the stores, and then go *there*." He made a tired, economical gesture towards the ditch. "Without us, what's left will last a little longer. Permission, madam?"

"But," she said at last, "Kassandros' men will butcher you."

"As God wills, lady. Today or tomorrow, what's the odds?"

"You may go," she said. He stood a few moments looking at her mutely as the rest began shambling away. She added, "Thank you for your good service."

She went in then, because of the cold; but a little later she went up again to watch them depart.

They had broken off branches from some scrawny pines that grew in the cracks of the stone, and as the gates creaked open they waved them in sign of peace. Slowly they eased themselves down the scarp, and plodded across no-man's-land towards the siege-works. The rough timber gate in the stockade was lifted open; they trickled through and stood in a clump inside. A single, helmeted figure came out to them, seemed to address them, and went away. Presently soldiers came among them with baskets and tall jars. She watched the bread and wine distributed, the stick-like arms reached out in eager gratitude.

She returned to her room in the gate-tower, to crouch over her little fire. A ribbon of ants was streaming along the hearth to a basket that stood beside it. She lifted the lid; inside, they were swarming over a dead snake. It was the last one left from the Thracian sanctuary of Dionysos, her oracle. What had killed it? The rats and mice had been trapped and eaten, but it could have lived on the creeping things. It was only a few years old. She gazed at the moving mass and shivered, then put the basket with its seething heap onto the fire.

The air grew mild, the breezes gentle. It was sailing weather; but the only sails were those of Kassandros' warships. The ration was down to a handful of meal a day, when Olympias sent envoys to ask for terms.

From the ramparts she saw them go into his tent. Beside her stood her stepdaughter Thessalonike, a legacy from one of Philip's campaign weddings. Her mother had died when she was born, and Olympias had tolerated her in the palace because she gave herself no airs, and was quiet and civil. She was thirty-five, tall and plain, but carried herself well. She had not dared confess that in Pella she had had an offer from Kassandros; she had come to Pydna letting it be thought it was her life she had feared for. Now, pale and lank-haired, she waited for the envoys, keeping her thoughts to herself.

The envoys came back, their lassitude a little lifted by the hospitality in the tent. Kassandros' envoy was with them.

He was a man called Deinias, who had done many secret errands for Olympias in the past and been well rewarded. How much had he told Kassandros? He behaved as if those days had never been, insolently bland. Florid, well-fleshed, his very body was an arrogance in that company. He refused a private parley, demanding to speak before the garrison. Having no choice, she met him in the central court where, while they were able, the soldiers used to exercise.

"Kassandros son of Antipatros sends you greetings. If your people give themselves up to him, they will be spared like those who have now surrendered. As for yourself, his terms are that you put yourself in his hands, without any conditions."

She pulled herself upright, though a twinge reminded her that her back was stiffening. "Tell Kassandros to come with better terms." A whispering sigh ran through the ranks behind her. "When Eumenes comes, your master will run like a hunted wolf. We will hold out till then."

He raised his brows in overplayed surprise. "Madam, forgive me. I had forgotten news does not reach you here. Do not set your hopes on a dead man."

Her vitality seemed to drain, like wine from a cracked jar. She kept her feet but did not answer.

"Eumenes was given up lately to Antigonos. He was sold by the Silver Shields whom he commanded. By the chance of battle, Antigonos seized their baggage train. Their loot of three reigns was in it; also their women and children— one cannot tell how much that weighed with such men.

At all events, Antigonos offered it back in exchange for their commander, and they struck the bargain."

A rustling shudder passed through the brittle ranks. Horror perhaps, the knowledge that nothing was now unthinkable; or, perhaps, temptation.

Her face was parchment-colored. She would have been glad of the stick she used sometimes to get about the rough places of the fort. "You may tell Kassandros we will open the gates without condition, in return for our lives alone."

Though her head felt icy cold, and a dazzle of darkness was spinning in her eyes, she got to her room and shut the door before she fainted.

"Excellent," said Kassandros when Deinias returned to him. "When the men come out, feed them and recruit any who are worth it. Get a trench dug for the carrion. The old bitch and her household will stay here for the time."

"And after?" said Deinias with feigned carelessness.

"Then . . . well. She is still the mother of Alexander, which awes the ignorant. The Macedonians won't bear her rule again; but, even now . . . I shall frighten her, and then offer her a ship to escape to Athens. Ships are wrecked every year."

The dead were shoveled into their trench; the thin, pasty-faced women moved from the fortress into the town house reserved for royal visits. It was roomy and clean; they got out their mirrors, and put them quickly away; girdled their loose clothes round them, and ate cravingly of fruit and curds. The boy picked up quickly. He knew he had survived a memorable siege, and that the Thracian archers, in the

secrecy of their guardroom, had made stew from the flesh
of corpses. The inner defenses of childhood were making
it like a tale to him. Kebes, whose fine physique had lasted
him well, did not check this talk; the haunted ones were
those who kept silent. All kings of Macedon were heirs to
the sword; it was well to know that war was not all flags
and trumpets. As man and boy gained strength, they began
to exercise again.

It was Roxane who had changed most to the outward
eye. She was twenty-six; but in her homeland this was
matronhood. Her glass had showed it her, and she had accepted it. Her consequence was now a dowager's; she saw
herself not as the last King's widow, but as the mother of
the next.

Pella had surrendered, on Olympias' orders, dictated by
Kassandros. This done, she sent to ask him if she might now
return to her palace rooms. He replied that at present it
was not convenient. At Pella he had things to do.

She would sit in a window that looked on the eastward
sea, considering the future. She was exiled now from Epiros; but there was still the boy. She was sixty; she might
have ten years or more to rear him and see him on his
father's throne.

Kassandros held audience at Pella. The Epirotes made
alliance with him; he sent an adviser to direct their King,
the young son of Kleopatra. He buried his brother Nikanor,
and restored his brother Iollas' desecrated tomb. Then he
asked where were the bodies of the royal pair, so foully
murdered. They led him to a corner of the royal burial
ground, where in a little brick-lined grave Philip and Eurydike had been laid like peasants. They were hardly to be
recognized, by now, as man and woman; but he burned

them on a ceremonial pyre, denouncing the outrage of their deaths, and had their bones laid up in precious coffers while a handsome tomb was built for them. He had not forgotten that kings of Macedon were entombed by their successors.

There were many graves around Pella after Olympias' purge. The withered wreaths still hung upon the stones, tasseled with the mourners' hair. The kindred still came with tears and offering-baskets. Kassandros made it his business to go among them, commiserating their losses, and asking if time was not ripe for justice on the guilty.

Soon it was announced that the bereaved wished an Assembly called, to accuse Olympias of shedding without trial the blood of Macedonians.

She was sitting with the other women at the evening meal when a messenger was announced. She finished, drank a cup of wine, and then went down to him.

He was a well-spoken man with the accent of the north; a stranger, but there were many after her long absence in the west. He warned her that her trial was to be demanded; then he said, "I am here, you understand, at the instance of Kassandros. He pledged your safety when the siege was raised. Tomorrow at dawn, there will be a ship for you in the harbor."

"A ship?" It was dusk, the lamps in the hall had not been lit yet. Her cheeks were hollowed with shadow, her eyes dark wells with a faint gleam in the depths. "A ship? What do you mean?"

"Madam, you have good guest-friends in Athens. You have supported their democrats." (It had been part of her feud with Antipatros.) "You will be well received. Let Assembly try you in absence. No one yet died of that."

Till now she had spoken quietly; she had not yet lost

the lassitude of the siege. But her raised voice was full and rounded. "Does Kassandros think I shall run away from the Macedonians? Would my son have done so?"

"No, madam. But Alexander had no cause."

"Let them see me!" she cried. "Let them try me if they wish. Say to Kassandros only to tell me the day, and I shall be there."

Disconcerted, he said, "Is that well advised? I was to warn you that some of the people wish you harm."

"When they have heard me, we will see what their wish is then."

"Tell her the day?" said Kassandros when this news was brought him. "She is asking too much. I know the fitful hearts of the Macedonians. Call Assembly for tomorrow, and give out that she refused to come."

The bereaved appeared before Assembly in torn mourning clothes, their hair newly shorn and strewn with ashes. Widows led orphaned children, old men bewailed the sons who had propped their age. When it was made known that Olympias would not appear, no one stood up to speak for her. By acclamation, Assembly voted for death.

"So far so good," said Kassandros afterwards. "We have authority. But for a woman of her rank, a public execution is unseemly. She would be able to address the people, a chance that she would not waste. I think we will make a different plan."

The household at Pydna was busy with small mid-morning tasks. Roxane was embroidering a girdle; Thessalonike was

washing her hair. (She had been told, on Kassandros' authority, that she was free to return to the palace; a distinction received with dread, and not responded to.) Olympias,
sitting in her window, was reading Kallisthenes' account
of the deeds of Alexander. He had had it copied for her by
a Greek scribe somewhere in Bactria, and sent it her by the
Royal Road. She had read it often; but today it had come
into her mind that she would like to read it again.

There was an urgent tap on her door. Kebes came in.
"Madam. There are soldiers asking for you outside. They're
here for no good; I have barred the doors."

As he spoke, battering and clanging began, with shouted
oaths. Roxane ran in with her sewing still in her hand.
Thessalonike, a towel wound round her hair, said only, "Is
he with them?" The boy came in, saying sharply, "What do
they want?"

She had been putting her book aside; now she picked it
up again. She gave it to him, saying, "Alexander, keep this
for me." He took it with grave quiet eyes. The battering
on the door grew louder. She turned to the women. "Go
in. Go to your rooms. And you too, Kebes. It is for me they
are here. Leave them to me."

The women withdrew. Kebes paused; but the boy had
taken his hand. If he had to die, it would be for the King.
He bowed and led him away.

The door was splintering. Olympias went to her clothes-
chest, dropped to her feet the house-gown she was wearing,
and put on the crimson robe in which she had given audiences. Its girdle was Indian cloth of gold, embroidered with
bullion and rubies. She took from her casket a necklace of
great pearls which Alexander had sent her from Taxila,
clasped it on, and walking without haste to the stairhead,
stood there waiting.

The doors gave way. A press of men stumbled in and
stood staring about them. They began pulling out their

swords, ready to ransack the house and seek such hiding-places as the sacking of towns had made them cunning in. Then, as they moved towards the stairs, they saw the silent figure looking down on them like an image on a plinth.

The leaders stopped. Those behind them, even those still at the gaping doors, saw what they saw. The clamor died into an eerie silence.

"You wished to see me," said Olympias. "I am here."

"Did you run mad?" said Kassandros when the leader reported back to him. "Do you tell me she was standing there before you, and you did nothing? Slunk off like dogs chased out of a kitchen? The old hag must have put a spell on you. What did she say?"

He had struck the wrong note. The man felt resentful. "She said nothing, Kassandros. What the men said was, she looked like Alexander's mother. And nobody would strike first."

"*You* were paid to do that," said Kassandros tartly.

"Not yet, sir. So I've saved you money. Permission to withdraw."

Kassandros let him go. Affairs were at a crux, commotion must be avoided. He would see the man got some dangerous mission later. At present, he must think of another plan. When it came to him, it was so simple that he wondered he could have been so slow to see it.

It was drawing towards evening. At Pydna they were looking forward to supper, not so much from hunger—their stomachs were still somewhat shrunken—as because it broke the tedium of the day. Alexander was being read to by his tutor from the *Odyssey*, the book where Circe changes the hero's men to swine. The women were making small changes in their toilet, to keep good manners alive. The sun hung over the high peaks of Olympos, ready to sink behind them and plunge the coast in dusk.

The little crowd came quietly along the road, not with the tramp of army boots, but with the soft shuffling tread that becomes a mourner. Their hair was cropped, disheveled and dusted with wood-ash, their clothing ritually torn.

In the last sunlight they came to the broken door, shored up by a local carpenter. It was ramshackle work. While passers-by stared, wondering what burial these people came from at such an hour, they ran up to the door and tore the planks apart.

Olympias heard. When the frightened servants ran up to her, she had already understood, as though she had known already. She did not change the homely gown she had on. She looked in the box where she kept the *Deeds of Alexander*. Good, the boy had it still. Walking to the stairs she saw the ash-streaked faces below, like masks of tragedy. She did not go through the farce of standing there, appealing to those unrelenting eyes. She went down to them.

They did not seize her at once. Each wanted his say. "You killed my son, who never injured anyone." "Your people cut my brother's throat, a good man who had fought for your son in Asia." "You hung my husband on a cross and his children saw it." "Your men killed my father, and raped my sisters too."

The voices rose, lost words, became a gabble of rage. It seemed they might tear her to pieces where she stood. She turned to the older men, steadier in their sternness. "Will you not see that this is decently done?"

Though they felt no pity, she had touched their pride. One of them lifted his staff for quiet, and cleared a place around her.

Above in the house the womenservants were keening,

Thessalonike moaning softly, Roxane wildly sobbing. She heard it like the noises of some foreign town which did not concern her. She cared only that the boy should not see.

The old man pointed his staff. They led her to a piece of waste-land near the sea, too poor for farming, where glaucous shore-plants grew in the stony ground, and a mat of flotsam edged the water. The stones that strewed it were smoothed by the sea's grinding, cast up in the winter storms. The people drew away from her, and stood round her in a ring, as children do in games. They looked at the old man who had appointed himself to speak.

"Olympias, daughter of Neoptolemos. For killing Macedonians without trial, contrary to justice and the law, we pronounce you worthy of death."

Alone in the circle, she stood with her head up while the first stones struck her. Their force made her stagger, and she sank to her knees to prevent an unseemly fall. This offered her head, and soon a big stone struck it. She found herself lying, gazing upwards at the sky. A cloud of great beauty had caught the light from the sinking sun, itself hidden behind the mountain. Her eyes began to swim, their images doubled; she felt her body breaking under the stones, but it was more shock than pain; she would be gone before the real pain had time to start. She looked up at the whirling effulgent cloud, and thought, I brought down the fire from heaven; I have lived with glory. A thunderbolt struck from the sky and all was gone.

3 1 5 B. C.

THE LYCEUM STOOD in a pleasant suburb of Athens, near the plane-shaded Ilissos stream beloved by Sokrates. It was a new and handsome building. The humbler one, where Aristotle had set up his strolling university, was a mere annex now. A long elegant stoa with painted Corinthian columns now sheltered the Principal and his students when they paced discoursing. Within, it smelled benignly of old vellum, ink and writing-wax.

It was all the gift of Kassandros, presented through his cultured Athenian governor. The Principal, Theophrastos, had long been eager to entertain their benefactor, and the auspicious day had arrived.

The distinguished guest had been shown the new library, many of its shelves consecrated to Theophrastos' works; he was a derivative but prolific author. Now they had returned to the Principal's rooms to take refreshment.

"I am glad," said Kassandros, "that you study history, and delighted that you compile it. It is for the scholars of each generation to purge it of its errors, before they infect the next."

"Aristotle's philosophy of history . . ." began Theophrastos eagerly. Kassandros, who had had an hour of learned garrulity, lifted a courteous hand.

"I myself sat at his feet, in my youth when he was in Macedon." Hateful days, tasting of gall, seeing the charmed circle always from outside, exiled from the bright warmth by the centrifuge of his own envy. He said meaningly, "If only the *chief* of his students had put his privilege to better use."

Cautiously, the Principal murmured something about the corruption of barbarian ways and the temptations of power.

"You suffered a grievous loss when Kallisthenes met his end. A brilliant scholar, I believe."

"Ah, yes. Aristotle feared, indeed predicted it. Some unwise letters . . ."

"I am persuaded that he was falsely accused of inspiring his students to plot the death of the King. The voice of philosophy had become unwelcome."

"I fear so . . . We have no one here who accompanied Alexander, and our records suffer."

"You have at least," said Kassandros smiling, "a guest who visited the court at Babylon in its last weeks. If you would like to call a scribe, I can give you some account of what I found."

The scribe came, well furnished with tablets. Kassandros dictated at a smooth, measured pace. ". . . *But long before this he had given way to arrogance and wantonness, preferring the godlike hauteur of a Persian Great King to the wholesome restraints of the homeland.*" The scribe would have no polishing to do; he had prepared it all in advance. Theophrastos, whose own career had been wholly scholastic, hung fascinated on this voice from the theater of great events.

"*He made his victorious generals fall down to the ground before his throne. Three hundred and sixty-five concubines, the same in number as Darius had, filled his palace. Not to speak of a troop of effeminate eunuchs, used to prostitution. As for his nightly carouses . . .*" He continued for some time, noting with satisfaction that every word was going down on the wax. At length the scribe was thanked, and dismissed to begin the work of copying.

"Naturally," Kassandros said, "his former companions will give such accounts of him as they hope will tend to their own glory." The Principal nodded sagely, the careful scholar warned of a dubious source.

Kassandros, whose throat was dry, sipped gratefully at his wine. He, like the Principal, had looked forward to this meeting. He had never managed to humble his living enemy; but at least, now, he had begun to damp down the fame he had set such store by, for which he had burned out his life.

"I trust," said Theophrastos civilly at parting, "that your wife enjoys good health."

"Thessalonike is as well as her condition allows at present. She has her father King Philip's good constitution."

"And the young King? He must be eight years old, and beginning his education."

"Yes. To keep him from inclining to his father's faults, I am giving him a more modest upbringing. Granted that the custom was an old one, still it did Alexander no good that all through his boyhood he had his Companions to dominate—a troop of lords' sons who competed to flatter him. The young King and his mother are installed in the castle of Amphipolis, where they are protected from treachery and intrigue; he is being reared like any private citizen of good birth."

"Most salutary," the Principal agreed. "I shall venture, sir, to present you with a little treatise of my own, *On the Education of Kings.* When he is older, should you think of appointing him a tutor . . ."

"That time," said the Regent of Macedon, "will certainly be in my thoughts."

3 1 0 B. C.

THE CASTLE OF AMPHIPOLIS crowned a high bluff above a sweeping curve of the Strymon, just before it reached the sea. In old days it had been fortified by Athens and by Sparta, strengthened and enlarged by Macedon, each of its conquerors adding a bastion or a tower. The watchmen on its ashlar walls could see wide prospects on every side. They would point out to Alexander, when the air was clear, distant landmarks in Thrace, or the crest of Athos; and he would try to tell them of places he himself had seen before he came here, when he was a little boy; but the years are long between seven and thirteen, and it was growing dim to him.

He remembered confusedly his mother's wagon, the women and eunuchs in her tent, the palace at Pella, his grandmother's house in Dodona; he remembered Pydna too well; he remembered how his mother would not tell him what had happened to Grandmother, though of course the servants had said; he remembered his aunt Thessalonike crying terribly although she was going to be married; and his mother crying too on the journey here, though she was settled now. Only one thing had been constant all his life: the presence of soldiers round him. Since Kebes had been sent away, they were his only friends.

He seemed never to meet other boys; but he was allowed out riding so long as soldiers went with him. It always seemed that as soon as he got to know them, to joke and race with them and get their stories out of them, they would be assigned somewhere else and he had a different pair. But in five years a good many turns had come round again, and one could pick up the threads.

Some of them were dour and no fun to ride with; but in five years he had learned policy. When Glaukias, the Commandant, came to see him, which happened every few days, he would say that these soldiers were most interesting people, who were telling him all about the wars in Asia; and soon after they would be transferred. When his friends were mentioned he looked glum, and they stayed on for some time.

Thus he had learned that Antigonos, the Commander-in-Chief in Asia, was making war on his account, wishing to get him out of Amphipolis and be his guardian. He had been two years old when Antigonos had come his way, and remembered only a huge one-eyed monster whose approach had made him scream with fright. He knew better now, but had still no wish to be his ward. His present guardian was no trouble because he never came.

He wished his guardian had been Ptolemy; not that he remembered him, but the soldiers said he was the best-liked of all Alexander's friends, and behaved in war almost as handsomely, which was rare these days. But Ptolemy was far off in Egypt, and there was no way of getting word to him.

Lately, however, it seemed the war was over. Kassandros and Antigonos and the other generals had made a peace, and agreed that Kassandros should be his guardian till he came of age.

"When *shall* I come of age?" he had asked his friends. For some reason this question had alarmed them both; they had enjoined him, with more than their usual emphasis, not to go chattering about what they'd said, or that would be the last he'd ever see of them.

There had always been two of them, until yesterday, when Peiros' horse had gone lame in the first mile, and he had begged Xanthos for one canter before they had to go home. So they had one while Peiros waited; and when they paused to breathe the horses, Xanthos had said, "Never a word. But there's a lot of talk about you, outside of here."

"Is there?" he said, instantly alert. "No one outside of here knows anything about me."

"So you'd think. But people talk, like we're talking now. Men go on leave. The word goes round that at your age your father had killed his man, and that you're a likely lad who should be getting to know your people. They want to see you."

"Tell them I want to see them, too."

"I'll tell them that when I want my back tanned. Remember; never a word."

"Silence or death!" This was their usual catchword. They trotted back to the waiting Peiros.

Roxane's rooms were furnished from her long travels. The splendors of the Queen's rooms in Babylon, the fretted lattices and lilied fishpond, were twelve years away; all she had of them were Stateira's casket and jewels. Lately, she hardly knew why, she had put them away out of sight. But she had plenty of ornaments and comforts; Kassandros had allowed her a wagon-train to carry her things to Amphipolis. He was sending them both there, he had said, only for their protection after all the perils they had undergone; by all means, let her make her stay agreeable.

She had however been very lonely. In the beginning the Commandant's wife, and some of the officers' ladies, had

made overtures; but she was the Queen Mother, she had
not expected a long stay, and she had exacted her proper
dignities. As months became years she had regretted this,
and put out small signals of condescension; but it was too
late, formality was coldly kept.

It distressed her that the King her son should have no
company but women and common soldiers. Little as she
knew of Greek education, she knew that he should be getting it; or how, when he came to reign, would he hold his
own at court? He was losing his tutored Greek, and falling
into the uncouth Doric patois of his escorts. What would
his guardian think of him when he came?

And he would come today. She had just had word that
he had arrived without warning at the castle, and was
closeted with the Commandant. At least, the boy's ignorance should convince the Regent of his need for schooling
and civil company. Besides, she herself should long since
have been installed in a proper court with her ladies and
attendants, not penned up among provincial nobodies. This
time she must insist.

When Alexander came in, dusty and flushed from his
ride, she sent him to bathe and change. In her long leisure
she had worked beautiful clothes for both of them. Washed,
combed, dressed in his blue tunic bordered with gold
thread and his embroidered girdle, she thought that he had
added to the grace of Persia the classic beauty of Greece.
Suddenly the sight of him moved her almost to tears. He
had been growing fast, and was already taller than she. His
soft dark hair and his fine delicate brows were hers; but his
eyes, though they were brown, had something in their
deep-set intensity that stirred her memories.

She put on her best gown, and a splendid gold necklace
set with sapphires which her husband had given her in
India. Then she remembered that among Stateira's jewels

were sapphire earrings. She found the casket in the chest, and put them on.

"Mother," said Alexander as they waited, "don't forget, not a word about what Xanthos told me yesterday. I promised. You've not told anyone?"

"Of course not, darling. Whom should I find to tell among these people?"

"Silence or death!"

"Hush. He is coming."

Escorted by the Commandant, whom he dismissed with a nod, Kassandros entered.

He noticed that she had grown stout in the idle years, though she had kept her clear ivory skin and splendid eyes; she, that he looked older and thin to gauntness, and that his cheekbones had a flush of broken veins. He greeted her with formal civility, asked after her health and, without awaiting an answer, turned to her son.

Alexander, who had been sitting when he came in, got up, but only on reflection. He had long ago been told that kings should not rise for anyone. On the other hand, this place was his home, and he had a duty as host.

Kassandros, noting this, did not remark on it. He said without expression, "I see your father in you."

"Yes," said Alexander, nodding. "My mother sees it, too."

"Well, you would have outgrown him. Your father was not tall."

"He was strong, though. I exercise every day."

"And how else do you spend your time?"

"He needs a tutor," Roxane cut in. "He would forget how to write, if I did not make him. His father was taught by a philosopher."

"These things can be attended to. Well, Alexander?"

The boy considered. He felt he was being tested, to see how soon he would come of age. "I go up to the ramparts and look at the ships and ask where they all come from, and what the places and the people are like, if anyone can tell me. I go riding every day, under guard, for exercise. The rest of the time," he added carefully, "I think about being King."

"Indeed?" said Kassandros sharply. "And how do you plan to rule?"

Alexander had given this thought. He said at once, "I shall find all the men I can whom my father trusted. I'll ask them all about him. And before I decide anything, I shall ask them what he'd do."

For a moment, to his surprise, he saw his guardian turn quite white, so that the red patches on his cheeks looked almost blue; he wondered if he was ill. But his face grew red again, and he only said, "What if they do not agree?"

"Well, I'm the King. So I must do what I think myself. He had to."

"Your father was a—" Kassandros checked himself, greatly though he had been tempted. The boy was naive, but the mother had shown cunning in the past. He finished ". . . man of many aspects. So you would find . . . Well, we will consider these matters, and do what is expedient. Farewell, Alexander. Roxane, farewell."

"Did I do well?" Alexander asked when he had gone.

"Very well. You looked truly your father's son. I saw him in you more than ever before."

Next day brought the first frost of autumn. He rode out with Xanthos and Peiros along the shore, their hair blowing, tasting the sea-wind. "When I come of age," he shouted over his shoulder, "I shall sail to Egypt."

He came back full of this thought. "I must see Ptolemy. He's my uncle, or partly. He knew my father from when he was born to when he died. Kebes told me so. And my father's tomb is there, and I ought to offer at it. I've never offered him anything. You must come too, Mother."

Someone tapped at the door. A young girl slave of the Commandant's wife came in, with a jug that steamed spicily and two deep goblets. She set it down, curtseyed, and said, "Madam brewed it for you, and hopes you will honor her by taking it, to keep out the cold." She sighed with relief at having remembered it. She was a Thracian and found Greek hard.

"Please thank your mistress," Roxane said graciously, "and tell her that we shall enjoy it." When the girl had gone, she said, "She is still hoping to be noticed. After all, we shall not be much longer here. Perhaps tomorrow we will invite her."

Alexander was thirsty from the salt air, and tossed down his cupful quickly. Roxane, who was at a tricky stage of her embroidery, finished the flower that she was stitching, and drank hers then.

She was telling him a story about her own father's wars —he must remember, after all, that there were warriors on her side too—when she saw his face tauten and his eyes stare past her. He looked urgently at the door, then rushed to a corner and bent over, retching and straining. She ran to him and took his head in her hands, but he fought her off like a hurt dog, and strained again. A little came up, smelling of vomit and spices; and of something else, that the spices had masked before.

It was from her eyes that he understood.

He staggered to the table, emptied the jug out on the floor, and saw the grounds at the bottom. Another spasm cramped him. Suddenly his eyes burned with pure rage; not like the tantrums of his childhood, but like a man's; like the blazing anger of his father which she had, once only, seen.

"You told!" he shouted. "You told!"

"No, no, I swear!" He hardly heard her, clenched in his agony. He was going to die, not when he was old but now;

he was in pain and afraid; but overwhelming even pain and fear was the knowledge that he had been robbed of his life, his reign, his glory; of the voyage to Egypt, of proving himself Alexander's son. Though he clung to his mother, he knew that he craved for Kebes, who had told him his father's deeds, and how he had died game to the last, greeting his men with his eyes when his voice was gone. If only Xanthos and Peiros had been here, to be his witnesses, to tell his story . . . there was no one, no one . . . The poison had entered his veins, his thoughts dissolved in pain and sickness; he lay rigid, staring at the roof-beams.

Roxane, the first qualms working in her, crouched over him, moaning and weeping. Instead of the stiffened face with the blue mouth, the white forehead sweating under the damp hair, she saw with dreadful clarity the half-made child of Stateira, frowning in Perdikkas' hands.

Alexander's body contracted violently. His eyes set. In her own belly the gripe became a stabbing, convulsive pain. She crept on her knees to the door and cried, "Help me! Help me!" But no one came.

2 8 6 B. C.

KING PTOLEMY'S BOOK-ROOM was on the upper floor of the palace, looking out over Alexandria harbor; it was cool and airy, its windows catching the sea-breeze. The King sat at his writing-table, a large surface of polished ebony which had once been crowded with the papers of his administration, for he had been a great planner and legislator. Now the space was clear but for some books, some writing things, and a sleeping cat. The business of Egypt went to his son, who was discharging it very capably. He had relinquished it by degrees, and with increasing satisfaction. He was eighty-three.

He looked over the writing on his tablet. It was a little shaky, but the wax was readably engraved. In any case, he hoped to live long enough to oversee the scribe.

Despite stiffness, fatigue and the other discomforts of old age, he was enjoying his retirement. He had never before had time to read enough; now he was making up for it. Besides he had had a task saved up, to whose completion he had long looked forward. Many things had hampered it in earlier years. He had had to exile his eldest son, who had proved incurably vicious (the mother, married too soon for policy, had been Kassandros' sister) and it had taken time to train this much younger son for kingship. The crimes of the elder were the one sorrow of his age; often he reproached himself for not having killed him. But his thoughts today were serene.

They were interrupted by the entrance of his heir. Ptolemy the Younger was twenty-six, pure Macedonian; Ptolemy's third wife had been his stepsister. Big-boned like his father, he entered softly, seeing the old man so quiet in his chair that he might be dozing. But his mere weight on a floorboard was enough to dislodge two scrolls from one of the crowded shelves that lined the walls. Ptolemy looked round smiling.

"Father, another chest of books has come from Athens. Where can they go?"

"Athens? Ah, good. Have them sent up here."

"Where will you put them? You've books on the floor already. The rats will have them."

Ptolemy reached out his wrinkled freckled hand and scratched the cat's neck above its jeweled collar. Svelte and muscular, it flexed its smooth bronze-furred back and stretched luxuriously, uttering a resonant, growling purr.

"Still," said his son, "you do need a bigger book-room. In fact, you need a house for them."

"You can build one when I'm dead. I will give you another book for it."

The young man noticed that his father was looking as complacent as the cat. Almost he had purred too.

"What? Father! Do you mean that *your* book is finished?"

"In this very hour." He showed the tablet, on which was written above a flourish of the stylus, HERE ENDS THE HISTORY OF ALEXANDER. His son, who had an affectionate nature, leaned down and embraced him.

"We must have the readings," he said. "In the Odeion of course. It's nearly all copied already. I'll arrange it for next month, then there will be time to give out word." To this late-born child, his father had been always old, but never unimpressive. This work, he knew, had begun before he himself was born. He was in haste to see his father enjoy the fruits of it; old age was fragile. He ran over in his mind the names of actors and orators noted for beauty of voice. Ptolemy pursued his thoughts.

"This," he said suddenly, "must kill Kassandros' poison. I was there, as everyone knows, from the beginning to the end . . . I should have done it sooner. Too many wars."

"Kassandros?" Dimly the young man recalled that King of Macedon, who had died during his boyhood and been succeeded by disastrous sons who were both dead too. He belonged to the distant past; whereas Alexander, who had died long before his birth, was as real to him as someone who might now walk in at the door. He had no need to read his father's book, he had been hearing the tales since childhood. "Kassandros . . . ?"

"In the pit of Tartaros, where he is if the gods are just, I hope he learns of it." The slack folds of the old face had tightened; it looked, for a moment, formidable. "He killed Alexander's son—I know it, though it was never proved— he hid him through all his growing years, so that his people never knew him, nor will he be known by men to come. The mother of Alexander, his wife, his son. And not content with that, he bought the Lyceum, which will never be the same again, and made a tool of it to blacken Alexander's name. Well, he rotted alive before he died, and between them his sons murdered their mother . . . Yes, arrange the readings. And then the book can go to the copy-house. I want it sent to the Lyceum—the Academy —the school at Kos. And one to Rhodes, of course."

"Of course," said his son. "It's not often the Rhodians get a book written by a god." They grinned at each other. Ptolemy had been awarded divine honors there for his help in their famous siege. He gently stirred the cat, which presented its cream belly to be tickled.

The younger Ptolemy looked out of the window. A blinding flash made him close his eyes. The gold laurel-wreath above the tomb of Alexander had caught the sun. He turned back into the room.

"All those great men. When Alexander was alive, they pulled together like one chariot-team. And when he died, they bolted like chariot-horses when the driver falls. And broke their backs like horses, too."

Ptolemy nodded slowly, stroking the cat. "Ah. That was Alexander."

"But," said the young man, startled, "you always said—"

"Yes, yes. And all of it true. That was Alexander. That was the cause." He picked up the tablet, looked at it jealously, and put it down.

"We were right," he said, "to offer him divinity. He had a mystery. He could make anything seem possible in which he himself believed. And we did it, too. His praise was precious, for his trust we would have died; we did impossible things. He was a man touched by a god; we were only men who had been touched by him; but we did not know it. We too had performed miracles, you see."

"Yes," said his son, "but they came to grief and you have prospered. Is it because you gave him burial here?"

"Perhaps. He liked things handsomely done. I kept him from Kassandros, and he never forgot a kindness. Yes, perhaps . . . But also, when he died I knew he had taken his mystery with him. Henceforward we were men like other men, with the limits that nature set us. Know yourself, says the god at Delphi. Nothing too much."

The cat, resenting his inattention, jumped into his lap and began kneading itself a bed. He unhooked its claws from his robe and set it back on the table. "Not now, Perseus, I have work to do. My boy, get me Philistos, he knows my writing. I want to see this book set down on paper. It is only in Rhodes that I am immortal."

When his son had gone, he gathered the new tablets together with shaky but determined hands, and set them neatly in order. Then he waited at the window, looking out at the gold laurel-wreath that stirred as if alive in the breeze of the Middle Sea.

AUTHOR'S NOTE

Among the many riddles of Alexander's life, one of the strangest surrounds his attitude to his own death. His courage was legendary; he consistently exposed himself in the most dangerous part of any action; if he believed himself to be god-begotten, this did not in Greek belief make men immortal. He had had several dangerous wounds and nearly fatal illnesses. One might have supposed that a man so alert to the contingencies of war would have provided for this obvious one. Yet he ignored it totally, not even begetting an heir till the last year of his life, when after his severe wound in India he must have felt his dynamic vitality begin to flag. This psychological block, in a man with immense constructive plans meant to outlast his life, will always be an enigma.

Had Hephaistion survived, he would presumably have been left the regency as a matter of course. His record reveals, besides a devoted friend and, probably, lover, an able intelligent man, sympathetic to all Alexander's ideas of statecraft. His sudden death seems to have shattered all Alexander's certainties, and it is clear that he had not yet recovered from the shock when, partly as a result of it, his own life ended. Even so, during his last illness he continued to plan for his next campaign till he could no longer speak. Perhaps he held the view Shakespeare gives to Julius Caesar: *Cowards die many times before their deaths; The valiant never taste of death but once.*

His responsibility for the murderous power struggle which followed does not lie in his personality as a leader. On the contrary, his standards were high in terms of his own day, and he demonstrably checked in his chief officers the unscrupulousness and treachery which surfaced when his influence was gone. Insofar as he was to blame, it was in not making a good dynastic marriage, and begetting an heir, before he crossed to Asia. Had he left a son of thirteen or fourteen, the Macedonians would never have considered any other claimant.

As it was, the earlier history of Macedon makes it plain that his successors simply reverted to the ancestral pattern of tribal and familial struggles for the throne; except that Alexander had given them a world stage on which to do it.

The deeds of violence which this book describes are all historical. It has indeed been necessary, for the sake of continuity, to omit several murders of prominent persons; the most notable being that of Kleopatra. After Perdikkas' death, she lived quietly in Sardis till she was forty-six, refusing an offer of marriage from Kassandros. In 308, probably from sheer ennui, she made overtures to Ptolemy. It seems unlikely that this prudent ruler meant to repeat Perdikkas' rash adventure; but he agreed to marry her, and she prepared to set out for Egypt. Her plans became known to Antigonos, who, fearing an obstacle to his own dynastic aims, had her murdered by her women, afterwards executing them for the crime.

Peithon allied himself with Antigonos, but became powerful in Media and seemed to be planning revolt. Antigonos killed him too.

Seleukos outlived even Ptolemy (he was a younger man) but when nearly eighty invaded Greece to attempt the throne of Macedon, and was killed by a rival claimant.

Aristonous, at the time of Olympias' surrender to Kassandros, was garrison commander of Amphipolis. Kassandros lured him out under a pledge of safety and had him murdered.

Pausanias says of Kassandros, *But he himself had no happy end. He was filled with dropsy, and from it came worms while he was still alive. Philip, his eldest son, soon after coming to the throne took a wasting disease and died. Antipatros, the next son, murdered his mother Thessalonike, Philip's and Nikasepolis' daughter, accusing her of being too fond of Alexandros, the youngest son.* He goes on to relate that Alexandros killed Antipatros his brother, but was killed in turn by Demetrios. This extirpation of the entire line reads like the vengeance of the Furies in some Greek tragedy.

Antigonos strove for years to conquer Alexander's empire for himself, till Ptolemy, Seleukos and Kassandros made a defensive alliance and killed him at the battle of Ipsos in Phrygia, before his son Demetrios, who was always loyal to him, could come to his help.

The remarkable career of Demetrios cannot be summarized in a note. A brilliant, charming, volatile and dissipated man, after notable achievements, which included the Macedonian throne, he was captured by Seleukos, in whose humane custody he drank himself to death.

The strange phenomenon of Alexander's uncorrupted body is historical. In Christian times this was considered the attribute of a saint; but there was no such tradition in Alexander's day to attract hagiographers, and allowing for exaggeration it does seem that something abnormal occurred, which the great heat of Babylon made more remarkable. The likeliest explanation is of course that clinical death took place much later than the watchers supposed. But it is evident that someone must have taken care of the body, protecting it from the flies; the probability being that this was done by one of the palace eunuchs, who had no part in the dynastic brawls going on outside.

Alexander's eight chief officers were known as the Body-guard; this is a literal translation of the Greek, but it would be wrong to suppose that they were in constant attendance on his person. Many held important military commands. They have therefore been described as staff officers in the list of Principal Persons. The title of Somatophylax, or Body-guard, is probably rooted deeply in Macedonian history.

Principal Sources

Quintus Curtius, Book X, for events immediately after Alexander's death: thereafter, Diodorus Siculus, Books XVIII and XIX. Diodorus' source for this period is a good one: Hieronymos of Kardia, who followed the fortunes first of Eumenes, afterwards of Antigonos, and was close to many of the events he describes.

ABOUT THE AUTHOR

MARY RENAULT was born in London, where her father was a doctor. She first went to Oxford with the idea of teaching, but decided that she wanted to be a writer instead, and that after taking her degree she should broaden her knowledge of human life. She then trained for three years as a nurse, and wrote her first published novel, *Promise of Love*. Her next three novels were written during off-duty time when serving in World War II. One of them, *Return to Night*, received the MGM award. After the war, she went to South Africa and settled at the Cape. She has traveled considerably in Africa and has gone up the east coast to Zanzibar and Mombasa. But it was her travels in Greece that resulted in her previous brilliant historical reconstructions of ancient Greece, *The Last of the Wine, The King Must Die, The Bull from the Sea, The Mask of Apollo, Fire from Heaven, The Persian Boy*, and *The Praise Singer*. In addition to the novels, she has written a biography of Alexander the Great, *The Nature of Alexander*.

TO ILLYRIA

EUXI

EPIROS

STRYMON R.

MACEDON

Amphipolis Abdera THRACE

Aigai Pella

MOLOSSIA

HELLESPONT

KOKYTOS R.

Pydna

Dion

Dodona

THESSALY

MT. ATHOS

ACHERON R.

MT. OLYMPOS

Thermopylai

AEGE

AITOLIA

BOIOTIA

SEA

Chaironeia

ARKADIA

Thebes

Marath

Tegea

Athi

Piraeus

SALAMIS

EUBOIA

Megalopolis

Sparta

PELOPONNESE

Isaura

RHO

CYPRUS

CRETE

Kyrene

MIDD SEA

Alexandria

DELTA

Pelusiu

GYPT

Memphis

Siwah
(Temple of Zeus Ammon)

NILE R.